The Peat Dead

By

Allan Martin

TP

ThunderPoint Publishing Ltd.

First Published in Great Britain in 2019 by
ThunderPoint Publishing Limited
Summit House
4-5 Mitchell Street
Edinburgh
Scotland EH6 7BD

Cover Image © Willy S
used under license from Shutterstock.com

Cover Design © Huw Francis

ISBN: 978-1-910946-54-1 (Paperback)
ISBN: 978-1-910946-55-8 (eBook)
Printed and bound in Great Britain by Clays Ltd, Elcograf S.p.A

www.thunderpoint.scot

Acknowledgements

My first and constant thanks must be to Vivien: my muse, my First Reader (and critic), my first believer, and my constant encouragement.

I also need to thank the friends who also believed in me from the beginning: Val Renahan, Duncan Martin, Jill Henderson, and Helen B (as well as for her advice and experience in police procedures).

Crime writers are surprisingly supportive of newcomers, and I'm grateful to the authors who've provided encouragement along the way, especially Alex Sokoloff, Craig Robertson, Alex Gray, Lin Anderson, Sarah Ward, Doug Johnstone (anonymously); and there are plenty of others.

Of course, this wouldn't have happened without Seonaid Francis at ThunderPoint recognising something worth reading, and suggesting how it might be more readable.

Dedication

To Vivien, Alison and Calum, with love.

Map of Islay

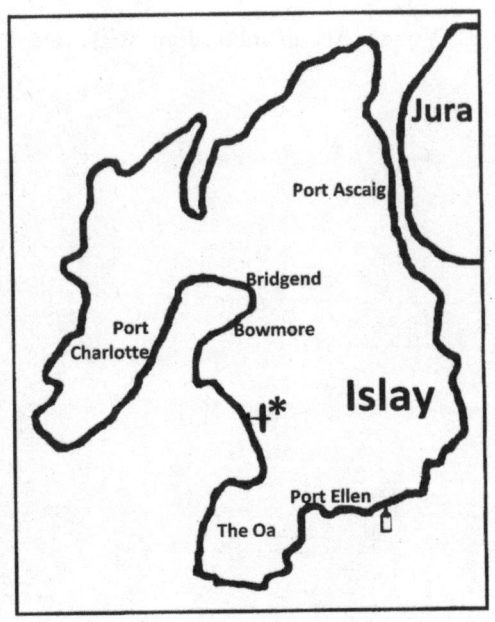

- ✈   Islay airport
- ✳   Excavation site
- 🍾   Lagavulin Bay

Prologue

Islay. The sun shines. In the air, the flavour of salt and of whisky. On the edge of the muir, two men work. With the long, sharp peat spades they are lifting thick shards, moist and deep brown, flicking them over to the top of the cutting, laying each aslant on the previous one, so that the wind will hustle through to dry them out, ready for the fire next year. Thomas and Robert McRae, men of Islay, Ìleachs, brothers.

Thomas is near the end of the line they have marked out for digging. As he lifts a long slab and twists the spade with age-old skill, the peat crumbles, scatters, falls to either side, spills back down the cliff-edge of the cutting. He turns to call to his brother.

"Rab," he says, "The peat's aa messed here. Something's up wi it."

So he's not looking as he slices the sharp spade into the dark peat again, and he feels this time that the blade has cut through an obstacle. Maybe a root. Instead of flicking the slab over, he pauses to inspect it on the spade. Again the peat crumbles and falls away. And on the bright steel of his spade a human hand, brown as the peat. As the hand seems to twitch (or is it a tic of his nervous arm?) it slides off the spade and falls, as if grasping for a handhold, to lie, palm upward, on the black earth.

Day 1. Thursday

1

Late morning, September.

The view from the fourth floor of the Oban Police Station was spectacular. You could see from the harbour all the way round to the Cathedral and the Corran Halls. You could see the ferries coming in and out, the top end of Kerrera, with the yachts clustered in the marina, and further off, the grey bulk of Mull. But Inspector Blue's office was not on the fourth floor, nor was it even at the front of the building. It was on the ground floor and at the back, and the view was of the kitchens of the Scotia Hotel.

Even so, there was sometimes, perhaps even often, something of interest to see from his window. He had recently witnessed the preparation of a boiled cod's head to a traditional recipe. The head had seemed very large, so that he could not imagine how big the whole fish must be. Davie the cook seemed to be removing the brain with a spoon, mixing it in a bowl with something dark and slimy, sprinkling in what could be salt, pepper, spices, herbs, maybe breadcrumbs too. The head had stared at the inspector balefully, before disappearing under the pan lid. Davie said to him later, in the bar, "You've to be careful wi cod. Bottom feeders. There's aye worms in them. Especially in the liver. For the Biled Cod's Heid you need to mix the brain wi liver, but you've to get the worms out the liver first. They spoil the taste." He'd asked if many people ordered it: "Aye, quite a few, they're taken by the novelty o it. But they dinna usually finish it. Plenty left for the Fish Soup next day – we just dinna say what's in it." Blue's stomach had churned as he remembered the tasty fish soup he'd often had in the bar of a lunch time.

His phone rang.

"Inspector Blue. How may I help?" There were strict instructions on how to answer the phone. No hellos, or other signs of familiarity. To the point, but with courtesy. Identify yourself clearly. Police Scotland are always ready to help.

"Excellent response, Blue, ten out of ten." Superintendent Campbell, Head of CID.

"Thank you sir, did you want something?"

The Super's office. The fourth floor, at the front. Divisional commander must have the penthouse. Of course, normally the view over Oban Bay was spectacular. But today heavy cloud hung over everything. A big ferry loomed out of the mist.

The boss as usual sat behind his wide polished wood desk. Files and papers at either side; in the space in the middle, one slim file. "Angus, come in, sit down. How are you doing?"

"Fine, thanks, chief." Campbell frowned, but who doesn't like to be called 'chief'? Informal but respectful, acknowledging the leader who can make contact with his troops. "Hope all's well up here?"

"Need you ask? Never is! Coffee?" The Super had a commensurately superior coffee machine with an Italian name. The coffee was good, made the trip upstairs worthwhile. Almost.

"Yes, please. What's going on now?"

"Rumours of an announcement on Britishness. Doesn't sound good." The government in London had recently announced that a *'Reclaiming Britishness'* project would soon be launched. This programme of as-yet-unspecified measures would enable citizens of a *'newly-self-confident Britain'* to rediscover the essence of their national identity, *'buried too long beneath continental bureaucracy and alien cultures.'*

"Hmm." Blue waited, but nothing more was forthcoming. He sipped his coffee. Strong and deep. "I guess there's something you'd like me to do, sir?"

"Yes, yes, of course." Campbell moved the slim file an inch to the right. "Islay. Unexplained death. Maybe more than one."

"Bloodbath?"

"Probably a perfectly natural explanation. CID need to have a look. Just in case."

Blue could not think of a natural explanation for several dead bodies. Why wasn't everyone they had being rushed over there?

"Accident of some sort?" A bus packed with screaming tourists rushing down the hairpins at Port Askaig and plunging into the Sound of Islay. "Maybe an epidemic?" A recent visitor from a distant land coughing a terrible virus onto the streets of Bowmore.

"No, no, Angus, they've just been revealed. Uncovered."

"Uncovered?"

"From the peat. Some peat-cutters found them. Early this morning."

"So they're not recent?"

"When did I say they were?"

"Er, you didn't."

"Exactly." Campbell glanced at the file, slid it one inch to the left.

"So how old are they?" asked Blue.

"We don't know. As yet. Could be very old, who knows, Middle Ages, Dark Ages, earlier. Like those bodies they found in…where was it?"

"Denmark. Bog bodies. Dyed brown by the peat."

"Sacrifices?"

"Maybe. Or executions. Maybe even a serial killer."

"Ours could be more recent. Can you get over there, check it out?"

"OK, chief. What about the shoplifting gang at the Co-op?"

"The Romanians?"

"Two of them. The rest are from Manchester."

"Where are we on that?"

"We're ready to round them up. Tomorrow afternoon. Sixteen-thirty."

"Don't give me jargon, Angus."

"Sorry, sir. Half past four."

"Good. Well, you may be back by then, otherwise Sergeant Bruce can handle it."

"When am I off then?"

Campbell looked at his watch. "Get home, grab a bag. There's a scheduled flight at twelve. Otherwise you'd have to get the bus to Kennacraig for the ferry."

"SOCOs?" asked Blue.

"Inspector Lennox is on it; they'll be over sometime this afternoon."

Blue got up and put his cup on the plastic tray on the window ledge. He knew the routine. "Just one thing, sir, any info on the subject?"

"Info? You're sailing close to the line, Blue."

"You're right, chief. Sorry." In order to encourage 'intercommunicability' throughout its empire, Police Scotland had issued a list of words to be used in reports and other 'intra-force transactions'. This document was regarded with contempt by most police officers.

"Quite so. Here's what was emailed this morning. Read it on the plane." He gazed at the file for a moment, then pushed it across the desk with a fingertip. Maybe just one sheet inside. And on the front was typed: 'Glenegedale Moss deceased'.

"Let me know what's happening, Angus."

"Yes, chief, ASAP." That wasn't on the list either.

2

The yellow Twin Islander 9-seater took Inspector Blue from Oban's modest airport to Islay in thirty minutes. There were only five passengers, so the pilot had to seat them to balance the plane. Blue observed them. An old man who fell asleep as soon as he boarded; a girl of anything between thirteen and nineteen; and two men who talked loudly in German – whisky tourists, mispronounced distillery names peppering their conversation. The plane flew low, and on a good day the views would have been fantastic. But this wasn't a good day. The sea was grey. The sky was grey. The distant land was grey. As if normality were on holiday, the tiny plane, wobbling on its axis, flew through nothingness and came out into another country. Mountains, bare and ancient, then flat lands of faded yellow-brown, and then asphalt of a runway that seemed too long for itself, and ended in the sea.

Climbing down from the plane, the flatness confirmed itself. A road ran past, perfectly straight, disappearing into gathering mist. Beyond, an imposing Victorian villa. Nothing else.

The terminal building was just one room, but offered everything. Except duty free. Though there was plenty of evidence of whisky about: bottles in tall glass display cases, framed posters on the walls. One caught his eye. Kilbrocheann. A squat dark bottle resting on a stack of peats, against a fiery red sunset.

He thought someone might have been sent to meet him; maybe on the islands things moved more slowly. In two minutes the only other person still there was the old man, who had lowered himself into one of the comfy seats and fallen asleep again. Blue took the five-second walk to the café end of the terminal and ordered coffee from the smiling ladies at the counter.

"Hello, would you be coming for a holiday here? I see you're ready for the walking." It was true, he was wearing walking shoes, trekking pants, fleece and waterproof jacket. That was one of the benefits of plain clothes; you could dress for the weather and the terrain. Not that he wore anything different in Oban. The chief had long since given up trying to persuade him to wear a cheap suit.

"Not as such."

"It must be the sales, then!"

Do I look like a shopper? thought Blue. "Sorry, I wasn't thinking of looking at the shops."

"Och, no, not the shops. We've precious few of them here. The sheep sales!"

"Ah, no, sorry."

"Then it must be the whisky!"

"Well, I am interested in the whisky, I must admit." Be a discreet businessman, probably in the spirits industry. Change the subject. "Is that a carrot cake? Looks good. Can I have a piece?"

"Jessie made it just yesterday. You'll be wanting cream with it."

By the counter was a shallow basket containing DVDs, home-made by the look of them: *Flying-boats over Islay*. Sixty minutes of planes flying over Islay, from the Second World War to the present day. He bought one of them too, along with a copy of *The Ileach*, Islay's fortnightly newspaper, and took a seat. The old man snored loudly and woke himself up, gazed at Blue and nodded vaguely, then sank into sleep again.

His thoughts drifted onto the bodies in the bog. He'd read the file before he even got on the flight; there was only one page, nothing more than a paragraph indicating that two men, Thomas and Robert McRae — were they brothers? — had been cutting peats, and came across the bodies. The site had been secured, and HQ at Oban were requested to send a scene-of-crime team, and a CID officer. It was signed by an Inspector Nicolson. The name meant nothing to him.

He remembered the bodies in the museum in Copenhagen. A man's head in a glass case. Just the head. Brown and leathery, a weather-beaten farmer. Strangled by persons unknown, the cord still round his neck. Sacrifice? Execution? Or just murder? What counted as crime back then? How many more were still down there, waiting to be wakened by the peat-cutters.

There were now a few more people hanging around: a middle-aged man in a fleece, a well-dressed woman, a young man in a denim jacket. Minutes later, when the plane from Glasgow arrived, Blue watched the passengers coming through. The man in the fleece held up a card with a large oriental character on it. A small group of young women came through talking excitedly; they spotted the sign and, giggling, headed for the man. One of them took the card and turned it the other way up — then they followed him out. The young man greeted his girl-friend with a lengthy hug, whilst the woman waved to an elderly lady, and led her towards the exit. A couple of young men in suits, a bald fleshy man with round glasses who would be a bank manager, if such things still existed, a big man with a heavy moustache and a limp, and a young couple, maybe from southern Europe, with rucksacks and binoculars. Soon they were all gone, leaving Blue and the old man, still sleeping.

He'd forgotten about the carrot cake. As he leaned over it, wondering how to eat with the plastic fork without getting cake all over himself, he sensed someone close by.

"Inspector Blue?" The accent was educated Glasgow. Maybe south side. Intelligent. Polite. He looked up. A young uniformed PC was stooping over him.

"Yes?"

"PC Bhardwaj, sir. Sorry I'm late. We thought you'd be on the ferry, so I was waiting at Port Askaig. I got over as soon as I heard."

"How did you know I was here?"

"Annie at the cafe phoned Bowmore, said they had someone who looked like a policeman." So much for the discreet businessman impersonation.

He hadn't made much impact on his carrot cake, so Annie insisted on putting it in a box, with an extra dollop of cream and another plastic fork. "You'll be wanting it for your dinner."

3

The police car was a small one, maybe a Clio, with four doors. The police transfers on the bodywork had either been stuck on carelessly, or someone had tried to rearrange them afterwards. "The patrol car broke down last week," explained Bhardwaj, "the garage lent us this one. We'll go up to the crime site right away, sir, if that's alright. The boss is waiting there."

They got into the car, and drove the twenty yards to the airport entrance gates. Looking left then right, Blue could see a dead straight road, disappearing into the mist in both directions. A white van with a cylindrical tube on top passed them at a leisurely pace from left to right.

"That'll be George Kelly," said Bhardwaj, "Plumber from Bowmore. Never drives over thirty mph."

He revved up the car and screeched onto the road, turning right, then after a few yards swinging left onto a minor road heading gradually up into the mist. To his left a large Victorian villa, maybe a hotel now, on the right a garage with rows of cars for sale outside. 'McCall's Motors' said the sign in big yellow letters.

A minute later he was thrown to the right as Bhardwaj took a 90-degree left onto a track that seemed to climb straight onto the moor. Soon they left the last swathes of mist behind, and came up to a temporary "Police – No Access" sign. Beyond it another police Clio sat by the track.

As they drew to a halt a uniformed female officer got out of the other car. She waited for them to exit their vehicle, then approached Blue. "Hi. Inspector Moira Nicolson." Tall, slim, short dark hair, hazel eyes, penetrating gaze. Fortyish, but he wasn't any good at guessing ages. Uniform clean and pressed. Green wellies. A look of efficiency. Something twitched at the back of his brain. The name was familiar, but he couldn't place it. Was there a Moira Nicolson in his class at primary school?

"Angus Blue." They shook hands.

"Good to meet you, Angus. I'll show you the scene. The ground's not too wet at the moment, but there's spare wellies in the car if you need them."

"I'm OK. Waterproof shoes. Thanks."

"This way then. Across the ditch. Watch in case it's a bit slippy."

Blue followed Nicolson across an old pallet bridging a drainage ditch at the side of the track. In a couple of minutes they were at the site. Along an edge about thirty yards long the peat had been cut in foot-long wet slabs, each turned over and laid partly onto the previous one to dry out in the wind. At the end of the cut there was a circle of police tape on posts, and within that things looked a bit more untidy. Part of the edge of the cut had crumbled away beneath the mat of heather and coarse grasses at the surface.

"This is Glenegedale Moss. You'll have passed over it as you came in on the plane. You've read my initial report?" When Blue nodded, she continued. "The McRae brothers, Rab and Tam, cutting peats here early this morning. Tam – that's Thomas – notices the peat's a bit disturbed. He goes for it anyway, and next thing is, he's hit something with the spade. Finds he's chopped off a hand."

"That would be quite a surprise."

"Yes, they called us right away. We secured the area and alerted Oban. You're first, SOCOs are on the way. I guess they'll be taking the ferry. Here we are, take a look. Down at the bottom there."

"I'm not seeing anything. Am I looking at the right spot?"

Nicolson fished in her top pocket and pulled out a slim cylinder. She pointed it at the peat bank, and a bright red spot appeared on the ground. "Laser pointer," she said, "Very useful. Look. There's the wrist where the hand came off." It was brown, the same colour as everything else, but once the red spot had hovered on it, Blue could see it just sticking out of the peat. An off-white hint of bone in the centre. "And there's a toe over there. It might be a second body."

He found it harder to see it despite the red spot. It might have been a stone at first glance. But when he looked closer, he could see the nail. "Yes, maybe too far away to be part of the same body," he said, "Unless it was chopped up."

He stepped back and looked at the peat face. He could see that above the arm and toe the texture of the peat was slightly different from the rest of the face. Not so smooth. And maybe it was even a little bit darker. Material disturbed when the grave was dug for the body. Or bodies. "Yes, I can see the disturbance," he said. "Maybe ten feet across. Big hole for one body. I suspect you're right about more than one. We'll have to wait for the SOCOs to dig it out, and see. They won't welcome all that exercise. By the way, do you know when they'll be here?"

"If they got the two o'clock boat they could be here not long after four. If they missed it, then they won't be here before it gets dark."

Blue was still studying the peat face. "Moira, can I suggest something?"

"Fire away."

"From what I've seen so far, I think it's worth calling in the forensic archaeologist. The SOCOs will all have done the archaeological training course, but there aren't many opportunities to use the skills. I'd suggest that we need an expert here. Her name's Alison Hendrickx, Dr Hendrickx, that is. With an X at the end. Her grandfather was Belgian."

"You know Dr Hendrickx then?"

"I've worked with her a few times. She knows her stuff."

Prior to unification, Scottish police forces had to borrow archaeologists from local universities. However, since then they had their own, Dr. Alison Hendrickx. Having specialised in the archaeology of crime scenes, she was now widely recognised for her expertise, and Police Scotland made a tidy income hiring her out, mainly to forces elsewhere in Europe. Her training work and lectures at the police college also brought in international business. But her first priority, which validated all the rest, was getting into the trenches, so to speak, in Scotland.

"Yes, I can see what you're getting at. I'll give Oban a ring, see if we can get her in." She took out a mobile and moved a few yards away to make the call.

Blue took the opportunity to look around. The mist was drifting away now, as if slithering back to some hidden lair, and the landscape slowly unveiled itself. He could see the airport, beyond it the sea. To the right the road, stretching off towards Bowmore, and above it the pale brown of the moor, with the black strips of the peat diggings standing out like scars.

The sun was out now, and as he let his gaze drift across the moor he caught a glimpse of reflected light. Light off glass. He saw a couple of figures out there, a long way off, too far to recognise. Were they watching?

He walked back to the car, where PC Bhardwaj was now sitting on a folding chair, a pair of powerful binoculars on his knee. He jumped up. "Yes, sir?"

"Constable…"

"Please, chief, call me Arvind."

"OK, Arvind, can I borrow your binoculars?"

"No problem, chief." He handed them over. "I keep a look out for birds. There are eagles here."

Blue pointed the binoculars and focused them, panned across the land where he'd seen the figures. But now there was nothing to be seen. Ramblers, birdwatchers, crime site ghouls? Did people already know there was a crime scene here?

Nicolson joined him again. "I've put in the request. They'll get her to call me back."

"Good. So what else is happening?"

"I thought we should see whether this is linked to any historic events, you know, old murders or disappearances. So I arranged a meeting with some folk from the Historical Society. I'm meeting them at the museum, over at Port Charlotte, at two-thirty. Do you want to come along?"

"Yes, that sounds useful."

"In that case I suggest we go straight over now." She glanced at her watch. "It's twenty past one now, so we can get a coffee there, and talk a bit more. Arvind will keep an eye on the site here."

They drove back down the track towards the road. Ahead of them, beyond the road, Blue could see waste ground with curious flat expanses of what looked like concrete, set here and there, like worn-out playing cards flicked onto the earth at random by some irritated giant.

"What are these things? Look like concrete floors," he asked.

"That's where the old air base was," said Nicolson, "Most of the buildings were knocked down after the war. All that's left are these floors in the middle of nowhere. And the airport."

They reached the road, and turned right, passing McCall's garage to turn right onto the main road.

"The airport?"

"There was a little airfield here in the 1930s. During the war it was converted into an air base and considerably extended. All sorts of stuff going on. That's why the runway at the airport's so long. They had big planes coming in. Even from America. So after the war that part of the base became the airport. They built this road too. Before that all the roads on the island were single-track."

A car passed them in the other direction. The driver, a middle-aged woman, raised a finger from the steering wheel, a hint of a wave, and Nicholson responded similarly.

"I suppose everybody knows everybody here," said Blue.

"Not necessarily. That's the Islay wave, most of the residents will do it, and the regular visitors. Dates from the time there weren't so many cars about, I guess."

They passed through Bowmore, the island's capital, with its round church, harbour and shops, and beyond the town found the shore of Loch Indaal, around which Islay curls like a sleeping giant. At Bridgend they turned left to follow the lochside towards Port Charlotte. Before reaching the museum they passed Bruaichladdich distillery, the first of Islay's distilleries Blue had spotted.

4

When he came to, the first thing he noticed was the floor beneath him. It was beneath most of him, as he was lying on it. It was cold and wet and hard. He touched it with his hand. It felt like concrete, coarse-grained with tiny ridges. His feet were bare and felt the cold floor too. At least he still had his shirt and trousers. He opened his eyes, and blinked. The darkness was total. It surrounded him like a living presence, a thick and hostile fog, soaking into his clothes, condensing onto his feet and hands, caressing his face, invading his nose and mouth like suffocating tentacles. He shivered, and tried to get up. Then he noticed the pain. First the stabbing from his left knee as he tried to raise himself, then the dull ache in his chest every time he breathed in, and finally, and worst of all, the waves of fire in his mouth, pulsating through his head. He put a hand to his cheek and gasped. The side of his face was swollen, his tongue felt a gap and a broken tooth, and the pain leapt out from it at him, seized his face, writhed with it. He groaned and forced his jaws together.

Now he remembered the two men. One had used a weapon, a cricket bat, sawn-off less than a foot below the handle. Used with the flat or edge, depending on what kind of damage he wanted to inflict. The other man just used his fists, and his boot. The rules of cricket didn't apply here.

He needed to get up, fought the pain to push himself onto his knees and then to stand. The darkness followed him, clinging to his arms and legs, draping itself over him. He raised an arm above him, and felt the ceiling, cold damp concrete too. Then he stretched out his arms into the blackness to find a wall. It was right next to him, he must have been lying against it. He felt cold brick and damp mortar. Now he groped his way around the edge of the room, to gauge its size. About six feet square he reckoned. In the first corner he came to he hit something metallic with his foot, heard a sloshing. Groping down, he realised it was a bucket. Had he used it earlier, or did they just not empty it very often? He couldn't remember. He found the door, solid steel by the feel, no hatch and no keyhole. And it didn't budge when he tried to push it. A cell, a dungeon, an oubliette. A tiny room with no light and no furniture. It smelt heavily of disinfectant, and behind that, the foul odour of urine, faeces and blood. He stopped moving and listened. Yes. The sound of the sea, of the waves swishing onto the beach. So, he was still here, still on Islay. And if he could hear the ocean, there must be a window, near the ceiling perhaps, or at the least a ventilation brick. So it must be night too, or he'd see what little light trickled into the cell along with the whisper of the sea.

He shouted, paused and listened. There was no response, not even an echo, as if the darkness had eaten up the words as they came out of his mouth. He shivered again, sat down with his back against the wall. The pain in his knee eased off a little. The man with the bat had used the edge of it on his knee, and the flat on his face. The other man's boot had focused on his stomach and his chest.

He heard voices outside, far off, muffled by the darkness, diluted by the swish-swash of the waves. Out there, life went on. Had his existence already been forgotten? Left to his tiny cell, black as the grave.

5

The museum was based in a big stone house overlooking the loch, next to an old church and burial ground. The only other vehicle in the car park was a camper van with Dutch plates, and blinds shut.

The heavy oak doors of the building were open and they went in, to be warmly greeted by the elderly lady behind the counter. "You've come awfy early for your meeting, Moira." Of course, this was an island. Everybody knew everyone's business.

"That's right, Nan," replied Nicolson, "We'll have a spot of lunch first."

There was a little cafe on the ground floor, with a view to the canted and crumbling gravestones. Pointers to more of Islay's dead.

Moira was greeted again, by a large and smiling woman. "Moira, it's yourself. And this will be Mr Blue, the top detective. We've heard all about you Mr Blue."

"Oh yes? What have you heard?"

"That you're here for a big case. And you like my carrot cake."

"So you'd be Jessie?"

"Moira, he's certainly a detective. So what'll it be? Today's soup is sweet potato and coconut."

The soup, served with a warm sesame roll, was good. As they ate, they talked.

"First thing I need to mention," said Moira, "your accommodation's sorted out, at the Victoria and Albert Hotel over in Port Ellen. It's ten minutes' drive from Bowmore, but the hotel's the nearest one on the Approved List." Police Scotland maintained a list of 'Police Approved' accommodation throughout the country for officers having to reside on expenses. No-one knew how the list was drawn up. "And we've got a car for you too. Iain McCall will deliver it to the hotel later today."

"Thanks, that sounds good," said Blue.

She looked out of the window, and seeing her head in profile, he suddenly remembered who she was. Moira Nicolson. More than ten years back, when he was just a graduate-entry constable near the end of his stint on the beat. A harassment case in Edinburgh. A sergeant claimed she'd been bullied, then denied promotion after she'd complained. The Federation took the case to the Court of Session. She won. He didn't know what happened after that. He assumed she got promoted. And here she was.

"Yes," she smiled, "I see the little light bulb over your head. You've worked out where you'd heard of me. This is where I ended up. My place of exile. My Constantsa."

"Sorry?"

"Constantsa, Romania. Where the Roman poet Ovid was exiled by the emperor Augustus. Maybe his poems weren't politically correct enough. Or it was something personal."

Blue remembered a Latin class twenty years previously. The poem was about a girl who got turned by the gods into a constellation. Each line was a struggle to understand. 'Come on, people, work for it!' urged Doc McLeod, 'Nothing comes for nothing in this life!'

"Ah." Back to the present. "You won the case."

"I did. But they never forgive a defeat. I got the promotion, yes, they couldn't avoid that, and quite a good payout too. Then here. Exile."

"Did you think of fighting it?"

"Oh yes, of course. I soon realised it would get me nowhere. They never forgive. Salve their consciences by giving me stuff. Laptop, top of the range camera, even sent me to Sabhal Mò Ostaig to learn Gaelic. Someone must have thought they all speak it here. But I'm not complaining. And this is a good place to be. Time to do plenty else than being a police officer. Not much serious crime either. Until now."

"That's if it is a crime."

"Oh, it's a crime all right," she said, "The wedding ring." For a moment Blue could not speak. Sadness assailed him, but he fought to stay focused.

"I heard of you too," said Moira quietly. "I'm sorry."

"Yes, of course. Please, the ring?"

"It was on the hand. Fourth finger, left hand. Forensics'll get it off, see if there's an inscription inside."

"Doesn't look like a historic case then?"

"Could still be nineteenth or early twentieth century. But yes, it could certainly be later."

"What did you do with the hand?"

"We brought it back, put it in the fridge. In an evidence bag. You can see it when you get to the station. Just one other thing. Until we know there's a relatively recent crime, as local commander I'm technically in charge of the case."

"Yes, that's true."

"But if there is a crime, I guess it'll be passed to you. In which case you can be assured I'll give you all the support I can."

"That sounds fine to me."

"Ah, there's Leonard!"

An elderly gentleman, thin and with a bushy white moustache, had just come into the café "Moira, my dear, there you are. We're all ready for you." Moira introduced Blue to Leonard Grange, retired judge, and current President of the Islay Historical, Literary and Philosophical Society. He led them back to the museum foyer, up stairs to a landing, and into a room overlooking the loch. In the centre was a large wooden table with chairs around it, and over in one corner one man and three women were watching a kettle as it came to the boil. They turned round as the visitors came in. Blue reckoned that they all qualified for free bus passes.

Inspector Nicolson introduced Blue to the others: Elspeth Forrest, the Society's librarian and archivist, a tall woman, with her grey hair in a bun; Liz McMichael, curator of the museum, short and stocky with dyed blonde hair; Ina McNiven, who took care of the genealogy work, a very ancient lady, Blue guessed as he shook her wiry blue-veined hand; and George Outhwaite, a big man, almost bald, his accent north of England: "Hello, lad, we weren't sure what 'twere about, so Leonard asked all of us to come. If it's about the war, then I'm your man."

Once they were seated, with tea or coffee, Inspector Nicolson began. "The first thing I have to say is that this is official business. We – the police, that is – are looking for your help, and for that help the usual donation will be made to the Museum."

"And we very much appreciate it," cut in Leonard, twitching a bushy white eyebrow up and down.

"Thank you, Leonard. This is official, so I have to ask you all for your absolute discretion."

She looked round the table. Each of them nodded.

"Thanks. Now, you've perhaps heard through the grapevine that something's going on up at Glenegedale Moss. The fact is, we've found some bodies under the peat." Liz McMichael gasped audibly, Elspeth Forrest frowned, and Leonard Grange stirred his tea. Ina McNiven showed no reaction – maybe she was deaf – and George Outhwaite perked up noticeably and waggled his ears.

She continued. "At least one, probably more. We'll have more details once our scene-of-crime officers have got to work. These bodies could be over a hundred years old, so this does *not* mean we're looking for a mass murderer on the rampage right now. Investigating bodies that turn up unexpectedly is simply routine police procedure. We need to establish who they are, when and how they died. Only then will we know whether a crime's been committed, and if so, whether the perpetrator may still be alive."

"Could they be prehistoric or mediaeval?" asked Liz, "Perhaps a plague pit."

"At the moment we're thinking nineteenth or twentieth century. I can't give you any more details at this point. But what we'd like to know is whether you can tell us of any death or disappearance of two or more people on the island during those centuries."

"Well," said Leonard, "I can say right away that there has been no documented multiple murder on the island during that period."

"You're quite sure?" asked Blue.

"Absolutely. Read my book *Islay Murders Through the Ages*. You can get it downstairs for only £5.50. Believe me, I researched it very thoroughly."

"Thanks Leonard," said Inspector Nicolson, "so it looks like we can rule out known crimes. That leaves unknown crimes, which for obvious reasons are harder to track down, and disappearances."

"And multiple burials," added Elspeth.

"How do you mean?"

"The plague pit mentioned by Liz is not so way off. Before vaccines and antibiotics, diseases like typhoid, typhus and cholera could easily claim multiple victims in a single locality, and these were sometimes buried in mass graves. Epidemics were quite frequent, often triggered by infected people from elsewhere. I can see if any of the outbreaks fit your time frame and location."

"That would be really useful."

"Disappearances could be trickier. We'd have to check the local paper and Kirk Session records. But there was a constant movement of people away from the island throughout the nineteenth and twentieth centuries, seeking work elsewhere in Scotland, or emigrating. So, a family present in one census but not the next, are more likely to be in Greenock or Melbourne than buried in the peat."

"That'll be true enough," said Ina McNiven quietly. "I know a lot of the family histories, of the island families that is. I'll have to be thinking about it." That must be the real Islay accent, thought Blue, not quite Lewis or Harris, but a lightness and a delicacy of speech nonetheless.

Nicolson turned to George Outhwaite. "Any thoughts, George?"

George, who seemed to have been dozing, shook his head as if to clear his brain for action. "Well, there were a lot of action 'ere during the war. All sorts, really. Commando training too. Planes coming and going day and night. Happen you've seen my DVD at the airport, Mr Blue?"

Blue struggled to remember.

"*Flying-boats Over Islay*. Lot of rare shots in there. Some beautiful planes. On sale here too. I can even sign one for you." He grinned.

Blue remembered. "Yes, of course, actually I bought one at the airport, George. Haven't had a chance to watch it yet. Looks interesting, though." He noticed Liz smiling to herself.

Leonard brought the conversation back to focus. "Well now, Angus, what's your role in all this?"

"None, unless there's been a serious crime within living memory. At the moment I'm just waiting on the sidelines to see if I'm needed."

"Thanks, Angus," said Inspector Nicolson, "I think we can leave it there. If you can all look into this over the next few days, that would be really helpful."

They agreed to reconvene at 2 pm on Saturday. On the way out Blue stopped by the book display. He bought a copy of *Islay Murders through the Ages*. Leonard insisted on signing it. He also bought another booklet, *A Short History of Islay*.

"Don't you forget to bring my DVD in," said George, "See, me and Leonard, we'll soon both be dead, so if they're signed, that'll double the value of them. Then get onto eBay and cash in!" He chuckled hoarsely.

6

As they made for the car, Inspector Nicolson's mobile beeped. "Text from Bob," she reported, "'SOCOs at the site.' That's good." She tapped a number and waited for a response. "Hi, Bob...Yes, fine, how's it going there?...Good..."

Blue whispered, "Ask who's in charge."

She nodded. "Who's leading the scene team, Bob?...Right...OK, we'll be along soon, Bye."

Then to Blue, "It's a Sergeant Dalvey."

Blue frowned. "Kevin Dalvey. Wonder why they sent him. Must be short-staffed at the moment."

"Is that a problem?"

"I'm sure it won't be. He usually stays in Oban, does lab stuff and ballistics."

"Well, we'd better go and take a look."

They set off, but they were not long out of Port Charlotte when Inspector Nicolson's phone rang. She pulled off the road onto the grassy verge between the road and the sea. To give her some privacy Blue got out of the car and watched the sea, dark and foreboding under the grey sky. After a few minutes Nicolson opened her window and held the phone out. "For you."

He took it. "Hello?"

"Hi, Angus, Alison here. How are you?"

"The better for hearing you, Alison. How about yourself?"

"Looking forward to a trip to Islay. I've just been telling Inspector Nicolson that it's been OKed, so I'll be on the first boat tomorrow morning. Means an early start, but the roads from Stirling will be clear at that time. Sounds like an interesting site. Who's in charge of the SOC team?"

"Kevin Dalvey."

"Ah. Better bring my hard hat and ear plugs. OK, got to go. I'll see you tomorrow."

They drove back to the site. There was now an outer fence of tape, ten or fifteen yards further out from the original one. Also a bigger "Police No Access" sign, blocking the track, and behind it PC Bhard-waj. As they approached, he moved the sign to let them past. They left the car behind a big white van parked by the track. They could see people at the site in white plastic overalls moving gingerly about. As they crossed the drainage ditch, a man came towards them. Fortyish. Overweight. Thick black moustache. Hostile expression.

Blue nodded, "Hi, Kevin, how's it going?"

The man grunted something inaudible to him and addressed Inspector Nicolson. "Sergeant Dalvey. I'm in charge here. I want everybody off my site except my team. At least fifty yards."

Moira Nicolson stared at him, expressionlessly, for several seconds, until he grunted, "Ma'am."

"Good morning, Mr. Dalvey. I'm Inspector Nicolson. I'm actually in charge here. Do you understand that?"

Dalvey's moustache twitched. He scowled and looked at the ground. "What I meant, is that I supervise the scene-of-crime."

"Thank you, Sergeant, the perimeter you already had is what I judged to be sufficient. I assume you've read the file. Where are we so far?"

Dalvey bristled. But he was now back in his comfort zone, wielding the power of expertise. "Hmm. Well, it's certainly far too early to give you any information. We're still examining the accessible area." He waved a hand vaguely at three white-clad figures on hands and knees at the point where the arm and toe had been discovered. "Then we'll have to take pictures. And we'll need a lot of the peat shifted."

"I hope you've brought your shovels, then," said Inspector Nicolson. "Thank you, Sergeant." And she turned away, and headed for her car.

"How are we supposed to see what's in there?" Dalvey shouted after her.

The inspector turned back. "Mr. Dalvey, when you learn how to speak politely to a senior officer, then I will think about discussing that with you. Please let me know when that happens. Now, was there anything else you wanted? I have work to do."

Dalvey twitched, and tried hard to restrain himself. When he spoke, there was a sullen edge to his voice: "Yes ma'am. My initial site assessment shows approximately three feet of peat over the level of the presumed incident. I'm therefore requesting some local police officers to dig out this material."

"Out of the question, I'm afraid. My local force is fully committed protecting the site, in addition to their normal duties. It may be possible to arrange for a mechanical digger. But, as you'll know, I can't authorise the expenditure for that without the paperwork, so I'll need your site assessment report before I do anything. Preferably within the next hour. Thank you, Sergeant. Please carry on." She turned away again, leaving Dalvey speechless. Blue could imagine the torrent of foul language his team would have to endure once they'd gone. He nodded again as they left, and Dalvey scowled at him with another grunt, before stomping back towards the site.

"Well, he's a charming customer," said Nicolson. "Is he any good at the job?"

"Yes, he's OK on the site, better in the lab. His main problem is himself."

"How do his team deal with it?"

"There've been several harassment and bullying complaints, especially from women. He's been reprimanded twice. They only send him out if there's no-one else available. Dealing with the public, or anyone else for that matter, isn't his forte. Neat work on the report; getting paperwork out of Dalvey's never easy. By the way, is the digging going to be a problem?"

"No, I don't think so. I'll call Archie McCormack. He's at the farm over there beyond that line of trees. He can be very precise with a digger. Won the ditch-digging prize at the Agricultural Show. Hopefully he can be ready to move as soon as Dalvey puts in a report."

"You didn't mention Alison to him."

"Let's do one thing at a time. I don't want to overload Mr Dalvey's brain. Not much we can do here at the moment, so I'll take you to the station."

7

They drove into Bowmore and pulled up outside an Edwardian villa on a road parallel to the main street. There were some terrace houses opposite, with a few shops at the ground level. Opposite the police station was a shop called 'The Spirit Well'. The window displayed bottles of whisky.

The villa's storm doors were open and Nicolson punched in a security code and pushed open the glass-panelled inner door to reveal a lobby, containing a reception desk, a battered coffee table and four old dining-room chairs. Spread on the coffee table were some well-leafed magazines: *Autocar, The Ileach, iScot* and *Practical Woodworking*. They went on through a door by the desk into a corridor, coming to an open doorway revealing a workroom. In the centre was a large dining table. At one end sat a female PC, tall and slim, brown hair in a pony-tail, filling in a form. At the other end a sergeant frowned at a computer.

Inspector Nicolson tapped on the doorframe. They both looked up and stared.

"This is Inspector Blue, from Oban," said Nicolson.

The sergeant, a large man with a weather-beaten complexion, got up laboriously, came over and offered Blue his hand. A firm shake. "Sergeant Bob Walker, sir, glad you've made it." A deep reassuring voice, but Blue wasn't very good at placing English accents. "Landing could be tricky, wi' the mirk out there. You've met Arvind, I guess, and" – he gestured to the WPC – "that's Deirdra Craig." She smiled – blue eyes – and gave a hint of a wave. "Clara's sorted you out an office, next to the boss's, in case you need it."

"Clara?"

"Clara Gilmour, our secretary-cum-receptionist," said Nicolson, "Part-time. You'll meet her tomorrow."

She led Blue along the corridor, past a kitchen on the left, and at the end turned right up a staircase. The wooden stairs creaked as they ascended. The dimly-lit corridor was floored with ancient lino, perhaps a shade of fawn. Nicolson opened the door before the end on the left. There was an old desk and two old chairs.

"We got hold of some of the furniture when the primary school was refurbished," said Nicolson, "Knew it would come in useful sometime."

"This is fine." Blue put his travel bag and rucksack on the desk. Dust moved around on it. "I'd better phone the Super now, let him know what's happening."

"Give me a knock when you're done. I'm just next door."

He was put through to Superintendent Campbell right away.

"Hi Angus, what's going on there?"

"Not much. I've looked at the site. Might be historic, might be more recent. SOC are there now. But there's a lot of peat to take off, so it could be a while before anything emerges. I've advised the local commander to call in Dr Hendrickx, and she'll be here tomorrow."

"Who's the local commander?"

"Inspector Nicolson."

"Nicolson, hmm, is that Peter Nicolson? Thought he was at Loanhead."

"Moira Nicolson." There was a pause. Memories reviewed.

"Ah. So that's where she is. Well, remember, she's the local commander, so until we've evidence of a crime, stay in the background. Get a feel for the place. Capture the spirit."

"Yes, sir."

"Good. Actually, Angus, talking of spirit, there is something else. When you've a minute, can you get over to the Kilbrocheann Distillery, and get me two bottles of the 21-year-old Madeira Cask Special. It might be a bit expensive, so use your credit card and I'll pay you as soon as you get back. Believe me, it's still a lot cheaper to buy it there than in the whisky shops in Oban."

Blue fumbled in his pocket for his notebook and pen. "Just jotting that down now, sir. Two bottles. 21-year-old Madeira Cask Special. Was that it?"

"Exactly. Good man. Keep me up to date on this one. And the quicker you can get some results the better. Then we'll know what we're dealing with."

He knocked on Inspector Nicolson's door, asked if he could see the hand. She led him down the stairs, into the kitchen, opened the fridge, took out a plastic container, prised the lid off. "Take a look."

The hand lay there, in its plastic shroud, palm upwards, as if waiting for some small gift to be placed in it. There was still a lot of peat adhering to it, but the gold ring stood out. Blue shuddered involuntarily. He remembered an old film where an evil hand scuttled around like a spider.

"Hmm. A man's hand."

"Yes, I think so too."

"Hope it doesn't escape."

"Don't say that, you'll give me nightmares." She put the box back in the fridge. "So what happens now? Is there anything else we can do?"

"Crucial thing is to get the peat off before the end of today. Now he knows he can't avoid it, Dalvey will get an initial site assessment to you ASAP. He doesn't like being away from home. Islands are his nightmare, he hates boats and large bodies of water."

"Let's have a coffee then, see how long he takes."

He felt the wedding ring on his finger, twisted it round, held it to his good cheek. The metal was warm. He remembered her hands on his face, in a different darkness, tracing every contour. Her lips on his cheek. Her body in his arms. He wept.

Blue sat in a wooden upright armchair facing her desk. It looked homemade, but felt solid enough. "Interesting chair."

"Made it myself. Time for creativity's another benefit of exile."

"It's solidly made. Do you do other furniture?"

"Whatever I feel like. Tables, benches, picture frames."

He glanced at the wall behind her, where a seascape hung, in a frame of worn grey wood, which itself looked like something from the sea. "Where do you get the wood?"

"On the shore. On the right beach all sorts of things get washed up. Wood that's ready seasoned by the sea."

"The right beach?"

"Oh yes, the sea is very particular where it puts things. You can get lots of driftwood on one beach, but just around the headland, there's nothing. Just like police work. You have to know where to look."

As she passed him his coffee – the superior instant type with bits of ground bean in it – the honk of an old car horn sounded in the room. She sat down and looked at the computer. "An email from Mr. Dalvey. With an attachment. I'll print it out."

The report was less than a page, indicating that the site had been located and taped, photographs taken, an initial examination made. Approximately 1.3 metres of peat would need to be removed from an area of about three metres by four, before any further work could be done. The case officer was therefore requested to engage a digger to carry this out, as any other method of removal would be less cost-effective.

Nicolson immediately phoned Archie McCormack, who readily agreed to the work. He would get straight over to the site. "OK, Angus," she said, "time to get you to your hotel."

8

They drove back past the airport and carried on along the straight road, zigzagging at the end into Port Ellen. They passed the massive bulk of the malting plant and pulled up in front of a whitewashed Victorian hotel, with a fine tower at each end, and an elegant portico in the middle. The Victoria and Albert.

"I hope it's OK," said Nicolson. "If you want to drop your stuff, we'll go back and see what's doing at the site."

Blue checked in, dropped his bags in his room, at the rear of the hotel, and had a quick wash. As he left again, the young man at the desk – Bogdan, said his name tag – called him over. "Sorry, sir, I forgot to mention, a car was left for you. Here are the keys. I think it's a Clio. In the car park."

It was a Clio, orange, with "McCall's Motors Courtesy Car" in big black letters on both sides. And a phone number. At least he'd know where to ring if it broke down.

They returned to the site in the police car. A yellow Lada estate was parked at the top of the track, behind the big white van used by the SOCOs. As they exited the police car, a uniformed officer emerged from the Lada. An older man, tall and thin, cadaverous. He looked at Blue suspiciously.

"Afternoon, boss," he said to Nicolson in a slow monotone, "or is it evening?" Then he seemed to notice Blue, and nodded vaguely. He had an odd tic in his left eye, so that he seemed to wink now and then at someone over Blue's right shoulder.

"Constable Blackett, this is Inspector Blue, Oban CID. We'll take a look at the site. Any problems here?"

"No, boss, not a soul's been here, no-one at all. Apart from our Oban colleagues. And Archie of course." The slow, monotonous, slightly metallic voice seemed somehow dissociated from the man, as if emanating from somewhere over his head. An ex-ventriloquist, perhaps, a useful man to have in some circumstances, thought Blue.

They walked over to where the SOCOs were standing watching the digger at work. Occasionally Dalvey would shout and gesticulate at the driver, and point repeatedly at a particular spot. He caught sight of Blue and Nicolson, and came over. "Is he deaf, or does nobody speak English here?" he shouted.

"He's not deaf," said Nicolson coolly, "and he speaks perfectly good English. But the more you shout at him, the less he'll co-operate. So I suggest you speak nicely to him, unless you want to be here for another week. If he decides to walk off, you and your team will have to get digging."

Dalvey opened his mouth to reply, then thought better of it. "Yes 'm," he mumbled.

"How much is coming off?"

"Down to a few inches above the exposed remains."

"Are you going to take some more off by hand when Archie's done?"

Dalvey looked at his watch. "It's nearly six."

"I didn't ask what time it was."

"I – *we* – haven't eaten yet. Once we've had an hour for tea, it won't be worth it. We'll start in the morning. Ma'am." Dalvey smirked. "And we'll want to see that hand too, it should never have been taken off the site. It'll be completely contaminated by now. I'll have to report that. Excuse me, ma'am." He gave a casual US-style salute, and turned back to watch the digger.

"He's insufferable," said Nicolson, as they walked back to the car. "You didn't tell him Dr Hendrickx's coming."

"You're right. It slipped my mind. I'll send him an email. I've had enough of him for today."

"Look!" said Blue. "Over there. In the airport car park. Someone's watching us." He pointed to the airport entrance gate, where the top half of a tiny figure could be seen among the parked cars, watching them through binoculars. A woolly hat, scarf and gloves meant that nothing of the body inside the clothes was visible. The waterproof jacket was dark blue or black.

"Could be anybody," said Nicolson, "Male or female. Maybe just a local. Anything unusual attracts interest here. Something to gossip about. Or a birdwatcher. We get plenty of them here. Maybe seen an eagle."

They both turned and looked up, towards the hills. No bird was circling on the rising air, seeking its prey.

Blue looked back to the airport. The figure was gone. He watched the car park but no car came out. "If we go down there, they'll have gone by the time we arrive."

"There's nothing more we can do here," said Nicolson, "Blackett's on watch overnight. I'll ask him to keep a lookout."

9

Inspector Nicolson dropped Blue back at his hotel.

It was half past six, but still light enough for a walk. Round the corner was the pier where the car ferry sometimes docked, the road leading down into the dark water. To his left, a long row of two-storey terrace houses faced the road and, beyond it, the beach. At each end of the bay were long harbour walls of dark weathered stone. Walking along the sand, he sensed the calm of the place.

At the far end of the bay the road turned off to the left. Towards the southern distilleries: Laphroaig, Lagavulin and Ardbeg. He passed a small stone-built church and a concrete-and-glass primary school, then left the village behind. Down to his right he could see the rocky coastline, to his left the land sloped upwards, and he caught sight of a solitary standing stone, glowing in the low-angled sunlight.

He walked for about fifteen minutes, then turned back. As he was crossing the road by the primary school, he stopped. He had an overwhelming sensation of being watched. But by whom? He looked at the blank windows of the houses, but there was no sign of movement. Not a curtain twitched. But at the bottom of the road he saw a figure, silhouetted against the evening sun flaming the water of the bay. It was watching him. He tried to shade his eyes, and the shadowy form seemed to grow larger as he struggled to make it out. A car horn sounded behind him, and he jumped aside to let it past. He looked again, but the figure was gone. He shook himself, and walked on. Who was watching him? Or had the figure actually been looking the other way, out into the bay? He hurried down to the corner, peered round. There was no-one in sight.

He ate in the hotel restaurant, read the *Short History of Islay*. Venison sausages, roast potato and parsnip, along with a bottle of Islay's own beer. And to finish, a glass of twelve-year-old Caol Ila. Caol Ila, the Sound of Islay, the narrow strait between Islay and Jura, where the distillery sat. He swirled the pale yellow-gold liquid in his glass and breathed it – he felt the vapour fill his lungs and coil its way up to his brain. He added a splash of water and breathed again. This time a whole galaxy of new aromas had been released: overtones, undertones, harmonics, whatever the experts called them. He never ceased to be impressed by the complexity of good whisky. Light and yet deep; sweet and yet spicy; vanilla and liquorice; the hint of peat and the smell of the sea. That was why he would never have more than one glass at a sitting – it always called to be savoured as if anew; a second glass would be merely drinking. Unlike some Islay whiskies, Caol Ila wasn't so smoky, and had a silky sweetness that appealed to his taste buds. Perhaps he'd try some of the others again. A shame to be on the island of whisky and not sample its treasures.

Back to his room to check his email, and start writing his report, which he would then update daily. Then he watched an episode of *Foyle's War* on the TV. Blue admired the Foyle character, unflappable and quiet-spoken, but willing to challenge anyone and demand the truth. As he lay in bed, his mind drifted again to the peat cutting, and the dead hand in the station fridge. He knew already that this was a crime, but was it recent enough to be his business? He hoped so. The dead deserved justice, for the sake of the living.

The news came on next. The UK education minister had announced that a new "British Studies" module would be introduced into all primary schools in England and Wales the following year. It would be taught as part of Social and Religious Education, for 10-to-11-year olds. New legislation was to be introduced at Westminster to make the module compulsory for Scottish schools too. *"Identity is as important as reading and writing,"* said the minister, as cameras clicked.

Day 2. Friday

10

Next morning he expected to see the SOC team at breakfast, but there was no sign. Neither was the white van in the car park. Must be staying somewhere else.

He was at the site by 8.30. Only PC Bhardwaj was there.

"Good morning, sir, looks like it's going to be a good day."

"Yes. Any trouble overnight?"

"Well, Boris didn't report anything." He sounded hesitant.

"Boris?"

"Oh, sorry, PC Blackett. Boris. Seems they've always called him that. You know, Boris Karloff, *Frankenstein, The Mummy*. Even has a Russian car. Yellow Lada estate – only one on the island."

"Ah yes." The dissociated voice.

"Since you ask, sir, there is something odd. Look, just over here." Bhardwaj pointed to marks in the damp earth of the track. Tyre tracks, parallel to the tracks made by Blue's car. "Compare them to yours. Quite a different pattern."

"Did you ask Blackett about them?"

"Didn't get a chance, he was off as soon as he saw me coming up the road."

Not helpful, thought Blue. Poor changeover. "Could the tracks be Blackett's?" he asked.

"No way. The Lada's got a very distinctive tyre pattern. Look! Over here, these are his tracks. These ones here are wider, deeper. A chunkier car altogether, Range Rover or something similar. And it didn't come up as far as his. You can see where he parked, there. And the other car stopped here – see the deeper marks where the front wheels started to reverse. Must have reversed all the way back down to the road."

"So this other car came up, stopped, and then some time later reversed down again."

"That's exactly it."

"That's good work, Arvind, very observant. We ought to photograph these tracks."

"Already done, chief." Bhardwaj produced a small digital camera from his pocket.

Blue was worried by this development. It could have been locals, simply coming up to have a look, and then clearing off when instructed to do so by Blackett. But it was also not unknown for officers on night watches to fall asleep. In which case, someone could have come up the track, taken a look at the site, then made off quietly without waking the sleeping policeman.

At quarter to nine they saw a police car making its way up the track. Blue signalled the car to stop. Moira Nicolson got out.

"Hi, Angus. I thought our SOCOs would be here by now."

"They can be a law unto themselves. Particularly with Dalvey in charge."

"I'll need to move the car further up, make room for the van."

"Just before you do, come and have a look at this."

Blue showed her the tracks, with Bhardwaj adding details from what seemed a comprehensive knowledge of all things automobile.

"Interesting," she concluded, "I'll have a word with Blackett. We'll get the SOCOs to take more photos."

Then she moved her car further up, avoiding the mystery tracks. She took two red cones from the boot and positioned them so that any other vehicle coming up would also keep clear of the alien tyre marks.

At ten past nine they saw a small blue car approaching.

"I think that's Alison, er, Dr Hendrickx's car," said Blue.

The car crept around the cones and parked further up, and a slight figure with short fair hair and rimless glasses, dressed for trekking the hills, got out and fished a rucksack from the back seat. She waved to Blue.

"Angus, hi, how are you doing?" She kept her gaze on him as she walked over.

"OK, Alison, what about yourself?"

"Just fine, till I heard Dalvey was here."

She turned to Inspector Nicolson: "Inspector Nicolson? Hi. Alison Hendrickx. Good to meet you."

"Please, call me Moira." The two women shook hands.

"Thanks for emailing the site report. Looks interesting. But we'll need to get the protocol sorted out with Mr. Dalvey. I've not found him welcoming in the past, and that's an understatement. Hope you've brought your trowel, Angus. I could use you on the peat face, as it were."

"Always in my travel bag." He pulled from his pocket a small masonry trowel, the point worn down to a gentle curve.

"He's a good digger, Moira. Very careful, patient, knows how to take orders." It was clear to Blue the two women were going to get on well. "By the way, when are the SOC team coming up?"

"Should have been here by now," said Inspector Nicolson.

"Where are they staying?" Blue asked.

"Don't know," said Moira, "Must have booked something from Oban. The Sergeant hasn't deigned to tell me."

11

Five minutes later Sergeant Walker arrived. But it was not until 9.45 that the white van came rushing up the track. When it reached the cones it simply drove over them, crushing them into the mud, and carried on. Blue noticed a big scratch down one side that hadn't been there the day before. The van halted abruptly and the team clambered out sluggishly and began to struggle into their white overalls. As Dalvey came over his face darkened. Blue thought, he's slept badly and has a headache. He needs to be careful.

"What the hell's she doing here?" shouted Dalvey. "I don't need her to tell me how to run my fucking site!" He marched towards Alison.

Inspector Nicolson stood in his way. "Sergeant Dalvey, good of you to join us."

He stopped, glaring at her. "I didn't ask for her, and no-one told me she was coming!" He was still shouting. Everyone else froze where they stood. White statues, thought Blue. Dalvey was swaying slightly. He must have put away quite a lot last night, and probably had plenty of alcohol still in his blood. He edged closer. He didn't want to encroach on Nicolson's authority but needed to be ready in case things got worse.

"I don't think it's necessary to shout, Mr. Dalvey," said Inspector Nicolson calmly, "I requested Dr. Hendrickx, as local commander, yesterday, after inspecting the site with Inspector Blue. The information in your report supported my decision. You did not seem to be in a receptive mood yesterday, so I emailed you my decision not long after we left the site yesterday. When did you read it?"

Dalvey just stood glaring at her, breathing heavily.

"I asked you a question, Sergeant. Please do me the courtesy of a response."

"I don't...I...I never got it. Maybe you sent it to the wrong address," Dalvey sneered.

"I don't think so, Sergeant. I put a delivery check on it – it was read at 7.08 pm. By you."

"We don't need her. Do you think I'm incompetent?"

"We're not discussing anyone's competence, Mr. Dalvey, only what's appropriate for this situation. And as the case officer, that's my call. I have judged that Dr Hendrickx's skills would be appropriate for this situation."

Dalvey looked around darkly. "Bloody women," he muttered, as if to some ghostly familiar.

Inspector Nicolson addressed the white statues by the van. "Who drove the van up?"

"He did," two of them said simultaneously, pointing at Dalvey.

"Did you see the cones on the road, Sergeant?"

"I'm not stopping half way down the bloody track. I decide where I park, not some idiot PC."

"Step closer, please, and let me smell your breath."

Dalvey took a step back, and looked around him again. He seemed to notice that they were all watching him. It occurred to Blue that he might suddenly run away. He wouldn't get far in the ill-fitting white overall. He pictured a large figure flailing its arms as it ran across the moor, eventually sinking into the bog...

"PC Bhardwaj, would you fetch a breathalyser kit from the car and test Sergeant Dalvey."

"You must be joking!" said Dalvey in disbelief, "A bloody breath test. From a fucking Paki. No way!"

"Sergeant Dalvey," said Inspector Nicolson, very slowly and clearly, but without raising her voice, "As local commander, I am relieving you from your duties as of this moment. The reasons are, one, suspected driving under the influence of alcohol, two, refusal to take a breath test, and three, racial abuse of a police officer. You will be escorted to the police station in Bowmore, where a breath test will be administered. A disciplinary report will be sent today to your superiors, and I will request that you be taken off this case forthwith. Sergeant Walker, would you take Mr Dalvey down to the police station in your car."

"Yes, boss, right away," growled Sergeant Walker, "Shall I cuff him?"

"I can get to the car myself," muttered Dalvey, then, to the inspector, "You won't get away with this. I've got friends, you'll see. What kind of coppers get sent out to this shithole anyway – women and Pakis. That nutter Blackett. What a bunch of losers." Then he turned away and ran to the van. He jumped in the open door, switched on and revved it up, did a rapid three-point turn which included smashing the back end into the passenger door of Blue's courtesy car, and raced off down the track towards the road.

The white-clad figures remained frozen, like improbable snowmen, but Blue knew immediate action was necessary. "Bhardwaj, with me! You drive!" He wrenched open the damaged passenger door with some difficulty, and by the time he had got into the seat Bhardwaj had already started up and was ready for his own three-point turn. Blue couldn't get the damaged door shut – it must have been bent out of shape – so he just had to hold onto it. A red warning light started flashing on the dashboard, accompanied by an insistent beeping.

Meanwhile they rushed on down the rutted and stony track, and swung right after the van. The door flew open again, but by this time Blue had his seat belt on and didn't fly out with it. The beeping was getting louder, and more rapid. As he pulled the door back, he shouted, "Can't we switch off this racket!"

Bhardwaj was gripping the steering wheel with intense concentration. "Yes, sir, I could do it in a couple of minutes with a pair of pliers, but I don't have a hand free at the moment. It might also invalidate the hire agreement. For the car. Iain McCall's not going to like the look of that door."

With some effort Blue managed to get the door shut and the beeping ceased. By now they had followed the van past the second-hand cars, where a burly man with a bald head and bushy red beard was staring at them open-mouthed – "That was Iain McCall there, actually!" observed Bhardwaj. They rushed past the hotel, and Blue noticed the bank manager type he'd seen at the airport, sitting at an outside table with a cup in one hand and a smartphone in the other, gazing at them over a document he must have been reading. Then they swung left onto the main road, heading for Port Ellen. The road ran dead straight for several miles, but the van had a good turn of speed, and Bhardwaj was hard put to keep up with it. It soon dawned on Blue that there was in fact no need to overtake Dalvey, since he had nowhere to go.

"He can't get off the island."

"That's right. I would have said his best bet was to go into Bowmore, lose the van, get the bus to Port Askaig, and try to sneak onto the boat as a foot passenger. Even at that he'd be very lucky to get away. But he doesn't know the island and is probably still a bit drunk, so he turned the wrong way. Whichever way he goes, it's a dead end."

"So all we have to do is stick with him. OK, Arvind, stick with him."

"Sir, the siren, where is it? You know, in case there's other traffic."

"This is a courtesy car, I don't think it comes with a siren. Just blow your horn if necessary."

At the end of the long straight, as the road nears Port Ellen it makes a 90-degree left turn, with a minor road going straight on. But the van was going too fast to take the turn, and flew straight ahead. A couple of walkers jumped into the long grass at the side of the road as the two vehicles raced past. Then they came to a T-junction, and the van heaved crazily to the right with a screeching of tyres on the road and shot off up a single-track road overhung on both sides by trees.

"We've got him now, Sir, this is the road to the Oa. His only way out is to drive off the cliff at the Mull. Terrible waste of all that expensive equipment."

"Can we get past him?"

"Not on this road, it's all single track. But we don't need to. If we just stay on his tail, he'll end up in the car park for the monument, and we'll have him trapped, like..." Bhardwaj hesitated, trying to think of an appropriate simile.

"A wasp in a jam jar?" put in Blue. An image from his childhood.

"Why a jam jar?" Bhardwaj did not share this memory.

"I'll explain later. Oops!" He saw a tractor turning into the road about a mile ahead. It was heading straight for the van – there was going to be an almighty smash. But it turned immediately into another field, and the van sped past with what seemed only a few inches clearance.

Now they were rushing uphill, with empty moorland on either side. They passed a sign, "Road ends in ½ mile at Car Park."

"Not long now, I think," commented Bhardwaj.

Almost at once, the van slowed and lurched to the right, onto the moor. It was clear Dalvey was going to try to drive round behind them, get back onto the road and make off again.

"Bad move," muttered Bhardwaj, bringing the car to a halt.

"Aren't we going to follow him?" Blue asked. "He's getting away."

"No need, chief, he won't get through the bog. Now we just need to collect him. We can get out here."

They got out the car and watched as the van slowed down and then sank into the moss until its underside rested on the ground. The door opened and Dalvey jumped out, still in his flapping white overall.

Good God, thought Blue, I saw this happen.

Dalvey stumbled towards them, yelling incoherently; they could make out the occasional fragment of abuse. The tirade was cut short as he suddenly sank up to his waist.

"The bog can be very deceptive," said Bhardwaj.

"So I see."

Dalvey scrambled out, water pouring out the arms of his plastic overall, and squelched towards them. "All right, you win," he gasped at Blue, "I surrender."

Blue nodded to Bhardwaj. "Help him into the car, Arvind."

"I didn't surrender to him," shouted Dalvey, "Don't touch me, you little git." He swung a chunky arm at Bhardwaj, who seemed merely to bend out of the way, then tap the side of Dalvey's knee with his toe as he rushed on past. Dalvey twisted round and fell to the ground shrieking and clutched his knee. "He's fucking dislocated it!" he screamed.

"You'd better cuff him, for his own protection," ordered Blue.

As Bhardwaj grabbed Dalvey's wrists and expertly slid the handcuffs on, they could hear sirens as the other cars finally caught up with them.

"That was neat, Arvind, where did you learn that?"

"Karate, sir. Black belt. West of Scotland Champion last year."

"Good to know that you can use it in the field. Well done."

12

Back at the station, Dalvey was locked in the interview room to sober up and come to terms with his situation. He was given a blanket to replace his soaking trousers. The breath test was borderline positive. A nurse from the medical practice up the road had expertly and, for Dalvey, painfully, snapped his knee back into place, and was now putting a white bandage round it. He'd been given some powerful painkillers, and his head was sagging over the table. He was weeping quietly.

Moira Nicolson was writing up her report on the incident, with Bhardwaj in her office to give details of the chase and capture. She had already sent a brief email to Oban, outlining the events, and requesting further instructions for the SOC team. Within minutes, Inspector Lennox, the SOC co-ordinator, had phoned to discuss the matter. He told her it was an incident waiting to happen, asked her to send in her report. "Tell Steve Belford he's in charge of the team now," he concluded, "and to defer to Dr Hendrickx until the scene's uncovered."

Blue went to his office to write up his report of the incident. Five minutes later there was a sharp rap on the door. A woman came into the room, middle-aged, thin, with lank straight hair dyed Burgundy and tied in a bun. She glanced suspiciously round the room, then at Blue.

"You'll be Inspector Blue then?" A superior Edinburgh edge.

"And I guess you'd be Mrs Gilmour."

"Ms Gilmour. Ranks of Inspector and above may call me Clara. I take it the hotel is to your satisfaction?"

"Seems excellent, thank you, Clara."

"And the office?"

"Fine."

"Any stationery items required, fill in the form and leave it on the reception desk." She turned and left the room without waiting for a reply.

After writing up his report, Blue decided to talk to Dalvey. He needed some sense of what was going on in the man's head. He made two mugs of coffee and took them into the interview room.

"Coffee, Kevin? I'd like a few words."

Dalvey took his mug in both hands, looked into it. "Thank you, sir. Are you going to charge me?"

"That's not my call, it's up to Inspector Nicolson. She's the commanding officer here. But I think you've got a lot of explaining to do. And apologising."

"I've told her I'm sorry."

"Saying sorry's easy. Meaning it, and proving it, is harder. That means looking at yourself, and changing what's there. Didn't that incident last year make you think about things?"

"Yes, sir, it did. I went to the rehab, at that place in Perthshire, got my drinking under control. The Drinking Discipline Programme. You're allowed 5 units a week, max one unit a day, and have to stick to that. And keep a record, so you become very aware of what you're drinking. But it's made me more, ah, irritable."

"So we noticed. But I think you had more than one unit last night. Is that right?"

"He must have spiked my drink, chief, that man in the bar."

"Start from the beginning, please. Which bar?"

"At the hotel at Bridgend. That's where we're staying."

"Did someone in Oban book you in there?"

"No, it was that Gilmour woman. I phoned the station here and spoke to her. She said she'd arrange it, said she didn't want us in the same hotel as the senior ranks. What a snob, eh?" So sharing information was not one of Clara Gilmour's skills, thought Blue.

"I don't think you're in a position to be critical of anyone, Kevin. Tell me what happened last night, then."

"We went for a meal at that Indian place in Bowmore, the one near the Co-op. I had a pretty good Vindaloo and a deep-fried banana fritter. I was driving, so I just drank that alcohol-free lager. Yon wee scratch on the van was from this morning. Anyway, we came back to the hotel. It was getting darker, so Andy wanted to go down to the shore to try and photograph some otters. The guy at the hotel said there was a cove where you could sometimes see them. Steve said he'd go along. Dave went to his room to talk to his girlfriend on Skype." You're not someone people want to spend their evenings with, thought Blue.

"So what did you do?"

"I'm not into wildlife – all these things just look like rats to me – so I went for a drink. Just my one unit, mind. I had a glass of that 4% lager. I was about halfway through when this guy walked past and bumped into the table, knocked my glass over. Of course, he was very apologetic, gave me twenty quid 'for the laundry bill' he said, insisted on buying me another drink. Well, it would have been rude to refuse, wouldn't it?"

"I doubt that's what they told you at the rehab."

"Er, no sir, but he just got me a glass of that very dark Islay stuff. Very tasty. I think he put something in it though. Vodka maybe."

"Wouldn't you have noticed?"

"After a Vindaloo you don't taste much, sir."

"How many more drinks did you have, Kevin?"

"Er, well, he gave me a whisky, just to go with the beer. I don't remember much after that. Just being sick in the middle of the night, then waking up with a real thumper of a headache. And late for work."

"Tell me about this man?"

"About your height, plumper – fat rather than muscle, I'd say. Ba face, balding, clean shaven, wee round glasses." It sounded like the bank manager type Blue had seen at the airport.

"Did he say anything about himself?"

"Said he was an accountant, came over now and then to work with the farmers on their tax returns. He said a name but I can't remember what it was. He'd noticed the activity at the site, from his hotel, he said, and was interested in scene-of-crime work. Watched CSI on TV, said that SOC work was so underrated."

"How much did you tell him?"

"I don't remember. Honest, sir, I don't. He just seemed such a good listener."

It was clear that this had not been a chance encounter. The man had been pumping Dalvey for information on the site. But why? Somebody was clearly very interested in what they were doing up on the muir.

Blue was heading for his car to get back to the site when his mobile rang.

"That, you, Blue? Any news yet?"

"Sorry, sir. We were delayed by a little altercation with Sergeant Dalvey."

"Dalvey! What the hell's he doing there?"

"He was sent to head up scene-of-crime. No-one else available, apparently."

"The man's an idiot, Angus. A dinosaur. Gives us a bad name. What happened?"

Blue explained briefly.

"Hmm. How did Nicolson handle it?"

"Expertly, I would say. She's very competent."

"Hmm, yes, that's what I've heard. Great pity we can't get rid of Dalvey. If we sacked him we'd just have to hire him by the hour at twice what we pay him now. As you know, when it comes to ballistics, he's unbeatable. Anything about guns. He's probably got an arsenal in his garage."

"We're lucky he's not running amok with weapons then."

"He did apply for the armed response squad once. Didn't get in though – his own shooting is hopeless. I didn't tell you that, by the way. So, where are we with the bodies?"

"Topsoil's off, Dr Hendrickx's here, I'm on my way up there now."

"Good. You'd be digging with them then, I'd guess."

"Yes, sir, I like to keep my hand in."

"Absolutely. Good idea to keep an eye on what's happening. Let me know as soon as you've got something, Angus."

13

Up at the site, Alison Hendrickx and the SOCOs were in a row, on garden knee-rests, taking the peat out gently with flat trowels, and transferring it to plastic buckets. PC Bhardwaj was on guard at the access to the site. As Blue approached the diggers, Alison looked up. "Hi, Angus, ready for action?"

"Yes ma'am, have trowel, will travel."

"OK. What about joining the end of the line there? We're lifting off the disturbed peat at the moment. We'll feel a change in texture when we reach the undisturbed stuff. Hopefully we'll find a surface compacted by the people who dug the pit – they'll have had to stand in it to dig the peat out. The area over and round any bodies will be simple, the tricky bit will be revealing the rest of the surface."

Blue remembered a case of Alison's in which a shoe-print and a cigarette filter found on the floor of a pit six feet deep convicted the man who had put his wife there before filling it in and building a garage on top.

"How much space do we need to clear?"

"Well, the digger took off an area from the cut edge of the peat, and in for about ten yards. That should be a lot more than we need. In fact, if you look at the ground, you can see the slightly darker peat forming a squarish patch about eight by ten feet – that's the hole they made to put the bodies in, so that's the area we need to clear."

"Quite a big hole, but I suppose the peat wasn't hard to shift. Any more bodies?"

"Not so far, but we're almost on top of the two we know. If there are others, they'll show up soon."

The work proceeded. Soon one of the SOCOs encountered another body. Ten minutes later one more emerged, and five minutes after that Blue himself felt his trowel slide through the peat and catch on something beneath. A little cleaning revealed an elbow, covered in cloth. Five bodies. Five dead people under the peat. Each with a name, a life, and a fate.

And they required some privacy, and protection from the weather. The white crime scene tent was fetched from the van and erected.

He must have dozed off again, but the tapping woke him up. From the wall. Someone was tapping from the other side. Another prisoner of the dark. He listened carefully. Could it be a code. But it didn't sound like Morse — just random tapping, to see if anyone else was there. Why hadn't he tried that? Feeling too sorry for himself. He stood up, winced again at the pain from his knee, felt his way to the wall from which he thought the tapping was coming, tapped back, making sure his wedding ring hit the wall. And the tapping came back, more excited. But it seemed the other prisoner didn't know Morse, so there wasn't much they could say to each other apart from hello. But at least that was something, knowing he wasn't alone. He tapped again.

And was interrupted by a scraping noise as the door opened. He could see dim light beyond it, and then a torch was switched on and the bright light shone in his face, dazzling him after his hours of darkness. He couldn't see anything, apart from the light.

Then a voice from beyond it. "Well, matey, you're a glutton for punishment, ain't yer? And my old pal Mr Batty here's been pining for a whack or two." The torchlight wavered slightly. "Hey, keep the light steady, can't you. Keep it right on his face."

He tried to avoid it, to dash out of the beam, but simply blundered into the wall. Then the pain exploded from his left arm, just below the shoulder. He fell to the floor, tried to huddle up small, knowing it was no use.

14

Half an hour later, Bhardwaj popped his head into the tent. "Car approaching, chief."

Blue got up, and, still wearing his white scene-of-crime overall, came out. Another of McCall's Clios, this time a blue one, had arrived at the barrier, and the driver jumped out. "Let me deal with this," whispered Blue to Bhardwaj, "I know him. Journalist."

The man, tall and well-built, with unruly red hair, strode up towards them and waved. "Angus! Good to see you. I was told you were here. Something must be up."

"Hi, John, how are you? PC Bhardwaj, this is John Striven, crime reporter, *The Nation*."

Striven shook Bhardwaj's hand. "Good to meet you, constable. Lucky man, to work with Angus here. Follow him everywhere. Learn from him. He's the best." He winked at Blue.

"Pay no attention, flattery is his speciality," said Blue.

"Cheaper than bribery!" added Striven.

"To what do we owe this pleasure, John?" said Blue.

"Come on, Angus, no pantomime puzzlement please. We are professionals all, are we not? Nothing happens today without leaving a footprint on social media. I just keep an eye open, and a crime tent always arouses attention. You're just lucky it's me, not some moron from the tabloids. So what's the story? Tent says murder. Especially with you standing outside it. Somebody told me there was a guy in a bar here last night shouting off about several bodies. 'Mass murder on Remote Island!' Mind if I take a photo?"

"Feel free to photograph anywhere you like apart from inside the tent. I'd recommend a scenic panorama over the airport."

"Come on, Angus, what have you got? You know if you don't say anything I'll have to make the most of what I've got. I could even just make it up, credit it to 'unnamed informants.' Although of course, as a professional, I'd be loath to do that."

"I'm only here as an observer, John, so I can't give you an interview. If you want an official statement, go to Inspector Nicolson at Bowmore. She's in charge."

"I phoned. 'A situation is being investigated. An announcement will follow in due course.' So, what have we got? Some bodies, looks like mass murder. Could the killer still be active? When's the next atrocity going to happen?"

"Alright, John, I'll tell you what I can. First, I can't comment on the number of bodies at the moment, but I will say it is small. Second, we don't know if it's murder or not, or indeed whether these deaths are recent or historic. Could be epidemic victims. You know, small-pox, cholera, typhoid, plague, that sort of thing."

At the word 'plague' Striven had taken a step back. "Oh. Where are you at the moment?"

"Still a while before we uncover the bodies. Maybe tomorrow. Given the contamination risk, it might take a while to get them off the site safely."

"Why are you here, if it's just a plague pit?"

"I didn't say it was a plague pit, but that's a possibility. I'm only here in case it's foul play, and wasn't over a hundred years ago. That's why, as I say, I'm just observing."

"You don't look like you're just observing."

"Helping out with the digging, that's all. Can't sit around doing nothing, can I? Why not come back the day after tomorrow? It'll be clearer then, I think."

"Hmm, we'll see," muttered Striven, "Thanks for the information. See you later." He took a few steps back, then pulled a smartphone from his pocket, and held it up.

"Say cheese." He took a picture, waved, and went off towards his car.

Blue phoned Moira Nicolson. "I hope you don't mind my giving Striven something. I know him, he'll play fair. But he's talked to someone who heard Dalvey spouting in the bar, and that's not good."

"How did he find out that anything was happening here?"

"Keeps an eye on social media. More than I do. By the way, have you had a chance to speak to Blackett about those tracks?"

"No, not yet. He won't be in till tomorrow now, he's not answering his phone."

He returned to the dig. The atmosphere in the tent was becoming more intense, now that the floor level had been reached. The bodies themselves had been left until the ground around them could be swept for clues. The men – and woman – kneeling on plastic boards, could regard the floor now as a crime scene with a dusting of peat on it. Take out the dust carefully and see what's there.

By one-thirty it was done. The finds were few: what Alison thought was part of a cigarette, wrapped in a piece of newspaper, and two bullets, from different places. These were all bagged for analysis. But now they knew this was neither an epidemic nor a historical event. Alison Hendrickx declared a half-hour lunch break. One of the SOCOs was sent to the airport cafe to fetch sandwiches, cake and coffee.

Blue phoned the Super.

"Well, Angus, what have you got?"

"Murder. Five bodies. Found two bullets so far and maybe a cigarette. Probably recent enough to be live. Just starting on the bodies now."

"Good summary. Email me a report once you've got the bodies out. The case is yours now. I'll email Inspector Nicolson."

"Thanks, chief. How are things at your end?"

"Have you seen the papers? This 'British Studies' module."

"Saw it in the telly. Sounds ominous."

"It gets worse, Angus. Every foreigner coming into the UK for a stay of more than sixty days has to take it, and get a pass or they don't get in."

"How does that affect us?"

"It'll be applied to those already here. Students, refugees, long-term residents, the lot. We're the mugs that'll have to enforce it. Find them, make sure they do the course, deport them if they fail."

"What about the ones who can't be deported? Refugees. People with no papers."

"Who knows! Maybe the Australian model. Set up a camp for them on the Falkland Islands."

By three-thirty the bodies had been cleared and photographed *in situ*. They were well-preserved, though hands and heads were quite brown, and the clothing well-stained too. Each man – they were all men – was dressed in a plain shirt and flannel trousers; the feet were bare. There was nothing in their pockets, and their clothes showed no obvious identifying features. Dr Sheena Halsetter, from the cottage hospital, examined them, and announced her conclusions body by body, each one the same: "Dead, but I think you'd already guessed that. Well-preserved if rather stained – peat does that, I suppose. Probably a long time ago. Shot through the back of the neck. Bullets exit through the front of the throat. Relatively painless, as these things go, if that's a comfort to anyone."

"Executions?" said Blue.

"Not for me to decide, but I'd tend to agree with that."

The ground beneath the corpses yielded three more bullets. So they had all five. The work was done. Blue watched as the bodies were slipped into bags, and loaded into a chilled van that had come over that afternoon. The van would set off for the next boat; and they'd be in the morgue in Oban that evening, ready for the post-mortems. Then the tent came down, and Andy McGuire, one of the SOCOs, was taking photos across the whole site. The others were pottering around putting stuff into the van. A roll of thick black plastic and three shovels were propped against it.

Alison offered Blue a coffee from a large flask. As they were sipping the hot liquid, Moira Nicolson arrived to see what was going on. "What'll happen now?" she asked Alison.

"They'll put plastic over the floor area, then a foot or so of peat on top. It means the scene is protected from the weather, but we can open it up again fairly quickly in case we want another look. Once the case is closed, they'll take up the plastic, and the digger can fill it all in again."

While they were both there, Blue asked Alison and Moira if they'd join him for a meal that evening, so that they could talk over what they'd found. He asked Steve Belford if the SOC team would like to come too, but they were keen to get the site covered and get the evening boat off the island. Home comforts beckoned.

Alison went back to the hotel – it turned out she was in the Victoria and Albert too – while Blue drove to the police station to update his report.

It was about half past five by the time he'd made a cup of coffee and got typing. By half past six, he'd completed the work, and emailed the report to Superintendent Campbell. He sat back to think about how he needed to organise the work on the case.

Fifteen minutes later his mobile rang. The Super. "Read your report, Angus. Interesting. Very interesting. Needs to be sorted out. Even if it turns out to be too old."

"Yes, sir."

"Well, I can help you there."

"I'm glad to hear that, naturally."

"Don't you want to know how?"

"I assumed you were going to tell me."

"Assume nothing, Angus. Remember the old saying: never assume, it makes an Ass of U and Me." Blue did remember it, but said nothing.

"You still there, Angus?"

"Yes, sir. You were going to offer me some help."

"Yes, I'm sending you Sergeant McCader."

Blue thought for a moment. He had never heard of him. "I don't recall Sergeant McCader."

"You wouldn't. No point trying. Just transferred from North East Division. I can't get you anyone else at the moment. So you'll have to take two of the local PCs, and make the best of it. I don't suppose they've much on there, anyway."

"OK, chief. By the way, when will Sergeant McCader arrive?"

"He's been alerted. Should be there tomorrow morning."

15

It was seven-thirty by the time Blue was back at the hotel. The first thing he noticed was John Striven sitting in the foyer with a drink. "Angus, how's it going?" he asked.

"Fine. We made faster progress than we thought, we've eliminated several possibilities."

"You mean, the plague pit?"

"Among others."

"I thought that was a red herring. It's murder, isn't it?"

"Come up to the station tomorrow morning, I'll be able to tell you more. Enjoy your drink." And he walked on up to his room.

He had arranged to meet Alison and Moira at eight at the bistro in Port Ellen, round the corner from the hotel, as he feared Striven would haunt the hotel restaurant. He and Alison were hungry, whilst Moira said she'd eaten at home already, but would be happy with a snack and a glass of wine. Since she lived on the edge of the village, she'd walked in. They sat at a table discreetly located in a corner. Striven might yet take a walk round and peer in. If he saw them, he'd certainly try to gate-crash the meeting, or decide to have a drink sitting at the next table.

"OK, Moira, Alison, thank you for coming. I wanted a chat about the case, see where we can go from here. Since it's clear now we're dealing with murder, I've been appointed case officer."

He paused, and Moira cut in, "Angus, I'll give you all the help I can."

"Thanks, Moira, I'd appreciate that. So, what have we got, then? Looks like multiple execution. That's rare for Scotland, let alone Islay. Can we start with the bodies, Alison?"

"Five bodies. Young men, I'd say in their twenties, but the PM will sharpen that up a bit. All look in good health, apart from being dead of course. All killed the same way, bullet through the back of the neck. The similarity in positioning of wounds suggests they were all killed by the same person, but again, we'll have to see if the PM confirms that. That's really all I can say at the moment."

"How long have they been there. Can you give us a rough dating?"

"Hmm. Right now I'd say 1930s to 1950s. The amount of staining on the bodies and their clothing from the peat would suggest at least fifty years ago. What they're wearing would fit the same time frame. Flannel trousers and open-necked casual shirts with integral collars would fit anywhere in that period."

"OK. Look at it from the other end. What was going on then that might produce a multiple execution?"

"Glasgow gang wars?" ventured Moira.

"That's certainly possible. But why bring the victims out here?"

"To be out of the way, where no-one would notice?"

"That's a problem. Their killings tended to be public. Revenge or warning. That needs a very visible body floating down the Clyde. Doesn't make a lot of sense to spirit folk away to Islay then quietly execute them."

"Could be a faction within a gang being eliminated," suggested Moira. "But you're right, it's not likely."

"Guns weren't a usual feature of gang fighting, especially before the war," Blue continued. "Knives, razors, clubs, iron bars. More firearms around after, it's true, but still not the weapon of choice. Alison, what about the way they were killed? Anything characteristic there?"

"That's an interesting one. It's classic KGB. Single shot in the back of the neck kills instantly first time, no bullets wasted. Very economical. But not common over here."

"So more likely a technique someone had picked up, perhaps during the war," said Blue

"Or an émigré Russian," put in Moira.

Alison gasped, a strangled cry. She was staring at the windows, which ran all the way along the front of the restaurant. Someone was peering in. A youngish man with dark hair under a black woolly hat, and a short beard. And in the dim light a woman nearby, tall, slim, with long blonde hair. The man was squinting and obviously trying to see what the restaurant was like. Eventually he turned to the woman and said something, and they walked off together.

Blue and Nicolson remained silent until Alison had recovered herself. "Sorry," she said, "Gave me a fright. He appeared so suddenly."

"He obviously didn't think The Palace Bistro was sufficiently palatial to eat in," said Moira.

"They came in yesterday, from Glasgow," said Blue, "I saw them come off the plane." He was relieved that it wasn't Striven peering in.

"They'll have to go to the hotels if they want to eat somewhere else," said Moira. "But Angus, what if it's nothing to do with gangs? Maybe political? I mean, haven't the Russians always tried to eliminate prominent émigré. You know, like Trotsky."

"We can't rule that out either," considered Blue.

"There's another problem if it was wartime," put in Alison, "The British ruling class's obsession with secrecy. A colleague from down south told me about a case they had near Salisbury Plain. You know, there's a whole city there that's not on any map because it's an army base. A young woman's body was found buried in a garden in Salisbury. Looked like she'd been killed in the mid-1960s. Seemed she was having a relationship with an officer at the base. But could he be tracked down? No. MoD refused to provide any information. 'Reasons of National Security.' End of case. He got away with it. Protected by his own."

"Would they have been more co-operative if he'd been a corporal?" asked Moira.

"Maybe. But probably not. What I'm saying is if it had anything to do with the base here in Islay, I wouldn't be surprised if you hit a blank wall."

"I'd agree with that," said Moira, "George Outhwaite couldn't get much information about the base out of the MoD. They eventually produced a plan, but there wasn't much detail on it."

"OK," said Blue, "to sum up, it looks like murder, looks like execution, probably forties or fifties, might be gang stuff, might be Russian agents, might be wartime, or it could be something else altogether. We can probably rule out aliens." This joke received the silence it deserved.

For a few minutes they ate in silence. Then Blue continued, "What about the finds, Alison? Can they sharpen things up a bit for us?"

"I would hope so. The bullets should point to the type of weapon, and that might suggest a typical user. I'm not an expert. But we do have one, if he's not in compulsory rehab by now."

"What, you don't mean Dalvey?" asked Moira.

"The very same. But he needn't come over here. He can examine the bullets in Oban, in the lab."

"That's a relief," said Moira.

"Quite," said Blue. "What about the other things, Alison?"

"The piece of newspaper round the cigarette may give us a date. But I daren't open it up till it's in the lab."

"How did you know it was a cigarette?"

"Just the shape and size. Probably half smoked and wrapped up to finish later. Maybe one of the diggers, or executioners, thought he was putting it in his pocket, but it slipped out or missed and trickled down into the hole. Or he took something else, like a hankie, out of his pocket, and it got caught and came out too. Could have been dark, so he didn't see it."

"You're saying *he*," said Moira.

"Only because I don't see women digging a pit and tossing bodies into it. But it's always possible. Then there's the ring; we'll get it off the hand in Oban, and hope there's something on the inside."

"Why wasn't it removed? All other identifying items were taken off."

"Maybe it couldn't be got off," said Alison, "Or no-one noticed it. We may not get an answer to that."

"Thanks, Alison?" said Blue, "What's your next move?"

"I'll pick up the finds in the morning, get over to the mainland, and get the analysis going. I'd also like to get to the PM and see what comes out there."

"That sounds good," said Blue. "Sooner we get some results the better. Meanwhile, we'll see what the museum people have got. I'll also have to write up a report for the Super. This evening has helped me a great deal there. You'll both have a copy, by the way. Any comments welcome."

They left it at that, and Moira excused herself fairly quickly. It was near ten, and Blue toyed with the idea of asking Alison for a drink at the hotel bar, but he was exhausted after a day out of doors, and needed to do some more thinking. He went to bed with the intention of jotting down the main points from the meeting, but was asleep within five minutes.

Day 3. Saturday

16

Blue was up at seven. There was no sign of Alison or John Striven at breakfast.

At eight he drove up to the site. He wanted to get a feel for the place, with fewer people about. As he got out of his car, he was met by PC Craig. She was sensibly dressed for night work in walking boots, black trousers and a dark blue parka. She was also wearing black gloves and a red woolly hat which she had removed as she came up to Blue's car. Her voice was strong, with a West of Scotland twang.

Blue greeted her. "Have you been here all night?"

"Aye, sir."

"Any incidents?"

She took out her notebook, and looked at it carefully. "Yes. 2.36 a.m.: a car stopped at the bottom of the access road. Nobody got out. At 2.41 I started to walk down the track tae take a look. I was only a few yards down when it drove off. I guess they saw the light from ma torch. So I didn't get any identification details. Sorry about that."

"That's all right. But if it happens again, don't go down yourself. Call the station and get someone else out. Even if they have to get out of bed."

"Probably just local youths. I'm nae feart o them."

"News of these bodies is probably out now, so we need to be more careful at the moment. Murder sites attract some weird people."

Craig consulted her notebook again. "And there was another, er, incident at 6.04 a.m. It was getting lighter by then, though the sun isn't up till about half past. I spotted a figure coming towards the site. Must have walked up over the moor fae the main road. Too far away to get details. Well muffled but I'd say a woman, that was my impression. Walked across the moor in this direction. Stepping very carefully. Then stopped. I think she was looking around wi her binoculars. Then she went across there towards the old road."

"Hmm. Do you think she was trying to reach the site?"

"I couldn't say, sir. She may have seen me standing here, watching her."

"Good work, Deirdra. I see Doctor Hendrickx's car here too."

Craig consulted her notebook again. "Aye, she got here at 7.40." That would explain why he'd not seen her at breakfast.

"Thanks. Good work. When are you due to be relieved?"

"Arvind or Boris should be up soon."

The car could have been Striven, up for a nose around, but not necessarily. And who was the woman?

Alison was at the edge of the site looking at the dark covering of newly shovelled peat. She looked up as he approached, smiled. "Hi, Angus. Thought I'd just take a look at the site again."

"Get a feel for the surroundings. How it sits in the landscape."

"That's about it. How did you know?"

"I didn't. But that's why I'm here too. You have to get a feel for the big picture. History, geography, politics, ways of life. And death."

They heard the drone of a plane. It came from the west, swung out into Loch Indaal and came onto the runway off the sea, taxiing to a halt just by the airport building. Tiny figures emerged and went into the building.

"That was the air base over there," said Blue, "It stretched as far as the foot of the track here."

For a few minutes Blue stared down at the space where the base had sat. His eyes were caught again by the off-white rectangles that were the floors of the vanished buildings. He must go down later and take a closer look.

Alison had wandered off. Soon she came back. "I'm heading off for Oban now. I'm booked on the nine-thirty boat from Port Ellen."

"Did you remember the hand?"

"Yes. I'm quite organised, you know." She laid her hand on his arm. "You take care of yourself, Angus."

"Yes, of course." He felt the warmth from her fingers.

Blue was just thinking of heading for the police station, when John Striven arrived. "Hi John," he said, "You just caught me. Weren't you going to see me at the station?"

"Thought I'd come up here first, have a quick look round. And here you are too."

"Well, I can give you an official interview. My case now."

"I'm glad to hear that. What have you got?"

"Five bodies in a pit. Looks like an execution."

"Wow, that'll make news."

"Not so fast. They're dated nineteen-thirties to fifties. The killer will by now at least be in his eighties. If he's alive at all."

"Hmm. So hardly a danger to the public. Are you going to investigate it? Or just leave it?"

"We'll treat the case as live. As the killer may still be."

"Not a hot scoop, then. More a historical interest piece. Page seven."

"Sorry. But at least it's your scoop. And you never know. We may get him. Or her. We'll certainly try. Even geriatrics should have to face up to what they've done."

"Any idea who the victims were?"

"At the moment, not the least. Young men. Short back and sides, flannels, open-neck shirts. No ID."

"Picnic. Fishing trip. Sunday School outing. Any clues at all?"

"There's some evidence from the site which may give us some direction. I can't tell you what at this stage, but keep in touch. This is one where we might need to be working together, if that's OK with you."

"I get it. Any readers notice five lads from your street suddenly disappear in 1956?"

"Something like that. But don't put it out till we've looked at the evidence. That might help us to pinpoint the date a bit better."

"Can I see the stiffs?"

"Sorry, they went off to Oban yesterday, for the PM."

"Thanks, Angus, at least there's something of a story there. Look out for it on Monday. See you later."

17

He decided to take a look at the remains of the airbase before going to the station. He parked the car at the airport and crossed the road, passing the big house, and the garage, to reach the waste ground beyond. He could see the white patches in the rough grass, and headed for one. It was an area of concrete flooring, about 10 yards square. Round the edge he could see where red brick walls had been, only one or two courses extant. Walking onto the floor, he could see the faint traces of other walls. Four small rooms on each side of a central corridor. Bedrooms, storerooms, or offices – there was no sign of how they'd been used. Maybe the war ended before they could be used for anything.

A little further on the road rose slightly, and on the left was a rusted rail. As he approached it he could see there was a stair – three steps leading down to a much bigger expanse of concrete flooring. Was this an assembly room, dining hall, dormitory or cinema? Again, nothing betrayed its former status. In one corner, a lead pipe protruded from the floor. He looked closer. It had been sawn off about an inch from the floor. The scrap metal merchants had combed the site.

Looking up the low incline of the road, he saw one of the wartime buildings still intact, and walked up to have a look. A small rectangular building, about ten feet long and six wide, with a concrete floor, red brick walls, and a flat concrete roof. A metal grille filled the doorway, secured with a large padlock. Next to the building was a hedge, with a gap leading into the garden of a bungalow. In the garden, an elderly man was sitting on a wooden bench reading a newspaper, a mug sitting beside him. He looked up as Blue came in.

"You would be with the police." Was it that obvious? "Did you find much up at the peat, then?"

"We're still working on it. Tell me, how did you manage to get one of those wartime buildings?"

"Well, that wasn't me, of course, it was my father's doing. I was just a boy then. This house wasn't there at that time, we lived over by Kildurrin." He pointed vaguely towards the sea. "We had to move when they built the base, not long after the war started. Everybody was just told to go – we had two weeks to find somewhere to live and get our stuff out of the house. Then, they just bulldozed it, furniture and all. We had to stay with my father's sister in Bowmore, at the grocery shop."

"Did they knock down all the houses?"

"All except the big one. That's the hotel now, became their HQ. Even Colonel Colquhoun – he lived in it then – had to move away. After that there was building work all through the war. All sorts of things going on there. Who knows what they were up to?"

"Did you see anything?"

The old man chuckled. "Young lads are always curious. We came out from Bowmore on our bikes, and watched from the peat up there. Me, Billy Duggan and Robbie McArthur. You couldn't get very near, they had a big metal fence right round, coils of barbed wire in front. Sentries patrolling night and day. Lot of hush-hush stuff going on. Planes coming and going all hours – day and night. All sorts." He took a slug of his tea. "Och, I'm sorry, would you like a cup of tea? I'm not being very hospitable, am I?"

"That's very kind of you, I'd love one."

"You'd be a milk and no sugar man, I'm thinking?"

"Yes, how did you know that?"

"Ah, I've an eye for these sorts of things. Sit yourself down, now." He levered himself up and made his way slowly to the open window of the bungalow and spoke to someone inside.

Blue sat on the bench, and for a few moments savoured the total stillness around them. The man came back. "Jean'll be out in a wee minute with your tea. Now, where was I?"

Blue remembered *Flying-Boats Over Islay*. "I suppose you could tell which planes were coming over. You know, what the engines sounded like."

"Oh yes, we young lads became real experts. We could soon tell which direction the planes were flying as well – we tried to guess what they were up to. They should have used us as spotters – mind you, I don't suppose you need someone to spot your own planes. Still, there were a few jerry planes too, you know, Heinkels and so on. Bombers that had lost their way mostly."

An elderly lady came round the side of the bungalow, with a tray. "Here's the tea, Sandy! And another mug for yourself, yours'll be cold by now. And there's a wee biscuit too." She handed one mug to Sandy and put a plate of biscuits next to him on the bench, then offered a mug to Blue. "You'll be the inspector, from Oban, then."

"Is it that obvious?"

"No, no, of course not. Sandy told me. He probably didn't introduce himself. He's Sandy and I'm Jean McRae." He wondered if they were related to Thomas and Robert, who found the bodies.

"How do you do. Angus Blue."

"Blue. Would you be one of the Jura or Colonsay Blues?"

"Yes, actually, I am. My great-grandfather came from Jura. He settled in Greenock in the 1870s, then moved to Glasgow later."

"So you're almost one of us. *Agus a bheil Gàdhlig agaibh?*"

"*Beagan*. Just a little. I went to an evening class for a year, I'm afraid I've forgotten most of it."

"It's dying out here on Islay now. Not enough of us to keep it going. I watch BBC Alba. They should have set it up thirty years ago, but in those days they still thought Gaelic was worthless. Are you interested in history then? Sandy tells me you were asking about the war."

"It's a bit of a hobby, yes. He was telling me about the base."

"Well, I'll leave you to it. Don't let him bore you to death now."

She patted Sandy on the head, and made her way back into the house.

"Were there many of the wartime buildings near here?" asked Blue.

"Yes, there was a big assembly building just down there." Sandy gestured down the road, and Blue could see, off the road a bit, a large white rectangle. "And round the corner was another one, not so big, we called it the 'secret bunker' – it was probably just a communications room, but there were soldiers guarding it all the time. And the…but you can see the map for yourself."

"You have a map?"

"No, not me personally. But a few years ago the Historical Society produced a wee booklet about the base, they'll have it at the museum. I think it was George Outhwaite who wrote the text. A few of us got together and we made a drawing of where we thought the buildings were, then the museum people surveyed the area and produced the map. Nobody knew what most of the buildings were, we just labelled them Building A, Building B, and so on. There's a lot more interest in that period now."

"That's true. Well, Sandy, you've been most helpful, thank you. And for the tea." He stood up.

"It was good to be able to help. Do come back any time if you need to know any more. And I think Jean will want to see how your people fit in with hers. There are some Blues in there, you see. So you're almost family!" He laughed and they shook hands.

18

Stay calm. Think. Now he remembered. He'd never been in that building, never even knew what it was for. On the edge of the base, inside the barbed wire. Always guarded. No windows. That's why he'd assumed it was some kind of storage facility for secret material – documents mostly, he'd supposed, but maybe other things too – weapons, chemicals, special equipment for spies or commandos, stuff captured from the Germans that needed to be examined. Though he'd doubted that would happen here – it would be sent on somewhere else, for the boffins to look at.

He'd believed that right up to the time he stepped in the door. He'd been puzzled – just a wide corridor, painted white, with four steel doors or either side. Heavy, blank grey-painted doors. Not even numbers on them. Two bare bulbs in the low concrete ceiling, each with a wire guard round it. And a human guard, a big man with a red face and a shaven head, slumped behind his grotesquely distended stomach on a wooden chair just inside the entrance, picking his nose. The guard flicked away his latest find, and looked at him with an expression of distaste. He didn't stand, he didn't salute. The two men who'd brought him came in behind him, shut the door.

This wasn't right. He'd been unsure of the two who'd come for him, distrusted them, but couldn't be sure it wasn't on the level. There was so much going on here. And after what had happened the previous day, anything was possible. Nevertheless, this wasn't right.

"What's going on here?" he'd asked, "I thought…"

The tall man shoved him forward violently, while the seated guard stuck out his foot, sending him falling onto the concrete floor. He scrambled round trying to get up, but something very hard hit him on the side of the head. He fell again, dazed, saw the two men looming over him. The shorter one, the one with the little ginger moustache, like Hitler's, was swinging some sort of club, and hit him with it again, and pain surged across his shoulder. Now the other man started kicking him. The guard remained in his seat, watching, laughing. He tried to curl up, protect his head with his arms, but that left the rest of him unprotected. He heard the man with the moustache again – he was the only one who spoke: "Come on, let's give it to him good and proper. Let's have some fun with the bastard."

How long the fun had lasted, he couldn't remember. Pain stretches time, draws seconds into minutes. Not long, he supposed, before he lost consciousness.

19

Blue went back to the station. Clara Gilmour nodded distantly as he passed. He dropped his rucksack in his office and went to see Moira Nicolson.

She was working at a laptop, a gently steaming cup on its slate coaster alongside. "Hi, Angus, have a seat, care for a coffee?"

"Thanks." Blue sat down again in the strange rustic chair. "Can we talk about manpower?"

"Yes, I've been ordered to lend you two of my people."

"Can you afford to lose them for a while?"

"Is that a trick question? Obviously I need all the people I've got all the time. If I said anything else, they'd soon be taken off me. I hope you'll leave me Sergeant Walker."

"Don't worry, I'm being sent a DS from Oban. Who would you suggest?"

"There's not much choice. Take Bhardwaj and Craig. Arvind's a good officer. He'll go far, I think. And Deirdra's quite sharp, and a bit of a computer whizz."

"OK, that sounds fine. By the way, did you have a word with Blackett?"

"Yes. Says he saw nothing, no car, not even the tracks. Wayne Blackett's not an easy man to work with. He was sent here after some odd incidents in Greenock. Nothing was ever proved, but it looked like he was selling information to a newspaper. That's only what the people there told me when he came here, about four years ago. To be honest, I've no cause to complain about him, he does the work, and some things he's very good at. Just doesn't give it everything."

"Hm. Tricky."

"Yes. Now, you'll be needing a room for your team. I've got Clara onto it."

Clara showed him a larger room next door to his office. There was a big table and two smaller ones, six upright chairs, a metal filing cabinet and a roll-over blackboard. She stressed that the furniture was borrowed from the Council and would have to be returned in good condition. He promised not to write on it, and received a withering look. "The main fault of male officers is placing hot mugs on wooden surfaces. Please ensure your team use the mats, Inspector."

Four cardboard coasters, two with robins and two with a smiling Santa, had been placed precisely in the mid-point of each side of the big table. He returned to his office, updated his report, and emailed it to the Super.

At ten to twelve his phone rang. "Angus, is that you?" Alison Hendrickx. She sounded breathless.

"Alison, good to hear from you. Are you OK?"

"No! Somebody tried to kill me, and he's still here!"

"Stay calm. Where are you?"

"On the way to Oban. I was off the boat, heading for Ardrishaig. I came up behind a guy in a red Range Rover going quite slowly. When the road was clear, I pulled out to go past, but then he decided to speed up, so I can't get past. Next thing there's a lorry come round the corner, one of those big ones that shift the logs around, heading straight at me. I hit the brakes, tried to get in behind the Range Rover. He wouldn't let me in, Angus! Slowed down to stop me! I couldn't get out the way of the lorry. I thought I was going to die. There was a lay-by on the right, I saw it, right at the loch-side, skidded into it, just missed the lorry, almost went into the loch, hit a waste-bin, stopped. Angus, he tried to kill me! And he's still here!" She hissed the words, as if afraid to shout.

Blue was stunned. For a moment he couldn't think of anything. With an effort he focused his thoughts. "Thank goodness you're alive. Are you injured?"

"No, but…"

"Good. That's good. Where is this other car now?"

"He's parked about fifty yards down the road, in an old passing place on the other side."

"Did you get a look at the driver?"

"Yes, it was awful. He was smiling at me. Smiling! Angus, he's the same man who peered into the restaurant window last night. I'm sure of it. He had dark glasses, and some sort of woolly hat on. But I'm sure it's him. He's still here! In his car."

"Describe the car."

"Red range rover. I told you."

"Registration number?"

"Can't see all of it, there's a bush in the way. But I'm pretty sure the first bit was PU15. Oh my God, Angus, the door's opening! He's getting out."

"Lock your car door. Turn on the engine. Describe him!"

"Yes, right." She cleared her throat. "Male, average height, slim build, wearing a black jumper, I think, and black trousers. It is that man! Oh God, he's staring straight at me. He's coming over!"

"Alison, stay calm…"

There was a tapping noise, and a scream. He could hear a muffled voice.

"Alison, what's going on? Can you hear me?"

For a moment there was nothing, then Alison, breathless. "Angus, thank heaven you're still there. It's the lorry driver. Come to see if I'm OK."

"Put him on the line."

There was a shuffling and a new voice on the line. Glaswegian. "Aye, who's this?"

"My names Angus Blue. Police Inspector."

"Then you need tae put yon bastard in the jail. Rich shites with their Chelsea effing tractors. Think they own the road and can play with other folk's lives. And they think 'cos they've got pals in high places they can get off anything. Bastards! I'll certainly give ye a statement, no need to ask. Ma name's Archie Glenn, I'll write my name and address and my phone number on a wee card and give it to the lassie here. She's had a rare fright."

"Is the car still there?"

"Ach, not now, he must have buggered off when he saw me coming."

Blue thanked Archie and asked him to pass the phone back to Alison.

"How are you now, Alison?"

"I'm OK. Still a bit shivery. The adrenaline's still there."

"I think Archie might have saved your life."

"He did that twice, by braking promptly, and then coming to see me."

"Right. If you sit tight I'll get the nearest patrol car out to you."

"No, I want to get away from here."

"I can understand. In that case drive straight to Oban. Go directly to the police station. Give them a statement, and Archie's contact details. I'll alert them to what's happened, and get a search on for that car."

"What if he's waiting for me somewhere?"

"There's constant traffic on that road, so as long as you keep moving and don't try to overtake anyone there's not much he can do. I suspect he's made himself scarce now. But if you see him again, call me and I'll get a patrol out to you. Are you sure it was the man we saw last night?"

"Absolutely. The way he looked at me. Angus, what's going on here?"

"I don't know. It could be this case. Five people dead, and you with much of the evidence in your car. Could be a geriatric executioner trying to cover his tracks even now."

"Don't joke about this please, Angus. That man wasn't a geriatric. You've seen him too."

"Sorry. I didn't want to scare you. But you need to be careful. As I said, keep an eye open for anyone following you. Contact me as soon as you get to the station. So I know you've got there safe and sound."

He stared at the fractured wood of his desktop. Someone had carved a name on it: 'Malc' – was that as far as he'd got when the teacher reached him? Then the tawse would come out, the pain begin. He had to focus. Alison had been close to death, he knew it. Would the man have tried to kill her? He began to see the images of that other incident, the one that had changed everything. He couldn't dwell on that, he forced himself back to the present. He put an alert into the system for a red Range Rover, PU15…, and the description of the man, adding that he was required for questioning regarding a serious road traffic incident. He wrote an email briefly describing the incident, and sent it to Inspector Peter Carroll at Oban.

He needed to get out of the office. He glanced at his watch. Not quite one. Why not go to the museum, get something to eat there, maybe have a look round.

20

He went to the museum cafe. Jessie recognised him immediately. "Mr Blue. So nice to see you here again. Soup of the day is broccoli and Stilton."

After his lunch, there was time for a quick look round. There was plenty to see, so he merely glanced at the earlier displays: tiny splinters of mesolithic flint, bronze age pottery, carved stones from the dark ages, ornamented wine cups used by the Lords of the Isles. He paused at a display on the Islay clearances. The pictures showed a land emptied by landlords driven by greed. Chiefs who had seized for themselves land owned by the whole clan, to fund a lifestyle beyond their people's imagining. So long ago, but it still made him feel angry. His own people had suffered back then too, though they had been on Islay's neighbour, Jura.

He skipped a couple of rooms and found himself in front of a dusty cabinet with black and white photos of Lancasters, Wellingtons, and Sunderland flying boats. *Flying-boats Over Islay* – must watch it, maybe on his laptop. The captions were typed in print almost too small to read, and now were beginning to peel off the backing paper. Below the aeroplane pictures, a couple of general shots of the wartime airfield complex, slightly out of focus. There was also the map Sandy McRae had mentioned. Marked on it were hangers for planes, workshops, dormitories, refectory and assembly hall. Most of the buildings were nameless. Offices, stores, communications bases, who knows what else? A whole city out there in the mist.

He imagined it, mist included. Doors opening to reveal rooms lit by bare bulbs, maps pinned to the walls, pilots with handlebar moustaches lounging in chairs waiting for the summons. No, scrub that one, this wasn't a fighter base. No bandits at two o'clock here. This was way behind the lines. Logistics, moving stuff around. Heavy transport planes lumbering out of the darkness after a long and freezing haul from Iceland or Newfoundland. What were they bringing, that mustn't come by boat, that can't be risked amongst the Atlantic waves and the U-boat packs. Stuff that was valuable. Equipment. People. Secret things. Inventions we still don't know about, because they didn't work. People whose names weren't on lists. Who went off again to be dropped behind enemy lines. Disappeared without trace.

Inspector Nicolson found him there. "Angus, there you are! The meeting's about to start. But now you're in charge of the case, I guess you should lead it."

"No, I'm happy for you to chair these meetings. You know the people better than I do – and what they can do for us. Just ask me to update them first."

They sat round the table, steaming mugs to hand, expectant.

Moira opened: "I should tell you all now that this is a murder case. It has therefore been passed to Inspector Blue. So, Angus, you could tell us where we are now."

"Thanks, Moira. Well, we have five bodies, young men. Shot. We don't know who they are, nor where they're from. But we've narrowed the probable date down to sometime between 1930 and 1960. So we're looking for five young men who disappeared between those dates."

He paused to let all that sink in. Liz McMichael and Ina McNiven glanced towards Leonard Grange, who duly obliged. "Inspector, thank you for bringing us into your confidence. Sadly, I've not much to report. We identified a number of epidemics, shipwrecks and fishing boat disasters. But few were in this locality, in most cases the destination of the bodies is clear, and none of those left fits into your revised time frame. Sorry."

"No, no, thanks for checking. Now we know this type of local disappearance is highly unlikely. That leads me to think we're looking for people from off the island. Maybe a group who came here, kept to themselves, perhaps hired a house rather than staying in a hotel. So when they disappear, no-one notices."

"You mean like a religious sect," said Liz, "Or hippies maybe?"

"Could they have been brought to the island clandestinely, as it were, to be killed and disposed of on the QT?" asked Leonard.

"That's also possible."

"Or were already dead when they came here?" asked Elspeth, "Killed somewhere else?"

"No, that's not an option. We are pretty sure that they were killed where they were found."

"Hmm. Nasty business," said Leonard, "I think the best thing we can do, Inspector, is to have a closer look at this period. But if these chaps were trying to avoid notice, it won't be easy."

"What about talking to some of the old folks who were around then?" suggested Liz. "Five people vanishing – might just trigger some memories."

"Good idea," said Blue, "A list would be really useful. Folk aged 80 and over who were on the island during or before the fifties, and who are still pretty much *compos mentis*."

"We can certainly put that together." said Elspeth.

"It would be harder if it happened during t'war," put in George, "Even ordinary news were suppressed. Papers censored, only allowed to print good news – how we were beating the Jerries. People think there were no crime then, you know, all of us pulling together like. Truth were exact opposite. You could easily kill half a dozen blokes then, and not a soul would know owt about it."

"Rest assured, Angus," said Leonard, "We'll do whatever we can."

Outside Blue checked his mobile. A text from Alison: 'In Oban HQ. Call asap. A.' He waved goodbye to Moira, got into his car and phoned Alison.

"Angus, thanks for your help. You kept me calm and sane. You really did, believe me."

"That's what I'm here for. Did you see any more of him?"

"No, not a thing."

"Alison, I don't want to worry you, but you should be careful. Don't be out on your own if possible, till we find out more about this guy. Where are you staying?"

"I'm with an aunt in Dalmally. Stirling's too far to commute from."

"That's good. What are you doing at the moment?"

"Getting on it. Examining the stuff."

"If it didn't sound patronising, I'd say well done, Alison."

"That's the title of a book."

"What?"

"A book for girls. *Well Done, Alison.* There was a series, I read them all when I was about twelve. By Sheila Stuart. I really enjoyed them, because it was like me, in them. I was Alison, doing all sorts of brave stuff. Though I don't think anyone tried to kill Alison in the stories."

Blue wasn't sure how to respond to that. "OK. Right, can you do two things for me? First, write these incidents down. That way you won't forget them, we've got a record, and further details might come to mind as you write. Second, I think you should have a chat with the Super. Bring him up to date on the case – say I asked you to do that. And include what happened to you. He may seem distant at times, but he takes an interest, and he's not a fool. He's done some hair-raising stuff in the past, too. And misses it, I think."

"OK, I'll talk to him. Thanks, Angus. You're a life-saver. Talk to you later."

21

He parked the car by the station, then went to Christie's on Shore Street and bought a one-cup sized cafetière. Then to a grocer's shop where he got some freshly-ground coffee. Finally to a baker's which yielded half a dozen generous pieces of their home-made chocolate chip shortbread. Crumbles in the hand and melts in the mouth, they told him. That sounded just right. Back in his office, he enjoyed a cup of good coffee and a piece of shortbread. The baker's description proved to be accurate.

Then he sat for a while with his head resting on his hands, thinking. The incident with Alison was a worrying complication. Could someone else be taking an interest in the case even before they had identified the victims? Was the mystery man connected to the killings? Grandson of the original killer? Not impossible. But there was also a ray of hope there too. If they could catch him, or even identify him, that would give another pointer to the identity of the victims, and maybe to the reason they'd had to die.

Now he had a case and a team to work on it. He emailed Bhardwaj and Craig, asking them to meet him at 9 a.m. the following morning. He noticed that an email had come in from Oban, with a PDF of Sergeant McCader's file attached. He printed it out. Only four pages, and not much on each one. Enver McCader. What kind of name was that? Born in Dundee, now 38 years old. Entered the police in 2008. What had he been doing before that? No indication. Promoted to Sergeant in 2012 – very rapid! Something told him this man was no ordinary policeman. As usual, the oddballs were being dumped on him.

Superintendent Campbell had made it clear to him years ago that, as an intellectual type whose presence was a puzzlement to him, he would be given all the assignments that called for a more creative approach – "thinking out of the box, Blue, that's what I get from you, and it's my job to put that skill to the right use." This meant giving him any case that was weird, historic, or looked unsolvable. This also applied to people, and he had worked with various foreign officers on secondment as well as officers in Scotland who were under a cloud for one reason or another or needed to be parked in a peripheral area for a while. Not that Blue minded this at all, he'd worked on some strange cases and met some interesting characters. So what was the deal with McCader?

He made himself another cup of coffee and spent a while at his laptop trying to find anything relevant in the Criminal Records Database. But the material that had been retrospectively digitised only went back to 1960, so he drew a complete blank there.

As he wondered what to do next, there was a knock at the door. It opened to reveal a small man, clean-shaven with a sallow complexion and dark hair cropped short, wearing a worn black leather jacket and jeans. The man stood in the doorway. "DS McCader, sir."

Blue sat up. How did someone like this get into the police force – from the look of him he would hardly command any authority on the beat. But he also knew that you never judge by first appearances. There was bound to be another side to Sergeant McCader. He got up, motioned him in, and shook hands. "Hi, Inspector Blue, good to meet you, take a seat. Cup of coffee?"

McCader sat down. "That would be very kind of you, sir."

The kettle was still hot, so the coffee was not long in the making. McCader took sugar, but no milk. A man who could do without a refrigerator was always useful.

"Thank, you, Inspector," he said quietly, "I do appreciate real coffee." This was positive too.

"Well," said Blue, "I'm glad you made it over. Any trouble getting here?"

"No, the bus goes right to the pier, and the ferry connects with the bus. Nice crossing." East coast accent, probably brought up where he was born. But a hint of something more exotic too. And he spoke in a quiet, self-effacing sort of way. A man who could become invisible.

"Good. McCader, that's an unusual name. What part of the country does it come from? Maybe up Sutherland way?"

"Actually, it doesn't come from anywhere, my father made it up."

"Ah." This was getting more interesting.

"He's from Albania. I was born there, only just. We came to Scotland in 1977."

"That's slightly at odds with the information in your file."

"Yes, sir." He did not elaborate. Best not ask too much now.

"Tell me about your previous posting. Aberdeen. What were you doing there?"

"Special operations. We uncovered a major drug ring connected to the oil industry."

"Some pretty big people were convicted, weren't they?"

"That's right. After it was over, it was felt it might be good for me to be somewhere a little quieter."

"Out of the public eye."

"Just so."

"I understand." This wasn't the first time Blue had been given someone to work with whom Superintendent Campbell – or Police Scotland – were less than open about. "Well, we'd better get down to work, er, Enver. First, are you fixed for accommodation?"

"Yes, a B&B here in Bowmore. Seems very comfortable, and the owners are friendly. By the way, I met a Sergeant Piłsudski at a briefing last year, and he mentioned your name, told me to look out for you and say hello from him if I ran into you. I didn't realise then that I'd be working with you."

"Ah, yes, Piłsudski." Images swept his mind of a cave on Skye, and a boat burning on dark water like a Viking funeral. He shook them away. "First thing you'd better do is read the report. Then we can talk it through."

Blue printed out the report and handed it to McCader, then led him to the next room.

"I hope this'll do for a base. We've two other people on the case team, PCs Bhardwaj and Craig. We'll have to see if we can borrow one of the computers from downstairs."

He left McCader settled into a chair, reading the report, and knocked on Moira's door, to let her know that McCader had arrived. She came with him through to the base room and Blue introduced them. Then she motioned him back to her office.

"Angus, about keeping watch on the crime scene. Blackett has texted that he's sick and can't do his shift tonight. You need Arvind and Deirdra tomorrow, Bob's been on duty here all day, so I've no-one else."

"Is Blackett's sickness genuine?"

"I don't know. I'm sure he has a few bogus sickies each year. But apart from turning up at his door with a doctor, there's nothing we can do. I think the best we can do is check the site at intervals. Will that do?"

"Yes, it'll have to. We need our manpower focused on the investigation."

"I'll arrange it. I'm off tomorrow, so I'll see you on Monday. Unless something urgent comes up."

As he sipped a fresh coffee, he glanced out of the window. Nothing happening in the street. But he snapped to attention as a red Range Rover slunk round the corner and drew in opposite the station. The windows were dark, he couldn't see inside. No-one got out. Were they watching him? And who were "they"? Time had slowed to a halt out in the street. Everything was still. Then the driver's door began to open. A man eased his way gingerly out onto the pavement. Blue could only see the top of a black woolly hat. What was going on here? Some sort of threat or warning? The black woollen dome hovered between the car and the open door.

The man finally managed to get himself out of the car. Now Blue could see that, although he was wearing a black woolly hat, and dark glasses to boot, he was probably in his eighties and had long white hair and a two-day stubble to match. He straightened himself with obvious effort, and, leaning back into the car, produced a long white stick. Easing himself round to face the pavement, he shut the car door and began poking his way forward with the white stick. He shuffled along the pavement and into the Spirit Well.

Blue was astonished. What was going on here? An alternative reality where the blind see? Perhaps on emerging from the whisky emporium he would throw his stick away. Was the driving test so lax here? He would have a word with someone about it.

He went through to the base room to see what McCader made of the case.

"It's an interesting one," said the sergeant thoughtfully, "It seems to me there's something we don't know going on here, something that connects then to now. Why does an old case raise any interest?"

"Perhaps the murderer is still alive, and someone, maybe family, is protecting him."

"Yes, family can be very protective, even over-protective. Sometimes it's the family more than the killer who want to hush up the crime. They're no longer interested in the killer's fate, but their own reputations. Who wants to be the relative of a murderer?"

Blue remembered reading the autobiography of the daughter of a famous Nazi. Her father's history had become her albatross.

"And there's something else," McCader went on, "The method of execution. Not gangland. More KGB. But that's puzzling. Killing five young men could be understandable in Soviet Russia, where there were plenty of reasons for young men to die, but it doesn't make sense here."

"Then what does the execution suggest to you?"

"Organisation. Maybe our KGB."

"The Secret Service?"

"They are just as ruthless in their own way as the KGB. If people get in their way, they can be threatened, blackmailed, killed. They work outside the law. I was in Northern Ireland for a while. I can't say any more."

"If that's the case, it's going to be a difficult one to pursue."

"Well, I can start on these PU15s right away. We should be able to identify all the owners from the DVLC database, and chase them up."

Blue returned to his office and phoned Alison. She was still working on the finds, and promised to call him in the morning. He was beginning to feel frustrated. Until they got some ID on the bodies, it was going to be difficult. He hoped the PM might throw something up. He supposed that would take place on Sunday or Monday. Alison's work on the finds might deliver some news too, but that would also take time.

He called Inspector Carroll in Oban, but was told he'd gone home. A sergeant explained they'd not had any sightings of the red Range Rover. Was that going to be a dead end? Just a one-off bit of sick mischief by a bored rich boy? Maybe it was time to give up for the evening, start afresh in the morning.

22

He needed to clear his mind. Change the subject. Go for a drive. Something really historic.

He drove out of Port Ellen, taking the road he'd walked the first evening. After a couple of miles the twisting road straightened out, and he passed the entrance to the Laphroaig distillery, its drive masked by woodland, then Lagavulin, with the ruin of Dunyvaig Castle silhouetted to seaward beyond, and finally Ardbeg, the smokiest of the Islay whiskies. It would be good to visit a distillery while he was here. He drove on a few more miles to Kildalton churchyard.

A walled enclosure, with a rusty iron gate, looked over a landscape emptied of habitation. The tall Celtic cross, cut in the Dark Ages out of hard greenish rock, was covered with vivid carvings of Bible figures. An object to incite wonder, to provoke worship. Its long shadow, cast by the autumn sun, stretched over lichened gravestones. Only the dead had not been cleared from the land.

Nearby stood the mediaeval church, a roofless testament to more of the departed. Inside its shell were gravestones of the chiefs. Carved out of the long slabs, life-size men like Norman knights, pointed helmets, chain mail hauberks, two-handed swords. So important in their time. Now nameless, and long gone. And of the nameless folk who followed them, and died for them, nothing at all.

Were there mass burials near here too? Villages on the coast wiped out by Viking raiders. Clansmen killed by hereditary foes. Young men doomed by pointless family feuds. Histories of killing.

Back at the hotel, he ate in the restaurant. Pan-fried salmon with mashed potato and leek, and a hollandaise sauce. And a 16-year-old Lagavulin. Heavier, less fruity than the Caol Ila, darker and suggestive of hidden depth. In the nose, a dense and guarded power, a memory of peat smoke. And on the tongue, an almost oily smoothness, and the warmth of the fire. A dram to dream by, to summon up the past. He felt a tear. Time to move on. He went up to his room, focused on finishing off the *Short History of Islay*. There was only a passing reference to the air base. He'd have to find the booklet about it that Sandy McRae had mentioned.

Then the news. This time the TV interview was with the UK

Home Secretary. She explained that, "There's no crisis, as some are making out, Jeremy. It's an opportunity, perhaps the greatest opportunity for this nation since the Second World War. But to really grasp that opportunity, we have to know exactly who we are. And be proud of it. The British Studies Module that we're introducing will ensure that our children know where they belong, and where they've come from. British Studies is a safeguard for our present, and a gift – a very precious gift – to our future."

Day 4. Sunday

23

Blue arrived at the police station at 8.45. Sergeant Walker was at the reception desk, reading a magazine. He put it down hurriedly, but Blue had caught the title. *Airfix Magazine.*

"Morning, Bob. You into model aeroplanes, then?"

"Yes, chief. When I were young, we moved down to Croydon, near the old airport. It had shut down before I was born, but my Dad was dead keen on planes. Used to take us out to Heathrow to see them. Every Christmas and birthday I got Airfix kits. You couldn't see the bedroom ceiling for all the little planes hanging there. I still keep my hand in."

"So what brought you up here?"

"Kids, I guess. I were ten years in the Met, made sergeant there. Got married. Angie was a nurse. But she's from up here, Scotland I mean. When she got pregnant we did some serious thinking. I'd seen a lot of stuff in those years, and there comes a time when either you're so used to it, you don't see the horror any more, or you've had enough. Me, I'd had enough, so when Angie said London wasn't a good place to bring up kids, I couldn't have agreed more. So here we are. And it's a great place for bringing up kids."

Blue recounted the incident he had witnessed of the blind man getting out of his Range Rover.

"Ah, that'll be Isaiah McKirdy. Lives just round the corner. When he turned eighty, his son – he's a builder in Lochgilphead – bought him that big car. Probably a tax write-off for his business. Isaiah's very proud of it, but he is 87, so he just drives it round to the whisky shop – he likes a glass now and then, only buys a bottle a week – and then on round the block back to his house. Drives slowly, doesn't reverse at all. And only if it's daylight, and not raining."

"You think he's safe on the roads?"

"That's not my decision, sir, you'd have to talk to Inspector Nicolson. But I understand he's been told that that's as far as driving goes, and he's not even to think about getting into third gear. I should also say that his eyes are not half as bad as he makes out."

"So the stick is what, an affectation?"

"I don't know about that, sir, maybe he feels it gets him some sympathy. I suppose it also gives him the opportunity to whack people in the ankles whenever he wants."

He met with his team – McCader, Bhardwaj and Craig – at nine in the base room. He introduced McCader, and brought them up to date.

"We don't have a lot of leads yet. I'm hoping Dr Hendrickx will get us something later today, and maybe the PMs will turn something up. But it does look as if we've got two lines of action here, first, five men being killed decades ago, and second, someone who doesn't like us asking questions today. The only lead we have on what's happening now is the car. We have descriptions of the couple but they'd fit plenty of people. Arvind, can you get onto the airport, see if we can get names for them? They came in on the Glasgow flight on Thursday just after I got here."

McCader indicated he had something to add. "About the cars. There are twenty-one red Range Rovers with a PU15 registration. Would have been far more if it had been a black one. We don't have any reports of one being stolen. However, two of them belong to a company called Euro Special Logistics Solutions, with an address in Northampton. The name is vague enough to make me suspicious. Usually companies want to tell you exactly what they do. I phoned them yesterday afternoon, but just got a young lad who said his dad would be in today. Looking at the others, I was able to get hold of ten of the private owners last night on the phone. They're all clear, as far as I can see. I'll try the rest today."

"Excellent! Deirdra, can you get one of the computers from downstairs and set it up here. See if there's anything on Islay from the thirties to fifties. Look for anything that might be relevant. Then see if there are any historic cases that could be linked to this one. Mass execution style."

He left them to get on with it, updated his report, then phoned Alison's mobile, and asked if she was all right.

"Yes, I'm back in the lab. I photographed the bodies and took some tissue samples to be going on with yesterday afternoon. The PMs are this afternoon. I was hoping for this morning, but Dr Saffraj wouldn't give up his Sunday morning golf. So it's two o'clock. I'll give you a ring after we're done."

24

At ten he drove over to Port Ellen and went to the little Baptist Church just round the corner from the front. His religion, though he never mentioned it, let alone press it upon his colleagues, had nevertheless occasioned both puzzlement and suspicion within the force. A common reaction was, "How can you be a Christian and a policeman? Aren't you supposed to forgive everybody and let them off?" He had often explained that forgiveness is linked to repentance, the wrongdoer's awareness of his wrongdoing, and that the difference between right and wrong behaviour was at the heart of Christianity. It was his competence at the job that provided reassurance to most of his colleagues.

There were only a few who were actively hostile, who feared his honesty and his commitment to finding the truth. Some of these were cops who felt they knew who the bad guys were, and were not averse to assisting the ends of justice, by planting evidence or falsifying their testimony in court. Others, and these were very few, were overtly corrupt, accepting "gifts" for overlooking offences, or selling in-formation from police sources to journalists, lawyers or criminals. These groups tended to avoid Blue. This was not difficult, given that Blue's oddball reputation consigned him to peripheral or unusual cases.

A different reaction was that of his superiors. When, as a Detective Sergeant, he had turned down what was considered a very gracious invitation to join the Freemasons, it was hinted that this might not be a wise response in terms of his career trajectory.

Alison once asked him how he could retain his faith after what had happened. He answered simply that without his faith he would have had nothing left, his life would have been without meaning. She knew not to press the point.

The church was well-attended, with the full age range. Hymns were sung with conviction, accompanied by piano, whistle and fiddle, giving the arrangements a Celtic ring. The minister, a tall man in his early thirties, with a dark complexion and long dreadlocks, was erudite, passionate, and humorous. His sermon addressed the need for Christians to engage with the world, to expose and confront injustice. My kind of preacher, thought Blue. He could remember sitting through services conducted by ageing ministers, preaching to the aged and the comfortable, that all you needed was to feel good about being saved, and God would do the rest. Cosy churches, inward-looking, ignoring the world, passing the time until death.

As the service ended Blue was greeted by those sitting near him and pressed to have a cup of tea in the church hall. Tea, coffee and fruit cake, liberally buttered, were served from a table at the rear. His profession, which seemed known to all, did not affect the warmth of his reception, and he found himself consuming enough fruit cake to see him through most of the day. He was soon approached by the minister.

"Hi, how are you? I'm David Sempleton; call me Dave."

"Hi. Angus Blue."

"Oh yes, with the police. I needn't ask if you're on holiday then. I'm glad you've come to visit the living as well as the dead. By the way, how's your work here going? Don't tell me if you don't want to. It's not every day we have a pile of corpses turned up on the island."

"News travels fast. We're making progress. Whatever happened, it was sixty or seventy years ago, so we don't have a mass murderer running round at the moment."

"Even with a zimmer?"

"Well, we can't rule everything out. Tell me, do you have anyone in the church who might remember the 1940s or 1950s? They would be in their seventies, eighties or even nineties now."

"Oh yes, we've a good few of those. What church doesn't? At least here they're not the majority. Let me think. Effie Cranston might be a good source, or Hamish McNeill. They're old enough, but both still very sharp. Hamish only comes in the evenings, over at Bowmore, but Effie should be here now." He looked around the crowded room. "Ah, yes, she's over there, guarding the teapot. Let's go over." He guided Blue to the table from which the drinks and fruitcake were served. Standing behind it was a small and thin but alert-looking lady who smiled warmly at them.

Once introductions were made and Blue had explained what he was looking for, she paused and thought for a moment. "Hmm. Aye, that's a long time ago, richt enough, but I was here then. I'm 90 this year, you know. But ma memory's still sharp, ye ken, I think I can help ye."

The minister offered them the use of his vestry, and ushered them into a small wood-panelled room, with a table and two chairs. There was a large wardrobe against one wall. Mr Sempleton adjusted the heat control on the radiator. "I know that Effie feels the cold, so I'll turn this up a wee bit. Let me know when you're finished, in case I lock up the church with you two in it."

25

Blue did not want to waste time. He sensed Effie was willing to reminisce, but needed to keep focused on what might be relevant to the case. "Have you lived long on Islay, Effie?" he began.

"I wisna born here, but you'd guess that just to listen to me. I'm fae Inverurie, up near Aberdeen. Ma faither thought the fresh air would be good for us. He felt Inverurie was no a good place to grow up in, but that was a long time ago. I'm sure it's got the benefit of all this oil money now. Maybe he just had itchy feet, and was after a new start. Anyways, we came over here, that would be in 1936, when I was thirteen. I can tell you it was a real change. I couldna understand fit the folks was saying."

"And you've been here ever since?"

"Aye, that's right. I was married here too, but that was no till efter the war. My man died ower twenty years past, so I've had plenty time on my own. The church has been a great thing for me. They always look after ye. Mr Sempleton, he's a real nice boy."

"What did your husband do, then?"

"Och, he was in the malting. His father had the farm up at Cruach, but his older brother got the runnin o it, and he didna just want to be a farm hand, especially for his brother – the twa didna get on. Aye, we had a good life. But the dust was no good for him. It was lung cancer took him. Some people said I should sue the company, and they must have got wind o it, as they gaed me a good settlin. And I keep active too, ye ken, I go to the old folks keep-fit on a Tuesday morning, and…"

"Did you have a job yourself, back then?"

"Oh aye, I worked at the bank, the Commercial Bank it was then. Straight from school. Of course I stopped when I was married. And when the children left home we turned the house into a wee B and B. I kept that going for a few years after Jamie died but my heart was no in it any mair, so I'm now in a wee sheltered house no far from here. Anyways, that's my history. Fit was it ye were looking for?"

"This may sound like a daft question, but do you remember anyone disappearing? As you know, we've found some bodies. They were all young men, and we think they died sometime between the thirties and the fifties. Maybe with a group of people from off the island."

"There was the Grace Mission. They had a revival here in 1954 or maybe it was '55, I canna mind which. That was a grand time, they were marching roon the streets wi banners and aa – they even had a pipe band – and a lot of folk stepped forward. But they wouldna be making awa wi folks, would they?"

"I don't suppose so. Anything else? Perhaps in the forties."

"Well, there was a group came over, it must have been not long after the war, maybe 1946. They set up over towards Ardbeg, just shacks really, doon by the shore. They were there just a few months, in the summer. Then the landlord must have got wind o it – he lived ower near Edinburgh – and sent folks to clear them off his land. Not that that land was aye used for anything."

"What were they like?"

"They seemed harmless. Very polite like when they came into Port Ellen to buy stuff, and get the papers. A few couples wi children, and some single men. Nice people really. The men had all been in the war, they were wanting a new life, away from the towns. There was a couple of lads who'd been affected, you ken, in the head, seen things fit you shouldna ever have to see. But the others looked after them."

"How many were there, do you think?"

"Oh, not that many, maybe fifteen or so. I only heard aboot what went on second hand, like. Geordie McKay, he was in the polis. He told us all about it – he wanted to impress us girls."

"So what happened?"

"A lawyer came, from Glasgow or somewhere. Gave them 24 hours to go. They said they were no fer going. The land belonged to everybody, they'd fought for it in the war. The lawyer went awa then. But the next day he was back, wi some men the landlord had hired in Glasgow. The lawyer said they were trespassing, so he was entitled to bring bailiffs to remove them. The polis were there too, in case there should be trouble. The lawyer said he was in danger from the hut folk, but the sergeant, it was Tam McMillan then, felt the hired men were the biggest threat. 'Scum of the earth', he called them, according to Geordie. Hard men, with heavy sticks, mair like clubs. When they arrived there, the hut folk gathered in front of the huts. One of them started to speak, but he'd no said more than a dozen words afore one of the thugs hit him with his club. Then the rest came in, knocking folk over and kicking them when they were down.

"One o the hut folk must a had enough. He pulled out a revolver – from the war I suppose – and shot one of the bailiffs, not so as he was dead, like, in his leg. That was when the police stepped in. Sergeant McMillan ordered them to stop fighting, or they'd all be arrested, he'd call the army if necessary. The lawyer and his thugs went off, said they'd be back. The man with the gun let himself be arrested. The polis had a van, the sergeant offered to take the hut folk into Port Ellen, said they could all stay owernight at the police house if they wanted. They were sort of shocked by it all. They collected a few things in bags and rucksacks, the women and the injured went off in the van, and the rest set off walking down the road to Port Ellen.

"Later that day the landlord's thugs came back onto the site and started smashing the huts up. Anything they found inside they tossed out and trampled. Then they set them on fire. These men were just savages, animals, and the man who sent them was no better. Aye, and we were to blame too."

"Why's that?"

"We did nothing. We didna stop it. We just let it happen."

"But you weren't even there."

"But we all knew what was happening. I dinna ken what we could have done, but we should have done something. It wasna richt, what they did." Effie wiped her eyes with a handkerchief. "It wasna richt, Mr Blue. If Mr Sempleton had been there then, I think he'd have stood up, but the ministers then were auld men, who widna rock the boat."

"What became of them, do you know?"

"They stayed owernight at the polis house. Not locked in, you mind. Apart from yon who fired the shot. He went to Oban for trial, we never kent what happened with him. The rest left on the morning boat. Connie Duff, her father was the piermaster, said they'd gone to Australia, but I dinna ken where she got that from."

"Do you think the same number left as had arrived?"

"I dinna ken that either. I saw them leave, so sad and broken. We were all weeping on the pier. I went out the next day – it was Saturday afternoon – with some pals to see the place. I canna describe it. The destruction. Personal things lying all round, trampled into the mud. I found a Bible there. I've still got it. I can even still mind the name and address in it: John Samuel, 13 Johnstone Street, Govan."

Blue thanked Effie for her information, adding his apologies that she'd had to relive it all."

Effie wiped her eyes again. "No, son, you've a job to do. And I'm happy that my memories can be useful."

There were still people in the hall when they came out. Mr Sempleton poured Effie another cup of tea. He asked Blue if the chat had been useful.

"Yes, indeed, very helpful. What about Hamish McNeill – do you have an address for him?"

The minister wrote it on his card. "Here you are. But he sleeps in the afternoon, so he may not answer the door. Your best bet is to come to the evening service. Five o'clock in Bowmore."

26

Blue took a walk round the bay to get some fresh air before driving over to Bowmore. No need for lunch – he felt he'd eaten a whole fruit cake – but a cup of real coffee would be welcome.

It was just after one when he got back to the station. He made coffee, and wrote up the key points of Effie's account. Then he went through to the base room. Bhardwaj and Craig were sitting together at the PC on one of the small tables, looking at the screen. McCader had gone out to get some lunch.

"Well, people, what have we got? Arvind?"

"Yes, chief. Got the airport. Shona was very helpful." Blue noticed Craig smile. "The couple booked their flight at the airline desk at Glasgow Airport, paid in cash. Mr and Mrs Smith. Guess that doesn't get us far."

"It shows they don't care about using an obvious alias. Assuming their name isn't Smith."

"It isn't. Shona spoke to the woman at the airline desk in Glasgow. She said they had some sort of accent, and talked to each other in a language she didn't understand. She thought they were Eastern European."

"Good, that takes us a little further. Deirdra, what about you?"

"No much luck, chief. Lots of info on Islay, but mostly sightseeing, accommodation, and whisky. Nothing on any disappearances. The only mass death I could find was Solam. A plague village. The story goes that some terrible disease was brought in by a shipwrecked sailor. So the villagers cut themselves off to contain the infection. People left food for them on a rock nearby. One by one, they all died. Only the ruins are left now. And a mass grave somewhere up in the glen. But that's over near Ardbeg, and in the mid-nineteenth century. No relevant to us."

"Interesting. But you're right, not relevant to us. Carry on with the killings across Scotland then. Maybe the *Scotsman* or the *Herald* have been digitised back to the thirties. You might even be able to round somebody up at Police Scotland HQ to look at the archives." He gave them a summary of what Effie had told him, and asked them to see what they could find, and to chase up John Samuel. "But don't forget to take your lunch break."

He sat at his desk and glanced at his watch. Ten past two. Alison would just be watching Dr Saffraj open up the first body. He shivered at the thought.

His mobile rang.

"Hello. Insp…"

"Angus, it's Alison. The bodies. They've gone!"

"Sorry?"

"Disappeared. Taken."

"Shit! Sorry! This doesn't sound good. Tell me what's happened. From the beginning."

"I'm at the morgue now. Got here at five to two. No sign of Dr Saffraj. Eddie – that's the attendant – was surprised to see me, said didn't I know the PMs were off and the bodies had been transferred. I asked what happened. He said about 4.30 a.m. he'd been woken at home and asked to open up, there was a body coming in. He's paid to be on call, so he got up and went over. There was a big black van there, and two men who greeted him politely and apologised for having got him up in the middle of the night. They had what looked like police ID cards. He let them in and told them to bring in the body. They said he must have misheard the instructions, they'd not come to bring a body, but to collect the five from Islay, for onward transfer. He asked for their authorisation, and they gave him a form. Issued by the Ministry of Defence."

"The MoD?"

"You heard correctly. It had also been countersigned by someone at the Met. They said they were MoD police. It was to do with national security, the bodies had to be taken to a secure site as they feared they might be seized by persons unknown. Naturally Police Scotland were aware of this. They also said Dr Saffraj and I knew what was happening, and he would still be carrying out the PMs, probably on Monday, at the safe location. They remained pleasant throughout, but when Eddie suggested he'd better phone Police HQ to make sure it was OK, they got nastier, said this was a secure operation and if he tried to phone anyone, he'd be guilty of a criminal offence, under the anti-terrorism laws, and they'd arrest him."

"That's nonsense."

"Eddie didn't know that. He was worried. So he gave in. There wasn't anything he could have done anyway, as two more men arrived, bruisers who could have squashed him in no time. Once they'd removed the bodies, they told him to go home, and warned him that any further action by him would be a breach of national security. So he went home, and came back in today as usual."

"What did you do then?"

"I phoned Police HQ right away, and, guess what, nobody knew anything about it. Then I phoned Saffraj; he said he'd had a message, purportedly from the police station, to say the PMs had been postponed, and they'd get back to him. Then I phoned you."

"OK. This is interesting."

"No Angus, it's frightening. What's going on here?"

"Somebody wants to stop us doing the PMs. I don't believe the national security stuff – who'd want to seize dead bodies? Can you phone HQ and ask them to get a statement from Eddie. Assure him that letting the bodies go was not his fault. Has he got the authorisation paper?"

"No, they took it off him as soon as they'd got the bodies. Said they'd take it to Police HQ personally."

"Damn!"

"But, while they were all busy moving the bodies, he surreptitiously photographed it with his phone."

"Clever lad. Ask him to send the picture to Steve Belford. Who did you speak to at the station?"

"Inspector Carroll. He sounded confused."

"Yes. He would be." Peter Carroll was a good investigator as long as procedures were followed closely. Making decisions on the hoof was not his forte, so he'd simply pass on the report to the Super.

"Hello? Angus?"

"Sorry. Yes, I'm still here. Why not get over to the lab and get on with the analysis of the stuff from here? The more that can be done today the better. Can you do that?"

"Yes."

"And once you're at the lab stay there. Text me when you get there, and I'll call you later this afternoon. Phone me if there's any problem. And keep an eye out for anyone following you."

"I'm already doing that."

"And Alison?"

"Yes?"

"Take care."

This was absurd. Who'd want to steal bodies? Rogue medical scientists? Trainee undertakers? And were they MoD, or just pretending. MoD. Another link to the air base, perhaps.

His phone rang again.

"Ah, Angus, there you are. I've had a garbled report from Peter Carroll. He thinks some bodies have been stolen from the morgue. Tell me what's going on."

Blue explained.

"This is an odd development, but remember, every development, however odd, moves the case forward. First thing to do is keep calm. No hasty moves. We need to know who was involved. Was it Ministry people, or people pretending to be Ministry people? I'll get Belford to send me a copy of the authorisation, and we'll see if we can identify the signatories."

"Yes, Sir."

"I'll call the fiscal too. Fatal Accident Inquiry with no bodies can be tricky. She won't be a happy bunny."

27

He went to the base room. McCader was sitting at the big table, pieces of paper spread in front of him. He motioned Blue over: "Getting interesting with the cars, chief. Remember two of them belong to a company, Euro Special Logistics Solutions, address in Northampton. I phoned again, got the father. Turns out to be a garage where the cars are kept. He claims he didn't know his address had been used to register them. Gave me the only contact he had, another phone number. An answering machine – no name, just 'leave a message after the beep.' Then I tried Companies House. Euro Special Logistics Solutions isn't registered there."

"It's just a name? What do you make of that?"

"It's the sort of thing any big organisation, government, criminal or commercial, would do to keep its more unorthodox activities at arm's length."

"This keeps on getting worse." He told them what had happened to the bodies.

"Crazy stuff," said Bhardwaj. "Not even vampires want corpses."

"The aim seems to be simply to hinder our investigation. Without bodies, it's much harder to prove a murder. Even though we've got photos."

"Is somebody trying to protect the killer, then?" said Craig, "That would suggest that he's still around."

"Maybe the killer was simply a hired hand," said McCader, "and they're trying to protect whoever paid him. If that was an organisation, they could just be attempting to keep their reputation clean. Stop any dirt getting out."

"Could it really be the MoD?" asked Bhardwaj.

"Government departments and agencies are very sensitive to reputational issues. Even more so than companies. There are not just civil servants in there, but also politicians. None of them wants to be tarnished by a scandal, even if it is sixty or seventy years old."

Plenty to think about there. Blue asked Bhardwaj how he was doing.

"Well, I got somebody at Oban to look in the archive. They have a record of a James Affleck charged with assault and illegal possession of a weapon on arrival from Islay. August 1946. He was sent before the sheriff, pleaded guilty, six months in prison. After that, no trace of him in the UK. I could try Australia?"

"No. Thanks, Arvind, but it's beginning to look like the hut people aren't involved in this. What about John Samuel?"

"Nothing from that period, sir, but Deirdra did get something." He looked over to Craig, "Deirdra?"

"Oh aye, I found a report from a news site in New Zealand." She read from her jotter. "Local councillor in the Christchurch area, name of John Samuel, died in 1994. He'd been a lifelong campaigner for land rights, from his time in Scotland on. Even says he'd been involved in the hut movement here after the war. Died a highly respected citizen."

"OK, that's good work, both of you. We can probably rule out the hut folk, at least."

"Bit of a negative sort of achievement, isn't it, chief, if it just rules something out?" remarked Bhardwaj.

"No, not if it narrows the area we need to do the real work in. Which it has. But to what?"

28

He made another cup of coffee, updated his report again.

At four the phone rang. The Super again. "Something unwholesome about this case, Angus, I can tell you."

"The authorisation – was it genuine?" asked Blue.

"Yes. Those people were indeed MoD police. Signatures genuine too. The MoD signatory, Harvey Atkinson, is a civil servant. The other, Commander Adam Farborough, at the Met, is Special Branch."

"So there's nothing we can do about it?"

"Well, maybe. Authorisation for a body transfer is a grey area vis-a-vis devolution. It may need an all clear from the Ministry of Justice here in Scotland. I had a chat with the ACC about it, he agreed we ought to report it to the Ministry, let them decide what to do."

"And have they?"

"Well, they're certainly not very pleased, especially after the way it was done, middle of the night and so on. They're going to protest to the MoD and the Home Office, and ask for an explanation. I doubt they'll get very far. The MoD will ignore it, the Home Office will promise to look into it, and nothing will happen."

"So how do we get the bodies back?"

"If, as I suspect, the bodies were taken straight across the border, I doubt we'll ever see them again. Wouldn't surprise me if they've already been cremated."

"That would certainly be final."

"And it leaves us all feeling we've been made fools of."

"Could they try to shut down the whole investigation?"

"Good question, Angus. It looks like they'd like to. But given the official protest from the Scottish Government, they'll realise that's not on. They could try to get hold of whatever material we've got using the anti-terrorism laws."

"So, what do you think we should do with it?"

"Hmm. Tell you what, get everything back over to Islay, hush-hush. I never told you to do it, understand? If they think it's still in Oban, they'll come to us there. Then we won't be able to find it. At least that gives you a few more days on it. And this is Sunday. They won't move till tomorrow."

"OK. Will do."

"Will do what, Blue?"

"What you just suggested." The penny dropped. "Sorry, chief, I forgot, you didn't suggest anything."

"That's it, Angus. But be careful. Farborough is a nasty piece of work. Be ready for anything. Anything."

Blue called Alison's mobile and asked her how things were going.

"Lot of progress, Angus. Steve and his people are helping too."

"Listen, Alison, I've just spoken to the Super. Can you put together all the moveable stuff and data files and bring it over here tomorrow. Don't drive, come over on the morning flight. It's safer."

"All right. Am I safe to go back to my aunt's this evening?"

"I'd rather you didn't risk it. Could you stay at the station this evening? Use the overnight room on the top floor. Get Abbie in the office to book the flight. Ask Inspector Raistrick to send you in a car to the airport. Can you do that?"

"No problem at all. I'd certainly feel safer. I can buy anything I need in Bowmore."

"Keep the receipts. It's police business. One other thing. Phone your aunt, tell her you're staying the night back at home, as you're finished with the case. Then she won't worry, and if anyone is listening in, it'll put them off the scent."

"Do you think people are listening in?"

"I don't know, Alison. We mustn't get paranoid, and I'm probably overstating the danger, but at the same time we shouldn't take chances. Do what you can this evening. I'll call you again later."

"Thanks, Angus. This is just so weird. Lucky I don't have a dog, eh?"

"What?"

"Nothing. Bye."

She doesn't have a dog, thought Blue.

He needed time to think. He walked down to the pier and breathed deeply, filling his lungs with salt and malt-laden air. He noticed the white bulk of Bowmore Distillery on his left, the name written in big letters on its seaward face. He must get those bottles for the Super at some point. But not now.

He debated whether it was still worth talking to Hamish McNeill. After all, it seemed the hut people were not connected to the five bodies in the peat. But it still might be worth hearing what he had to say. And he might touch on something else that was relevant. He already knew in his bones that it was something to do with the airbase. And the war.

29

By then it was nearly five o'clock, so he went to the evening service at the Bowmore Baptist Church, which was on the main road, almost parallel to the police station.

The church itself occupied the ground floor of a two-storey building, the flat on the upper floor forming the manse. There were people he recognised from the morning, along with others, including several teenagers. The service was less formal, with a discussion about the morning's theme instead of a sermon. At the end no-one showed much sign of leaving, and a young woman with a baby sitting next to him told him that they were now going to have a meal together – "just soup and a roll" – and he was welcome to join them. He noticed now that tables were being set up at the rear.

Mr Sempleton appeared. "Hi, Angus, good to see you here, I see you've met Anna. Why don't you both come over to the back, there's someone I'd like Angus to meet." He led them to one of the tables, where an elderly man was already sitting. He was a big man, with the ruddy face of one who'd lived in the open air, and a bald head. "Angus, this is Hamish McNeill. Hamish, Angus is with the police. He's trying to find out where those bodies in the peat came from."

"Ah. The Peat Dead. Yes, that would surely be God's curse upon the sinful," intoned Hamish in a voice that left no room for disagreement. "No doubt they followed a life of lust and depravity, and have paid for it with divine judgement. Their souls now will surely be enduring forever the tortures of Hell. Aye, the torment of eternal fire. Eh?" He stared at Blue with a look that penetrated his skull.

Blue didn't know how to react. "Er, yes, well."

"Surely the Peat Dead bear the curse of Cain, and if you disturb their unquiet rest…" He paused.

Blue waited. Then he saw Hamish's stern look dissolve into a loud throaty laughter.

"Heh, heh," he chuckled, "It never fails, eh, Mr Sempleton, it always gets them. Sorry, son, I just can't resist it. Ever since I played the messenger of doom in the church play back in 1962, I can't let go of the part." He pulled out a big handkerchief and wiped his eyes.

"You're an old rogue, Hamish, sure you are," smiled Anna. She spoke with an Irish accent. Hamish beamed.

"I must go to the kitchen," said the minister, "and help Sam, that's

91

my wife, Mr Blue, with the soup. It's our own Cullen Skink this evening."

"Were you catching the fish, too?" asked Hamish.

"Sort of. Offcuts from the smokehouse. Wait till you taste this, Angus." He went off towards a door at the rear of the room.

"So what can I be helping you with, Angus?" said Hamish.

"We think these men whose bodies we found died during the forties or fifties, and we'd like to know if anyone remembers any odd events. Were you around here then?"

"Oh yes, I've lived here most of my life. Apart from when I was in Canada, that was from '52 to '67. But I never really took to it. The work was all right, there was plenty of it – cutting trees – and the people were good, too. But I always missed the water, and there's not much of that in Alberta. So I came back."

"So you were here up to 1952?"

"Well, not quite. I was called up in 1944, when I was eighteen. Into the navy, of course. This being an island, they assumed we knew all about the sea. Sadly, far from the truth. Most of us couldn't even swim. The only one on the ship who knew what he was doing was the first officer, and he came from Leith."

"What about the captain?" asked Anna, "Surely he could drive it?"

"The captain! Admiral Wavy-Hair, we called him. He was related to some bigwig, so he was put in command, but he hadn't a clue, just let the rest of us get on with it. Spent most of the time combing his hair or being sick. Ah, those were the days."

"You were on active service?" asked Blue. Curiosity was distracting him.

"Arctic convoys. Russia and back. Hell on earth. I thank the Lord that He brought me through it. Well, most of me." And he held up his left hand to reveal that most of his fourth finger was missing.

"What happened?" asked Anna.

"I was chipping ice off the rails. You had to do that or the ship – she was just a destroyer – would have capsized with the weight. With a hatchet. I got too enthusiastic and the axehead skited off the ice and took my finger clean off. I was wearing gloves, but it was so cold I didn't feel anything at first. I took off the mitten to see what damage had been done, and the finger fell out and bounced off the rail into the Atlantic. I'm sure a shark snapped it up right away. They took me down below and bandaged it up. But I still feel it there – it itches when the weather's damp. A phantom finger they call it. It also ruined my career as a concert pianist." He roared with laughter again.

"You've got to laugh, haven't you? But that finger probably saved my life."

"How was that?" Blue asked.

"When we got back I was taken off active duty as wounded, sent right back here, to the base at Bowmore. Where the flying boats were. Not that I had anything to do with them. I was in the supplies office, filling in forms and counting everything you can think of. Tins of corned beef, car tyres, teaspoons, balaclavas, you name it, we had it. Somewhere. Two months later I heard that my ship had been torpedoed, up near the North Cape. Only six men saved."

"Oh my God," cried Anna, "how awful." The baby, peacefully snoozing, woke up, and stared fearfully up at her. It was thinking of crying, but she pre-empted the squall with soothing words and a rocking motion.

Soup and rolls came, Mr Sempleton said the grace. The rolls were warm and the soup rich with cream and smoked fish, potato and leek and onion. Then tea, and serious talking could resume.

"I've been thinking about those chaps in the peat," began Hamish. "Do you have any clues?"

"We heard there were some hut folks here in the late forties," said Blue, "Perhaps it could have been something to do with them. Did you come across them?"

Hamish thought for a while. "The hut folk. Yes, I remember them. I admired what they were doing. It was wrong to chase them off. Someone said they'd gone to New Zealand. Probably did well for themselves there. The landowners are our curse. Parasites! I'd shoot the lot of them, myself."

"Did you meet those hut people?" asked Anna.

"Well now, I did go out to see them once, with Johnny Barclay, we went on his motor bike. They were good people mostly, though some were, how can I say it, damaged. Hospitable too, invited us to share their lunch. Tinned fish and potatoes. I'm not sure how they intended to live, they were vague about that. The war did a lot of harm to people. Made some of them capable of anything. Even murder. And there were plenty of weapons about in those days too. Ones that weren't handed back in at the end, and ones that were taken from Jerries. Even pinched from our own armouries. I did my best at the Bowmore base, but still the amount of stuff that disappeared, you wouldn't believe it. And the worst offenders were some of our own NCOs and officers, they were making money hand-over-fist selling our own supplies on the black market. One of my colleagues in the office, Shorty Blair, complained about that to the commander, said we all knew who it was. I'd warned him not to. Golden rule of the forces, keep your head down and mouth shut at all times!"

"What happened?" asked Anna. Even the baby looked interested.

"He just disappeared. One day he was sitting at the desk opposite me. Next day, he wasn't. They said he'd been transferred, Egypt, ship had left that morning. I thought it was more likely he was knocked over the head and thrown in the sea. Sure enough, three weeks later, his body was washed up down at Kintra Bay. It was hushed up, but the word got around."

Time had run out for the baby, and Anna excused herself. The dishes were being collected in, and Blue took the opportunity to make his farewells. He thanked Hamish for his help.

"Any time, son, any time. I've got plenty of it, or not much, depending on how you look at it!"

30

In the darkness he clung onto her, to the feel of her in his head. To the memories that made her real for him, made her part of him. They didn't know how much time they'd have together. Fighter pilots had a high mortality rate.

When they'd got engaged everything had seemed so different. He was working then in Glasgow, as a clerk in the offices at the Central Station, and Rowena worked at the main branch there of the British Linen Bank, just around the corner from the station. They must have passed each other unknowing many times before they met at a ceilidh in Queen's Park Church Hall. It turned out they only lived a few streets from each other, he with an uncle and aunt and she with her parents. Sunday afternoons soon became a precious time for them. In due course he proposed and she accepted. That was January 1939, the fourteenth to be exact. Not a day he could forget. And then they talked and planned and loved each other. Enjoyed the present and looked forward to the future.

Then the war came. He volunteered in November 1940 and joined the RAF. He was trained to fly at the base at Lossiemouth, on the east coast, and wrote every week to her. He was soon moved to an airfield on the Lincolnshire coast; he recalled the flat and empty land, the cold winds from the east, the dark clouds of German bombers flying like migrating birds, seeking out the industrial centres of the English Midlands. Occasionally there was leave to visit his family on Lewis, and Rowena in Glasgow, and on one of these visits, during a walk around the little loch in the Queen's Park, they decided to get married as soon as they could. That happened on the 4th April 1942, he in his uniform, she in white, a dress she made herself from other dresses cannibalised. He felt a different man after that, more complete, more ready for the imagined future, and keener that the war would be over so that they could make it real.

Then, towards the end of 1942 he was unexpectedly transferred to Islay for 'escort duties'. That usually meant flying out over the Atlantic to lead in the big planes lumbering over from Newfoundland or Iceland, but sometimes there were convoys to watch over as they assembled and moved north. He'd heard about the conditions the convoys had to endure, and both of them knew he was lucky to be well behind the front lines. And yet, who might know what could happen next. A transfer to the Middle East or to the developing fronts in Europe was likely. But it hadn't happened so far. He was beginning to think things would work out as they'd planned.

He sat up, jolted out of his thoughts by a piercing scream from the corridor. He heard a desperate voice calling out, begging, "Please, please, not again, for God's sake tell me, what have I done?" Then he recognised the voice. And began to wonder how he and the other might be connected.

31

Back at the police station, Blue called in on the base room. McCader was still phoning people up about the cars. He'd eliminated most of the names on the list. "I told Arvind and Deirdra they could go at six. I'm just about finished here too. For tonight at any rate. I'll go for a walk, then have an early night. I need to phone the wife too. The family are still in Dundee. If this post's confirmed, they'll come over to Oban too. I'd love the kids to learn Gaelic at the school."

Twenty minutes later Blue was at his hotel. He typed up his conversation with Hamish. At eight he phoned Alison, and asked how things were going.

"Really well, actually. Works wonders if you know you're not going anywhere. I'm just writing it all up now. I'll email the report as soon as it's done."

"No. Don't do that. Sorry to be so abrupt. Just bring it with you."

"OK. The flight is booked, and the car, so I'll see you tomorrow."

"Till tomorrow. I'll get someone to meet you at the airport. Take care."

After his lasagne in the restaurant, he tried the ten-year old Bruichladdich. The liquor gleamed translucent saffron as he swirled it in the glass, to his nose it was light, unpeated, with a hint of honey, and on his tongue surprisingly rounded, with an earthiness that lingered, a completeness that he couldn't define.

Then he watched the news on the TV. There was an interview with a pompous Cambridge historian with a knighthood, who had been appointed chairman of the British Studies working party. "You see, Jeremy, identity isn't about questioning and critique, it's about certainties. The certainties that make us who we are. So the figures that we take to epitomise our identity must genuinely be heroic, people we can respect, identify with, even to some extent emulate. Historians who look for their faults, or just try to dig up dirt on them – this so-called 'revisionist' history – are actually harming millions of British people, by trying to kick away the props that support their identity. I would call it abusive." He smiled smugly. Who were these key figures, the interviewer asked. "Only the best, those who utterly epitomise the qualities of Britishness. Alfred the Great. Richard the Lion-Heart. Edward Longshanks. Queen Elizabeth the First. Wellington. And of course, Churchill, perhaps the greatest Briton of them all." The interviewer ended the interview by reminding viewers that *Churchill: The True King Arthur* was the title of the historian's best-selling biography of the great man, and held up the chunky volume as he was faded out.

Day 5. Monday

32

Blue was up at 6.30. At 7.45 he got a text from Alison, "At Oban airp." He decided to collect her himself.

He was at Islay's airport by 8.20. There were a few people sitting around, presumably passengers on the return flight to Oban. Or like himself, just waiting for somebody to arrive. The bank manager type was there too, studying the *Telegraph*; perhaps he was an accountant, as he'd told Dalvey. There was look of precision about him – the expensive raincoat and black document case on the empty seat by him, the crisp pin-stripe suit, gleaming white shirt and perfectly knotted tie, the hair carefully combed over the bald patch. Not the sort who'd accidentally bump into a table in a bar.

He was working up a pretext to talk to the man, when his phone rang.

"Hi, Angus, Moira here. The site's been trashed! During the night. I drove up there at nine last night, and it was quiet. Bob checked it again on his way in this morning just before eight, saw right away it had been got at. Looks like somebody drove a digger all over it, shovelled everything around. Bob's still there questioning the locals, see if anyone saw anything. I'm getting over there now."

"They must have heard something at least. It's not as if you can hide a digger. Is it?"

"Angus, this is Islay. Anything that looks like farm or construction equipment can be hidden in plain sight, just parked in a field or on a bit of waste ground."

Blue noticed people coming through the door from the runway. "OK, got to go, Alison's arrived. I'll go straight to the site from here."

Alison came through last. She looked pleased to see him. "I thought you'd send Arvind or Deirdra."

"I decided I'd come myself. Just to make sure you were here."

"Thanks, Angus." She squeezed his hand. "I'm relieved to be here."

"He pulled out his phone, and whispered to her, "Just let me photograph you from a few angles. Big reunion. OK?"

"Er, OK, if you want." Puzzled but acquiescent.

He took shots of her from a number of angles, moving the phone at the last moment to put Alison into the corner of the frame, and capture all the passengers who were now lined up waiting to go onto the plane. Then he led her outside into the car park.

"Thanks. I just wanted pictures of all the people going out."

"Oh. I thought you wanted to take some pictures of me. What a disappointment." Was she joking?

"The site was trashed during the night. It might have been one of them."

"Oh no! How bad is it?"

"Don't know. Let's go and see."

It was a mess. Trenches had been cut through it at crazy angles and holes left where peat had been dug out then dumped elsewhere. The heavy plastic sheeting at the ground level had been ripped right out and piled in a heap in one corner.

"Well," said Alison, "Not much chance of getting back to that in a hurry."

"Can it be done?"

"Oh, yes, it could, but it would need so much time and manpower, expert manpower, that it's unlikely to be approved. My advice would be to forget the site, and hope we've got enough from the stuff we already got up. Apart from the bodies, that is!"

Five minutes later Moira arrived. "Hi Alison, good to see you, you've had a nasty experience. How are you doing?"

"Rather relieved to be back over here, But this doesn't look good, does it?"

"No, it doesn't. Let's hope Bob can find some witnesses."

"When's the first boat out, Moira?" asked Blue.

"9.45. I see what you're suggesting. The culprit could be sitting at the pier at Port Ellen right now. But how would we identify him, or her, before Bob gets any descriptions?"

"Unless they've changed clothes, they'll be wearing something worn and unobtrusive. Nothing that would attract attention. Might have mud or peat on their shoes. They must have known someone would see them. Counted on the fact they'd not be noticed – they'd look like someone you'd expect to see, in the distance, on a digger. And probably a man. I suspect a woman in a digger would attract attention anywhere."

"I can get Calmac to hold the ferry, but they don't like it, and it would take all day to interview everybody waiting. And what if he just lies low till the afternoon boat?"

"I'm inclined to think he wouldn't hang about, so it's worth moving now. What about this? Send someone to Port Ellen, Arvind and Deirdra if they're in. They can note the occupants of each car and the reg. number, ask them how long they've been on the island and what for. We can chase up any suspects later."

"What about the foot passengers?" asked Alison, "Shouldn't they be checked too?"

"Yes, I guess so. Though I suspect they'd want a vehicle, for a quick getaway at the other end."

Moira already had her phone out, and a minute later, reported, "Arvind was in at eight, Deirdra's just in. They're off to Port Ellen right away."

"I don't suppose it could have been a local having a lark?" said Alison.

"No, we've never had anything like that. Frustrated youths are more likely to race old cars from one end of the island to the other and back again. I'd better get back to the station."

"We'll follow you."

33

At the station, Blue scheduled a case meeting for ten. Then he downloaded from his phone the pictures taken at the airport of the people waiting for the Oban plane. There were only seven of them. One was a slim woman wearing stiletto heels – unless she had a good disguise he didn't see her up for it. Two of the men looked very plausible candidates, a large man with short-cropped ginger hair and a beer gut hanging out over greasy jeans, and a short, thin individual, with a pock-marked face and dark hair tied in a ponytail. Then there was the bank-manager type who he suspected had bought drinks for Dalvey; he'd noticed where the phone was pointed and tried to turn away from the shot, but not quite quick enough, so Blue had a good profile of him. Was he hiding something? Swindling the farmers? Or the tax man? He extracted head-and-shoulders images of each person from the pictures, and emailed them to Inspector Carroll in Oban, asking if he recognised any of them. Carroll knew all the villains in the North West by sight, both big and small.

At 9.30 Bhardwaj and Craig got back from the ferry. They had noted particularly three of the cars, each driven by a single man in ordinary clothes whose reason for travelling was vague.

Ten minutes later the newspapers arrived. Blue flicked though *The Nation*. On page 7 was a short item by John Striven: "Peat diggers reveal mass murder – 70 years ago!" He had stuck with what Blue had given him, but had added an appeal to readers: "Who could these mystery men be? Get in touch with us if you think you know." Blue frowned – he'd asked Striven to hold off the appeal for a bit. Still, now it was done, and it might turn something up. He wasn't going to let that ruin his day.

The meeting started at ten. Round the table were Blue, Nicolson, McCader, Bhardwaj, Craig, and Alison Hendrickx. Craig was frowning slightly. Blue wondered if she needed glasses.

"Well, let's begin. Our case is the Peat Dead."

"The Peat Dead. Cool. Sounds like a rock band," said Bhardwaj.

"Is it a quote from a book?" asked Moira.

"Not a book, from someone I met." He brought them up to date. His exposition was concise. He did not use the blackboard.

When he had finished, Inspector Nicolson spoke: "If I may say so, inspector, that was a masterly survey of the facts."

"Thank you, inspector, flattery is a powerful social lubricant. Deirdra, what do you make of all this?"

Craig was taken by surprise by the question. "Er, aye, we've a lot to do, I'm thinking."

"So where do you think we should start?"

Craig frowned again. "Aye, well, there are two parts to this, aren't there, one in the forties, one now. Maybe we should divide our efforts, treat them as two cases." She spoke slowly, thoughtfully.

"That's a good approach. So, let's do it. Sergeant McCader will focus on what we can call the Now case, and PCs Bhardwaj and Craig on the Then case. But we won't forget that the two are linked. Every additional lead from Now tells us something more about Then. And *vice versa*. Questions?"

"What about the removal of the bodies, chief?" said Bhardwaj, "What does that tell us?"

"That we've touched a nerve somewhere. If it is MoD, is there something they want to cover up, or stop us finding out? The best way to hinder a murder investigation is for the bodies to vanish."

"Could they stop the investigation altogether?" asked Inspector Nicolson.

"I don't think so. It's public knowledge, it was even in this morning's paper, so it can't just be hushed up. But they might try to get it transferred to themselves. On grounds of national security."

"Ah. Then they could produce their own explanation? Even concoct evidence to back it up."

"This is about the wartime base, is it no, chief?" asked Craig, "Why else would the MoD be interested?"

"It does look that way," answered Blue. "So, now we are further on. They have shown us their hand, at least to some extent. The business with Dr Hendrickx is more sinister, and we need to track down that vehicle, and the man in it. Enver, what have you got?"

"The likely owners are Euro Special Logistics Solutions. I think this company is a sub-contractor, operating on behalf of someone else."

"So what does it do?" asked Moira Nicolson.

"Undercover surveillance or other illegal activities. Sometimes legal things. More often not."

"Murder?"

"Oh yes, it could include murder. Though it's not all that common."

"Like Dr. David Kelly after the Iraq war?"

"Well, who knows?"

"So who are their people?" asked Alison.

"Probably freelance operatives who take on any work which a government, or maybe a corporation, wants to distance itself from. They have no ideological baggage, it's just a job. The client can make things happen which can't be traced back to it."

"Who could they be working for?" asked Blue.

"If there's a link to the theft of the bodies, it does point to a government agency rather than friends or family of the culprits. The MoD seem to have made their interest clear."

"But we can't prove they are behind this man," said Moira Nicolson.

"No. Not at all," said McCader. "And probably never will. Even if we find him and question him, he won't tell us anything important because he doesn't know it. He's been given an assignment, and has carried it out. He doesn't want to know who it's for or what its purpose is."

"And there's nothing much we can charge him with so far," added Blue.

"He tried to kill me," put in Alison.

"Even with a witness, we'd be unlikely to prove anything more than dangerous driving."

"So we're at a dead end there?" said Moira.

"Not quite," said Blue. "If we continue our investigation, they may try something else."

"Which may be nastier that what we've already seen?"

"These are people who live in the shadows," said McCader, "They come out of the darkness only to strike."

A shiver ran through the room. Nobody spoke. Blue could hear the clock on the wall ticking.

After a pause, he broke the silence. "OK then, let's now move on to the Then case. I'm glad to say Alison's back, to bring us up to date on the forensic work. Alison?"

"Thanks, Angus, I think we've got all we can from the material, at least for the moment." She tapped at her laptop, and the projector threw onto the blank wall an image of her desktop. "So, first, the bodies. As you know, they've been purloined. That's a pity, we could have got more from them. On the positive side, we do have two things. One, detailed photographs – I've put all five of them on the pinboard by the window." She pointed to the five A4 size colour photos, each showing the face of one of the dead. The eyes were closed, and the staining of the faces was evident. A tan gained without sunlight. Faces once alive. She paused while they stared over at the images, then went on: "I've numbered each one, and as we find out who they are, we'll add the names. And the second thing is, we'd already taken DNA samples. If we get a name, we can test it, provided we can locate some living relatives."

"Good," said Blue, "What about the bit of newspaper?"

"We've unfolded and scanned it, restored some colour balance. But sadly, there's nothing specific in the text that dates it." She clicked the mouse again. Closely packed and grainy text. They strained their eyes trying to read it. "It's a sermon."

"You mean a religious thing?" said Craig, "Why put that in the newspaper?"

"It happened all the time then. When Scotland was thought of, and thought of itself, as a Christian nation, sermons were news. I guess too that in wartime they were useful if they helped morale. Suitable messages of course. David and Goliath. God on our side. Anyway, here's what's on the back," said Alison, clicking again. "Not very helpful either. Looks like an advert." A drawing of a tin, with an outline fish on the label, just one word, 'SCRUMPTIOUS!'

"It could be any fish at all," said Moira.

"Then there's the cigarette," Alison continued, "No brand name visible. Chemical analysis might narrow that down, but it would take a while, we'd have to send it off to the lab at Gartcosh. We did get some DNA, however."

"That might be useful," said Blue, "And the bullets?"

"Yes, Dalvey was allowed in to look at them. Anxious to please, ever so 'umble. 7.62 by 25mm Tokarev cartridges. Here's one of ours on the left and a new one on the right." The slide showed the battered head of a bullet lying on a white sheet of paper, with a ruler below it, and facing it a gleaming brand-new cartridge, the copper-coloured bullet peeping out of a grey metal case. "The most probable weapon associated with this cartridge is a Tokarev TT-33 semi-automatic pistol." The image showed a pistol of the type spies in films were always brandishing. "It was used by the Russians from the early '30s up to the '50s, so it fits into our window. Very common apparently."

"So the executioner could have been a Russian?" asked Moira.

"Yes. Or just used a Russian pistol."

"OK," said Blue, "What else is there, Alison?"

"Just the ring from the severed hand. Average gold wedding ring. No distinctive features. Inscription inside: 'MM–RS 4 April 1942'.

Probably the initials of the couple and the marriage date."

"That could give us a lead," said Blue, "Thanks, Alison. We're getting closer to these people."

He glanced at his watch, moved things on. "I think we should be looking more closely at what was going on during the war. If what George says is correct, people could have been killed, and the whole thing hushed up. The site's proximity to the air base is suggestive. And what Hamish told me about someone disappearing after reporting thefts could be an indicator too. Moira, can we get the museum people together again? Maybe this afternoon?"

"I'll ask Clara to get onto them, and let you know. I'll suggest two o'clock."

"Thanks, that would be good. Deirdra, we need to have a picture of what was going on here during the war. Can you round up any information you can find about that?"

"Will do, chief."

"Meanwhile, there are still people around who remember that time. We need to tap into their memories. See the time through their eyes. I'm waiting for a list from the museum folk."

"What about the killing itself?" asked Moira, "Are we looking for one person or more?"

"The profile of the shots suggests the same man fired all of them. However, it wouldn't be easy for one man to corral five people to the edge of a pit, then kill them all one after another. Maybe we're talking about one executioner, and two or three others to keep the victims rounded up."

"That sounds reasonable," said McCader.

"Anything else?"

"Yes," said Moira Nicolson, "Alison may be a target, and we should think about how we can keep her safe. I've offered to put her up at my place while she's here. I hope that's OK."

"Alison. Is that OK with you?" Blue asked, rather hesitantly.

"Yes, I've already told Moira that would be good. I'm very grateful."

34

Blue checked his phone, which he had switched to silent for the meeting. There was a text from John Striven: 'Info. Call.' He hit the call button.

"Angus, hi. I got the article in this morning's edition, thought I might as well put in the appeal too."

"So I noticed."

"Yeah, well, do you follow me on Twitter or Facebook?"

"No."

"Oh. Well, the article was put up on the paper's website and Facebook page yesterday – taster for today's edition. And it's getting some interesting responses. Plenty of theories. Lot of support for alien involvement."

"Aliens?"

"Yeah. OK, sounds whacky but you never know. Jez Ufospotter…"

"Sorry, I didn't get that."

"Jez Ufospotter. Yes, daft name. Big UFO expert. You wouldn't believe what's on his website."

"That's probably true."

"Says he's given up on the police, they don't listen to him."

"You don't say. Anyway, what's his theory?"

"He thinks all five were abducted by aliens, then returned to earth with super powers. You know, x-ray vision, invisibility, that sort of thing. Brainwashed to work as spies for the aliens. But the government was onto them. They know all about the aliens, but pretend they don't exist. Anyway, the guys are seized by government forces – probably a special anti-alien unit – tried in secret as alien spies, and executed. Naturally that will be denied."

"Naturally."

"This happened during the war. There was a lot of alien activity during the war. So much secret stuff going on that people assumed any odd lights or noises or even people that didn't quite look like people were all just hush-hush war programmes and ignored it. You get the picture."

"Is that it?"

"No. There's another theory, from biffo@alienmaster."

"Don't tell me about his website, please."

"OK. He thinks that your five guys just had a meeting with the aliens."

"By appointment?"

"I can see you're getting into the spirit of it. No, they were probably out hiking or camping somewhere, getting away from it all."

"During the war?"

"OK. Maybe soldiers on a night march. Anyway, the point is, the aliens come and find them."

"'Take me to your leader?'"

"Yeah. Or maybe they just want to find out what's going on with the war. So, they have a meeting, and…"

"Then the squaddies get executed as spies."

"No. They get executed because they met the aliens. Remember we're not supposed to know they exist. So any witnesses have to be got rid of. Get it?"

"Yes, I understand. Why didn't the aliens just hypnotise them to forget?"

"You're not taking this seriously."

"Are you?"

"I'm a journalist. I take everything seriously. And there's a third theory."

"There would be."

"Yeah. They weren't killed for meeting the aliens. Only because they accidentally witness a meeting between government agents and the aliens."

"Negotiating to get a franchise agreement on an alien death ray machine?"

"Now, now, Angus. This is stirring up a massive online debate amongst UFO-watchers. You may have some of them over there soon, looking for evidence."

"That's the last thing we want. Was that what you wanted me to call you for. Aliens?"

"No, that was just novelty background material to raise the tension level. I kept the real info to the end because it's not so exciting. But I guess you'll find it more useful. I've got a possible ID on one of the victims!"

"Ah. Go on," said Blue cautiously. "Nothing to do with aliens, I hope."

"Dear me, Angus, no wonder Jez doesn't trust the fuzz. No, not an alien in sight. Just an old lady in Wales who thinks one of them might be her Dad."

"Didn't think the *Nation* had many readers in Wales."

"You'd be surprised. Her grandson saw it on the website. Glyn Ellis. He's a student at Strathclyde Uni. Engineering. He knew she was interested in what happened to her Dad. He talked to her then emailed me. I think you ought to hear it."

"I'm listening."

"His name is, was, Dafydd Thomas. From Llangeirick, North Wales. In the air force. He's home on leave in 1941 and gets married to his childhood sweetheart Mary Jenkins. Eight months later their daughter is born. That's Glyn's granny, Evelyn. He's on leave again later, and there's a son, Owen. At some point Dafydd is posted to the air base on Islay. Glyn doesn't know when, he'd need to ask Granny. But Dafydd writes letters to Mary. Every week."

"Do the letters still exist?"

"Evelyn may still have them, Glyn's not sure. Anyway, to cut a long story short, the last letter Mary gets is in November 1944. It's heavily censored as usual but everything seems OK. Then, nothing. Nothing at all. After two months, Mary writes to the base commander. She's worried sick. A month later she gets a reply: Dafydd has been killed on a top secret operation behind enemy lines. The usual guff: bravest of the brave, his country will always be grateful to him, she can be so proud, etc., etc. But Mary is suspicious."

"Why"

"Dafydd is a cook, for one thing."

"A crook?"

"I said cook. He's also very short-sighted, has to wear glasses. And has a bad leg, from an accident when he was seven. What use is a short-sighted commando with a limp, whose only skill is cookery? His wife just knows he's not commando material, or secret agent material, or anything like that. So she asks for details. Naturally they refuse to provide any. When the war's over, she writes to the War Ministry, asking where he's buried, so she can visit the grave. They say they don't know where he ended up, but they think he was cremated by the Nazis in a POW camp. That's all they know. But Mary just doesn't believe them. It doesn't ring true. And the letter contradicts itself. They don't know where he was, but he was definitely cremated."

"What did she think happened?"

"What she told her children, that's Evelyn and Owen, once they were grown up, was that she thought there had been some sort of incident or accident at the base, and they were covering it up because they didn't want to admit that loads of servicemen got killed before they were anywhere near the Nazis."

"You mean like aircraft fuel accidentally exploding, people being run over by trucks in the blackout…"

"Trigger happy sentries, or even guys with shell shock going bananas with a Tommy-gun. Or something more sinister."

"Aliens?"

"No, no. Secret experiments. Try out the new gas, or biological weapon, on a few squaddies. If they die, cover it up, get rid of the bodies, pretend they died in action. Who knows any different?"

"You think that's what happened here?"

"No idea, though it's odd you've got five bodies together. We now know all that sort of stuff did go on."

"Well, it's certainly a lead. We'd need to talk to Evelyn."

"I'm going down first thing tomorrow to see her. Why don't I send you a copy of my recording?"

"What's this, newspapermen helping the police?"

"Symbiosis, Angus, we need each other."

"I'm not so sure about that. I've seen downright lies purveyed by newspapers, and on TV. What happened to journalistic integrity?"

"Come on Angus, we're not as bad as some. And you're not the only one who wants to chase this case. Even a page seven story that runs for weeks is good copy. Holds readers like a mini-series on telly. Besides, by the time you arrange to send someone down, then they spend two days on a bus trying to get there…"

"We could ask the local police to talk to her right away."

"They wouldn't touch it. Nobody likes historic cases, they're just a waste of money, and in these times of austerity…"

"Alright, I give up. I guess you're right. OK, send me what you get. We can have a chat once you're back. I might even be able to give you more on this end of the case."

"Now you're talking, Angus. And by the way…"

"Yes?"

"Keep an eye open for those aliens. It's the time of year. Nights getting longer, sun getting lower. Weird lights in the sky."

"Thanks for that, John. Keep in touch."

35

It was the Welsh accent, distinctive even in the anguished voice, that called into his head the picture of the man he knew with the voice that was normally quiet and musical, who, like himself, had married earlier in the war, who like himself, still spoke the language of his forbears. He knew that even talking to the man was frowned upon by his superiors. "Look here," the Wing Commander had said, "as an officer, you have to maintain a certain decorum, you know, old chap. Being seen in the Officers' mess, keeping up the squadron's end at billiards, not mixing with the lower ranks, know what I mean. Look, I understand you and this Welsh chap have got plenty in common – Celtic fringe and all that – but dammit it all man, he's only a cook!"

Nevertheless the cook, when he chose to sing, possessed a voice that descended like oil upon stormy waters. At the occasional musical shows organised for the Islay bases, his singing of old Welsh songs always brought the crowded hall to silence, and often moved to tears the toughest of men.

He even knew how to cook, too. Perhaps because of his short sight and his bad leg, it was the only task that could be assigned to him, but it was a happy coincidence that it was in the kitchen that one of his talents lay.

The Wing Commander's words did not prevent the two men getting together now and again, talking of the wives they'd left behind and for whom they awaited the war's end, and the lives they'd had before the war transformed them from people into numbers. It was Dafydd's plan to train after the war to become a teacher. With his leg, working the farm would be difficult, and his father had already decided that it was his younger brother who would take it on. He understood his father's decision, and knew too that the money would be there to help him get to Cardiff to do his teacher training.

He leant his head against the cold metal of the door. The voice came again in a whimper, "Please, not my leg, not there." It was followed by a loud crack and another agonised scream. Then another voice, which he also recognised: "Pipe down, you little Welsh bastard. Or Mr Batty'll want to have more fun with you."

36

Blue went into the corridor. He could hear muffled voices from Inspector Nicolson's office: Moira and Alison. He tapped on his door and went in. The two women looked up at him. Did they look slightly guilty? Had they been talking about him?

"Ah, Angus," said Moira, "I had a call from Elspeth, two this afternoon's OK, but all she could round up were George and Ina. Leonard's gone to Glasgow to see Scottish Opera do something about a harem."

"*Die Entführung aus dem Serail.* Mozart. Very jolly."

"And Liz has her sister and family over from New Zealand."

"That's fine, three's better than none. I've some good news. My journalist friend brought me a name. Dafydd Thomas. A cook who died on a secret mission." Blue summarised what he'd learned from John Striven. "His daughter is still alive. So are other relatives. We can do a DNA comparison. His great-grandson is at Strathclyde Uni. Is a great-grandson OK, Alison?"

"Yes, absolutely. I'll phone Gartcosh, ask them to look out for it. If he can pop into a police station and give a sample, we could have a result in a couple of days."

"Good. The other thing we need to follow up is what Hamish McNeill told me, that there might have been some sort of organised racket at the base. Admittedly Hamish was talking about the flying-boat base at Bowmore, but the base by Glenegedale was on a bigger scale, so there could have been a bigger racket."

"That's going to be tricky to prove," said Moira, "even if there are rumours it'll be hard to find witnesses still alive and willing to talk. And the MoD aren't going to co-operate, are they? Provide names and so on."

"You're right. Still, even rumours might help us uncover something. By the way, anything from Bob yet?"

"Yes, but not much to go on. Several people saw the digger at work, and just assumed it was Archie. It was his digger. He found it this morning parked on the road near his farm."

"I guess that confirms the driver was a man. Any prints on it?"

"Bob's dusted it. But I don't think we'll get much. Archie was clearing a drain this morning, so he'll have smudged everything. Even if the phantom digger-driver wasn't wearing gloves."

Blue frowned. "Stealing and using a digger, that would need somebody with the right experience. So I'd guess someone was sent over from the mainland to do it. In which case they arrived yesterday, had a look round to locate a suitable digger, did the job, then got out this morning."

"So they could be on the list Arvind and Deirdra made this morning," said Moira.

"What if someone else were here earlier and located the digger for him?" said Blue.

"That's possible. Archie always leaves his in the same field, even leaves the keys in it, too."

"What I'm thinking is, what if he didn't come in a car. With a car, there's always the chance that we'd check the vehicles at the ferry, and catch him there, if we moved quickly enough. Getting out on an early plane would be a good bet. And it's possible we wouldn't even have noticed the damage till after that."

"Archie's digger and the site are both within walking distance of the airport. But how would he know that? Ah, I see what you're getting at – somebody else had been here earlier and told him where they were."

"Exactly."

"Clever. Does that mean he could have walked right past you when you were at the airport waiting for Alison?"

"Yes, and no. Yes, he could have walked right past me. But no, not without being recorded. I took pictures of all the passengers waiting for the plane."

"And I thought he just wanted to take my picture," said Alison.

Moira left to drive Alison over to her house. Blue popped into the base room. Only Bhardwaj was there. He was still working on the names from the ferry terminal. Craig had gone to Roy's store to see what material they had on Islay during the war. And McCader was out too; Bhardwaj didn't know where he'd gone.

37

At midday Inspector Carroll phoned. He had identified not one, but two of the men waiting for the plane. One of them, the big man with the cropped hair, was "Ginger Joe" Donnelly, a small-time crook from the East End of Glasgow, who moved to Oban after a nasty assault saw him jailed for six years. Presumably his home patch had become unsafe. He had since been involved in plant theft, no, not flowers, said Carroll, real plant: building and agricultural machinery – compressors, tractors, harvesters – anything moveable. He'd spent a couple of short periods in jail. A likely candidate.

"Who was the other?" asked Blue. "Was it that youth with the ponytail?"

"He did look shifty, so I checked him out. One of my WPCs recognised him, he's in a rock band, they sing in Gaelic. Play all the big festivals. He's very well-known. So I'm told. No, it was the bald chap with the glasses. Turning slightly away. Gregory King. Chief Inspector, Special Branch now, I think. I was at a lecture he gave at the Police College, must have been about eight years ago. He was still an inspector then, in the Met's anti-terrorism squad. Now, what's he doing on Islay, I wonder?"

"Any ideas, Peter?" asked Blue, though he knew that ideas were not Peter Carroll's strong suit.

"Maybe he has a holiday home there."

"Yes, we'll check that." Why would a Special Branch man be skulking around Islay, chatting up Dalvey? This was surely no coincidence.

"By the way, Angus, what do you want us to do about Ginger Joe. Shall we pick him up?"

"Hmm. The evidence is circumstantial at the moment, but pretty strong; we've got a photo of him here. However, there's nothing that ties him to the digger. What I really want to know is who put him up to it."

"I think a visit can be arranged. It's always good to talk to our customers regularly."

"Can I ask a favour there, Peter? I'd like one of my team here, Sergeant McCader, to go with one of your people to talk to him. He knows the ins and outs of the case."

"I can't see any objection to that. When's he likely to come over?"

"Soon as possible?"

"No problem. Just let me know when he'll arrive."

Fifteen minutes later Bhardwaj reported that all of the people they'd noted at the ferry terminal seemed *bona fide* and had alibis for the night the trashing was done. Blue asked him to get onto Shona at the airport again and get a list of the passengers on the Oban plane. He asked Craig to see if she could find any record of Dafydd Thomas. There must be databases of military stuff.

38

Half past one. Time to get to the museum for two. Moira was already there, along with Elspeth, Ina and George, so they started immediately. Blue outlined developments. He omitted the vanishing bodies, and explained that the focus was now on wartime activities at the airbase, and the possibility that the murdered men may have stumbled across some sort of criminal activity.

Elspeth reported that they'd not found much that would be helpful: "The only thing that might be of interest is a group who set up a hut settlement near Ardbeg. That was in 1946. After a few months there was a run-in with bailiffs, after which they gave up and left. There's only one paragraph in the *Oban Times*. We also have the old police station log book. There's a report from a Sergeant McMillan, let me see," – she consulted a notebook – "here it is, I quote, 'numbering about 16 persons,' had arrived on 15th May on the morning steamer at Port Ellen. Later on he says that after a fracas two persons were sent to the hospital in Oban, one was detained on a charge of assault, and thirteen left on the morning boat on 3rd September. So it does seem he counted them in and counted them out."

"That's useful," said Blue, "I got something on that from Effie Cranston and Hamish McNeill yesterday, so it's good to have the documentary side too." He noted raised eyebrows from Elspeth and Ina "We could also check with Oban and see what they've got. But it doesn't look like it was them. The wartime period is where we need to focus now."

Elspeth slid a sheet of paper across the table towards Blue. "Here's the list of names of old folks you asked for. There's fifteen altogether, but you've already spoken to two of them."

"We could interview them too," added Ina, hopefully.

"Thanks for the offer, Ina," put in Moira, "but we'd prefer to do that, it's more secure in court."

"So there will be a trial?"

"It would be a possibility," said Blue, "if we could identify who did it, and if he's still alive and has all his marbles. On the face of it, that's unlikely, I must admit. But you never know."

"We could check the newspapers again for the wartime period," said Elspeth, "though I doubt we'll find much. I can also have a look in our archives, see if there's anything else."

"Thanks," said Blue, "That's very helpful. Could you track down this for us too, see if you can put a date on it?" He passed over a scanned image of both sides of the newspaper fragment. He turned to Ina: "Ina, what's the best way to track down service personnel from the war? To follow up a name."

"Oh, there are various databases, Inspector, but we've got a subscription here to FindYourForbears.com. It provides access to several databases, including the ones run by the War Museum. I can give you our login ID and password, if you'll give us copies of everything you get, to add to our files here."

"It's a deal. You drive a hard bargain, Ina."

Ina smiled. She wrote a few words very carefully on a spiral-bound notepad, then pulled off the sheet and passed it to Blue.

"You've not asked me to do owt yet?" said George, feeling left out.

"George, we need to tap into your expertise on the base itself. Could you come in to the police station tomorrow morning and brief the case team on what was happening there?"

George perked up. "Pleased to be of service, Inspector. I've not been called as an expert afore."

"Good. Is ten OK?"

"No problems, Mr Blue. I think you'd find my little booklet useful. *Islay during World War Two*. It includes a map of the base, too."

"Yes, I'd like to buy four copies while I'm here, so that we can do our homework this evening."

"I can expect some cracking questions tomorrow then? I'll be signing them copies too!"

Kilbrocheann Distillery was not far beyond Port Charlotte, so he decided to head over and pick up the two bottles for the Super. Like all the old Islay distilleries, Kilbrocheann was on the coast, with the name in great black letters on the seaward face of the long white-washed building. He drove in under a dark archway to a parking area enclosed by a high and ancient stone wall. From there a cramped and timeworn gateway led into a dusty courtyard. It was like something from the middle ages – dark stone walls pierced by tiny windows. Small doors without signs. He stood still, closed his eyes, breathed deeply. A scent of ages.

A low doorway in a corner of the courtyard led into the distillery shop, an unexpected space, well-lit with cafe-style tables and a counter running down the side. An exhibition was being prepared: blank boards were stacked against the walls, and a roll of tartan cloth propped against a chair, while on the round wooden tables plastic-covered pictures and cards with captions were piled. Two young women were sorting them and moving them to other tables where they were carefully laid out. A staple gun and large pair of scissors lay in readiness.

"Hi. Can I help you?" one of them asked. An educated Central Belt voice.

"I want to buy some whisky."

"Aye, well, that's not an unusual request here." He felt himself blushing.

"Anything in particular?"

"Yes, wait a minute." He pulled out his notebook, and flipped the pages.

"You're looking like a policeman when you do that. Does he not, Jenny?" This was a voice that belonged more to the islands.

"Aye, he does right enough, Mary. Honest, we didnae dae it, officer." They laughed.

"Er, I'd like two bottles of the 21-year-old Madeira Cask Special," he read out, "It's for my boss, so I've got to get it right."

"Oh, right. A Special," said Jenny. "I'll have to get Billy to fetch that, we don't keep them in the shop. Normally people order them from the catalogue here, then wait. But the plus side is, you get a free glass of whisky while you're waiting." She called over to the young man who was fixing up the display boards, and he went off.

"Sorry, I'm afraid I'm driving, I'll have to pass on the dram."

"Well, that's a shame. Would you prefer a non-alcoholic whisky then? We do that too."

"Sounds good. What do you call it?" This must be cutting edge. Non-alcoholic whisky. Was it really possible?

"We call it Lapsang Souchong. Deep amber, rich and smoky. With or without milk?"

His bottles of whisky came in dark wooden boxes. Mary slid them carefully into a distinctive canvas bag, with a picture of the distillery on it. "Normally the bag is £4.50, but when you buy a Special it comes free. And you get a Kilbrocheann Distillery whisky glass too. One of the ones with a wee lid to keep the smell in. And since you're buying the whisky for someone else, I'll put in another whisky glass for yourself, plus a miniature to drink one evening. When you're not driving."

Blue was getting a bad feeling about how much the whisky would cost if there were so many freebies thrown in. "How much will that be?"

"Oh, just £299.98 altogether!"

Blue gasped. What was the Super's salary, he wondered.

"You look as if you've had a shock. Have another miniature. On the house."

"Er, thanks. Here's my credit card."

39

Back at the station, he updated the team, including the identification of Ginger Joe Donnelly as the probable site vandal, and DCI Gregory King as another passenger on the plane.

"King? He's dangerous," said McCader at once.

"Do you know him?" asked Blue.

McCader considered his response. "I came across him at one point. He's a fixer. If there's an awkward problem, he fixes it. He usually brings in people to do the work, but he can do it himself if necessary. He may look harmless, but he's not. Believe me, sir, he didn't come to Islay for a holiday."

"So the bodies from the peat might be an 'awkward problem'."

"Yes, it would seem so."

Bhardwaj had a list of passengers from the plane. It didn't include either King or Donnelly. "I asked Shona about them, when they checked in. She reckons the 'Dolan' on the list was Donnelly, and the 'Jones' was King. Don't suppose that takes us any further."

"Shows they were both trying to hide their identity," said Blue, "Enver, could you go over to the mainland tomorrow and have a chat with Ginger Joe? Try and find out who was employing him for this job."

"Yes, chief, I can go right now if you want. Then be back tomorrow evening."

"That's even better. I'll drive you over to Port Askaig. How much time do you need to get ready?"

"Ten minutes. Just give me a shout when we're going."

He gave Craig the sheet from Ina with the access details to the databases, and asked her if she'd got much information on wartime Islay. "Sadly, chief, there's not a lot. I found one book at the shop about the war in the Hebrides, but that only had a wee bit on Islay. The histories of Islay don't have a lot either, they tend to sort of slide past it. There was a wee bit too on the military history sites. So this booklet may be the best source we've got."

"Not quite. George himself is available, and I'm sure there's a lot in his head that's not in the book. He's coming over tomorrow so we can tap his brains, so I hope everyone can get through the booklet today."

"Homework!" said Bhardwaj, "I love it!"

Blue got back to his office and sat down. The phone rang. The Super.

"Ah there you are, Angus, any progress?"

Blue outlined where they had got to.

"Good work. Nothing's come up yet about those bodies. At least, nobody's told me. And the CC's keeping a low profile – not available, at a meeting all day. Oh, one other thing. My whisky. Did you manage to…?"

"Exactly as requested."

"Well, done. Do bring it back in one piece."

"Or two."

"Sorry?"

"Two bottles, chief. You wanted two."

"Yes, very clever."

"Actually, I could send it over this afternoon with Sergeant Mc-Cader. He'll be on the next boat."

"Excellent! To be delivered directly to me, understand. I'll wait till he gets here."

"Yes, sir. Of course."

"Good man. Knew I could count on you, Angus."

He picked up McCader, who had only a lightweight rucksack. He gave him the bag with the whisky bottles in their boxes. "When you get to Oban, can you go straight to the station, and give this bag to Superintendent Campbell? To be delivered only into his hands. Guard it with your life."

"I won't let it out of my sight, chief."

Once they were on the road, he took the opportunity to ask Mc-Cader what he thought about the Britishness programme.

"Well, chief, I feel Scottish sometimes, and Albanian sometimes, but British, hmm, I just don't know what that's supposed to mean. With Scotland, and Albania too, it's easy: the landscape, the history, the language, the music – I grew up whistling Albanian folk tunes on the way to school – literature, all sorts of things that make a place real, that makes it home. I've got friends in England who are happy being English too. The only people I met who were fanatically British were in Northern Ireland, and their take on Britishness wasn't something I'd want to export. It was all about negatives, things they were against."

Blue could remember being at a football match when he was young.

A vocal minority of the crowd waving Union flags and chanting hate slogans.

After a long and gradual upward gradient, they finally topped the road's summit to see the Paps of Jura rising bare and grey in the weak sun.

"That's Jura, where my people, my family, came from. Diurachs," said Blue.

"Have you been there?"

"A few times, when I was young. Haven't been for a long while. Keep telling myself I should get back."

"Perhaps while you're here. It seems so close."

"We'll see."

"Were your family estate owners then?"

"No. Not at all. Quite the opposite. They lived in a farming tounship – something smaller than a village – about half way up the right hand side of the island. Then, in the early nineteenth century they were moved by the landowner, to the coast, where they became crofters – they had a small plot, a few animals, topped it up with a bit of fishing. Must have been a hard life."

Now they reached what seemed the end of the land, and the road tipped over into a precipitous hairpin-cornered descent down into a hollow cut into the cliffs. Port Askaig. A hotel, a shop, a pier and a waiting room. And a parking area, for the cars queueing for the little ferry across to Jura, or for the big one to Kennacraig or, occasionally, Oban. With the ferries using Port Askaig at some times and Port Ellen at others, visitors to the island had be very careful to turn up at the right place for their boat back. Blue had checked the timetable earlier on the internet. "You're in luck, Enver, you won't need to sit in the bus from Kennacraig. The next boat goes, via Colonsay, all the way to Oban."

40

He drove back at a more leisurely pace, this time paying more attention to the places he passed. First the signs for Caol Ila and then Bunnahabhain distilleries, both places he'd like to visit. He toyed with the idea of just nipping in to one of them right now – Caol Ila was only a mile off the main road – but corrected himself with the thought that these weren't places to dash around. The pace of whisky requires otherwise.

Back at the station, he was updating his report. There was a knock on his door. PC Craig.

"Got a match on Dafydd Thomas, chief."

"Great stuff, Deirdra. Fire away."

"Dafydd Thomas is a pretty common name in Wales. Three from the parish of Llangeirick alone. But this one seems to fit. In the 212th RAF Regiment. Called up September 1940. Given leave to get married in October 1941. Disnae say where he was based, but does say he died on active service on 16th November 1944. Doesn't say where. That's all there is."

"OK. The regiment is a positive pointer. That date could be very useful. In fact, can you find who else in that Regiment died on or around the same day? More of our dead may be in there."

"Aye, chief, will do."

She's very competent, thought Blue, doesn't waste time, gets the job done.

Six-thirty. Blue drove back to his hotel. He had a meal there, and a glass of 12-year-old Bunnahabhain. Not peaty, but the liquor, the colour of burnished gold, had a sweet heaviness that lingered on the palate for a long time. Not a dram to be taken lightly.

Then he read George's booklet. It confirmed what he had already learned about the base from Sandy McRae. It was large, mostly concerned with training and reconnaissance. George added that 'special operations' had been carried out from there, without giving any details.

On the news a fawning reporter interviewed the Prime Minister about the British Studies module. "You see, Nick, people need to know who they are, where they came from. The past is so very important here, and that's why we have to make sure that people get it right, from the beginning. You see, all sorts of people are presenting a past that, frankly, they've just made up. And we can't have that. We need to make sure that people have the truth, the real truth, from the people who really know it, the experts. Facts, not opinions. Not negative stuff either, carping about whether some drunken soldier machine-gunned a camel in 1923. No, the positive things, the things that made us what we are. Right back to King Canute defending England from the Vikings. And the Magna Carta, that was the invention of democracy, Nick. And moreover, it was by the people whose descendants make up our House of Lords today. Elizabeth the First, who saw off the French and the Spanish. Yes, the women, as well as the men – let's not forget Florence Nightingale, you know the Angel of the, er…Anyway, my job's a tough one, Nick, but I still find time to read, we've all got to do that. I've recently been reading *Churchill: The True King Arthur,* and believe me, it's a great book. It makes me proud of our brave island nation. And immensely proud too, that I, like Churchill, am leading it through a time of trouble, a time when there are enemies not only on foreign shores, but even in our own country. So I'm hugely grateful that Churchill's biographer is chairing our working party. Their work will be definitive, Nick. It will make us proud to be British again."

Day 6. Tuesday

41

Blue was at the police station just after eight-thirty. He emailed Elspeth Forrest the date of Dafydd Thomas's death, suggesting the newspaper fragment might be from around that time.

He called the team, minus McCader, together at nine – Moira Nicolson and Alison Hendrickx were there too – and brought them up-to date. He asked Craig to keep looking for people who'd died the same day as Dafydd Thomas, and then turned to the list of old folk from the museum group. "We'll need to start interviewing these people today. But let's hear what George has to say first."

George Outhwaite arrived early, not long after half past nine, clutching a large black document case, so Blue asked him to talk right away, whilst everyone was still together. He didn't have a PowerPoint show, but a big pile of photographs, maps and documents sat in front of him. "Good morning, ladies and gentlemen. I've been asked to talk about what were happening in Islay during the last war. RAF had two bases, one at Glenegedale, where the airport is now, and the other at Bowmore, using the distillery buildings, and the water in the loch, 'cos it were flying boats based there."

He went on to describe the routine activities of the two bases. The Glenegedale base, RAF Port Ellen, opened in 1940 on the site of an airfield established in 1935. It was used for reconnaissance, covering the North Atlantic, and also for training. Three new concrete runways were built, aligned in different directions. 1,500 personnel were based there. Not far away, the Bowmore base of RAF Coastal Command housed Sunderland flying boats on coastal patrols, looking for U-boats and other suspicious craft. As he talked, George rummaged through the pile of photos and handed out pictures to pass round the table.

He concluded with conditions in Islay during the war: "For many folks it weren't so bad, since they could get food straight from the farms. Lives were simpler then too, most of what folks ate were basic stuff. Eggs, butter, bread, milk and so on. It were folks in the cities who really had to put up with food shortages."

The talk only lasted half an hour, for which Blue was grateful.

"Thanks, George, that was great. From what you've said, I'm thinking our case may have had nothing to do with the routine activities of the base. What else was going on, but not talked about: secret or criminal activities?"

"Criminal activities, Mr Blue? Well, there were a lot of thieving for sure. Stuff were always going missing. In wartime, when you had folks in the forces who'd never in normal times been let anywhere near 'em, it were bound to be worse. Though of course, that were never admitted by them as were in charge. In the war you could never admit owt were going wrong – that were treason of course. So I suppose it were quite possible some chaps were caught thieving and shot for it, if that's what you're thinking."

"OK. What about secret stuff, then. How much do you know about that?"

"Secret stuff? Well, it were a war, so everything they did were secret really, d'you see what I mean?"

"Let's approach it a different way. There would be regular, routine activities, training, reconnaissance, and so on. Then there might be special operations, you know, commando raids, dropping spies into occupied territory. Maybe they tested new weapons. Or meetings of top brass. All that stuff would be kept very quiet."

"Hmm, I get it now. Aye, there were rumours of testing weapons, but nothing you could put your finger on, like. As to commando stuff, yes, there were definitely summat there, but again, it's all rumour. 'Cos it were secret, like."

"What sort of rumours have you heard?"

"Well, old John McClay, he's dead now, died four years back, but he were 89, he did tell me a few things he'd heard. About them spy drops and secret raids. He worked at the base you know, he were a joiner and they was always wanting joinery work, fitting out buildings different like and opening up new uns. They paid him hardly owt, he said, but…"

"So what about the secret ops?"

"Ops? Oh aye, you mean operations. That's what old John called them. Operations. Mind you, this is only what he told me. That's why it comes with a health warning like."

"Thanks, George," said Blue, "we appreciate your concern that what you tell us, as an expert, is completely based on the facts. But sometimes rumours have a kernel of truth, so we need to pay attention to everything we can get, even if we're not 100% convinced of its authenticity. Do go on."

"Thanks, Mr Blue, that's very helpful. Clears my mind, like. Well, John did say as how all sorts of folk were flying in and out all the time. Foreigners as well as our lot. Of course there were Yanks and Canadians and Australians, a lot of them came for the training. But also more exotic folks, Frenchmen, Norwegians, Poles, and so on. And some he didn't know where they came from. Obviously he couldn't just ask them – that weren't allowed, they'd suspect you was a spy like – but John, he were a real nosey type. Always were, all the time I knew him, always wanted to know a bit more than the rest of us."

"Did he say anything about any Russians, George?"

"Russians, well, I don't rightly know, I didn't expect you'd ask me about this, you see. I'd have to listen to the tapes again."

"You recorded him?" said Moira.

"Oh aye, course I did. I told you, he were right old like. And I weren't going to even try to write it all down. He were quite happy about that. I got two tapes, you know, them cassettes. It were only a year before he died, so he were 88 then."

"Could we listen to the tapes?" asked Blue.

"Of course. I'll bring 'em in."

"I can send someone back with you to collect them, if that's OK."

"Yes, that's all right by me. They're at the museum, in the archive room."

"Just one thing, George." This was Moira. "Did you record anyone else's memories of the base?"

"Let me see, aye, I think I did. Well, more no than yes, I suppose. Not long after I came here it were. There were an old chap who used to come to the Society's meetings, and when he heard I were interested in the war like, he pulled me aside after one of the meetings, into yon room with stuffed animals – we had more of them on display then. Said he knew lots about the base, would I like to hear it. Some of it were 'hot stuff', so he said. That were how he spoke, real posh like. Well, of course, I said yes, and he said, there'd be just one condition, that I didn't make any of it public till he were dead. Said there might be folks who wouldn't like what he said, and he didn't want the hassle if they was to complain. Well, I agreed to that, and we set a date and all. Anyways, next thing Amanda Tompkins – she was on the committee – comes in and tells us to leave, she's locking up. Old Daniel – Daniel Stamford, that were his name – he'd been quite high up in the RAF you know – he didn't look pleased, I think he thought she'd been eavesdropping like. She'd been a Girl Guide leader, very solid built like, she could knock you over just with her bosom, stood no messing from anyone, even a retired Group Captain – I think that's what he were anyhow.

"We'd arranged to meet three days after, on the Friday morning. But, d'ye know, on the Wednesday he were dead! Heart attack, the doctor said. So that were it for our meeting. A real shame, it were, I'm sure he had all sorts to tell me. There were a real big funeral, all sorts of folk, with gold braid, medals. One of them made a speech, saying what a hero he'd been during the war. There were a brass band too, and…"

Blue interrupted: "So you never got to talk to him at all?"

"No, but there were one odd thing. On the Thursday morning – that were after he'd died, except of course I didn't know that then – in the post were a letter from him. Well, not a letter as such, more of a note. See, when a letter is just one sentence like, I wouldn't call it a letter at all. I mean, would you, Mr Blue?"

"No, 'note' is a much better word for it. So what was in the note?"

"Just said he'd see me Friday. That were all. But there were a little book with the note. I could make no sense of it, letters and numbers, some sort of code, I suppose. I took it to the committee in case any of them could do owt with it. Amanda said she'd have a look. A few days later, she said she'd cracked it, it were notes on the various bottles of wine he'd drunk. She said he were a real connoisseur, French wine. Course in them days ordinary folks didn't drink wine every day like they do today, we used to…"

"What happened to the book, then?"

"Oh, Amanda said her cousin, he were a connoisseur too, could he borrow it, to add the information to his own notes, she said. Well, given that Daniel were dead, I couldn't see any objection. Couple of months later, I asked for it back. She said she'd get onto him and get it back right away. But next week she were gone too."

"What? Dead!?" said Alison.

"No, no, love, she'd just moved away. Back to the south of England. No-one knew exactly where, never left a forwarding address."

"So you never saw the book again?"

"No, I never did."

Moira Nicolson asked, "Had you copied any of it?"

"Funny you should say that, I did photocopy a bit of it. Just two pages, well, it would be four pages 'cos it were laid open like, then the copier ran out of paper."

"Do you still have those pages?"

"I do, as it happens, they should be in here somewhere." He pulled from under the pile in front of him a battered A4 size exercise book, bulging with extra sheets of papers stuck in, flicked through it, and pulled out two sheets of paper folded together. "Here we are, feel free to copy them." He passed them over to Blue.

Blue could sense there was a need for a break. "George, that's been really helpful. Thank you so much." He started clapping, and the others joined in.

George beamed. "Glad to help, Mr Blue. Any time."

"I think it's time for a break now. George, PC Bhardwaj will follow you to the museum to collect the tapes. You'll get them, as well as the photocopies, back as soon as we're finished with them. I can guarantee that."

George and Bhardwaj left, and PC Craig offered to make coffee. This was not a usual occurrence.

42

They sat round the table sipping hot coffee and contemplating the imitation KitKats spilling out of the packet in the centre of the table.

"Group Captain Stamford knew something big," said Alison.

"What makes you say that?" asked Moira.

"He had a watcher. Someone keeping an eye on him. That costs a lot of money, so you only get one if you know a really big secret."

"You mean Amanda?"

"Exactly. She would have been keeping an eye on him at the meetings, spotted him buttonholing George. Probably listened in, realised what he was up to, stepped in to interrupt before too much was said. And I'll bet his death wasn't an accident. Most likely she thought the secret was likely to be compromised, and took steps to make sure it wasn't. Maybe with an injection. She goes to his house, asks him to look at something, and while he's focused on it sticks the needle in. Fast-acting drug triggers a heart attack, so unless the local doctor is looking for a puncture mark it's a straightforward death. Old man. Heart attack. Case closed."

"How do you know about all this, Alison?" asked Moira.

"It was in a book I read a few years ago. Memoirs of a secret agent. Mind, I think a lot of it was made up. Especially the bits with the women. But there was a bit in it just like what happened to the Group Captain."

"Interesting," said Blue. "Sending the notebook could suggest he was worried about what might happen to him."

"It sounds plausible to me," added Moira.

"George said Amanda didn't leave the moment he was dead," went on Alison, "What if she hung around to make sure there were no loose ends? She may have kept an eye on George, to see what he knew."

"There's a danger here that we start seeing dirty deeds where there aren't any," said Blue. "We need to see those sheets George photocopied."

"I'll get Clara to make copies for all of us," said Moira.

"Thanks Moira. We'll reconvene once Arvind gets back."

Half an hour later Bhardwaj was back, with a plastic bag containing two tape cassettes. Blue reassembled the group, to look at the excerpts from Daniel Stamford's notebook. They began with the first one:

44

1-3 BS C. Chandel 28 h a2 b l f 4*
15-3 AMcL   C. Rechonne 36 l a1 p l m   3*
17-3 Op 63 Stav 3d r100 5*
29-3 BS   C. Lepelisse 33 m a4 b p m 4*
12-4 PM C. De Ruteuil 39 l a1 b l n 2*
26-4 BS   C. Thoronnel 35 ckd –

"Any ideas?" asked Blue.

Moira Nicolson spoke first, "It could well be a wine diary, as Amanda said. If the C stands for Châeau, that is, then the name and year of vintage could follow, and the stuff after that is maybe what he thought of it, you know, heavy, light, hint of blackcurrant, undertone of vanilla, all that guff they spout in wine lists. Then the 1-3, 15-3 and so on could be the date he drank it. And the 44 at the top is the year, 1944."

"OK. What about the initials after the date?"

"Whoever produced the bottle for him? Drinking companion, fellow connoisseur? Bound to be some amongst the senior officers. AMcL certainly suggests a name."

"Yes. But then there's an anomaly. Op 63."

"Maybe they listened to music instead of drinking," suggested Alison. "No wine available. Where did they get the wine from anyway?"

"Colonel Colquhoun's cellar perhaps," said Blue, "Or people bringing it in. I guess that even during a war people of his class could lay their hands on good wine."

"Dates of a secret operation, perhaps," put in Craig. "For instance, what if 'Stav' is an agent parachuted into occupied Europe. Stavros, he could be Greek, could he no?"

"Or it could be Stavanger, in Norway." That was Bhardwaj, "Where they were dropped."

"What's '3d' then?" said Blue, "Three men dropped, or three planes down? This is not going to be obvious. Let's look at the next one."

Bhardwaj put up the next image, much the same as the first, apart from one entry in the middle:

2-4 Op 66 Din 2d r100 5*

"Dinard," said Nicolson, "in Brittany."

"Or Dinant," said Alison, "That's in Belgium."

"Who knows?" said Blue, "Next please."

The third page was similar, but on the last page there was one odd item:

No-one could offer an interpretation of this.

"But Dafydd Thomas was killed the next day," said Craig. "That's surely no a coincidence."

"You're right, Deirdra," said Blue. "What's on these sheets is important, but I'm not sure how. We'll have to think about it. And see what's on those tapes, that may make it all clearer."

He was very tempted to sit through them himself. He could anticipate the magical shiver that runs through the body when something turns up in an interview. Sometimes just the single word that makes all the linkages come together, flips all the switches so that the current runs straight through to the light bulb in your head. But that wasn't his job here. Somebody had to keep all the leads together. And that was a different kind of thrill, a gradual but growing sense of connectedness, that fragments of information were slowly but surely, by sometimes tiny increments, attracting meaning to themselves. More than that, they became real as tiny slivers of lives lived by real people. The whispers of the Peat Dead. He sat in silence, closed his eyes. For twenty seconds no-one moved.

"Can we go now, sir?" said Alison.

"Sorry. I was thinking."

"Looked like hard work, too."

"Alison, could you do something for me?"

"Anything, Angus. Just say it." Was there an edge to that?

"Er, well, could you and Arvind each take one of these cassettes and listen all the way through it. Note any passage that might be interesting to us. Organised crime on the base, executions, Russians, anything else that looks like a lead of any sort. Is that OK?"

"No trouble. Glad to help. I was beginning to feel at a loose end. Thought I might have to visit the hairdresser. Are there any clothes shops here?" Was she joking? Focus.

"I don't know if we've got any cassette players," said Moira.

"Don't worry," said Alison, "If not, I'm sure we'll find some in a charity shop or a school."

43

Back in his office, he glanced at his mobile, which had been on silent during the meeting. A text from John Striven, a mobile number for Glyn Ellis. He was about to call the number, when the phone rang.

"Inspector Blue. How may I help?"

"Seen the news, Angus? On the TV."

"No, chief, never watched it, so I cancelled the licence."

"I think you'd better see this. You've got a computer, haven't you, watch it on that. MoD have held a mass funeral for our bodies. Watch it, call me back."

It didn't take long for Blue to find the item on the BBC News website: "Forgotten heroes commemorated." It had happened the previous afternoon, but the news had not been released until the morning. No location was given, nor the names of the dead, who were described as "five commandos who died in World War Two, and whose bodies have recently been recovered." The coffins were drawn on gun carriages through the streets of a town, preceded by an army band and followed by a column of marching men with rifles. People in the streets waved Union Jacks. The parade moved towards a big cathedral. He paused the clip and opened another window to look at pictures of English cathedrals. There it was, Salisbury. That figured – near to the bases on Salisbury Plain. Inside the cathedral, a bishop celebrated the giving of life for one's country. *Dulce et decorum est, pro patria mori*, as the Roman poet Horace once said: It is sweet and fitting to die for one's country. "The old lie" Wilfred Owen had called it, though the bishop failed to mention that. Then a fadeout transition to the burial, at an unnamed military cemetery. Five coffins lined up, each covered by a Union flag. Several middle-aged men in gold braid and medals, standing in a solemn row. The Minister of Defence giving a short eulogy. Heroes who died of wounds received on a courageous mission behind enemy lines. Bodies only recently recovered, deserve now to be buried with honour, and to lie forever undisturbed. There was certainly a message there, thought Blue. Then a volley of rifle fire from a row of soldiers, their squat weapons looking like toys. Finally a lone trumpeter played *The Last Post*. The actual burial was not shown.

Blue watched the clip a second time, then looked for any other reports. He found one on the website of a London-based broadsheet, reporting that the men, still unnamed, had been on a mission to destroy a "top Nazi installation" somewhere in occupied Europe. They had succeeded in laying the explosives, and were heading back to the rendezvous where they were to be picked up by a plane when they were attacked by German troops. There was a fierce firefight in which two of the men were killed and the other three badly wounded. However, with the help of local Resistance fighters, all the Germans were killed, and the plane was able to land and pick up the commandos, including the two dead. They were flown back to their base in Scotland, but by the time they arrived the three wounded men had also died. All five were hastily buried with the intention of having a more proper burial once the war was over, but the burial records had been lost. The bodies had recently come to light when they were accidentally uncovered by a farmer. Names had not yet been released, as families were still being informed. The Nazi installation they were attacking had been completely destroyed. Their mission had been a success.

Blue phoned Campbell.

"Well, Angus, what do you make of all that, eh?"

"I don't think we're going to get our bodies back, chief."

"That's the least of it. We're under a lot of pressure from the Home Office to drop the investigation completely, now that the mystery has been, and I quote, 'solved.' Apparently the CC's furious, thinks we've been made to look an utter bunch of numpties."

"Bit odd, isn't it, to have a funeral before the families of the dead have been informed. And why have a funeral at all? Why didn't they just dispose of them quietly?"

"That might have made more sense. I guess there's a political agenda here. With the British Studies course in the news, someone somewhere couldn't resist the temptation to make a patriotic drama out of it. And if we're sceptical, we'll be accused of betraying the heroes and their families."

"But the whole story's patently false, chief. Our victims were executed. No other wounds. We have photos showing that clearly."

"Listen, Angus, I need an up-to-date report on where you are with this. All the information you've got, but not too detailed. Our Minister of Justice is with us on this, but she needs to know exactly what's going on. Can you do that for me? Pronto, if I may use that word."

"I'll get onto it immediately, sir."

"Good man. Keep at it."

He knew somebody had written a book called *One Step Forward, Two Steps Back*. Or was it the other way round? He looked at the clock. After twelve. With a bit of luck a student might be on his lunch break. He called the number. He was lucky.

"Hello? Who is this?" A light voice with a pronounced Welsh lilt.

"Glyn Ellis?"

"Yes, who is this?"

"Hi Glyn, this is Inspector Blue, Police Scotland. I wonder if you can help me."

A pause, then recognition. "Ah. You're guy who found those bodies in Islay. Mr Striven told me. I think he's gone to see my Gran today. I really do hope he can track down my great-Granda. I mean, you're working on this too, aren't you?"

"Yes, we're trying to move it on at this end. Glyn, what I'm telling you now is confidential, so please don't repeat it to anyone, OK?"

"Don't worry, I won't."

"Good. We've got DNA samples from the bodies and we'd like to compare them with your DNA, as a possible direct descendant. That will prove whether one of them is Dafydd Thomas. Would you be willing to give a small sample? They'll just take a swab from your mouth, quite painless."

"Yes, of course, I'd be happy to. What do I do?"

"Just go to any police station, and tell them you need to leave a DNA sample. Explain that it's for Inspector Blue of Oban CID. They'll sort out everything else."

"I don't have a lecture till two, so I can do it right away. How long will it be before we know…?"

"Only two or three days. We'll phone you as soon as we have a result."

"Great. I do hope it's positive. Gran needs some closure on this. If my phone's off, I'm in a class, so just text me a yes or no. Just so I know."

"OK, will do. Thanks very much, Glyn, this is a real help to us."

It was still too dark, back there at the base, all those years ago. But some tiny flames were beginning to flicker. He knew now even without the DNA result that Dafydd Thomas was one of them. And others would come forward too, into the light. But not without help, his help.

He went through to the base room. Alison was sitting in one corner, typing into her laptop. No-one else was there. "Hi, Alison, did you locate any cassette recorders?"

"Yes, at the secondary school. I'm going round to get them in a minute. And I need some fresh air. Want to come too? Then we could get some lunch."

Blue felt he'd like some fresh air too. And lunch. Or was there more to it? Had he agreed just a little too quickly?

They walked round past the distillery to the school campus tucked behind it. A middle-aged receptionist looked at them suspiciously, before producing a bulging plastic bag, "With the compliments of Mrs Truscott. Please return them in working order." Alison had to sign a receipt before the bag was handed over.

Then they walked down to the pier. There was a light breeze blowing in from Loch Indaal, carrying a thin drizzle. Blue felt the wetness on his face and was glad of it. He took some deep breaths, and smelt the salt on the wind, along with the distinctive smell that you only find near a distillery. Like the vapours of whisky, hanging in the air, swirling with the wind. He could be intoxicated just by breathing.

"Makes you feel alive, doesn't it?" said Alison.

"Alive, and grateful," answered Blue.

"To think I could have been at a forensics conference in Tenerife today, instead of Islay in the rain."

"Oh, I didn't realise you had…"

She put a finger to his lips. "Shh. Where do you think I'd rather be?"

They walked out of the town, along the shore, as far as the Gaelic Centre, a modern building set on a little headland, with a balcony jutting over the water. They had coffee and scones, and talked about books and music and archaeology.

As they came back into Bowmore, Alison excused herself: "I want to go to Roy's and get a book – maybe they've a Daphne du Maurier, I'm rereading her at the moment – then I've a couple of other things to get. See you later, and thanks for the lunch. Oh, by the way, I had a text from Gartcosh. Glyn has given his sample, and they expect to receive it later today."

44

Waiting is always the hardest bit. Blue wasn't good at it. He made coffee. If he smoked, and if smoking were permitted inside the station, that would been the time for it. He would draw in two heavy lungfulls, and along with the nicotine and tar and all the other carcinogenic stuff would come enlightenment. Alternatively a glass of good whisky, slowly sipped, gradually infusing his whole being with warmth, then the waiting wouldn't matter, only the peat smoke and the malt. He remembered reading about the difficult choices that had to be made way back, when the barley crop was poor. How much to put by for eating, how much for seed, how much for malting. Sometimes the people starved so that there was still whisky made. *Uisge beatha.* Water of life and death.

One-thirty. Time to get on with the report for the Ministry which the Super had requested. But he didn't resent the task. It gave him another opportunity to marshal the evidence they had garnered so far. By three the report was done, and emailed to Campbell. Ten minutes later the Super was on the phone.

"Good work, Angus. Gripping, if I may say so. Wish I were there with you. This will do fine for the top brass. Oh, and thanks for getting the whisky to me. Good plan to send it with McCader. He looks ready for anything, I'd say. I don't know if you know whisky, Angus?"

"I like a Bruichladdich or a Caol Ila now and then."

"Hmm. Interesting choice." The Super was reassessing Blue. Knowing whisky was worth extra brownie points. "Then you'll realise what you got me was the very best us ordinary folk can buy."

Blue didn't think the price of these bottles counted as ordinary, but kept his counsel. "I hope it lived up to your expectations, sir."

"Indeed it did, indeed it did. Exquisite."

He checked his email. A message from John Striven, sent from his iPad. "On train back. Can't talk. Pic attached. Speak to you tomorrow am." Attached were two JPG picture files, digital photos of an old black and white photograph, front and back. The front showed two young men standing in front of a square white tower three or four storeys high, perched on a rock with a broad bay in the background. Blue recognised it, but couldn't put a name to it. One of the men was short, with dark wavy hair falling down onto his forehead, and what looked like thick glasses. The other was taller, lighter hair cut short, a neat parting on the right hand side. Access to hair-oil was still possible, then. The rear side simply had the words "Me and Pete Bishop, Sept 44" He printed both images onto a single A4 sheet.

He went into the base room. Alison and Bhardwaj were listening to the cassettes through headphones, occasionally pausing the tape and making notes. Craig was studying the screen of her PC, a ballpoint pen clutched in her right hand resting on a pad. He showed her the picture. "Oh aye," she said, "that's Carraig Fhada lighthouse, near Port Ellen. You take the road behind the maltings, past the old Port Ellen distillery."

"Thanks, Deirdra. Any results yet?"

She looked at her pad. "I got forty-two names for 16th November. Place of death given for twenty-seven of them, France, Italy, over Germany – that's RAF – and so on. Six down as 'lost at sea.' Three left, just no place of death given. They are Dafydd Thomas – that's the name you gave me – Terence Darwin, and Gilbert Cartwright. You know what we've got for Dafydd Thomas. 212th RAF Regiment. It's the same regiment for Terence Darwin. Gilbert Cartwright was in the Somerset Yeomanry."

"Terence Darwin sounds like a possibility. See what you find on him in the genealogy databases. But before that, check out this name, Peter Bishop."

He waited whilst she accessed the site and typed in the name. "Died on the 16th November, according to the site. Regiment? Aye, 212th again. Wow!" Blue had not seen her this animated before. Deep fires. She scribbled on the pad.

"Does it say where he died?"

"Hang on, I'll check. Shite! Sorry, chief. Computer's hung. I'll have to restart. Maybe a data overload. Databases can aye get caught up in themselves, so to speak."

They waited while the screen went blank, then with an audible electronic pop the computer started up again, and went through the tedious booting up procedure. A couple of minutes later, she murmured, "Right oh, I think we can get back to the database now. Let's see what we've got here. Aye, here it is, now the name, Peter Bishop." She typed the name and they waited again, whilst a little wheel in the middle of the screen went round and round and round.

"About time! Here it is. Peter Bishop. Died 16th November 1944, 18th Tank Regiment, Northern Italy. That's gey odd. It didn't say that afore. You saw it, chief, it said 212th RAF Regiment, and no place of death given."

"Quickly, go back to Dafydd Thomas."

"OK, doing it right now…Ach, it's just hung again." Anxiously they waited whilst the shutdown and boot up processes churned through. Craig connected to the database again, but this time a message came up, 'Sorry, this site is temporarily closed for maintenance.'

"Something's up with it. The second time I looked at Peter Bishop his data was different. I'd jotted down the first info here on the pad. Maybe the database was in the middle of a memory reshuffle, you know, movin the data around on the disks. If you go intae the database in the middle of that, you can get daft results, because of data being stored in temporary locations."

"I'm not so sure," said Blue, "Anyway, see what you can do on the genealogy sites. Try that one again later."

Now he was pretty sure they had three names: Dafydd Thomas, Peter Bishop, and Terence Darwin. Perhaps Darwin had been the photographer at the lighthouse. But it still had to be proved. This was going to be harder if someone was trying to cover it up by changing the data on the database. He suspected that next time PC Craig got into the database, all three names would be linked to other regiments and places of death far from Islay. They also had a date: 16th November 1944. He felt sure too, that the reference in GC Stamford's wine diary for the 15th was significant. He glanced at his watch. Nearly five o'clock. But he felt no desire to stop working. He sensed that this was a crucial day in the life of the Peat Dead case. A lot of small breakthroughs were being made. The pace of the investigation had subtly moved up a gear.

He also had images of two of the possible victims. He interrupted Alison and Bhardwaj. "Sorry to interrupt. Alison, this is a photo of Dafydd Thomas and Peter Bishop, taken here during the war. Do these two look like any of our bodies?"

"Let's have a look." She took the printout and went over to the pinboard, where Blue, Bhardwaj and Craig joined her. She studied the picture and compared with each of the faces, and finally announced, "Bingo! The one with the glasses I would say is number 4. Obviously the body doesn't have glasses on, but look at the hair – it's the same. I would say, provisionally, that it's Dafydd Thomas. The taller one I think matches image number 5 – the shape of the face and the short hair, even the parting is still visible. I would guess that's Peter Bishop."

All four stared at the two faces. Somehow the naming, even if tentative, made the dead men more real.

45

It was one of those warm September days when everything becomes relaxed. It almost seemed as if there wasn't a war on. There was no sound of planes, nor the clanging of hammers and buzzing of saws, none of the shouts and curses that accompanied most work at the base. Things didn't usually slow down on Sundays, but today was somehow different. He wished so much that Rowena could be there with him, and walked out by himself to be alone with the thought of her.

He left the base and followed the road up the shallow valley to the junction with the old single track road that before the war had been the main road, and turned left to go to Port Ellen. He'd almost arrived at the village when he saw three men coming towards him. As they got closer he soon recognised Dafydd by his characteristic lopsided gait. He was chatting to the two others, and they didn't notice him until he was quite close.

As soon as they did see him, they stood to a relaxed attention and saluted. He returned the salute and greeted Dafydd, asking him where they'd been. The Welshman introduced his companions, as Peter and Terry and they all shook hands. "We've been down to Port Ellen, for a walk along the beach. There's an odd-looking little square lighthouse we had a look at. You'd find it interesting, sir." He'd smiled at the last word, added us Dafydd was with his pals who knew you didn't speak with familiarity to officers.

"Thank you," he'd replied, "I'll be giving it a look then." He'd given them a nod and moved on.

A couple of minutes later he heard the sound of a vehicle engine, and stepped off the road on to the rough grass verge to let it pass, turning as he did so to see it was a jeep containing a driver and an officer. The jeep drew level with him and pulled to a halt.

He'd recognised the officer was an army colonel, stood to attention, and saluted him.

"Stand easy, Flight-Lieutenant," said the colonel, a well-built man with a red fleshy face and thick black moustache, "Can we give you a ride anywhere?"

"No thank you, sir, I'm just out for a walk. To get a bit of fresh air. But thank you for the offer, sir."

"Don't mention it, old chap. By the way, those three fellows we just passed, walking to the base. You must have met them a minute ago. Do you know who they are? They're air force, so you may have come across them."

Something in the over-studied casualness of the man's voice made him suspicious of this apparently innocuous inquiry.

"No, sir. Other ranks, by the look of them. Sorry I can't help you, sir."

The man's voice grew harder. "Are you sure you don't know them? Weren't you talking to them?"

He knew now to be very careful. He'd heard there were senior officers who were obsessed with uncovering traitors, or simply men who weren't enthusiastic enough about the war, who could then be branded as fifth-columnists. He knew the theory too, had heard it often enough in the mess: punish a few harshly, even if they're not guilty – it'll keep the rest in line.

"Yes, sir, I was asking them where they'd been."

"And...?"

"They'd been walking, to Port Ellen."

"Why?"

"I'm supposing, sir, to get some exercise, relax a little."

"Do you suppose we should be doing that sort of thing when there's a war on?"

"Well, sir, it's my view that if men have a little time for relaxation, it makes them more effective at their work."

"Flight-Lieutenant, once you're a Squadron Leader, you can start to have views of your own. Show me some identification."

He handed over his security pass, the folded card with his photo and details, and the blue stripe giving him access to the runway and hangar areas. The colonel studied it closely, then handed it back with a scowl. "There's a war on, Flight-Lieutenant, don't you ever forget that. One other thing, you're not Irish, are you?"

"No, sir."

"Where are you from?"

"Lewis, sir."

"Where the hell's that?"

"Further west, sir, and a little north."

"Close to Ireland then."

"Not really, sir, we're closer to Ireland here, sir."

"That wasn't a question, and it wasn't a request for your opinion. Next time you talk to me like that you'll find yourself on a charge. And there are plenty places a damn sight worse than this that you could be sent to. Just you remember that. All right, drive on, Smithers!"

He'd saluted again as the jeep drove off, but the colonel's gaze was fixed on the road ahead.

46

Blue spent the next hour updating his report. Then he popped back into the case room. Bhardwaj and Craig were still there.

"Anything else turned up?" he asked.

Craig responded first, "Aye, chief, as you suspected, they've changed the data. But I got more stuff from the genealogy sites. I'm no quite done yet."

"Good." He turned to Bhardwaj. "Arvind, how did the tapes go?"

"We've got some real leads, chief."

"Where's Doctor Hendrickx, by the way?"

"Oh, she went off once we'd finished. Said she had plenty to do this evening."

"OK. Thanks, guys, we'll hear what you've got at the meeting in the morning. Ten o'clock."

Back in his office, Blue checked his phone. A text from McCader: "Saw JD this afternoon. On 1st boat tmrw." He called McCader's mobile, asked how it had gone.

"Progress, chief. I went round to his house with DC Tom McEwan, one of Inspector Carroll's people. Joe was none too pleased at the visit, and had a big dog – nasty-looking brute – slavering around his living room, which he refused to put somewhere else, until Tom produced a Taser and offered to count up to five. That got the canine out of the way. Joe was quite startled when asked about his trip to Islay, denied he'd ever been there. His picture at the airport forced a rethink, then he said it was just a holiday. I asked where he'd stayed. Said it was a B&B, he couldn't remember the name, or even where it was. Tom then started opening drawers and cupboards and just glancing in, that made Joe very uneasy.

"I thought it was time to open him up, so I said there was a multiple homicide, and we knew he'd covered up the site – that made him an accessory after the fact to five killings. I didn't say how long after the fact. He got very worried then, especially when Tom began to rummage about in a sideboard, when he suddenly said, 'I didn't kill anyone, I only just messed it up a bit.' I told him we knew that, we wanted the details. He wasn't sure what to say, until Tom pulled a shoe-box out of the cupboard. 'Put that back!' he shouts. Of course, Tom opens it, and there's a black automatic. 'Now you're in real trouble, Joe, here's the weapon,' says Tom, 'We'd better talk more down the station. Hope you've got someone to feed the dog for the next twenty-five years.'

"Once we'd cuffed Joe, Tom called for a search team and a dog handler. They found some boxes of pills in the kitchen, and an old wardrobe at the back of his garage was full of pirate DVDs. And they hadn't even started looking for hiding places."

"So what did Joe have to say about his visit here?"

"Oh yeah. Said he didn't know anything about murder. Didn't even know he had a gun. Claimed a friend had left the box ages ago and he'd forgotten about it. Also forgotten who the friend was. Anyway, he said he'd been contacted a couple of weeks ago on the phone by a woman who asked him to do a job. Pinch a digger, then go to a site nearby and mess it up. She'd phone later to tell him where the digger and the site were, and she'd book him on the plane. Five hundred quid. Easy money! He took the evening plane over, found the digger just where she said it would be. It was too early to do the job, so he walked into Bowmore, bought himself half a bottle of cheap whisky, for later, and spent the rest of the evening in a pub. At closing time he walked back to the digger, got into the cab, and drank his whisky – to keep warm – while he waited. Just after dawn he drove it – the key had been left in it – to the site, did the trashing, left the digger on the road nearby, and made his way back to the airport. As soon as it opened, he had a wash and got some breakfast at the cafe, then waited for his plane. That's it."

"So he was only in contact with the woman twice?"

"Yes. First time when she asked him to do the job, second time when she told him where the digger and the site were. She sounded English, he said, but with a bit of something else. His flight was booked on the web by a Julia Crabtree with an address in Highford, Essex. We checked the address – it doesn't exist. Joe collected the ticket at the airport in Oban."

"How was he paid?" Blue finally asked.

"Cash in an envelope through the post. Half before, and the rest after."

"I guess we'd find plenty of witnesses for Joe's evening here, but there's no point if he's told us everything. Do you think he has, Enver?"

"Yes. After all, we were threatening him with all sorts. We can charge him with plenty now, but none of it adds up to murder."

Now it was well after seven. Blue was feeling exhausted. The pace of the investigation must be catching up with him. He went back to the hotel, and had a plate of lentil and bacon soup and a roll in the restaurant, washed down with a glass of bland but chilled lager. Then he went to his room.

He updated his report again. He knew other cops who waited till the case was ended before touching the keyboard. That was mainly because they saw the writing simply as a chore, like having to wash the dishes after a good meal. But Blue saw the constant updating as a dialogue with himself about the case, a constant review of the evidence and the theories, and a means of getting his head right inside it. He felt they had put several more pieces into the jigsaw, though there was still a lot of empty space. This case wasn't going to give them a big breakthrough, the sort of thing that enables the detective to put everything together five minutes before the credits are due. This was real police work, the accretion through hours of work of hard facts. But the facts only meant something if you had a theory that joined them up plausibly, a story that sounded right. And then you had to find a few more facts to confirm it.

He watched the news on TV. The funeral was the main feature. Then an interview with the Minister of Defence. "This event made me proud to be British, Jeremy, proud to be British. What we have today owes so much to heroes like these men, willing to sacrifice everything for their country. For Britain. Think back to dark days of the Blitz, Jeremy. Without the inspired leadership of Winston Churchill, and his War Cabinet, those brave men's deaths would have been wasted. They saw how each individual fitted into the bigger picture. How each sacrifice brought gain in the fight against the enemy. How Britain would remain Great."

Day 7. Wednesday

47

He didn't wake until eight. He'd needed the sleep.

He reached the station at 8.55. Clara Gilmour greeted him absent-mindedly, and continued sorting papers in front of her into two piles.

He went up to his office and checked his mobile – he'd heard it ping while he was driving over. Text from John Striven. "Call asap." He hit the shortcut number for Striven.

"John, hi, Angus here. How did it go with Evelyn Davies yesterday? I got the picture, by the way, thanks."

"At least that's one thing that's worked out. She'd been got at, Angus. Warned off. They've threatened her. Bastards!"

"Tell me the story."

"Oh yeah, well, I got down there, to the house, and as soon as she opened the door I knew. She just looked so sheepish. Offered me tea, Welsh cake, biscuits, the lot. I took a cup of tea, and asked what had happened. She said someone from the MoD had been in touch, said they'd found her father's body, he'd died a hero's death on a commando raid in Germany. The body was going to be buried that day. They were sorry she couldn't be there, for security reasons they couldn't release the news just yet. There would be a memorial service later for the families. She realised that any connection with the bodies in the peat was a mistake on her part, and now thought it was quite possible Dafydd had been a commando.

"I said to her that was what they'd said before and she hadn't believed it, so what had changed her mind. She said she'd thought about it more. I said what was there to think about? Then she said, 'Sorry, you'll have to go now.' As I passed her going out of the lounge, she whispered, 'They're watching me, across the road. They said something bad would happen to my grandchildren if I talked to you.' Then she slid the photo, folded in two, into my jacket pocket, and whispered, 'I never gave you that, you stole it while I was getting the tea, see.' Then shoved me out of the door, and shouted after me, 'And don't come back and bother me again, d'you hear?' My taxi was waiting outside, so I got straight in, then had a quick look round. No cars in the street, but in the upstairs window of the house opposite I caught a flicker of sunlight reflected off binoculars, or a camera lens. They were up there all right, making sure she did what she was told."

"Well, John, at least we know what they're up to, and we got the picture. We're chasing up Peter Bishop. And we've got DNA from Glyn Ellis, hoping for the result today. How are you going to play it in the paper?"

"I don't have an interview with Evelyn sitting at the heart of a 'They found my Dad' human interest story. What worries me is that a tame hack will be told to knock up a 'They found my Dad the Heroic Commando' piece, and it'll appear in one of the tabloids with pictures of that fake funeral. I'll have to leave it a couple of days, make them think I've got nothing, then do it as an investigative piece. Maybe you could help me there."

"We'll do what we can. You could put them off the scent with an 'Aliens were on Islay' story."

He went through to the base room. Alison was typing at her laptop. Bhardwaj was listening to something on headphones. Craig was reading a book. He went over to Alison first. Before he could speak she put a finger up to silence him.

"Guess what?"

"I don't know, Alison. Your cat gave birth to kittens?"

"I don't have a cat. Let me give you a clue: DNA test positive!"

"A body and Glyn Ellis?"

"Yess!" She punched the air, something Blue had never ever seen her do before. Then she went over to the pinboard, took a laminated label with the name "Dafydd Thomas" written on it, and stuck it on the board, below the photo. "I had the label ready. I knew it would be positive."

"Good. One down, four to go. Now we need something on Peter Bishop."

"I've found him!" called Craig. She put down the book and flicked through her notebook.

"OK. What have you got, Deirdra?"

"Well, these were young men, so I've left out anyone under sixteen and over thirty from the searches. Peter Bishop's a common enough name, so there's still plenty left. I've went through the birth entries, then looked at the death registers, and took out any Peter Bishop who died before or after the war or even during it but not on active service, and whose age couldn't be matched with the births. That only left seven, all in the war museum database. But now the real Peter Bishop, if I can call him that, has been disguised. He's no longer with the 212th

RAF Regiment. However, the thing is, we ken his disguise, since we saw the data being changed. If *they* realise we saw that, they'll have to move him again, then we've lost him. But I didn't think they did, so I looked for the Peter Bishop who was in the 18th Tank Regiment, and died on the 16th November 1944, in Northern Italy. I used that information with another database that contains records of British armed forces postings and deaths from as far back as they can be got. What it gives us is an age at death and a date of birth, if known. Then we can identify which one of thae births is the right one."

"But will they have changed this database too?" asked Alison.

"I'm assuming that *they* are not stupid, and will have altered the same details in this database as in the other one, but left everything else. After all, if they change that linkage, we can't follow it. Or so they think."

"And have you?" asked Blue.

"Aye. Well, actually, not quite. I've got it down to two birth records. That gives us the names and address of the parents. They're probably dead now, but it gives us a starting point to find them, or find a relative to do the DNA match. And finding people is what the cops are good at. Or should be anyway. Right, chief?"

"Yes, indeed," said Blue. "That's good work, I'm very impressed. So what do you suggest doing next?"

Craig glanced down at her notes, in tiny but very precise handwriting, then back up at Blue. "With your permission, chief, I'll make some calls, and find some relatives. They may have something on what happened to their grandfather or whatever he was during the war. That should enable us to pin down the right one."

"Even if it's not clear which one it is," put in Alison, "all we have to do is take DNA from both families, and see if either of them matches the bodies."

"Sounds good to me," said Blue. "Once that's done, can you do the same for Terence Darwin, that other name we got yesterday. Died 16th November 1944. Check him on the war museum database again. If they've changed his regiment we know he's ours."

"Aye, righto chief!" said Craig. She turned back to the computer, licked her lips, and rubbed her palms together. Go get 'em, he thought. What was it Sherlock Holmes used to say? The game is on, was that it?

"The game is afoot!" said Alison. Blue hadn't realised he'd been speaking out loud.

"Though he was actually quoting Shakespeare," she went on, "who uses it twice. The well-known reference is in Henry V, who says 'The game's afoot,' towards the end of his speech to the English troops at the Battle of Agincourt, but it also appears in Henry IV, Part 1, in a less gung-ho context. However, Sherlock buffs have noted that in the recent TV series, Sherlock says 'The game is on!', subtly shifting the meaning of the word 'game'. That's probably where you got it!"

"Ah, I stand corrected of tampering with the great quotations." He noticed out of the corner of his eye PC Craig grinning.

"That's fascinatin, Alison," she said. "How dae you mean that the meaning o 'game' is changed?"

"It originally referred to the hunt, and meant that a target animal had come out of cover and was making a run for it. So the hunters can see the quarry and give chase. But hunting references are frowned on now, so the other meaning of 'game' is brought in, to mean 'the contest has begun' or something like that."

"I didn't know you were a Sherlock buff," said Blue.

"There's plenty about me you don't know," smiled Alison, "But actually I'm not a Sherlock buff. I just proof-read my baby sister's final year dissertation. 'Literary allusions in the Sherlock Holmes canon.' I can give you a much longer lecture on it sometime."

Blue struggled to focus, but was out of his conversational depth. "I look forward to it. But what about the tapes, Alison? Anything interesting?"

"Didn't Arvind tell you that yesterday? So that was the wrong question. You need to ask what it was that was interesting. Asking the right questions is important, isn't that right, Constable Craig?"

Craig was trying hard to maintain a straight face. "Er, yes, Doctor Hendrickx, if you say so."

"You're in a good mood today," said Blue.

"I had a lovely evening." she answered.

Blue felt unaccountably jealous. "What did you do?"

"I went with Moira for a walk. We walked out from Port Ellen, past the school, and up to the standing stone. It leans slightly, so Moira took a photo of me trying to push it right over. Then we went back to the house and played Monopoly. There's an Islay edition."

"Monopoly's a bit hard with just two of you."

"No, Alasdair was playing too, Moira's husband. He's a really nice guy. Have you met him?"

"Er, no, not yet."

"Well, you'll have to come round and play too. Or maybe you prefer Cluedo?"

This was getting a bit out of hand, but he found himself saying "I'd love to. And any game will do. Whether it's afoot or not."

"I'll suggest it to Moira. Now for the tape." She poked Bhardwaj in the arm, and he jumped, then saw who it was, and took his earphones off.

"Sorry, I was concentrating." He noticed Blue. "Sir!"

"Right then, report please," said Blue.

Alison had become serious again: "We got just three bits which are interesting, and Arvind was typing them out. He's converted the audio on the cassettes into digital files, so we can extract those bits. John McClay is difficult to interpret at times, and he has a very hoarse voice and a persistent cough. He doesn't sound at all well, in fact. But then, he wasn't. Nearly done?" she said to Bhardwaj.

"On the last few lines. Should have it ten minutes, chief."

"Excellent," said Blue, feeling a lot calmer. "Drop me a copy when you're finished, and we can look at it at the meeting." He looked at his watch. Ten to ten. Just time for a cup of coffee.

48

McCader was back for the meeting, looking as if he'd had a perfect night's sleep and was ready for action again. Moira sat in too, as well as Craig and Bhardwaj. Blue reported on the work on the names, and McCader on his interview with Joe Donnelly. Then they moved on to the tapes.

Bhardwaj produced hard copies of the extracts, and handed them round. "I've edited out of the printed text all the coughs, throat clearances, sniffs, and meaningless sounds, but I've not tried to interpret the words that aren't clear. George is the interviewer, you'll recognise his voice. Mr McClay doesn't always understand what he's saying, and he's also a little deaf. Here's the first one. Follow it on the sheet, transcription No. 1. GO is George, JM is John McClay."

> *Transcription No. 1*
> *GO: So, John, you were telling me about the various foreigners on the base. Where d'you reckon they came from?"*
> *JM: Eh?*
> *GO: The foreign people. Where were they from?*
> *JM: Well, from all over the place. France. You recognise them right enough, Mr George, the Frenchies. Dutchmen too, or maybe Belgians, I wouldn't be knowing the difference. And there were a few from Denmark, or was it Norway? They were there for the training, you see.*
> *GO: What others were there?*
> *JM: Eh, what's that?*
> *GO: Others, were there others?*
> *JM: There were others, yes that would be right. French, Belgians, or maybe they were Dutch.*
> *GO: We've had them already, John, what about Poles? Czechs?*
> *JM: Oh yes. Poles. There were certainly a good few of them. Poles, from Poland. Czechs too, yes, but then again, I wouldn't really know the difference, it's just what I was told. I mean if you were to hear some people talking, could you yourself be telling whether they*

149

*were Poles or Czechs? I suppose it's the same if you
had a Lewisman and a Diurach, could you be telling
the difference? Well, I suppose I could, but you, Mr
George, well it would not be easy for you. The Gaelic
is very different. But with these Poles and Czechs and
so on, well it's not easy, now is it?*
GO: No, I suppose it ain't. Any others?
*JM: Here's a really interesting thing for you, Mr
George. Even though I'm not sure I could tell a Pole
and a Czech apart, I was always able to spot a Rus-
sian.*
GO: Was there a Russian there?
*JM: The Russian bear. Yes, in the cartoons the Russian
would always be a bear. Slow-witted, but persistent,
obstinate, never giving up.*
GO: So there was a Russian?
*JM: Yes, of course there was. He even looked like a
Russian. Wore a fur hat. And a long overcoat. It's
very cold in Russia. He didn't need the coat here. But
he was a Russian, certainly. I saw him myself.*
GO: What kind of Russian? An officer?
JM: Yes, all the foreigners were officers.
GO: So apart from them, were there others too?
JM: Eh?
…

"That's the first one," said Bhardwaj. "It tells us there was a Russian."

"One Russian," said Blue. "All the others are plural. But he always
refers to the Russian in the singular."

"He does seem emphatic that there was a Russian there," said Alison, "Even asserts that he saw the man himself, and describes him."

"OK," said Blue, "Arvind, let's hear No. 2."

Transcription No. 2
GO: So you were putting up partitions in Building 7b.
JM: Eh?
GO: You were putting up walls.
*JM: Walls? No, we were putting in partitions. Walls and
partitions are two very different things, Mr George.
Walls are outside, and partitions will be inside.*

GO: *So what happened?*

JM: *I was putting in the partitions, you see. It was a big dormitory, and they were wanting separate little rooms for each person. Anyway, this officer comes up and says to me, 'Comrade worker!' That's not the sort of greeting you forget, now, is it, Mr George? Well, of course, I says to him, 'Sir,' and then he says, 'No, not Sir, you will call me Comrade Major.' So I says 'Certainly I will, Comrade Major.' And then he's asking, can I make his room bigger. I'm explaining that all the rooms are to be the same size. So he says, 'No, no, to each according to his needs. My needs are greater, comrade worker, I am larger person and have bigger job.' Well, now, that wasn't very fair, was it? But of course I wouldn't be saying that to him, now would I? So I just says that I do what I'm told. He didn't like that at all. 'Well,' he says, 'Now I tell you, comrade worker, it must be bigger. It is for me, Fululugh Bululugh [Pronunciation of the name not clear.]...*

GO: *I didn't rightly hear his name, John. Can you give it me again?*

JM: *I'm not sure I'm remembering it right, Mr George, in those days we weren't so used to foreign names. I'm just telling you what it sounded like.*

GO: *That's all right, John, carry on.*

JM: *As I said, he says, 'It is for me, Fululugh Bululugh, Commissar of the People's Army.' He was swaying a bit, I think he was drunk too. They like their vodka. Ivans, we used to call them. Not that I ever saw many. In fact, just the one, and that was him. And his name wasn't Ivan. Anyway, he was swaying slightly, sort of like a tree. I didn't like the look of him. He was a big man, you know, a real bear. With a big moustache, just like Stalin. Only lighter.*

GO: *Stalin?*

JM: *Yes, you could say it was startling. And a nasty look about him too. So now Colonel Kilphedar comes along, to see how the work is doing, and he sees the major. 'Now,' he says, 'What's the problem, Major? No need to discuss it with the workmen. I think we*

*can sort it out over a drink, eh?' At that the Russian
perks up, I can tell you. 'Spot of whisky do the
trick?' says the colonel, 'Why don't we pop over to the
mess?' And he leads the Russian away, just like he's
a sheep, and not a bear. A Russian sheep. That's a
good one, isn't it, Mr George?*

*GO: I think you mentioned a Greek earlier, what can
you tell me about him then?*

...

"Right," said Blue, "Any comments on that one?"

"He's a commissar," said McCader, "A political officer. Their job was to impose political correctness and punish anyone who was out of line."

"So what was he doing there?" asked Alison. "I don't suppose there was any need for a commissar at the base, especially if he were the only Russian."

"Possibly a liaison officer," said Blue, "sharing information. Reporting back to Moscow."

"A spy?" asked Bhardwaj.

"Sort of. Everybody did it. We had liaison officers in Russia to try and see what they were up to, so I suppose they did the same here."

"He might be our executioner," said McCader. "He would probably be carrying a Tokarev pistol. And he's the only Russian we've come across so far. Making himself useful, as it were."

"What about the name? Any ideas there?" asked Blue.

"Sounds awfully garbled," said Alison, "Could start with F, V or even B. They do sound a bit similar."

"It's certainly a possible lead.," said Blue. "OK, Arvind, then let's have No. 3."

Transcription No. 3
GO: Were the foreign officers on special missions too?
JM: Which two?
GO: No, not two, any of them.
*JM: Well, they would all be there for something, Mr
George, wouldn't they? Even the Russian, Bululugh,
or whatever it was.*
GO: What was he doing?
*JM: Mostly drinking it seemed. One of the other joiners,
was it Roddie McBrayne, now, I can't rightly remem-*

*ber, well, anyway, whoever it was, he told me that a
Polish officer told him the Russian had killed several
Polish officers after the Russian invasion in thirty-
nine. The Poles wouldn't speak to him. Later on,
there was an incident of some sort. I was there one
morning, and it was clear something had been happening the night before. You could tell that the officers
were tense. Of course they were not supposed to tell us
anything, but you overhear bits and pieces. You know,
if you're working on a partition that isn't very thick,
you can usually hear what's going on at the other side.
If you put your ear to it.*

GO: And?

JM: And what?

GO: What happened then?

*JM: There's no need to be getting impatient, Mr George.
Patience is a virtue, as the Good Book tells us. The
thing was this, you see. One of the Polish officers had
challenged this Russian to a duel. The Russian says,
'Yes, that's fine.' The Pole says, 'When?' The Russian says, 'Now!' pulls out his pistol and shoots him.
Right there. The Pole was only wounded, but it was
enough to put him out of the war for a while. It
caused a real upset, all the officers were talking about
it.*

GO: The Russian. Was he punished?

*JM: I never heard any more. I suppose it was all hushed
up, that's what they used to do with anything funny
that was going on. But, now that I'm thinking about
it, I never did see that Russian again, the comrade
major. Mind you, I was out of things a bit myself, you
see, I slipped on a plank and broke my arm. I was off
for three months then, and…"*

GO: And you didn't see the Russian again?

JM: Wasn't I just telling you that, Mr George.

…

"Anything on No. 3 then?"

"Suggests he was a nasty piece of work." said Moira.

"May have done some killing before," said McCader.

"It does seem to back up the other two," said Blue. "Thanks,

Arvind. And Dr Hendrickx. Anything else?"

"There was one other thing," said Alison. "There was a point where John said that all the workmen had been told to take three days off, it was the anniversary of something, and the RAF people didn't want to be disturbed during the celebrations. John thought they didn't want the civilians to see them having a big feast and then all getting drunk. But what if it were something else that they didn't want witnessed? A quiet execution, for instance?"

"That's interesting," said Blue. "Brings us onto the reason for the killing. We've spent a lot of time on the victims, and now we've a suspicion about the killer. But we need to think of the reason too. There are a few possibilities. One is crime, possibly theft of war materials. Hamish McNeill mentioned a colleague who disappeared after complaining about supplies being stolen. It's possible that our victims died because they complained about some major criminal activity. Or maybe they themselves were the criminals, discreetly executed after a secret court-martial."

"If it was a court-martial," asked Moira, "surely there would be a record somewhere?"

"Even if they exist," said Alison, "I suspect records of wartime court-martials would be classified. I doubt we'd see them, particularly if they reveal a story that conflicts with the official tale of how our victims died."

"Yes," said Blue, "That could be a dead end. However, things are looking positive. We've opened up some new ground this morning. Now let's see what we can dig up. Deirdra, can you keep chasing those families? Arvind, can you start interviewing the old folks on the list from the museum?"

"I'll give him a hand," added Alison. "If it's all right with you, Inspector, sir."

49

Blue motioned McCader into his office. "Enver, thanks for the report. Did the whisky handover go to plan?"

"Perfect, chief."

"That's a relief. Now, how do you feel we can progress the Now case?"

"Two lines at the moment, I think. One, I can get back to the garage man in Northampton, see if he can describe any of the drivers connected to Euro Special Logistics Solutions. Maybe that'll give us more on Range Rover Man, possibly other possible accomplices. Two, I can chase up this Julia Crabtree, do some phoning to Essex. Perhaps she was the woman with Range Rover Man when they looked into the restaurant. I've got your description there, we can see if anybody down there's seen her. DVLC should have a photo, if she got a driving licence using that name. While I was in Oban I checked on sightings of the vehicle. Not a sausage. Looks like he may have gone to ground. Waiting up for the next mission, I'd guess."

He updated his report, then looked into the base room. Craig was working at the computer, McCader was on the phone, Bhardwaj and Alison Hendrickx were out, presumably interviewing the old folk. Everything seemed very quiet, so he decided to go get some fresh air.

He went up the main street to the round church at the top. As he came back down he noticed, parked at the bottom of the main street, near the pier, a yellow Lada Estate. That must be Boris Blackett's. He passed it and walked on to the end of the pier.

It was raining slightly now, but it was good to breathe the salt air again. From the end of the pier he looked back at Bowmore distillery, whose long white buildings lay on the seafront just next to the pier. The bay here was where the flying-boats had been based, and the distillery buildings were taken over by the sounds and paraphernalia of war. Probably a great deal of damage done to the buildings and their contents too. This was where Hamish McNeill had worked then, too, noting the corruption that was covered up.

He bought a sandwich for his lunch at the Co-op, and walked back to the station. Sergeant Walker was at the reception desk, filling in a form. He greeted Blue jovially. "Morning, chief, not such a bad day, eh?"

Blue took the opportunity. "Bob, what do you think about this Britishness business?"

"Well, I dunno about that, sir. If you'd asked me what I was when I were in London, I'd have said English. Up here, well I'm getting to be Scottish now, I guess. The wife and kids certainly are. Kids even speak some Gaelic! I mean, British is like the Empire, or the war, ain't it?"

"So what about this programme the government's bringing in?"

"Oh, that! Well, that's an easy one, sir, it's just a dodge to stop people getting in, you know, immigrants and so on. Memorising old kings and queens, I mean, that's a lot of old baloney, ain't it? If you ask me, it's just so's they can ask people tricky questions at the ferry ports if they don't want 'em in. You know, who were the third son of Henry the Second? See what I mean?"

"Yes. By the way, who was the third son of Henry the Second?"

"Don't ask me, I haven't a clue. I've got better stuff than that to clog my head with."

"Thanks, Bob, that's very helpful. By the way, what can you tell me about Boris Blackett?"

"I couldn't say very much, chief. Keeps himself to himself. Does the job. Not interested in promotion, but I think he wants off the island. Not really an island type, if you know what I mean."

He made his way up to his office. But as he entered, he paused. Things weren't quite right. He looked at the papers on his desk. They were more or less as he'd left them earlier, but somehow not quite. Someone had been in the room. He went back down to the entrance, and asked the Sergeant who'd been in during the morning.

"You'd have to check with Clara for the morning – you just missed her when you came in, she finishes at twelve." He opened a hard-covered A5 sized notebook and looked at the bookmarked page. "There's no-one logged in the book for this morning – we record any visitors who come past the desk here."

"Who's in at the moment?"

"Well, I think Deirdra and Enver are upstairs. Arvind and Dr Hendrickx are out talking to some old folk. The boss's gone to a Community Council meeting. And Boris's over at the distillery. A crowd of Germans did the tour, wouldn't leave after their two free drams. Got quite rowdy, Sheila said – she's the receptionist – so I sent Boris over to sort 'em out. 'Bout what you was asking earlier, sir, Boris, he's very good wi' crowds and drunks. Never raises his voice. But he can look quite menacing when he wants."

What was going on? Someone had been in and had a rummage round during the time he'd been out. How long had that been? He looked at his watch – 12.15. He must have been out for nearly an hour. He climbed the stairs. McCader and Craig were still in the base room. But they'd not noticed anyone in the corridor, they hadn't been out of the room.

50

He was wondering what to do next, when he heard voices along the corridor, and went out to see Moira Nicolson coming up the stairs, followed by Elspeth Forrest.

"Elspeth's on the Community Council," explained Moira, "I'm usually in attendance – there are usually some questions for me, you know, parking, dog-fouling, noisy youths. Elspeth's got something, so I asked her to come back afterwards. Come on in and we can have a look."

Blue followed them into Moira's office. "Good to see you, Elspeth. So what have you got?"

"We've managed to identify that newspaper fragment." She took a small leather-bound notebook from her handbag and selected a page. "It's from the *Oban Advertiser*, Saturday, 11th November, 1944."

"Well, that date fits all right."

A sermon preached in the Free Church in Oban by Rev. Josiah Carstairs. His text is 2 Samuel, chapter 10, verses 11-13. Joab, the Israelite general, is talking to his brother Abishai, who leads the other half of their army. They're up against a huge host of Ammonites and Syrians: 'If the Syrians be too strong for me, then thou shalt help me: but if the children of Ammon be too strong for thee, then I will come and help thee. Be of good courage, and let us play the men for our people, and for the cities of our God: and the LORD do that which seemeth him good. And Joab drew nigh, and the people that were with him, unto the battle against the Syrians: and they fled before him.' He's quoting from the Authorised Version – we call it the King James Version now – that was the version all the protestant churches used then.

"So what's Mr Carstairs' point here?"

"He's suggesting that if the allies help each other, and if everyone puts all their effort into it, then God will help them too, and they'll beat the enemy who seems to be stronger."

"Do you think that passage was torn out for a reason? Is it telling us something?"

"Unfortunately, I don't think so. It's not the whole sermon. It looks more like a piece was just torn off the corner of the page, without reference to what was printed on it. In those days newspaper wasn't just thrown away. It was all recycled for household uses: window coverings, tablecloths, firelighters, toilet paper."

"What about the advert on the back?"

"It's for tins of minced fish. Stuff you'd use to make fish cakes and sausages. Included fish no-one had heard of, bits of shark, whale and so on. But I don't think that has any relevance for us either."

"Thanks, Elspeth. At least that date is useful. Did you turn up anything else?"

"Yes and no. I had a look in the boxes of photographs we have in the storeroom. We've been working through them, cataloguing them, it's a mammoth task. We haven't done the wartime boxes yet, so I brought them over." She had been carrying a canvas shopping bag when she came in, and now pulled out of it a flat cardboard box, slightly bigger that A4 in footprint, and about three inches deep, and laid it on the desk, followed by another. "There we are. Two boxes. You'll know better than I will what you're looking for, but if you want to do it now, I'm happy enough to hang on, and give you any further information I can."

Blue could have got one of the team to do this, but old photographs fascinated him. He never ceased to be amazed by the thought that these images were windows on a reality that had passed. Moments in real lives, preserved for eternity. "OK, let's do it. Moira, would you like to take one and I'll take the other?"

"What are we looking for?"

"Anything that throws light on what we know so far."

Most of the pictures were general scenes of the island during the war. Unidentified buildings, an armoured car in Bowmore, some girls standing outside the post office.

"Let's take out any with RAF personnel, or groups of officers," Blue suggested.

After half an hour, a dozen photos were piled on a space in between the two boxes. Moira produced a copy of the photo from Evelyn Davies, and put it on the table. "This'll help us too, Elspeth," she said. "We know what two of them look like."

Soon the pile was reduced to just two. One was a seven by five inch picture of a group of about thirty men, standing in front of a large plane. They all wore similar uniforms, RAF rather than army, and were smiling at the camera. It was a sunny day; the picture was very sharp.

"Look!" said Moira, "There they are. Dafydd Thomas and Peter Bishop." The other two craned forward to squint at the picture, then had to lean back again as their own shadows obscured it. "Wait a minute," said Moira, rummaging in her desk drawer and extracting a large magnifying glass. The thick rim had a set of built-in LED lights. Now they could look closely at the picture.

"I think they're with that guy on the left," said Moira. "There's a little cluster of three within the bigger group. What d'you think, Elspeth?"

"Yes, you could be right."

"Could that be Terence Darwin, I wonder?"

"We could scan the picture," suggested Elspeth, "blow up this part, see if he looks like one of the bodies."

The other picture showed eight men standing in front of a brick wall with a door in it. They wore army field uniforms, but with different flashes on the shoulders, and little flags on the upper chest. To the left of the door was a sign 'Dormitory No. 4' and above the door was painted roughly 'Chez Nous'. The men themselves looked somewhat exotic. One was sporting a Gallic moustache, and another had a swarthy complexion and dark curly hair of a length prohibited in the British army. These two were also smiling. Most of the others had serious or even grim expressions.

"Can you focus on the flags?" asked Blue. "What countries have we got there?"

"OK," said Elspeth, peering through the magnifying glass, "there's the Free French, and Greece, two Norwegians, two Poles, a Belgian, and what's the last, ah, hammer and sickle, Russian. Look how the Poles are at the opposite end of the group from the Russian. Can't have been fun sharing a dorm with one of the people who'd invaded their country in 1939. Especially if that's *our* Russian. Could it be him?"

"We do have a description of him," said Moira. "Large and with a light-coloured Stalin moustache."

All three of them looked closely at the man, seeking to elicit from his picture any sign that he could be the killer. He was a tall man, perhaps in his mid-thirties, well-built and with a pale squarish face, and light hair cut short, almost a crew cut. They had to look hard to see the moustache, but it was there, though its light colour somehow made it un-Stalin-like. He stared at the camera with completely expressionless eyes.

"It's him," whispered Moira, as if the man might hear her. "Look at the eyes. There's no emotion in them. Compare him with the others." Sure enough, the faces of the other men, even if not smiling, conveyed some emotion: satisfaction, hope, pride, determination, sadness, comradeship. These were men ready to fight for their countries, ready to do anything to expel the occupiers, glad of an opportunity to make a contribution. All but the Russian. If there was any expression there, it was boredom.

"Is there anything on the back?" asked Blue.

Elspeth turned it over. Again they craned forward. There were pencil marks, giving a year 'probably 1944' and a box number. But there was also some faded writing, grey now rather than its original blue, written with a fountain pen. Names! Just a single line: *Lisowski Wilk Sjosted Madsen Klaark Lefevre Samaras Burovkin*

"Burovkin," said Moira. "Bululugh. Same number of syllables, and starts with the same letter."

"It looks like that could be him," said Blue. "Elspeth, where did these pictures come from?"

"Let's see. Box 23. We were given these a few years ago by Billy Duggan's widow. After the war it seems he and some pals went round the site of the base looking for souvenirs. The site was guarded, but I suppose local kids could sneak in and out."

51

He was wakened later by more noise, thumping, and groaning. Then another voice: "Hey, what the hell are ye doing, lads? Get off us, will ye. If you want a fight, put yon bloody bat down and face me like a man."

The response to that was a loud crack, and a groan. Then a voice he knew now: "You're a tough 'un, you Geordie bastard," he sneered. "Your little pal Taffy, he screamed easy enough, when Mr Batty just tickled him. We couldn't leave it there, though, could we, got to give every one of you a fair shot, heh. Mr Batty don't have favourites, he likes to have fun with everybody. You Geordies must be tougher than the bloody Taffs. I see we're going to have to break a few little bones here, to make you sing."

The thumps and groans continued.

Then another voice, "Come on mate, isn't that enough? I reckon you've broken all the bones in that arm."

"Hey, Les, you're my pal, but don't you bloody tell me what to do. These bastards is traitors, and deserve all they get. And it don't matter what gets broken. They won't need any bones pretty soon. Ain't you enjoying yourself?" And he laughed.

He knew then that he wasn't getting out. They were going to kill him. He could only think of one reason why.

52

He thanked Elspeth for her help, and left her to have coffee with Moira. The base room was empty, so he left the pictures for Craig with a note to scan them. Then he ate his sandwich and had a cup of coffee, and thought about things. It was the pictures, first the one of Dafydd Thomas and Peter Bishop, and now the two he'd just seen. Faces of the living. The victims, probably at least three, maybe even all of them. And, he felt sure, the killer. The expression on the man's face, the emotionless stare into the camera, told him that this man could kill, without stress, without guilt, without sadness, without nightmares.

Two o'clock. He was about to see what McCader and Craig had got, when there was a sharp knock at the door, and Moira Nicolson came in. She looked serious.

"Hi Moira, what's up?"

"Angus, an old man's been run down in Glasgow by a red Range Rover. Registration number starting with PU15. He's in hospital now, in a bad way. Glasgow knew we had an interest in the car, emailed me the details." She had printed out the information from Glasgow, and passed it to Blue.

There was silence in the room for two and a half minutes while he read it.

"So, what have we got?" said Blue. "An old man, no name yet, lives in a flat in Argyle Street, near the Art Gallery. He's crossing the street to go to the newsagent when a car jumps a red light, knocks him over, then whips into a side street and disappears. A woman checking her shopping list sees what happened, spots the registration number, notes it down. The old man's in the Western Infirmary, condition critical." This was important. Blue didn't think a freelance agent would be a careless driver, or let his car be stolen by joyriders. *Ergo*, he had run down the old man deliberately. But why. There was an obvious answer: the old man was connected to the case.

"That's our car, isn't it?" said Moira. "The man who tried to kill Alison."

"Seems likely. We're lucky. Second time he's not succeeded."

"Could the old man have been a witness to the execution?" asked Moira.

"It's certainly a possibility," said Blue.

"Why do it now?"

"Perhaps they thought we were getting close to him, decided to eliminate him before we found him."

"But we weren't on to this old man."

"Maybe they thought we were. Or that he might respond to the appeal in the *Nation*. Didn't want to take the chance. But if we didn't know he was there before, now we do. They've led us to him. So now we need to know who he is, and to talk to him while he's still alive. Who's in charge of the case?"

"Email from a Sergeant Glen, case officer's name is…ah, Inspector Taylor."

"Hmm. Don't know the name. I'll phone, see what he can tell me."

There was a number at the bottom of the email. Blue called it, and asked to be put through to Inspector Taylor. Then he leaned away from the phone, as electronic muzak enveloped his ear. He switched the phone to conference. A monotonous riff filled the room. They couldn't even think.

After about half a minute it suddenly stopped in mid-note. "Taylor!" barked an impatient voice. No 'How can I help you?' here, noted Blue.

"Hi, this is Inspector Blue from Oban. I'm sorry to disturb you…"

"No, you're not. You don't care if I was doing something important or not. You imagined I was just sitting here waiting for your call, ready to jump to attention for you. Well, here's news, pal, I wasn't. So if you waste my time I'll put the phone down. Now, who are you and what do you want?"

"This is Inspector Blue from Oban…"

"I already know that," the voice snapped back.

"And this is Inspector Nicolson, from Islay," said Moira.

There was a sharp intake of breath at the other end. Inspector Taylor had not realised this was a conference call and now did not know how many people might be listening, only that there were at least two. The tone changed, now more wary. "Well, I am in fact very busy, can we get to the point right away?"

"We're running the bodies in the peat case here. You may have heard of it. We think an incident yesterday which you informed us about was connected to this case."

"I didn't inform you, that was Sergeant Glen. I certainly don't have time to spend on historic cases. I've enough to do dealing with today's crime."

"We think yesterday's incident *was* today's crime, and if that man dies, it's murder," said Blue.

"Just looks like a hit-and-run to me. Someone driving a car that's too powerful for him. Or probably her."

"I think you'll find that presumption is not borne out by the statistics," put in Moira. "Shall I quote them?"

"I don't have time for that, what makes you think this was murder, Green?"

"Blue."

"Whatever. Get on with it."

Blue bit his lip. He could feel himself becoming angry. But he needed information from this man, he had to stay calm. Moira laid her fingertips on his arm, with a warning look. Don't be riled. He drew a deep breath. "The car was involved in a serious incident a few days ago. We think this was an attempt to silence a key witness involved in my case here."

"What do expect me to do about it?"

"Nothing at all, apart from giving us what you've got on it."

"Sergeant Glen can do that. But as far as I'm concerned, this is a road-traffic incident. I don't have the time or the officers to divert onto it."

"Thank you, that's most helpful. I'd also like to interview the victim. I will be happy for one of your officers to accompany me."

"We'll do that when we've time and let you know."

"No. You won't. Let me repeat that this is an active inquiry and I am the case officer. I'm afraid that I must insist. If you have any specific objection I would be glad to hear it. If you would prefer me to make the request via my Super to yours, I can do that."

There was a loud click. Taylor had hung up.

For a few seconds they both stared at the phone. It remained silent.

"Well," said Moira, "What a cheek! I should report him. We can't let him just stop the investigation."

"He can't, and he knows it. As far as he knows, I've picked up the phone right now to speak to my superior. So he doesn't have long to decide what to do. Let's wait for a minute."

Thirty seconds later the phone rang. Blue flicked the conference switch again, and answered. "Inspector Blue. How may I help you?"

"Oh, er, this is Sergeant Glen, Glasgow, sir. Inspector Taylor asked me to call you. I believe you're looking at the Argyle Street incident."

"That's right. We suspect it to be an attempted murder, linked to a case we're pursuing here on Islay. Any details would be helpful."

"No problem, sir. Let's see." Papers could be heard shuffling. "Yes, we now have a name, Lesley Greeley, aged 93. Address in Argyle Street, ground floor flat, shared with his wife, Dorothy Greeley. Current medical status critical. The doctors are not hopeful."

"Thanks. Do you have someone by his bedside, in case he says anything?"

"No. I raised it with Inspector Taylor as soon as we got the report in, but he vetoed it. No manpower to spare on a traffic incident. Sorry, sir, nothing more I can do there." He did sound genuinely sorry.

"Fair enough. Sergeant, I'm coming down to see if I can talk to the victim and his wife. Will someone from your division be accompanying me?"

"The inspector has asked me to do that, sir. When are you coming?"

"Hold on a minute," Nicolson stuck a post-it note in front of Blue – 'Next GLA flight 18.15 arr. 18.50'

"The next flight departs here at quarter past six. It gets into Glasgow at ten to seven. I can get a taxi over to Stewart Street."

"No need to do that, sir, I'll pick you up myself at the airport and take you straight to the hospital."

"That's very helpful, Sergeant. How will I recognise you?"

"The uniform may be a bit of a giveaway, sir. Apart from that I'm rather large and have short grey hair and a walrus moustache. Will that do?"

Blue laughed. "Perfectly, Sergeant, I'll see you this evening."

53

Blue led Moira through to the base room, and told McCader and Craig about the Glasgow incident.

"This is interesting," said McCader. "They're rattled. They don't know what we know, and are trying to guess. They were afraid our enquiries would lead us to Lesley Greeley, and decided to take him out first. But, as you said, chief, they've led us to him. We need to find out as much as we can about him."

"Hopefully he'll still be able to tell me something when I get there this evening," said Blue, "If he had a role, and they seem to think he had, what was it? Executioner, accomplice, or the man who gave the orders? An accidental witness, or somebody who just found out about it. Whoever he was, they wanted him silenced, and that tells us that whatever it was about, it's something they want to hide, whoever *they* are. Something they're willing to put resources into, and willing to kill for. Anyway, how are your enquiries moving?"

"Managed to talk to Arnold Dearton at the garage. Claimed he couldn't remember exactly what the ESLS drivers looked like. Said they were all men, the description of Range Rover Man might be one of them, but couldn't swear to it. They always came at night to collect the vehicles, and hardly spoke. He never saw them when the cars were returned, they were just left in a corner of the forecourt during the night, and the keys pushed through the letterbox. He sounded pretty unwilling to talk about it. I think someone's warned him about telling us anything. I'm still working on Julia Crabtree, hopefully I'll have something before you're off."

Blue asked Craig where she was with the name searches.

"Aye, making progress all right, chief. Peter Bishop. Born Newcastle, August 1920. Never married, so no chance of tracking a widow or weans. Younger sister, still alive, 87 now, lives in Whitley Bay, that's on the coast, near Newcastle. We went there for a holiday once, when I was wee. It was freezing. Anyway, I've phoned her up, she's happy to give us a sample, so I've arranged for a lab at Newcastle Uni to take it. I hope that's OK, Sir, it's just there was nobody about, I felt we just had to move things on."

"No, that's exactly the right thing. By the way, what did you say about payment? To the lab, I mean. They don't do it for nothing."

"Yes, sir, er, I said you'd be in touch later today to confirm it. I've got a job number."

"Deirdra, you are fantastic. I need to be in Glasgow this evening, so Sergeant McCader will be in charge. Give him the details and he'll do the paperwork. When can the sister give the sample?"

"Elsie – that's her name – Elsie Bishop, hopefully she's did it this afternoon. The University's right in the centre of the city so it's no hard to get to."

"That's great, well done!" He could see Craig beaming at this.

"That's not all, chief. I'm onto Terence Darwin's people too. He wasn't married when he disappeared, but his girlfriend was pregnant. His son was no born till after he was dead, but I've found him, in Nuneaton, Warwickshire, that's not too far from Birmingham. He's retired now, but he was out when I phoned – I had a lovely chat wi his wife – an he'll phone as soon as he's in. There's a lab at Birmingham Uni who'll do the test."

"Good work, Deirdra! These are important steps forward. Now, see what you can find about Lesley Greeley."

After the meeting, he told Moira about the suspicion he had that someone had been in his office. She was concerned, and suggested getting the keys for the base room and Blue's office. She phoned Sergeant Walker, who said that he didn't know where the keys were, but Clara would.

"I'll make sure we get keys tomorrow. If Clara can't find them, I'll have Gregor from the ironmonger's replace the locks. I'm really sorry, Angus, I should have thought of that before you got here, but it's never been a problem before. Meanwhile, why not pile your files in the corner of my office and I'll lock it whenever I'm not in."

Blue's files were soon piled up in Moira's office. He was going to have to go back to the hotel to pick up stuff for an overnight in Glasgow. He hadn't fixed up anywhere to stay yet, so he phoned his cousin Janice who lived in the city's northern suburb of Bearsden.

"Hi, Janice, it's Angus here. How are you doing?"

"Jeez, Angus, when was the last time we heard from you?"

"Er, yes, quite a while. Still, I'll be in Glasgow this evening. Any chance of putting me up?"

"We never hear from you for years, and now you want put up for a night, or is it more? Of course we'll put you up. Do you want to share a room with the kids or the dog?"

"I'll take the dog. Is it still the same one? The big black one that drools over everything?"

"That's the one. Only older and slobbers even more. Do you still remember where we live?"

"Er, it's up past the cross, to the right, and then left after the shops, or something like that. Anyway I've got your phone number. I've got the address, so I can get a taxi. I've to see a man in hospital first, so I'll get to you later in the evening."

"Are you still in Oban?"

"Yes. Or rather, no, I'm in Islay at the moment."

"There's been a murder, eh?" she said dramatically.

"Well, yes, five of them. Maybe another in Glasgow too."

"You'll be busy then. By the way, have you got yourself a girlfriend yet? Time you were getting settled down again."

"Not as such. No."

"You're a no-hoper, Angus. We'll see you tomorrow. Love you." And she hung up.

He spent the next hour on his report. He needed to get it up-to-date before leaving for Glasgow. He felt there'd be a lot to add once he got there. Then he drove to Port Ellen to pick up his overnight things from the hotel. He got back to the station just before five. Bhardwaj and Alison Hendrickx were back by then, so he called them together to bring everyone up to date. He explained that Mc-Cader would be in charge until his return. He asked Alison if they'd got anything useful.

"Not today, I'm afraid," explained Alison. "We only managed to get to five people. Plenty of scones and jam. Several cups of tea. Met some interesting old folk. Lots of anecdotes about the forties and fifties, but nothing with a real bearing on the case. Fascinating, nevertheless. But we'll carry on again tomorrow, and we should get the whole lot done by Friday."

"Great. I'll leave you to it, then. Deirdra, anything on Lesley Greeley?"

"Aye, chief, I've made progress there. You gave his age as 93, so that gave me a starting point. Found a few Lesley Greeleys born in England in 1921, but only one of them got married in 1946 in Glasgow, to a Dorothy Simson, born in Oban in 1926, and he's still alive. He's that old man, is he no?"

"Yes that certainly looks like him. See what else you can find on him." He turned to McCader. "Enver, what about Ms Crabtree?"

"A very elusive lady. We had a credit card number from the airline. But it's from one of those banks that only exists online. No telephone number on the website. There was one of those contact forms, so I sent them an email, but nothing back so far. I thought she might have an account at a high street bank in Highford, so I tried them all. How many times can I listen to somebody telling me my call is so important to them that I'll have to wait another ten minutes, and then offering me six choices, then another six. When I finally get to speak to the branch, they ask me to email a scan of my ID before they'll talk. That happened four times before I got one of them to admit she might have a current account there. But no-one at the bank can remember seeing her, they think she may have applied for the account online. They'll have to consult head office, which may take a while, and they'll need a letter from a senior officer before they can consider releasing any confidential information. What a waste of time! Don't say anything, yeah, I know it's got to be done. And at the moment there's no-one else to do it."

"That's the spirit, Sergeant. What are you going to try next?"

"I'll try the public library. I've also put in a request to DVLC for a copy of her driving licence, if she's got one. And the local council. She'll have needed some sort of ID to get the credit card, so there'll be traces of her somewhere. The trouble is, I'm pretty sure it's not her real name anyway."

"Well, stick with it. If we can get an image of her, that would be a step forward. That is, if it matches the woman with Range Rover Man."

As he was putting his jacket on in his office, Alison came in, without knocking. She offered him a lift to the airport.

Outside, dirty-looking cloud hung heavily over the island. As they drove, Alison asked him how he thought it was going. "We're getting there. Slowly but surely. Thanks for your help, Alison. I appreciate it."

He went to the airline counter to pick up his ticket, only to find he was booked onto a flight for the following evening. Clara must have got the dates mixed up. Luckily there was a seat free on this evening's flight, so he was able to change, though it almost doubled the price.

Alison waited with him till the flight was called. Then she kissed him on the cheek. "Do take care, Angus."

54

The flight was on time, into Glasgow at 6.50. Since Blue only had hand luggage, he was quickly through to the arrivals area, and found that Sergeant Glen was indeed true to his own description. Santa Claus in a police uniform. Without the beard.

"Come this way, sir, we'll get you to the hospital in no time. By the way, have you somewhere to stay? We can arrange that if necessary."

Blue assured him that he would be staying with relatives.

"Ah, yes, everyone has relatives in Glasgow. Sure they do."

A blue police Range Rover was waiting for them, and sped off as soon as they got in, sirens wailing.

"What's the emergency?" asked Blue.

"Well now, sir, partly it's just that the boys like having the siren on, and partly I think you'd be wanting to get to the hospital before Mr Greeley's passed away. I hear it's touch and go at the moment."

To which argument Blue could hardly demur. And in ten minutes they swept into the grounds of the Southern General hospital, at the south end of the Clyde Tunnel.

"I thought he was in the Western," said Blue.

"Yes, sir. He was moved here this afternoon. At the Southern, or whatever fancy name they call it now, they can keep him alive just a little bit longer. They've got all the technology there, as new as you like."

They raced into the hospital precinct, and screeched to a halt by a building standing on its own, away from the gleaming new tower block forming the main hospital. There was no sign at the door, but there were lights on inside.

"Come on, sir, no time to lose. Malky, park the car!" said the sergeant, jumping out of the vehicle and making for the door. Blue had to run to keep up. Sergeant Glen paused at the entrance to punch in a code, the doors opened, and they found themselves in a dim lobby, quite empty. There was a desk at one side, and the Sergeant reached it in one stride and pinged loudly a bell on its corner. After a few seconds he pinged the bell again, and this time a WPC appeared from a door behind the desk. Blue thought from her physique that she might be a wrestler or weight-lifter. She nodded to the Sergeant, then turned to Blue.

"ID please. And who are you here for?"

They showed their warrant cards. "Inspector Blue is here for Mr Greeley," said the Sergeant.

"Up the stairs and on the right," was all the WPC said, folding her powerful arms as she watched them go.

They went up the stairs, and turned right into the short corridor at the top. There was a room on their left, with the door shut, but through the windows from the corridor they could see a figure in bed, tubes coming out in all directions, and two drips by the bedside.

A young doctor materialised behind them. "Are you for Mr Greeley or Mr Dorman?"

"Lesley Greeley," said the sergeant.

"How's he doing?" asked Blue. He couldn't let the sergeant do all the talking.

"Not very well. We've done all we can, but I doubt he'll last the night. At least he's comfortable now."

"Can I talk to him?"

"You're welcome to try. We've given him a lot of morphine, so he won't necessarily be on this planet. But you can't do any harm, it's past that now."

They went on into the room. The only things suggesting Lesley Greeley was alive were the tubes. Not that anything appeared to be moving through them, but Blue reasoned that if he were dead they would have removed them, and indeed, Lesley Greeley too. He had thick bandaging round his head and a brace on his neck. The rest of him was covered by a white coverlet, apart from one arm, which lay on the coverlet on the side next to Blue. It was encased in plaster.

"Let's see if he's awake, shall we, sir," said the sergeant, and, before Blue realised what he was doing, rapped his knuckles on the plaster.

The old man opened his eyes and slowly turned them towards the two policemen. Blue's stomach turned. He had seen bodies before, but not a man who looked already dead before he actually was. Greeley's skin was grey and his lips black, his breathing a hoarse grating.

"Mr Greeley," asked Sergeant Glen gently. "Can you tell us about the accident?"

Blue put his hand on the sergeant's arm, and motioned that he should sit back. He leaned forward over the dying man. "I'm Inspector Blue, from Islay," he said clearly to him. "Tell me about the five men who were killed in 1944. Tell me as much as you know. You've no reason to hide it now."

"I'm dying, ain't I?" said Greeley, "They don't say nothing to me 'ere. Won't let my wife see me either. I don't even know where I am."

"Tell me about the killings while you still can, Mr Greeley. Get it off your chest. Let it out."

Greeley looked at him as if from a great distance. His pupils were dilated. For perhaps twenty seconds he stared at Blue. Then he seemed to focus. "Jerry agents, the colonel said. Been thieving, we was told, war materials. Vital stuff. Petrol, equipment from the planes. Said it would persuade 'em to confess."

"Who did?"

Greeley drifted away again. His eyeballs bulged ominously and Blue was ready to hit the red button on the console by the bed. Then he seemed to calm again.

"It was just another job to him, you know, just like washing your socks. 'Cept for him it was killing. I said to him, 'We're not supposed to kill them,' and he said, 'course we are, that's what we're here for. What else would we be doing in the middle of the night?' We had their hands tied with bandages and their mouths gagged. Me and Tony, we had to go along with it. He said he'd kill us too if we didn't."

"Who said that?"

"The Russian. Burriekin. Cold as ice. And we thought we was cool. He showed us all right. Bang, bang, bang, they was all gone, and into the pit. Was that enough bangs for all of them? Bang, bang, there's a couple more. One for each of them. He was good, done it before, plenty times he said. A master of his craft. Ha, ha, ha!" His eyes showed he was half way to another place.

"Who were the five men?"

"Eh? Heh, heh, heh." He was laughing at some private joke, an amusing spectre teasing him on the point of death. Nudging him over the edge. He pulled back. "The flight-lieutenant, he was a nice guy, didn't deserve it. None of 'em did. We had to fetch him from his digs, you see, Tony and me. In the dark. Real cloak and dagger. Will there be a judgement?"

"A judgement?"

"Will I be judged? For what I've done. That was a long time ago. Even now I can see them. Are they waiting for me? Can you keep them away from me?"

"Who was the flight lieutenant?"

"Mc something. Mind you, they're all called that out there. What was he doing, eh, whispering to the little girl like that, in that language of theirs? We knew he was hiding something. He was the ringleader, that's what the colonel said."

"Which colonel?"

"Colonel Blimp, was that him? I can't remember. I wanted to forget them, but they still follow me, they don't give up, never have." He was looking at the door now, his eyes staring. "Can't you see them?" He turned again to Blue. "We went back, next day, to his digs, but we couldn't find nothing. Not a sausage." He stared away again.

Sergeant Glen tapped his plaster cast again. "That car that hit you. Did you see the driver?"

"The grim reaper, that's who he was. Telling me my time was up. Bang! Just like those boys back then. And what'll Dora do? Where is she, please, you have to tell her, you have to tell her. Dora, where are you!" he shouted, though it came out with a strangled hoarseness. "They're waiting for me, out in the dark. Help me, Dora, help me." He slumped back in the bed.

A nurse leaned past them and took his wrist, checking his pulse. Blue hadn't noticed her at all. She must have come in later. "He's not dead," she said, "but that's enough excitement for now." An Irish voice, quiet but authoritative.

"How long do you think he's got?" he asked her.

"You'd be better asking the doctor that, but I don't myself think he'll live past tomorrow."

"Thank you," said Blue. They left the room.

Outside, in the corridor, Blue said to Sergeant Glen, "Sergeant, sorry if I seem ignorant, but what is this place? It's certainly not a normal ward."

"Er, no, sir, this is our secure ward. It's used for suspects injured during capture, whom we need to keep an eye on, and for victims of crime who might be in danger. We don't tell people about it."

"So why was Mr Greeley brought here yesterday?"

"As I said, sir, they've got…"

"This is just between us, Sergeant. Tell me the truth."

The sergeant paused and looked at the floor for a few seconds, the back at Blue. "Well, sir, I think your phone call yesterday did have a stimulating effect on the boss, Inspector Taylor that is. 'We'd better get him moved,' he said, 'just in case.'"

"Thank you, Sergeant, for your candour. It was a wise move to bring him here. I believe there are people out there who want Mr Greeley dead."

"It doesn't sound like he's going to last long anyway, sir."

"And his wife needs to see him. Before he dies."

"I'll see what we can do in the morning."

"No, this needs to be done now. Can you get her right away. I'll wait here. He's only got hours."

"But Inspector Taylor said…"

"Is Inspector Taylor here?"

"No, sir, he plays bridge on Wednesday evenings. Nothing gets in the way of that. Not even murder. Everything has to wait till Thursday morning."

"Not today, Sergeant. He's not here. I am. So get in that car, and bring his wife in. Dorothy, or Dora, she's called. I'm sure you know where she lives."

"Yes, sir, of course. Thank you, sir."

55

Blue went back into the room. "I just want to sit with him," he said to the nurse, seeing the concern in her face, "till his wife comes. That's all. No more questions." She nodded and pointed to a chair by the bed. He sat down, and she left the room as silently as she had entered. Sitting in the silent dimness of the room, he noticed that one of the machines surrounding the bed was making a sort of gentle pulsating noise. Its reassuring regularity enabled him to relax, and he had soon dozed off.

He awoke with a start. Had someone turned the door handle. He squeezed his eyes and looked at the door. It was still shut, but in the window set at head height was framed a head whose shape he recognised from Islay airport – Chief Inspector Gregory King! What the hell was the Special Branch man doing here?

He hurriedly pushed himself up from the chair, but had to turn and move it back to get past a trolley parked by the bed, with a sensor of some sort on it. By the time he faced the door again, King had vanished. Blue tiptoed to the door as fast as he could and went through into the corridor. No-one was to be seen. He went along the corridor to the other end – there were only another three rooms, two of them empty and the third, at the far end, occupied by a young man with bandages round his chest and his eyes. He seemed asleep. There was no sign of either the doctor or the nurse.

He was debating with himself whether he could leave Lesley Greeley long enough to go downstairs and check the lobby when he heard voices from down there. Sergeant Glen! Just what a policeman should sound like: authoritative and reassuring, in command, yet willing to help. The sergeant came up the stairs slowly, assisting an elderly lady.

"Inspector Blue, this is Mrs Greeley. Mrs Greeley, the Inspector's looking into what happened to your husband."

Mrs Greeley was indeed frail, but still had her wits about her. She looked at Blue appraisingly as they shook hands. "They tried to kill him, you know. I told the other inspector, but he wouldn't listen. He insisted it was just a 'traffic incident'. I hope you've got some better ideas."

"As it happens, I do, Mrs Greeley. But I think you'll want to see your husband first. Once you've seen him for a while, and if you're willing to leave him for a little, I would like to talk with you."

The old lady nodded. "Yes, good. I'll go and see Les first." She allowed the sergeant to lead her into the room.

A few moments later Sergeant Glen came out again. "You were right, sir. Good idea to fetch Mrs Greeley. We'll see if she needs a lift back. I'll ask PC Smith to come in from the car. No point him sitting out there."

"That's fine," agreed Blue. There were some chairs on the landing at the top of the stairs, so he sat down. He phoned Janice to say he'd be late getting out to them. He could hear Sergeant Glen and PC Smith talking with the WPC at the desk in the lobby. Then the sergeant came up the stairs. "If you don't mind, Malky, that's Constable Smith, and me'll wait downstairs with Kayleigh, PC Baines that is, and have a cup of tea. There's a wee kitchen there. Can I get you something too, sir?"

"That would be great. Milk, no sugar. Thank you, Sergeant."

As the sergeant went off down the stairs again, Blue went over what Lesley Greeley had told him. He and someone called Tony seemed to have been ordered by a colonel to lead the five men to a place of execution. Except he didn't realise the men were going to be killed. And it was indeed the Russian, Burovkin, who did it. Greeley was too close to the name to be mistaken. As far as he knew, the men had been stealing war materials. The ringleader was a flight lieutenant McSomething, who lived in digs somewhere, and spoke some Gaelic. But there were plenty of questions raised. What was the men's crime? Who was the Colonel? Who was Tony? Who was the unknown flight lieutenant? Who was the little girl, and what did he whisper to her? Why did they search his digs, what were they looking for? He jotted the points and the questions down in his notebook. Then he closed his eyes to think about it.

He was wakened by a door opening. Mrs Greeley was coming out of the room, helped by the nurse, who led her towards Blue. She lowered herself into the chair next to his. The nurse smiled, and headed off along the corridor.

"He's sleeping now," she said, "He woke up a bit and he knows I'm here with him. I've spoken to the nurse, and I know he's dying. He said it quite often, recently."

"What?"

"That they'd get him. That they were coming for him."

"Did he say who were going to get him?"

"He wouldn't talk about it. Something that happened during the war. Before I met him."

"He's not from these parts, is he?"

"No, he's from somewhere north of London. Dunstable, I think that was it. We never went there, so I don't know what it's like. Les had no interest in going back. 'My life's with you now, Dora,' he'd say."

"How did you meet him?"

"Oh, that was after the war. He was in Islay during the war, and when it finished, he got a job driving a taxi in Glasgow. He was based at the Central Station, that's how he met me. I lived in Milngavie, and one evening I'd missed the train and...well, you can guess the rest. In a year we were married. Then, three children, seven grand-children now, and we're even great-grandparents too. Emily, she's just two now. It's been nearly thirty years since Les retired, you know. We had a good life. I don't know what'll happen now."

"Can you tell me about Tony?"

"Yes, it's all to do with Tony, isn't it? He stirred it all up again."

"Sorry, who is Tony?"

"Tony Rogers. He was a pal of Les's in the war. Went back to England afterwards. Never married. I think he was in Australia for a while. He came to visit us a couple of times not long after we married. Bit of a spiv, I thought, an easy smile, but his eyes were always hard. I never liked him. About ten years ago he visited us again. He was living in Nottingham then – maybe that's where he came from. That's when he spoke about it."

"What do you mean?"

"Tony was working on a book. About his wartime experiences. He thought he'd make some money on it. He said there were secrets he could reveal, would make it a best-seller."

"Do you know what they were?"

"No. It didn't really interest me. Les was more interested, but he didn't like the idea at all. He thought all the wartime stuff was in the past, and it should stay there. Said it was a bad idea to rake it all up again. He tried to persuade Tony to give up the idea. But Tony was determined. We were having dinner together at the time, he said to Les, 'Come on, mate, it's just history. You can have a cut of the pro-ceeds if you help me with it.' Les said, 'No Tony, that stuff's better locked up for good. If you open the box' – that's exactly the words he used – 'if you open the box, we'll all end up dead.' Well, Tony, he just laughed, and Les, he said, 'This ain't a laughing matter, pal, I'm serious. It'll get us killed.' I can tell you, it made me feel quite creepy.

I asked them to talk about something else."

"So did Tony write his book?"

"He never published it, if that's what you mean. He wrote a draft. But then he was killed. In a road accident. His car went straight on at a bend, right into a stone wall. Near Buxton, I think that's near Derby, Les would know, late one night in October 2002, or maybe it was 2003. I know it was October because all the Hallowe'en stuff was in the shops. They said the brakes had failed – it was quite an old car. Les was really cut up. Said Tony had saved his life once, in the war I suppose. He left us £20,000. That was such a surprise. Plus a box full of old papers and stuff. Rental agreements, pension stuff, and some share certificates – they turned out to be worthless, the company had gone bankrupt years ago. And the draft of his book was in there too."

"What did you do with the stuff?"

"We got a new kitchen with the money, and had enough left over for a Mediterranean cruise. Most of the old documents we got rid of, but Les couldn't make up his mind what to do with the book. First he was going to throw it away, then he thought he'd burn it, then he changed his mind again, decided to keep it. He said it was a kind of insurance. I'm not sure what he meant by that."

"So what did he do with it?"

"First he kept it in his desk, with the gas bills and so on. But after that man called, he decided to hide it."

"What man?"

"Well, this was only last week. A man turned up at the doorstep. Said he was a publisher. He'd heard about Tony's book, was keen to publish it. He knew Tony had left stuff to us, and wondered if Les knew anything about it. Offered us a share of the royalties, if we had the manuscript, that is. He said it would sell well, these 'what really happened' memoirs of the war, from ordinary soldiers, were very popular now. Well, Les said to him that he didn't know anything about any book Tony had written, and even if Tony had written anything, he wouldn't want it published. It would all be about the past, and it should be left alone. The man seemed quite sympathetic to that. He said that was fine, sorry to have bothered us, and he was off."

"What was his name?"

"Sethman, no Statham, Reginald Statham. I can't remember the company. He gave Les a card."

"What did he look like?"

"About your height. Average build, a bit flabby. Bald head. Glasses, round black ones. Looked a bit like a bank manager."

Blue showed her on his mobile the image of DCI King at the airport. "Does this look like him?"

"Yes, that's him. I'd swear it. Do you know who he is? Is he really a publisher?"

"No, he's not a publisher. Les was right to be wary of him. So the draft is still safe?"

"Oh, yes. Why is it so important?"

"Because I think that it includes details of a crime committed during the war, a mass murder…"

"Les wouldn't murder anybody! I can't believe that."

"No, no. I don't believe either Les or Tony murdered anyone. But they may have witnessed it. The crime has recently come to light, and…"

"And you think that's why Les was knocked down?"

"It's a possibility."

"And they're after the draft of Tony's book?"

"It looks that way."

"Who are these people? Why are they doing this?"

"As to who, we're trying to find out. As to why, it seems they don't want this old crime to come to light."

"But why go to all that trouble about something that happened so long ago?"

"That's what I don't know. But Tony's book might help there. The clue might be in it."

"Then you'd better have it, Mr Blue."

"That would be very helpful, thank you, Mrs Greeley."

"That publisher man – he was one of them, wasn't he?"

"Yes, I think he was."

"When do you want the draft?"

"As soon as possible. That man is still around. I think they'll be back to look for it. Possibly when there's no-one in."

"How would they know?"

"They're probably watching the house."

"You'd better get it right now then. I can't leave my man. I'll stay with him till he goes. But I'll tell you where it is, and you can fetch it now. Before it's lost."

"That would be excellent. Thank you."

"Come closer, Inspector." Blue bent down to her, and she whispered the location of the draft in his ear. She gave him a ring with three keys on it, then walked back to the room to join her husband.

56

Blue went down the stairs. Sergeant Glen and PC Smith were sitting in the lobby. The sergeant was on the phone, and PC Smith, a tall, thin young man with brown hair cut very short, was reading a magazine. *Weight-Lifting Illustrated.* There was no sign of the WPC who manned the desk.

"Sergeant, I need to fetch something for Mrs Greeley. Can I borrow PC Smith and the car?"

"No problem, sir. Malky, can you drive Inspector Blue over to the Greeleys' place?"

"Aye, gaffer, nae hassle."

"Shall I go upstairs and keep an eye on things?" asked the sergeant.

"Good man. Thanks. Come on, Malky, let's go."

PC Smith looked relieved to have something to do. "Nae problem, boss, Ah think ah've memorised yon magazine. All thae muscles on lasses, it's no right."

PC Smith drove Blue through the tunnel, then onto the Expressway, alongside the river Clyde. Soon they turned off and were onto a long street with tenement blocks on both sides. "We'll be there in a minute, boss," said PC Smith.

The Greeleys had the ground floor flat on the right of the entrance, and Blue noticed a light flickering in one room. The door to the entrance passage was not locked, and they hurried in. As they reached the door to the flat, Blue realised they were too late. There were two locks, a deadlocking Yale-type and a mortice lock. These would have been tough to force, but the forcers hadn't bothered to cover their tracks. There were holes where an electric drill had been used, and splintered edges to the door and the frame, where chisels and jemmies had been employed. Blue pushed, but the door didn't move. He tried the keys but the Yale wouldn't turn in the socket. "Malky, I wonder if you could get this door open for me?" he asked.

"Nae hassle, boss." PC Smith gave the door a mighty thump with the flat of his foot near the locks, and with a scrunching noise, it swung in.

The flat had been ransacked. In every room, every cupboard and shelf had been emptied, the contents tossed onto the floor. In some places, floor boards had been ripped up. In the living room, a pile of stuff had been stacked on an armchair pushed against the wall and set alight. The curtains were closed, but this was the flickering Blue had seen from outside. The fire was well ablaze and scorch marks stretched up the wall to the ceiling. The intention was clear – to destroy the flat and its contents. But had they found the book?

Blue grabbed a rug from the floor and threw it over the fire – that might delay it a little. He called to PC Smith, "Malky, the extinguisher from the car. And call it in."

PC Smith came through with an extinguisher. "Found this one in the kitchen, boss. Fire started there too. I'll deal with it." He handed Blue the extinguisher and dashed back to the kitchen. Blue fired the extinguisher at the flames and as the CO2 hissed over them, he heard a tap running and then a sizzling and fizzing as water was tossed over the burning material in the kitchen.

As he heard PC Smith calling for police and fire assistance, he left the smouldering pile in the living room and looked in at the kitchen. A similar smoking heap sat sulking by the cooker. Lucky the Greeleys were all-electric. Any gas outlets could have been opened and the whole flat would have blown up, bringing down those above too, and, at this time of night, there would certainly have been fatalities.

Blue went out of the flat, back into the passage, and turned towards the rear door. He went through into the back green. He always carried with him a small LED torch and as he panned it round he saw the neatly cut grass, the clothes poles, with lines strung between them, and then, on the left, the old wash-house, where the communal boiler and sink would have been. The third key on the ring Mrs Greeley had given him, an ordinary Yale-type, opened the wooden door, revealing gardening tools hanging on the walls, and a lawn mower in one corner. In the other corner was a big chest made of dark green plastic. He lifted the lid and looked inside: there was a bag of compost and an assortment of flower pots, plastic watering cans and other pieces of garden equipment. He left the lid propped against the back wall, grabbed the top edge of the narrow side with both hands, and dragged the chest away from the corner. Then he took a trowel off the wall, got down on hands and knees and shone his torch into the corner. The wash-house floor was of stone slabs, each about a foot square. He used the blade of the trowel to lever up the stone in the corner until he could get his hands round the edge and pull it right up and over.

There, beneath it, was a package wrapped in an empty compost bag. He lifted it out, and opened it. Inside was another plastic bag.

Inside that, wrapped in a piece of cloth, were three spiral-bound notebooks, a little bigger than A5 in size. He wrapped the cloth back round the notebooks and thrust the package into the poacher's pocket in his jacket, put the slab and the chest back, and returned to the flat.

The fire brigade had arrived and PC Smith was in charge of the situation. And relishing it. He was directing the firemen into the flat.

"Well done, Malky, keep it up," said Blue, "I'll take the car back to the hospital."

"Nae problem, boss. I've got it all in hand. Here's the car key."

As Blue came onto the street, he spotted Sergeant Glen on the pavement talking to a fireman.

"Came as soon as Malky called, sir," he said. "Did Mrs Greeley leave the gas on?"

"All-electric," said Blue. "Arson. We'll need SOCOs in as soon as the firemen are done."

"Right, sir, I'm onto it. I'd better tell Inspector Taylor too."

Something puzzled Blue. Why set fire to the flat once they'd ransacked it? That would only draw attention. Then it clicked. "Who's at the hospital?" he called to Sergeant Glen, who was talking into his mobile.

"Don't worry, sir, PC Baines will be there."

"I'll get back anyway."

57

In ten minutes Blue was back at the hospital. The door was open, and the lobby was empty. He ran up the stairs. On the landing, nothing but a suspicious silence.

Then he heard a whimpering sound. Lesley Greeley's room. The light was on. He ran in. The young doctor was kneeling on the floor bent over a still figure. The nurse whom Blue had seen earlier.

"They're all dead," said the doctor, his voice breaking. He looked up, and Blue saw the tears in his eyes.

Both the Greeleys had been shot cleanly through the head, Lesley as he lay in bed, Dora in the chair by the bed. He wondered if they'd both been asleep. "Who did this?" he said to the doctor.

"I d-don't know. I never saw any of it. I was through in the office writing up a report on Johnny Dorman – he's in the room at the end. I came back to check Mr Greeley, and found them."

"How long ago?"

"Maybe ten minutes. Poor Maeve, she was so good with them." His voice trailed off. "I never heard anything, Inspector, why didn't I hear the shots?" Now tears ran freely down his cheeks.

"Probably used a silenced weapon," said Blue. "Have you called for help?"

The doctor looked dazed. "No, I…I just…" Blue noticed he was holding Maeve's hand.

He had his mobile out as he left the room. As he dashed down the stairs he met PC Baines coming up.

"Oh my God!" she gasped, "What the fuck's happened here?"

Soon after the SOCOs had got to work, Inspector Taylor arrived. A burly man, bull neck, short-cropped hair, bad expression. It was nearly midnight and he was furious. "You caused all this, Blue, with your accusations. If you'd left well alone this wouldn't have happened. And I had to leave a winning hand on the table. I want you out of here, right now."

"No problem. I wouldn't want to cramp your style. Don't you want a statement from me?"

"You weren't here when this happened, you weren't first on the scene afterwards, so your statement's only necessary to confirm the times. Email it to me tomorrow. I don't want to see you here again.

Got that?"

"Suits me. I've got a case to solve on Islay. In respect of which, I'd like any reports on this case forwarded to me. I'll make the request through my Super to yours."

Blue turned to go, then hesitated. "Oh, just one other thing, Inspector, what was PC Baines doing, when this crime was committed?"

"What do you mean?"

"She was out when I arrived. And the door to the unit was open. She only came in again after a short while. Wasn't she supposed to be on guard? This is a guarded facility, isn't it?"

"Yes, of course it is. You bloody know that already," Taylor snarled.

"Well, it does look like something, or somebody, failed here. Big time. Who's in charge of it?"

Taylor opened and shut his mouth. More than once. He turned his gaze to the floor. He tugged at his chin, as if trying to extend it. He was working out how to survive.

"All right Blue, I'm sorry I got a little angry. Been a long day. We need to talk."

"Can we do that tomorrow morning? I need some sleep, and you need to get on with your job here. I can be at Stewart Street at nine."

"Yes, yes, that's fine." Taylor was plainly relieved. "Need a lift? I'll have one of the cars take you."

"That would be very helpful. Thank you."

By the time a police car delivered Blue to Janice's door it was after one. Nevertheless, Janice and her husband Bill were still up. A glass of whisky at 1.15 am was not Blue's usual nightcap, but he needed to unwind, and it was a 10-year-old Laphroaig. Light and mildly acidic, smoke on the tongue, an aftertaste of bitumen or pungent herbs. A distinctive taste that had gained Laphroaig many followers.

Janice was eager to hear what he was up to now. He kept the details of the case to a minimum. Bill was wanting to know more, but Janice was more interested in his personal life. "It's a few years now since, you know…" she began.

"Yes, I know. Time I was hitched up again."

"Well, yes, you need someone to look after you, wash your socks, and so on."

"I have a washing machine."

"You know what I mean. You can't cuddle up to a washing machine."

"Yes, I know what you mean." His voice faltered.

"It's time there was someone else," she said, more gently now.

"It's not something I think about a lot. I have plenty to do."

"You can't spend all your time working, Angus. What'll you do when you retire?"

"Read, travel, write, walk, play music, wash socks."

"What will you write?" asked Bill, "Your memoirs? You must have a few good stories there. You know, Oban mafia, that sort of stuff." Janice shot him a you've-let-him-off-the-hook stare.

"That's not encouraged. Might give something away, or stir something up, or just make us look daft. No, it'll have to be something fictional, I think. Maybe one of those historical detectives."

"Like Brother Whatsisname?"

"Perhaps around 1700. Plenty going on then. Bad harvests, financial disaster at Darien, lead-up to the Union, spies all over the place, grasping landlords, corrupt politicians, assassination, bribery, and a pile of everyday crime."

"Just like today, eh?"

Day 8. Thursday

58

Blue woke early from a dream of bandaged ghosts. For a moment he was puzzled by the package resting on the bedside table. Tony Rogers' book. Sitting up, he took the books out of their protective cloth. Written on the front of each one was 'Memoirs of a RAF man who never Flew,' and a volume number, 1, 2 and 3. Books 1 and 2 were filled with handwriting in blue biro, book 3 was about three-quarters filled.

He read the first few pages of Book 1. The handwriting was not easy. Chapter 1, 'Into the RAF I go,' described how Tony, in 1942, at age twenty, had been advised by his father to avoid the army at all costs – 'You're just cannon fodder' – and choose between the navy and air force, adding that, 'If you go for the air force, make sure you don't go up in the planes. You'll end up dead for sure.' He chose the RAF, and as a mechanic at a garage, his technical skills ensured that he was assigned to ground staff. He was first at an aerodrome in Norfolk, but soon transferred to Islay.

Blue flicked through the rest of the notebooks, noting the chapter headings. Naturally, there was nothing like 'I witness an execution'. The handwriting did not permit him to skim the text. By this time he could hear Janice up and about. The notebooks would have to wait till he could give them more time.

Janice taught at an FE college in the city. They were worried about the impact of the British Studies module. "We could lose half our students, Angus. All those Chinese hotel managers we're training. Why do they have to memorise the life of King Alfred, for God's sake. I don't even know who he was!"

Blue reached the Stewart Street police HQ at 8.45. He was directed to Inspector Taylor's base, where he was greeted, politely, by the inspector himself. Taylor asked him to write a statement covering the events of the previous evening, and suggested they meet at ten. It took Blue forty-five minutes to write the statement. He printed it out and left a copy for Taylor, then phoned Sergeant McCader.

"Hi, Enver. What's doing?"

"Arvind and Alison are out interviewing the old folk again. Deirdra is trying to get more on Greeley and track down Burovkin. I'm still after Julia Crabtree. And we're hoping to get DNA results for Pete Bishop and Terence Darwin later today. What's happening at your end?"

"Plenty!" He summarised the previous evening's events.

"What do you think's going on?"

"They didn't kill Greeley when they knocked him down. Distracted us with the fire while they finished the job. Very professional. Eliminating a possible witness from 1944. Maybe even the last one."

"Unless Burovkin's still around. It's just possible."

"Trouble is, if he's still alive, they're better placed than we are to find him."

"I know a couple of people who might be able to give us a pointer there. I'll make some calls."

"Thanks, Enver. Talk to you later."

Blue went to Taylor's office.

"Take a seat, Inspector." Taylor spoke in a neutral, formal tone.

"Thank you." Blue sat down.

"This is a bad business." Taylor knew he could no longer pretend this was a traffic incident. "We're under a lot of pressure here and this case isn't helping. I need to know what it's all about. You set all this in motion, with your bodies from the peat. I don't know why people can't just leave things alone."

"Do you think those peat-cutters who found the bodies meant to do it?"

"Of course not," snapped Taylor.

"Do you think we as policemen should just have ignored them?"

"No. But once it was clear it was a historic case, why waste time and resources on it?"

"Don't you think dead people deserve justice?"

"If the killers are clearly either geriatric or dead, you should just drop it. There are plenty of live criminals who need stopping."

"I'm sorry, I don't agree. Justice must be seen to be done. No-one should get away with it. Even if they're over a hundred, they should answer for what they've done. Taking responsibility is the basis of morality."

"I don't have time to bandy words, Blue. I've got work to do." Taylor was shouting, clenching his chunky fists with anger.

"Listen to me, Mr Taylor," said Blue, trying hard not to raise his voice. "You know as well as I do that these cases are connected. I'm willing to work with you on this. But you need to change your attitude if you want that to happen. Think about it."

Taylor glared at his tidy desktop for a long time. Blue said nothing. Finally Taylor looked up. "All right, we're wasting time as it is. Tell me about your case and how it impacts on mine."

Blue's review of the case took ten minutes. He didn't mention that he'd found Tony Rogers' book – he didn't want an argument over who should have it before he'd read it. Taylor listened, occasionally nodding. He had calmed down, and was making an effort to focus on the case.

"All right, Blue, who do *you* think killed our victims yesterday? This Range Rover Man?"

"He's the most likely. Unless there's more than one. If he's the man we saw in Islay, there may be a woman too. And DCI King's also involved. He was in the ward last night, I didn't just dream that."

"King! That scumbag. I hate those people. They've stopped chasing villains, and are just fixing political stuff. Shielding MPs or Royals from scandals. Covering up whatever's not convenient. Victimising people who get in the way. They think they're above the law."

"Usually they are."

"Bastards!"

"On that I completely agree with you."

Taylor nodded. "He'll be the co-ordinator. In the hospital to see what was doing. Do you think he saw you?" Now there was comradeship in his tone.

"I'm pretty sure of it. He probably summoned the killer then. What about PC Baines? What's she saying?"

Taylor frowned at his desk. "Not enough. If she spent less time pumping iron and even tried doing the puzzle page in the *Daily Record*, she might be able to use her brain a bit more. She says she had a phone call from neurosurgery saying that there was a vital medication there for Mr Greeley, could she pop over and get it. Says she can't remember the caller's name. She went over to neurosurgery, where they told her there was no medication, and they hadn't called. Then she came back here."

"Do you believe her?"

"Don't know, sounds a bit pat."

"Did she just leave the door open and go?"

"Says she shut it. But admits she was in a hurry."

"Can't get the staff these days, can you?"

Taylor glared at Blue and his face gradually became redder, until

Blue feared that he was about to explode. He had already pictured the blood all over the office walls and was wondering how to avoid the worst of it, when Taylor suddenly burst into laughter.

"Yes, can't get the staff. I see what you mean. Hmm!" He cleared his throat noisily. "One bit of good news, though. That doctor who was in the ward, Jamieson, remembers King coming in. Says he claimed to be a consultant from neurosurgery, even had a white coat and an ID card to prove it. Wanted a quick look at Mr Greeley and an update on his condition. The doc didn't recognise him, but it's a huge hospital, and on top of that some of the consultants are based in Gartnavel or the Western or one of the others. So the doc gave him the update and directed him to the room. Then he had to check on Dorman. By the time he came out again the consultant was nowhere to be seen. But he identified King from the picture you left us."

"Can we confront King?" asked Blue.

"No point. He'll simply deny it, these people always do. Next thing is, somebody from the Home Office calls to say he's on secret business and we've to take all trace of him out of the investigation. National security. Bastards!"

"Has that happened before?"

"How do you think I know just how it goes? You wouldn't believe how often these guys try to push their snouts into our business. Sometimes on cases that are completely trivial. For instance, last February…"

"You're right. There's no point in trying to pin King down till we've got more on him. What about CCTV. I noticed a camera in the lobby. Is that the only one?"

"Yes, there are none upstairs. And the footage is useless. Somebody must have given the camera a nudge – it was pointing at the ceiling."

"That's a pity. What about forensics?"

"Still waiting for the report, should get it later this morning. This case is now top priority. We're circulating your description of the suspect. And we're on to the vehicle – owners, a company called, er," he flicked through a file, "here we are, Euro Special Logistics Solutions. A man at a garage in Northampton. Says the driver told them it was stolen the day before the hit-and-run, and he'd reported it to the police."

"Did he say who the driver was?"

"He said he looks after the cars on behalf of a company based abroad. Can't remember the name. They send the drivers. But for the insurance, they had to have details, and after a few threats, he produced a photocopy of a driving licence." Taylor put a grainy image on the desk between them. "Scanned copy. Name: Kazimir Blasić. Croatian. Have a look." He turned the sheet round and pushed it towards Blue. The tiny photo showed a man with a thin face, close-cropped hair and a suggestion of moustache and beard.

"Yes," Blue said finally, "that's him. Got more hair since then."

"I've sent the details we have to Interpol, to see if he has any form. Talking of hair, one other thing. SOCOs found a hair on Mr Greeley's bed. Long, brown, dyed blonde. Probably female. Not Nurse Doyle or anyone else in the ward." Blue thought of the woman with Blasić when he'd looked in the restaurant window.

Blue realised there was no time to waste. It seemed as if Taylor was just going to wait till some sort of evidence turned up. But if they didn't do something the killers would simply vanish. "Inspector, you've got more experience of this than I have. Do you think some sort of trap might catch them?"

"You're right," said Taylor, "I do have a lot of experience. What are you thinking of?"

"The aim was to remove a witness to a 1944 murder. But what if the killing had been witnessed?"

"But it wasn't."

"No, but they don't know that. What if we suggested there was a witness? Doctor Jamieson. If they think he'd seen the killer, as well as King, they might decide to take him out. And we can be ready for them."

"Hmm. I get you. A trap with Dr Jamieson as the bait."

"I'm only suggesting, it's really up to you. It would need clever handling."

Taylor smiled to himself. "Yes, it might just work, with the right co-ordination and leadership. But how do we let the killers know?"

"Maybe if you made sure PC Baines knew about it."

"Why Baines? She's hardly competent."

"I think there's more than that. What if she's the link with them?"

"What! With the killers? I can't believe that. That would be gross disloyalty. More than gross, grosser!"

"I'm sure she's not a killer. But it's possible she's passing information to King."

Taylor seemed stung by the suggestion of Baines's disloyalty. "But why would she do that?"

"Has she applied for promotion?"

"Yes, last year. I had to turn it down, she really wasn't up to it."

"Perhaps King offered her a Sergeant's stripes if she worked with him. Maybe the MoD Police. There's work there for a female heavy I'm sure."

"I gave her plenty of feedback, suggested areas she needed to sharpen up – mind you, plenty of them – and this is what I get in return. Hmm. Listen, why don't, I tell Baines to keep a special eye on the doc, as he's a key witness?"

"Good idea. What about putting her on the same shifts as Dr Jamieson?"

"Yes, that's neat. We'll put a heavy guard on the doc's home. And escort him to and from the hospital. That way they'll see the ward as the easiest place to get at him."

Blue had some time free while the operation was being set up. He called the Super, but he was in a meeting. Then he went to the canteen and had a cup of tea and a piece of carrot cake, and thought things over. As with most cases, progress was coming in small but significant increments. Lesley Greeley's death was a setback, but would not derail the progress. And he knew they were on the right trail. "The game's afoot," he muttered to himself. He didn't think Henry V would have made a good detective. Too impulsive. All that speechifying. He probably liked killing people too. Was there a good Shakespearian detective? He'd have to think about that.

Blue's phone startled him. John Striven.

"Hi Angus, what's going on down there? Another bloodbath? What's the connection with your case?"

"Nothing I can tell you right now, I'm afraid, John. Not my case. It's just linked to it. You'd better talk to Inspector Taylor."

"Oh no, not Taylor. He's hopeless."

"Is he really?"

"No, not really. He's just rude, won't talk to us hacks. Then complains when we don't show him in a good light. By the way, are you getting more names for the bodies?"

"Dafydd Thomas is a definite. And we're close to two more. Get back to me tomorrow."

Blue looked at his watch. 11.28. The operation was due to start at twelve, when Dr Jamieson and PC Baines would both be on duty. Nothing for it now but to wait.

59

There was nothing he could do but wait. Another man was brought in. He heard the thump as the guard tripped him up and he fell. "Hey, what d'you think you're doing? I'll have you on report for this. What's your game?" English, but he couldn't tell which part. Though he knew who the man was, he'd seen him two days previously. They'd flown out together on an escort job. What was his name?

"I've had enough of this," came the voice again, "I'm going to the base commander right away. This will be the last..." There was a loud crack, and a dull thud.

"Christ, Tony, I reckon you've killed him. You shouldn't have hit him so hard. We were told just to lock them up, not beat them up. They'll want them for a trial."

"Don't panic, Les, 'e ain't dead. Look, 'e's still twitching. I used the flat of the bat, see. If I'd wanted to kill him, I'd have used the side, that would've cracked his head right open, like a boiled egg. Heh, that's a good 'un, ain't it. Just like a soft-boiled egg!"

"Come on, Tony, let's get him into a cell, then, before he wakes up."

He wished he could get a message to Rowena, even if only to say goodbye. He didn't want her to spend the rest of life mourning him. Why should they both die? He wanted to wish her a good life, and a happy one. He tried to concentrate hard, to send a telepathic message to her. If his love was strong enough, perhaps she would feel the message in her heart. He thought hard: Rowena, mo graidh, my love, my only love, my sunlight, my songthrush. He let the thought fly to her as the tears flowed again.

60

Ten minutes later, Sergeant Glen came into the canteen. He spotted Blue and came over. Soon they were in a car heading for the hospital.

Everything was in place. Before Baines's shift started at midday, John Dorman, the only patient left in the ward, had been moved elsewhere, and a couple of officers disguised as patients installed. Armed officers lurked silently in two of the empty rooms. Blue and Sergeant Glen were in the office along with Dr Jamieson. He'd agreed at once to be involved. "Maeve would have wanted it." All three wore Kevlar upper body armour. There was also a 'nurse' on duty, a member of the Special Operations Unit, and not known to PC Baines. Across the road from the unit, Taylor was installed in a first floor room, with two other officers, a camera with a long lens, and a marksman.

Blue and Glen had a laptop patched into the CCTV system, so they could watch the lobby. The camera, an older type, was repositioned and fixed tightly in place with a locking nut. At twelve o'clock sharp, they saw the door open and PC Baines enter. She greeted the officer finishing his shift, and he left. She made herself a cup of coffee and sat down behind the counter with a magazine. Blue's bet was on *Weight-Lifting Illustrated*.

A quarter of an hour later Blue strolled down to the lobby.

"Hi, it's PC Baines, isn't it? I recognise you from yesterday."

"Yes, sir, nasty business, sir."

"Yes, that's why I'm here again. Need a chat with Dr Jamieson about what he saw. I'm pretty sure we can learn something to point us to these killers."

"Yes, sir, that would be good."

"By the way, the doc told me to let you know there are two new patients in, they're not to be disturbed."

"That's OK, sir, I usually stay down here where I can keep an eye on the door."

"Excellent. See you later then." And he came back up.

Five minutes later, they saw Baines make a call on her mobile. Glen picked up the walkie-talkie and whispered, "She's phoning now, sir."

"OK," said Taylor, "We'll trace it."

Next came the waiting. It was possible that nothing would happen, that their suspicions about Baines were unfounded, that she was simply a good weight-lifter who wasn't such a good police officer. It was also possible that, even if Baines reported the situation to King, nothing would happen until after dark, when a better getaway would be possible. Blue knew King was not a fool. But his options were limited. He could send someone to eliminate Dr Jamieson, or he could try to get the whole case shut down. With three murders, that wouldn't be easy. If he chose to have him taken out, the hospital was the best place. And if he knew the doctor was talking to Blue, there was a danger that Blue would connect too many details. All that would encourage him to act quickly. If he was going to do anything.

He didn't think Baines could use the 'I was called away by a bogus summons' routine again, so she would have to let the killer in through the main door. That would mean the killer, or killers – there could easily be two or three – must have a plausible reason to come into the building, probably with fake IDs, as King had done earlier. That way Baines could claim afterwards she thought they were legitimate.

Nothing happened for half an hour. Then Taylor phoned Baines and asked her to see if Blue was making progress with Dr Jamieson. He explained that he couldn't reach the phone in the doctor's office, maybe it was off the hook. Blue had been forewarned, and was waiting for her at the top of the stairs, ostensibly stretching his legs. "Yes, tell him it's going far better than we expected. The doc is pretty observant, he should have been a cop. I think I've got enough to nail the bastard, and the people behind him. We're just having a break now, then we'll carry on. Believe me, Constable, we'll winkle out everyone connected with yesterday's events, and make sure they get everything they deserve. No matter who they are."

Blue nodded to Baines and went back into the room. Baines went back downstairs. Blue saw her take out her mobile and make another call. Then she picked up the landline and called Inspector Taylor. His office number had been patched through to his mobile. She reported that Inspector Blue did not think he was making much progress. Then she stared at the CCTV camera, and Blue could see the realisation dawning that it was pointed down at her and not up at the ceiling. She fetched a chair and positioned it under the camera. Blue could see her frowning as she tried to nudge it upwards, without success. She eventually gave up.

And again they waited. Blue glanced at his watch. 1.30.

About ten minutes later, a figure appeared at the door and buzzed for entry. A youngish woman in a white medical coat. She held up an ID to the small window in the door and Baines peered at it carefully. Then she let her in. The woman had a shoulder bag, open at the top, from which she took a large envelope, of the sort that X-ray photos would be held in. She showed the envelope to Baines, who pointed to the stairs, then went through the door behind the counter and shut it.

Blue felt sure it was the woman he had seen with Blasić on Islay. Tall and slim, around thirtyish – Blue wasn't good with ages – with hair fixed firmly in a tight bun. She wore her white lab coat over a dark-coloured blouse and jeans. He signed to Glen, who whispered "Attacker! On alert!" into his walkie-talkie.

The woman dipped a hand into her bag and extracted a silenced pistol. Then she walked up the stairs and out of the picture.

Dr Jamieson crouched behind the desk at the end of the room, while Blue and Glen were positioned against the wall next to the door. Nobody breathed. Nobody moved. "Heading your way!" came a whisper on the walkie-talkie.

There was a knock on the door, and a voice, "Dr Jamieson?" Almost sounded English, but not quite.

"Who is it?" called the doctor.

"I've brought the X-ray prints that Dr Bancroft ordered this morning. He wants you to give a second opinion. It'll only take five minutes."

"OK. Just wait there. I'm coming."

But Dr Jamieson did not move. Blue counted to five, then stretched a hand over and began to press the door handle down. As soon as it moved the woman fired three rapid shots through the thin plywood door. Had Dr Jamieson been standing behind it, opening the door, he would have taken two bullets in the chest and one in the stomach. Except that he wasn't.

She kicked the door open, intent on finishing off Blue as well. But suddenly the corridor was full of light and an avalanche of ear-splitting sound burst over them. For moment she seemed disoriented, then uttered an unintelligible curse, and turned to run. A jet of white liquid hit her face. She fired wildly along the corridor twice, then ran for the stairs wiping frantically at her eyes. She didn't seem to see where the staircase began, and fell down out of sight.

Three of the armed officers hidden in the rooms ran down the stairs after the woman. "Subject down!" shouted the first, and the others slowed down, and lowered their weapons. Blue, now out in the corridor, could see an officer in helmet and bulletproof vest putting a high-powered pepper spray gun back in its case. It looked like one of those giant water pistols he had seen kids playing with. Meanwhile the doctor emerged from the office, and shouted to the men, "Get her up here to the washbasin, quickly!"

The woman reappeared from the staircase, handcuffed and held fast by two officers. Her eyes were red and puffy and she appeared unable to see anything. Blue noticed she had a cut on her forehead, perhaps from the fall down the stairs. The officers led her into the room indicated by the doctor. Blue went down the stairs and saw PC Baines standing as if frozen behind the counter.

"She said she had X-rays," she stammered.

Blue ignored her and opened the main door. Inspector Taylor and two of his officers came in.

"Get scene-of-crime, fast," he ordered one of the men. Then he turned to Baines: "Kayleigh Baines, I'm arresting you on suspicion of being an accessory to murder."

"You don't understand," she gasped. "It's secret stuff."

"We'll talk about that later," said Taylor, and nodded to the other officer, who completed the caution, then turned to Blue. "Hi, Angus. You did well."

61

An hour later, Blue was back in Taylor's office at Stewart Street. Taylor had introduced himself as Donald – "Not Donnie or Don, you understand." He was satisfied with the way things had gone.

The woman had been charged with the attempted murder of Dr Jamieson. There could be little doubt about that, as there were eight witnesses. Taylor was sure her hair, when compared to the strand found with the body of Lesley Greeley, would be enough to convict her of the three killings. No ID was found on her and she refused to say who she was, or, indeed, anything. When she was invited to present her hands for fingerprinting, she went berserk, swinging her handcuffed arms in all directions. The procedure had to be carried out forcibly.

"Anything on her?" Blue asked.

"Clean! Not even a bus ticket."

"Did she walk to the hospital?"

"I'll bet not. She'd want to get away sharpish. So either she left a car nearby, or somebody was waiting to pick her up. We had a checkpoint at the hospital gate from the moment she entered the building, checked every car in and out, but nothing suspicious, and certainly no Blasić or King."

"It's a cold day. She didn't have a coat. Apart from the lab coat, which I suppose she would have dumped after the job. Where was her coat?"

"If she had a car, it'll still be at the hospital. So where's the key? Right, there's one thing we could still try. Excuse me a moment." Taylor dashed out of the room.

He was back in two minutes. "I've sent the metal detector over. They'll scour the ground near that building to see if she hid a car key anywhere. They're checking the cars out as we speak. Looking for a hire car, or one belonging to an obscure company."

"She's not from this neck of the woods. When the lights went on, that curse wasn't one I recognised."

Ten minutes later the woman was in the interview room, being questioned by Taylor, with Blue alongside. Her eyes were very red and she kept blinking them. But she refused to speak, and her face betrayed no emotion. After ten minutes of fruitless questioning, Taylor gave up, and sent her down to the cells.

"What do you think?" asked Blue.

"She thinks somebody's going to get her out. I've spoken to my Super about it. He's spoken to the Ministry of Justice already, and they've made it clear, no-one has authority to take her."

"What about Baines?"

"Claims she was told it was some sort of top secret security operation. The Greeleys were Russian spies, or something. I don't think we'll get much out of her, they didn't tell her anything. Couldn't identify King. Says she only talked to him on the phone. Didn't even realise the phoney consultant was him."

"What about the calls she made?"

"Both to the same number. Anonymous pay-as-you-go mobile. Too quick to get a fix on the location. But we've got recordings. Do you know his voice?"

"No, I've never spoken to him."

"Don't worry about that. My Super has, and he recognised the voice right away. Said he'd recognise 'that smarmy bastard' anywhere. I think 'patronising git' came into it too. He's double-checking with a couple of other people he knows have met King."

"Have we enough to nail him?"

"The timing of the calls is circumstantial but will take us some way. The content isn't very helpful. Listen." He tapped a few keys on his laptop. "Here's the first…"

> *Ring tone.*
> *Man: Yes?*
> *Woman: My uncle's in bed here. Mr Black is with him.*
> *Man: Tell me if he seems to be waking. Thank you.*
> *End of call.*

"…and the second."

> *Ring tone.*
> *Man: Yes?*
> *Woman: He seems to be awake now, and he's talking.*
> *Man: I'll send a friend round, to see him.*
> *Woman: How will I…*
> *Man: You will. Goodbye.*
> *End of call.*

"Not exactly a clever code is it?" said Taylor, "but anything more complex would have foxed poor Baines. Should I call you Mr Black from now on?"

The phone rang. Taylor flicked the speaker switch, and barked into it: "Taylor!"

"Sergeant Deans, sir, reporting from the hospital." Blue noted that Taylor had a procedure for people reporting to him. Say who and where you are and wait for the OK.

"Well, Deans, what have we got?"

"They've found the key, sir. Under a brick round the corner from the ward. We're pacing the grounds now, to see if any parked car beeps when the button's pressed. Nothing so far, though."

"Wait a minute," put in Blue, to Taylor, "Surely they'd realise that a checkpoint would be set up as soon as the murder was discovered. I doubt she'd have parked within the hospital precinct itself. Anywhere just outside?"

"Good point. Deans, try just outside the grounds. Let me think. Yes, start at Lidl." Taylor replaced the phone. "Just next to the hospital is a Lidl store with a big car park. It's right on the road into the Clyde tunnel too. Perfect for a rapid getaway. She could either be at the airport or on the motorway south within minutes. We need that car, Angus. By the way, what are your plans?"

"I'd like to get the evening flight back to Islay, if it's OK with you, Donald. It goes at five."

"No problem. Just after three now. I'll get you booked onto it right away." He picked up the phone again. "Tracey, can you come in for a moment?"

A minute later there was a knock at the door, and a girl came in whom Blue reckoned was about fourteen. Her blue skirt and top might have been a school uniform. What was she doing skipping school? Taylor's daughter? Granddaughter? Taylor introduced her. "Angus, this is Tracey, our secretary and general do-it-all. She'll take your details and book the flight. Tracey, this is Inspector Blue. He needs a flight this evening."

"Yes, sir, where are you going?" The voice matched Blue's assessment of her age.

"Islay please. There's a flight at five. Here's my card. The address is there too, Oban Police HQ."

"No problem, sir. Ah, weren't there were Pictish kings called Angus?"

"Yes. How do you know?"

"I did Scottish History at Glasgow Uni. Comes in useful now and then. I'll print off the ticket and let you have it as soon as it's done." Then to Taylor, "Will that be all, sir?"

"Thanks Tracey," said Taylor, and the girl left.

"Don't say anything, Angus, she looks like a wee girl. But she's efficient. Never puts anything off. Always notes down what she's done. Her diary has saved us a few times."

Ten minutes later Tracey was back, gave Blue a brown envelope containing his ticket details and the printout of his boarding pass, and wished him a pleasant flight. Blue had just extracted the printout to check the details, when Taylor's phone rang again.

"Taylor!"

"Donnelly, sir, repo…"

"OK, what have you got?"

"Got the car, sir. Just like you said, in the Lidl car park."

"Good. Don't touch it. Get scene-of-crime over there now. I'll be there in ten minutes." He put the phone down. "Come on, Angus. Bring your bag. I'll drop you at the airport after."

62

By the time they got there the car, a small grey hatchback, had been examined and dusted for prints. A scene-of-crime officer approached Taylor. "Sergeant Morris, sir. Treasure trove! Prints on the door handle, steering wheel and car radio buttons. Coat on the back seat, pockets empty, handbag under the driver's seat, with documentation, overnight bag in the boot, with clothing, plus spare pistol and ammo." He produced a packet of disposable gloves and pulled out a pair for Taylor.

"Give Inspector Blue a pair, too, Sergeant."

"Yes, sir." The sergeant pulled out another pair and gave them to Blue, with raised eyebrows. Inspector Taylor treating other officers as equals wasn't what he was used to. He reached down to the cardboard box at his feet, and pulled something out. He turned back to Taylor. "You might find these interesting. Don't worry, they've been dusted." He handed Taylor a wallet and a passport.

Taylor flicked through the passport first. "Croatian passport in the name of Iulia Vrasko." He passed it to Blue, and moved on to the wallet. "Wallet containing some English and Scottish banknotes, and some Euros, quite a lot by the look of it."

"Three hundred and sixty pounds and eight hundred Euros, sir."

"Hmm. Enough to get away quickly without leaving a card trail."

"She wasn't planning on going too far, sir, take a look at what's behind the cash."

Taylor pulled out a folded piece of paper, and opened it out. "Boarding pass for a flight to Islay this evening. Guess there'll be an empty seat, then, Angus." He passed it to Blue, intent on extracting the cards which were visible in another section of the wallet.

"Travelling under the name of Julia Crabtree," said Blue, studying the boarding pass.

"And here's a UK driving licence for Ms Julia Crabtree, of Old Barn House, East Lane, Highford, Essex. Credit and debit card in the name of J Crabtree. Essex library card ditto. All quite new."

"The address is as fake as the name," said Blue. "She's the woman who hired our site-wrecker."

"OK, Sergeant," said Taylor, "Can you get this stuff back to the Station. Get the car in too, and pull it apart. Thank you. Right, Angus, now I'll drive you to the airport."

As they drove along the motorway, they discussed what had happened. "It seems," began Taylor, "that King has commissioned these two Croats to do some dirty work. Obstructing your investigation of the wartime Islay killings, and eliminating a potential witness. I know I don't have much time for cold cases, but this one must be pretty hot if they're willing to kill to keep it quiet. What is it about that case?"

"Frankly, Donald, we don't so far have any idea. I don't understand why they'd go to all this trouble to cover up the executions. If the men were criminals, no-one's going to be that fussed. Relatives may wonder if the punishment was too harsh I suppose. If they were mutineers, the main interest would be to historians, unless the families wanted to clear their names. Even so, it wouldn't be that big a rumpus. There's something else we aren't seeing."

"And presumably which neither of our Croats knows about either. They will have been hired simply to do what King told them. And by the way, Angus, be careful, there's still at least one of them out there, who may not be too pleased that we've got his partner, and may be heading for your neck of the woods too."

"Unless he's already there, and she was going to meet him."

63

Taylor dropped Blue at the entrance to the terminal building. He went through the security check, then bought a coffee, sat down at a gate where nobody was waiting, and phoned Superintendent Campbell. He gave him a full account of what had happened.

Campbell was impressed. "That's good stuff, Blue, very good. The game's afoot, eh?"

"Well, not that one, chief, we got her. But Vrasko was headed for Islay, so it may be that Blasić is on his way too."

"You'll need to be careful. Eyes peeled. But it may be their first priority is to get rid of any remaining witnesses from back then. We'll have to keep a watch for elderly people being killed, anywhere in the UK I suppose. Nothing we can do to prevent it, except circulate Blasić's details."

"I'll get Sergeant McCader on to that."

"Good. Those murders in Glasgow have stirred up a hornet's nest, believe me. The Ministry of Justice want to release a definitive statement regarding the Peat Dead. But they need the whole story. How close are we?"

"We're getting a bit more of it each day, chief. I think we're almost there."

Next he phoned McCader, brought him up to date, and asked him to send everything he had on Julia Crabtree to Inspector Taylor, since he was pursuing the case against Iulia Vrasko, and to circulate Blasić's details to other UK police forces with a request to keep a lookout for him. Things on Islay were quiet, by the sound of it. He set a team meeting for nine the following morning. There was quite a lot of information that needed pulling together and sharing.

He was relieved to see that neither King nor Blasić were on his plane, and there were a few empty seats. There was time to have another look at Tony Rogers' book. The memoirs were, as far as Blue could tell, fairly honest. Tony made no attempt to paint himself as a hero. He came across, even in his own words, as work-shy and dishonest. He frequently feigned illness to avoid work, and admitted that he cut corners in servicing the planes. How many had crashed because of that, Blue wondered. He also boasted about obtaining goods which he knew to have been stolen, and even pointed out how he had installed previously used parts in planes, and sold off the new parts on the black market. The war was, for him, simply a series of opportunities to benefit himself.

As the plane came down out of the cloud, he had just reached an interesting episode:

I'd got this nice racket going, nicking hydraulic fluid. Here's how it went. I'd syphon off the fluid into jerry cans, then pass them to a contact – I'll just call him 'Jasper' here, that wasn't his real name, of course. He got the stuff shipped on to Glasgow for sale. I've no idea how he did it – that's the kind of thing you don't ask – but it made both of us a tidy sum. Something for a rainy day, or for after the war. Mind you, I wasn't the only one at it, there were all sorts of rackets going on. Some guys made a fortune out of it. I suppose I was hoping to do the same, because I got to taking a bit more than I should have done, and it got spotted. Some pen-pusher must noticed a discrepancy somewhere because I was suddenly visited by a couple of MPs, who threw me in the clink.

This was a bad moment. I really thought I was for the chop: at best a court-martial, at worst a firing squad. Goodbye good times. But my luck was in. Instead of all that I was brought before this Colonel Dawkins. I can tell by the look on his face, he thinks I'm scum, and he's looking at a paper – I guess that's the report on me. But, after a while, he looks at me, thoughtfully like, and he says, "My, but you're an enterprising lad, aren't you? Very resourceful, if I may say so, but lacking any strategic sense, and that could be quite fatal. However, we don't want to waste your, ah, talents, so I'm going to assign you to some special duties."

Of course, I'd heard of 'special duties' before – that meant cleaning out latrines, removing body parts from planes which had taken hits, all the other jobs nobody wanted. Imagine my surprise when it turns out to be a lot nicer than that. The colonel wants me to keep an eye on men he thinks are 'unreliable'. "Chaps who might hinder the war effort," he says, "could even be fifth-columnists. Need to be watched."

As it happens, these 'chaps' are mainly officers, so he fixes me a job, serving booze in the officers' mess. What a doddle. Of course, I have to keep a discreet watch on the 'suspects', as he calls them. Especially if they've had a good bit to drink and start talking too much. Sometimes he even gets me to follow one of them when they go home on leave. What a lark that is, all expenses-paid, hotel rooms, booze, all sorts of opportunities to move stuff around, do a few more deals.

The colonel wants reports, of course. And he likes to see that his suspicions are always correct. No problem, I can easily make up the sort of guff he wants to read. Captain so-and-so met in a bar a shifty-looking character with a foreign accent, who slipped him a brown envelope. The colonel loves it, tells me how good I am. Then he gets Captain so-and-so sent out on a high-risk mission or posted to a dangerous front-line location. Usually, he doesn't come back.

64

As he came into the little terminal, he found both Moira Nicolson and Alison Hendrickx waiting for him. Moira shook hands and Alison gave him a hug. Time paused for just a moment.

"Good to see you back, Angus," said Moira. "Why don't you come back with us for a spot of dinner?"

The house stood at the edge of Port Ellen, so he was able to walk to it from his hotel. A detached villa of greyish stone, standing in a large garden. Next to it was a stone building with large doors at the front. As he walked up the drive, he could also see further out-buildings at the back.

"Former manse," explained Moira. "Needed a bit of work, but it's very comfortable now."

"Is this where you make your furniture?"

"Yes, the workshop's round the back."

A tall man with white hair and neatly-trimmed beard met them at the door. "*Hallo, a h-Aonghus, ciamar a tha thu? Is mise Alasdair.*"

Blue scrabbled in his brain for fragments from the Gaelic evening course he'd been to several years back. "*Ah, hallo. Tha gu math, tapadh leat.*" Were they going to talk Gaelic all evening? What if Alison spoke it too? What else had they done at that class?

Alasdair smiled. "I can see the Gaelic's not your mother-tongue, but you did very well. Moira said you had a bit. It's nice to meet you." His voice had the soft cadence of the Western Isles.

They avoided talking about the case over dinner, a slow-cooked casserole of venison in red wine, followed by whole apples, cored and stewed, served with cream infused with sweet spiced rum. Blue felt himself nodding off, and realised that the adrenalin which had kept him going for the last two days had switched off. A powerful espresso temporarily revived him, and he was able to pay attention to Alasdair talking about his work as a translator from German. His current project was a series of crime novels by Hubert Valkerius.

"Sorry, I've not heard of him," said Blue.

"Don't worry," said Alasdair, "He's only published in German at the moment. His hero, *Kommissar* – that's inspector – Brack, is a police officer in the Austro-Hungarian Empire. He travels to various parts of the Empire to assist local police with difficult cases, in the early 1900s. He comes from a modest background, but in order to be promoted he has to pretend that he has some noble blood. Sometimes he even calls himself Count von Brack to be able to question members of the upper class."

"That sounds interesting," said Blue. "I can read German, as long as I've a dictionary to hand, so I'll look out for his work." He noticed Alison's eyes opening wide as she stared at him.

"It must be fascinating to translate a series of books, and watch the characters develop," she observed.

"Do they reach the First World War, and after?" asked Blue, "That must have been a challenging period."

"Not so far, but I've talked to Hubert a few times now, and he says he's working on one set during the war. But the one after that will take place during the chaos in Hungary after the end of the war, and then during the 1919 communist regime. These were difficult times for a policeman who tries to serve justice and avoid political involvement. In practice, it couldn't be done, because different political groups had different views of what constituted justice. Laws changed dramatically depending on which group was in power, and the police were regularly purged to remove those who were regarded as unreliable."

"How does Inspector Brack manage to survive, then?" asked Blue.

"He makes his own view of justice clear, and tries to avoid cases which are mainly political. He's tolerated because he's a good policeman, and he's honest. And there are still tricky crimes that need Brack's skills. But it's not easy for him, and he has some close shaves."

"So how would you describe his style as an investigator?" asked Alison.

"That's an interesting question. I run the books past Moira to make sure I've translated him plausibly as a policeman. Maybe she should answer that."

Moira laughed. "I think I know Inspector Brack quite well now. He's not heroic. Quite quiet. Puts his cases together bit by bit, so that you feel he's inching towards a solution, but that he's bound to get there. He can stand up for himself too. And he's also politically aware. He's not afraid to say what he thinks is wrong with the society he lives in, although that can get him into trouble."

"A bit like you, Angus," said Alison, smiling.

Blue felt himself blush and mumbled something incoherent.

The meal was finished off with a glass of whisky, a ten-year-old Ardbeg, light and smoky, with a lingering hint of honey on the tongue. After that Blue felt in serious danger of falling off his chair asleep, and made his thanks and farewells, refusing a lift to his hotel. As he walked back, he breathed deeply, smelling the sea in every breath, and every so often a drift of warm whisky as the breeze caught the smoke from the malting plant. What kind of policemen was he? At least he didn't have to pretend to be an aristocrat. But how did he seem to others? Or to one other.

Day 9. Friday

65

As usual when he'd had plenty to drink, Blue slept badly, and he was awake by six. He finished Tony Rogers' book by breakfast time, and noted the parts he needed to share with the team.

He was at the police station in Bowmore by 8.30, greeting Clara Gilmour at the reception desk, only to receive a brief scowl by way of response. "Oh yes, this is for you. Took me a lot of trouble to find it. Someone had taken it from the box." She gave him a key, then turned back to counting biros from one cardboard box to another.

The meeting started at nine. Nicolson, McCader, Bhardwaj, Craig and Alison Hendrickx were there. Alison sat next to Blue. He could detect a faint smell of the sea around her. He needed to concentrate. He opened with an account of events in Glasgow, concluding, "These events make our case more urgent. We've got one of them, but there's still at least one out there, maybe more. And we don't know what King is up to."

"What do you think they'll try next?" asked Moira.

"I guess if there were other surviving members of the execution squad, they will try to eliminate them too. That would include Burovkin, if he's still around."

"Could he have gone back to Russia?"

"That's very unlikely," said McCader, "Having done jobs like this – and he may well have been used for other killings – the British would not want to lose control of him. He'd know too much. Burovkin himself may have known that any Russians returning to the USSR after working with the Allies were treated with extreme suspicion by the Soviets. In many cases they were simply shot out of hand. The best thing for himself and the British government would have been for him to stay here."

"But they'd keep tabs on him?" put in Alison.

"Yes. They'll certainly know where he is. They'll have given him a new identity, and will be monitoring him. If they deal with him as discreetly as Stamford, he'll just be another very old man who dies. I've got a contact who'll peep into some classified files for me. He owes me. Deirdra tried looking for Burovkin on the databases but, as we would expect, there's nothing. By the way, Alison's theory about what happened to Group Captain Stamford – I'm pretty sure she's right."

There was silence in the room for a moment.

Blue broke it. "Vrasko was coming here," he said. "It's possible she was going to meet Blasić, maybe King too. So we need to be vigilant."

"Being on an island gives us one advantage," said Moira Nicolson. "We can at least keep an eye on who's coming and going. I'll have the folk at the airport and ferry ports keep a lookout for them."

"Couldn't somebody just come in on a wee boat, boss?" asked Craig.

"Yes, you're right, Deirdra," said Moira, "but I can ask people we know to keep an eye out for boats moored away from the usual places."

Blue turned to Alison: "Alison, where are we on the DNA?"

"Thanks to Deirdra, we've two more positive IDs. No. 2 is Terence Darwin, and No. 5 Peter Bishop. We have two still to identify. No. 1 has the ring with the initials M. M. and No. 3 is still unknown."

"Tony Rogers' book may throw more light on that. Good work, Deirdra. Arvind, anything from the interviews with the old folk?"

"Yes, chief. Dr Hendrickx and I have interviewed twelve of them so far, so we're almost done. We've found several crimes committed during the war which were never even investigated – two rapes, several serious assaults, and lots of theft, some of it on a fairly large scale. Most of the problems were with members of the forces. For instance…"

"Sadly, right now we're not going to look at these cases, although after this particular business is sorted out, Moira, you may want to go through the details and see whether you think any are worth following up. Did you get anything that might be relevant to our case?"

"Yes, there was something." Bhardwaj glanced down at his notes. "Eliza Grant, aged 89, of Bowmore. I can play it, if you like, won't take long." Blue nodded. Bhardwaj tapped a few keys on his PC and in few seconds they heard the surprisingly strong voice of the old lady.

> *EG: There was one time, late in 1944, I think it was November, we were just out walking, along the shore beyond the distillery. It was a lovely afternoon – even the planes seemed to have stopped flying. So we just walked and talked. And Arthur – that was my boyfriend, he was in the RAF – he said there'd been a*

big meeting. Top brass, very hush-hush. So I said to him, why are you telling me, then? He said, well, he couldn't give me details, but it could change the outcome of the war. Could be over by Christmas, even. I was so pleased to hear that, you can't imagine how much we looked forward to it all being finished. So I said, that's great. And he said, but you've not to tell a soul. And I haven't, not till now, that is. How do you know about it, I said. I escorted one of them in, he said. I could tell he was dying to tell me the whole story, but that's all he would say.

AG: Did he ever say anything about it later?

EG: He never had the chance. That was the last time I ever saw him. Two weeks later, an officer came to see me. He said Arthur's plane had failed to return from a mission. Probably crashed into the sea. I was heartbroken, I really was. I thought I wouldn't meet anyone else. I did of course, and we were married for fifty years. But back then, I felt it was the end of the world.

AB: What else did the officer say?

EG: It was quite odd really, I mean, him coming at all, because they never usually sent even a note to a girlfriend. You had to be a wife to get any information, and then it was usually just a letter or telegram. But I soon realised what he was up to. He wanted to know what I knew, if Arthur had let anything slip. He asked what I knew about Arthur's job, and such. I wasn't stupid, I just said he'd never said anything, and I knew not to ask. He asked me the same sort of question a few times, in different ways, but I always said the same thing. He seemed to be happy about that, even left me a box with some things that were hard to get – soap, thread, things that are so ordinary now – he said it was a gift from the RAF. He was sorry for my loss. Wished me well for the future.

AB: Did the officer give his name?

EG: I suppose so. I don't remember. I was thinking of Arthur, somewhere out in the sea. He was very well-spoken, posh I would say. Definitely a toff. That's what Arthur used to call them. Said they used to

> *spend their evenings eating and drinking. Wine, bran-*
> *dy, port, cigars, the lot. And when they got bored*
> *they'd go off and shoot deer up on the moors. And*
> *anything else that moved."*
>
> AG: *What was Arthur's name, by the way? His sec-*
> *ond name.*
>
> EG: *Oh, let me think. I just called him Arthur for so*
> *long. Came from somewhere near Leeds. Walforth.*
> *That's it. I can still hear that officer saying it in that*
> *posh voice of his. Arthur Walforth.*

"So, what do we learn from that?" said Blue.

"He's number 3, isn't he?" said Alison, "Arthur Walforth."

"It looks that way," said Blue, "But we still need to track him down. Can you get onto that, Deirdra?"

"Four down, one to go," commented Bhardwaj.

"What else does Eliza tell us?" said Blue.

"There was some sort of meeting," said Alison, "Important people. Pity Arthur died or he might have told her more."

"He was killed," said McCader bluntly. "The girl was lucky they believed she knew nothing. Or she'd have been killed too."

"What makes you think that?" asked Blue.

"There's a big meeting. Then he's dead. Then some bigwig wants to know if he gave anything away. It's too much of a coincidence. He was killed to keep the meeting secret."

"Are you saying he might have accidentally overheard something?" asked Moira.

"Yes, ma'am, either that or he just got wind of what it was about. I've worked with these people. They don't change. The elite who think it's their destiny to rule, and everyone else's to obey."

"Yes," said Blue, "people forget that Churchill was an aristocrat and an imperialist. He thought Britain – or rather, his sort of people – had a right to rule a large slice of the world. He certainly didn't want the masses getting involved."

"So what was the meeting about?" asked Alison.

"What about the D-Day landings?" suggested Bhardwaj

"They'd already happened," said Blue, "By late 1944 it was clear the war was moving into its final phase. And also who was going to win."

"So anyone who *might* have heard or seen anything is eliminated, just to be on the safe side," said Moira. "The chef who cooked the meal, the waiter who served it, the pilot who escorted them in. And so on. I guess, from that point of view, just five is a very modest number to kill. Or are there other little heaps of bodies under the peat? Is that why they want to keep it quiet? Because they're afraid that we might find the others."

"My God," said Alison.

"Let's not get carried away," said Blue. "We've not encountered any people who disappeared that we haven't linked to our bodies. We don't have lots of people coming forward to report missing relatives. Unless that happens – or someone uncovers more corpses – let's work on the basis that ours are the only ones."

66

Blue spread Tony Rogers' three notebooks on the table on front of him. "I mentioned Tony Rogers' book in passing earlier. Here it is. I've read it all. It adds another piece to the jigsaw. Tony says that he was told to spy on officers thought to be 'unreliable'. Then his boss added other duties. These included softening up suspects for interrogation. That seems to have included anyone who questioned the war or how it was being run. Tony refers to them as 'jerry-lovers'. He describes some of the techniques he and his colleagues used. I won't read them out. He was now working closely with someone who became a good friend."

"Lesley Greeley?" asked Moira Nicolson.

"Bang on. Tony and Lesley became something of a double act. Searching, torturing, sometimes just plain old beating up. Always 'jerry-lovers' – that made everything they did all right. Here's the bit we want." Blue opened one of the notebooks at a point marked with a yellow post-it, and read:

This was about the middle of November 1944. One day Col. Dawkins calls Les and me into his office. "Got a job for you lads this evening," he says. "Caught some of those Fifth-columnist chaps. Five of them. Stealing war materials. Need to deal with them."

I says, "Need help getting a confession, then?"

Col. D. looks at us like we're insects. "We know they're guilty. But we'd prefer a confession – makes the court martial much simpler."

So I say, "Yes, sir, whatever we can do, sir."

Then he says, "I want to give these fellows a real fright, so we're going to pretend to execute them."

So I say, "My shooting's not so good, sir."

"No, no," he says, "you save your bullets for jerry, I've got someone else to do that. You just look after the prisoners. Soften them up a bit, know what I mean?"

The first thing he wants us to do is bring these guys in. Says they can't let the MPs do it, it would give the game away and they'd clam up. Plus this is all very hush-hush. fewer people who know, the better. So we, Les and me, we have to go one evening after dark, and bring each one in, pretending they've got to see a senior officer about a special mission. They haven't heard of him, of course, but orders is orders. We have to do each one separately, can't just round them all up, so each one doesn't know we've got the others. We take them to this building on the edge of the base, there's a guard outside and another one inside. Nasty looking characters, thugs both of them. We do them over a bit, have a bit of fun. I got hold of an old cricket bat, sawed most of it off, makes a great weapon. You can get a really good swing. After that we chuck them into a cell. Each of them in solitary, of course.

Then this big Russian guy turns up, makes my flesh creep. Even looks a bit like Stalin. Brings a bag of clothes. So we get the guys into the new clothes, then drag them out of the cells, and give them a few whacks. We tie their hands behind their backs and gag them, then shove them into a van that's waiting outside. It takes us up the track onto the moor, not very far, and we see there's a hole already dug. We bundle them out and the van drives off.

So we line them up in front of the pit, not saying what's going to happen. Two of them are officers, and one of these is hardly conscious. I must have done in his head quite bad when we first got him in. He doesn't seem to know what's going on, so we have to drag him. The little Welsh guy is whimpering, the others keep quiet. We line them up, grinning at them. They must be shitting themselves. Next the Russian takes out his pistol, puts it behind the Welsh guy's neck, and just shoots him. He pitches forward into the pit.

"Wait a mo!" Les says to the shooter, "We ain't supposed to kill 'em. Just frighten them. To make them confess. No-one said anything about killing them."

Well, the Russian just looks at Les, with no expression at all. Then he says to him, "What do you think we do out here, comrade? Of course we kill them. You want to join them, eh? No problem to me. I kill many men. Women, children, babies. Another two, no problem."

I told Les to shut up. "Don't worry," I says to the Russian, "we're OK with that. All in a day's work, eh?"

"Yes," says the Russki, "very good." He smiles at me. Then he just shoots the rest. Pop, pop, pop, just like that, as Tommy Cooper would say, and it's done. Single shot and they fall forward into the hole. Easy. He's an expert. Apart from the last one, that is. That's Flight Lieutenant McSomething. He turns round and looks the Russki right in the eye. They just stare at each other – it's weird. Then he turns round again, and the Russki shoots him too.

Next thing is, he tells us to get into the pit, and take the ropes and gags off them. I was scared now that he'd shoot us too, so I do that as fast as I can. Then he says, "Fill it in," and points to a couple of shovels by a big pile of peat. I really did think we were for it as soon as we were done.

It took ages, and while he's watching us he produces a bottle of vodka and drinks most of it. So when we're nearly done, he says, "Need more vodka," that's all, and wanders off. After a couple of minutes Les says to me, "Let's get out of here." So we bat the earth down a bit, shoulder the shovels, and clear off, fast as we can.

The next evening the colonel summons us again. Wants us to go back to the flight-lieutenant's place and give it a good go-through. See if he's got a diary, anything like that. "These educated chaps," says the colonel, "they've a nasty habit of writing things down. Things that shouldn't be written down. Should be a crime in wartime. Aiding the enemy." We go back there, give the old lady and the little girl who live there a good scare. But we don't find anything.

Next week me and Les were transferred. We never saw the colonel, or that Russian, again.

Blue shut the book, and put it down. "There we are. All so matter-of-fact." There was a silence in the room. Revulsion at the ordinariness with which murder was seen, and the casual efficiency with which it was carried out.

"That tells the story," Blue continued, "But it still leaves two questions unanswered: One, why did the men have to be silenced? Tony and Les thought they were fifth-columnists, but as far as we know, the ones we've identified were nothing of the sort. And two, who was the fifth man, Flight Lieutenant McSomething? We need to fill in those gaps. We're under pressure to produce the whole story. Arvind, can you and Alison finish off the interviews? If that's OK, Alison? I appreciate that you're still here helping us."

67

As he flopped into the chair in his office, Blue thought to himself that even the case meetings were becoming exhausting. It was time for a coffee. Updating the report occupied him for the next hour. He was just shutting down his PC when the phone rang. John Striven.

"Hi, Angus. I've seen what happened in Glasgow. Do you follow violence or does it follow you?"

"That's far too clever a question for me to answer. How do you know what's happened?"

"Taylor's boss, Superintendent McDonough, aka The Doughnut, just gave a press conference here. Murders at the hospital, then the operation yesterday to trap a 'dangerous terrorist'. Pat on the back for Taylor for organising a 'slick and successful operation'. He didn't make any link to the bodies found on Islay, which I'm not complaining about. Nor did he say how a triple murder happened in a so-called 'secure ward.'"

"I'm sure you asked."

"Naturally. He alluded to a rogue police officer, forced to provide information because the terrorists threatened to kill her aged parents. Makes a good story, but we all got it. What's happening over there?"

"Obviously I can't give you any details regarding the current operational situation."

"But?"

"But I would say the arrest of Iulia Vrasko yesterday has progressed matters significantly."

"And in English please?"

"This is off the record?"

"Of course. You know me, Angus."

"Yes, I do. And I didn't tell you this. We're close to identifying all the bodies from the peat, as well as the circumstances of their deaths. The Glasgow deaths were linked, I'm glad McDonough kept that quiet. It's possible there's a concerted attempt to undermine this investigation, and I don't think it's over yet."

"You seem to be suggesting these 'terrorists' are going to pop up in Islay next."

"We have to be alert to such a possibility."

"That means you think there are more of them."

"We think Ms Vrasko had one or more accomplices. We don't

know where they are at this point in time."

"But you know who they are."

"I didn't say that."

"Do you know who they are?"

"We have our suspicions."

"You're hinting that it might be worth while for me to come over there now?"

"It's obviously up to you to decide where your journalistic efforts should be directed."

"Nuff said. I'll be over as soon as I can."

He went through to the case room. The door was locked. He knocked, and a moment later PC Craig opened it a fraction. "Oh, it's you, chief, come right in." She shut the door firmly and went back to her seat at the computer.

"Why have you got the door locked?"

"We were warned about keeping it locked by the boss, I mean, Inspector Nicolson. Sensitive information."

"Yes, there's a lot of stuff that we don't want to lose. Where's Sergeant McCader, by the way?"

"He went out about quarter of an hour ago. To call somebody. Said he wouldn't be very long."

"So, any progress with the name hunts?"

"Aye, I'm getting there. Walforth is not a very common name, and we've a geographical location too. I think I've got the Arthur Walforth that Eliza knew." She peered at her notes. "Born 1921, in Tadcaster, Yorkshire. Joined the RAF 1940. Promoted from Pilot Officer to Flying Officer 1942. Lost on a mission November 1944, that's what the database says, anyway. He had two brothers and a sister, so I'm trying to identify some of their descendants."

"Good. When you've done that I think it's worth having a look at the couple whose initials we've got on the inside of the wedding ring."

"Yes, sir. Actually I've done a bit of work on it already. I've went through UK marriages for the 4th April 1942, or other marriages involving British servicemen. I've listed all the couples with the initials MM and RS. That's as far as I got, when I had to switch to the other bodies."

"If Tony's right in saying that one of the five was a McSomething, that gives us a good pointer. By the way, Deirdra, how are you enjoying this work?"

"Aye, it's very interesting, right enough. Better than trying to talk sense into numpties who let their dogs shite on the pavements, know what I mean? But I'm getting fed up being indoors as well. I'm beginning to feel like I just work in an office. All the others are getting out and about. Not that I'm complaining, chief. I ken the work has to be done."

"Yes, sadly it does, and you're good at it. But that doesn't mean you'll get stuck indoors all the time. Remember that."

"Yes, chief, thanks."

They heard a siren outside. Blue went to the window.

"An ambulance," he said to Craig, "How many do they have on the island?"

"Just the one. Sounds like it's heading towards Bridgend." The siren grew fainter as the ambulance raced out of town.

The door opened, and Moira Nicolson came straight in.

"Angus, there's been an accident, on the road out towards Bridgend."

"Ah, we heard the ambulance."

"It was Sergeant McCader."

"What?"

"Enver. It seems he was struck by a van as he was walking out of the town."

"Is he…?"

"No, not dead, but he doesn't look good. According to witnesses – and we have two – the van ran at him at speed from behind. He was thrown into the air. Thankfully he landed on the grass verge, and not the rocks. There were people with him almost immediately and the ambulance was called."

"The witnesses?"

"Agnes Finnarty and Mary McLennan were having a chat about ten yards down the road. They say he was walking out along the roadside towards the Gaelic Centre, in fact, he'd waved as he passed them. Then this van – a big white one – came past them at speed and went straight at him. Bob is at the scene, went there as soon as the 999 call came in, recognised Enver right away."

"Did they get any details of the van?"

"Not the number, but the van was easy to spot. The name was on it. It was George Kelly's. The plumber. Lives in Port Charlotte. We're trying to find him now."

"You don't think he was driving the van?"

"No. George is well-known. He wouldn't run anybody down.

Drives too slowly. Anywhere." Blue remembered the van passing as he and Bhardwaj waited to exit the airport, on the day of his arrival.

"He may have had a heart attack at the wheel. Got his foot stuck on the pedal."

"Do you think that's likely, Angus? Just as he's driving up behind one of our case team, at a crucial point in the investigation."

"I'd like to talk to the witnesses at the locus. Could you ask Bob to hang onto them? I'll go now."

"I'll come too, Angus. This is technically my case. And, if you're OK with it, we should take Deirdra with us too, we may need all the people we have. Boris can man the station."

Blue thought, McCader must have walked past Blackett as he left the building. Could Blackett have phoned someone, and told them?

68

PC Craig at the wheel, they were there in five minutes. The road ran by the shore, with a rough grass verge about two yards wide between the asphalt and the sand of the bay. Further round the curve of the beach Blue could see the Gaelic Centre. Turning towards the town, there were no buildings on the seaward side of the road, but on the other side, the cottages of the town began just about twenty yards away. It was by the gate of the first of these that Agnes and Mary had been talking. They were standing there again now, talking to Sergeant Walker. Blue could see the black skid mark on the road at the point where the van had hit McCader then changed direction and accelerated rapidly off towards Bridgend.

"Drove away at some speed," said Blue, "but we might still be able to catch them."

"Go for it!" said Moira, "I'll get Arvind over to help here."

As they set off again, Blue said to Craig, "We need to see where they went, maybe even locate the van. I doubt they'll be sitting in it waiting for us, but you never know, so we have to be careful. And we don't know how many there are. Could be Blasić, or him and King, or somebody else altogether. Where do you think they'd go from here?"

"They'll have three choices at Bridgend," said Craig. "They could turn left towards Port Charlotte, or right to Port Askaig. But there's also a single-track road that turns off just before Bridgend, heading for Mulindry."

"Does that road go anywhere after that?"

"Aye, it loops round to join the Port Askaig road at Ballygrant. That's not far from Port Askaig."

"Let's take that one. I'm guessing their aim is to get out of sight as fast as possible and then lose the van. Once they're away from it we've lost them again."

"Right on, chief. They could be off across country, an with rucksacks and walking poles, they could be back in Bowmore in a couple of hours, and just be taken for walkers. Nothing suspicious at all."

They turned right just before the main junction at Bridgend, and headed down a narrow road bounded by straggling trees. The road twisted and turned, so it was impossible to see what was ahead.

Soon they came up behind a tractor. When the driver, a young man in a flat cap, saw the police car behind him he turned into the next passing place. They drew alongside and stopped.

"Hi, Alex," said Craig, "sorry to push you off the road. Have you seen George Kelly's van recently?"

"It's awfa curious you should be saying that, Deirdra," came the slow reply. "He passed me maybe five minutes ago. Seemed in a awfa hurry – and that's very unusual for George. Flashing his lights and sounding the horn. Now I think of it, it didna look like George was at the wheel at all, I'm thinking it was someone younger."

"Was he the only person in the van?" asked Craig.

"Yes, I think so. Did he steal it, then?"

"Looks like it," said Craig. "I'll call you later."

"Now that's an offer I didna think I'd hear, Deirdra. Would that be about the Young Farmers Harvest Party then?"

"No! I'll be wantin a description of the man in George's van. But right now we're trying to catch him. See you later, Alex." And they drove off.

"Local farmer, sir. Alex Kinnoul."

"The tractor was a bit of a give-away. Outdoor work – just what you wanted, eh?"

"Aye, too true, chief. Sounded like it might have been Blasić in the van."

"Yes. He may be armed, so we need to be careful."

As they came round a sharp corner, Craig slammed on the brakes as they saw the van parked right across the road, but the car slewed sideways on the muddy surface and slammed side on into it. Both Blue and Craig were belted in, so neither was injured, though they had both got a jolt, Blue in particular in the passenger seat. Craig jumped out, and then Blue scrambled across the driver's seat and out the door. He flexed his left shoulder and arm. He would have some impressive bruises by the morning.

Craig was already photographing the scene with her phone, so Blue peered into the van. It was empty. No key in the ignition either. He cautiously made his way round it, but there was no sign of anyone. The bird, or birds, had flown. He asked Craig to see if the car was driveable. She got in and started it up, then gingerly drove it off the van – with some screeching and scraping of bodywork – and parked at the side of the road. "Yes, chief," she confirmed, "it's OK. Just the doors on that side a wee bit bashed in."

Alex Kinnoul in his tractor came up. "I heard the bang," he said.

"You've been lucky there. You could have crashed straight into it. Aye, that would have been very nasty all right. I'd better pull yon van off the road, otherwise neither of us will be getting past."

There was no point now in rushing on, so Blue asked the young farmer for a description of the van driver.

"Well, now, he had the window shut, so I couldna see very much. But I'd say a youngish chap, dark hair, and maybe a beard. From off the island, I'd say."

Blue produced the grainy picture copied from Blasić's driving licence. "Could that be him?"

"Hmm, yes, it's not very clear, but that could certainly have been him."

"Thanks. By the way, is it possible to walk from here back to Bowmore? I'm wondering where that man could have gone."

"Well now, about half a mile up the road there's a wee path that comes into Bowmore near the Round Church. Quite an easy walk, would take you about two hours, I'd say."

69

Blue and Craig left Alex towing the van off the road, and drove back to Bowmore, pulling up by the spot where McCader had been hit. Inspector Nicolson and Sergeant Walker were still there, and stared as the battered car came to a halt. "Good heavens, Angus," said Moira, "you certainly seem to be getting through our cars. Mr McCall will be very pleased at the amount of work we're bringing his body shop."

"It's Blasić," said Blue, "we have a description from Alex Kinnoul. Did either of the women here see him?"

"No. The van had passed before they took a lot of notice. He can't have been revving up unduly at that point, or Enver would have heard him."

"That may have saved Enver. Blasić abandoned the van on the Mulindry road. He may walk from there across country into Bowmore. We might be able to catch him on the path. Who have we got?"

"Good question, Angus, I'm afraid what you see here is what we've got, apart from Arvind, who's on his way, and Boris, who's at the station. I've already asked Oban for a SOC team, but they won't be here till at least half past three."

They heard the whine of a siren, and the ambulance rushed past them and on towards Bridgend.

"I hope that's not more trouble," said Moira.

"Once Arvind arrives," said Blue, "I'll go with him and Deirdra, and see if we can catch Blasić."

"He could well be armed. Maybe we should wait till backup arrives. I'm assuming Oban will send us something now that we know it was deliberate. And that it's Blasić."

"Even if they rush them here by helicopter, it'll still be a while. And that's unlikely, unless he's actually killed someone."

"Excuse me, folks." It was Sergeant Walker. "I've just had a call from the emergency centre in Glasgow. Someone has dialled 999 and reported a dead body here. Or rather, over at Portnahaven."

"Any details?" asked Moira.

Walker looked at his watch. "At 12.12, that's about eight minutes ago now, somebody dialled 999. A woman's voice. Said she thought there had been a murder on Islay, at Portnahaven. Kirk Lane, half way up from the pier. Said she'd seen a body through the window, a man, sitting at a table, but not moving. Just in case he wasn't dead, the centre called out the ambulance first. Then they called my mobile. Said there was no answer at the station."

"That's odd. Oh God! George Outhwaite lives in Kirk Lane. What if…"

"We need to get there then," said Blue, "and fast, or the paramedics will have trampled all over everything."

"Don't worry, Angus, they know me, and I know them. They'll be careful. But we do need to get there. Why didn't Boris answer the phone? Where has he got to?"

"What if the call is a hoax? An attempt to send us all over the island, while Blasić vanishes. What if King is in touch with Blasić, learns what happened with the van? He's not stupid, and guesses that we might try to catch Blasić on his walk into town. So he gets one of his other minions to make the call. Maybe there'll be another in five minutes reporting an explosion at that bird sanctuary up at the top of the island."

"Gruinart Bay."

"Yes, or a fight breaking out at Ardbeg distillery. Then we're all out of town, and Blasić nips in, collects a car, and disappears."

"So what do we do?"

"What I think you were hinting at earlier, Moira. Trust the paramedics. If we get a report as soon as they arrive, we'll know right away whether it's a crime or not. If not, the ambush is still on. What do you think?"

"Yes, a few fake 999s could make us look really foolish if Blasić slips through our fingers. So, we'd better wait."

Five minutes later, Bhardwaj screeched to a halt. Blue peered into the car. "Where's Alison?"

"Oh, she's still at Grace Keltie's, past Kilchoman. We were getting some good stuff from her when your call came. Alison wanted to hear all of Grace's story. I've to collect her later, she said. Grace will keep her well-supplied with tea and pancakes."

They stood uneasily, waiting. Blue had a bad feeling about the way things were going. Sergeant Walker put out cones to protect the skid marks for the SOCOs. Blue had a word with the two witnesses, but they had nothing more to tell him than Moira had already given him. The whole thing had been over in seconds. But they were quite shaken by it. Blue was just suggesting they go and have a cup of tea together, when Nicolson's mobile rang.

"Hello…Yes…OK…Right, you know the drill, Donnie, don't touch anything, I'm on my way."

She looked serious. "It's not a hoax, Angus. It's George. Dead. Shot in the head. Not long ago."

"So it's not just Blasić." said Blue, "there's someone else. Blasić could have gone over to Portnahaven, killed George, then come back, stolen George Kelly's van, run down Enver and then ditched the van. But it's not plausible. There's too much there. An accomplice fits the facts better. Either King himself, or another creature of his."

"Which means that Blasić may not be trudging into Bowmore at all. The accomplice could have killed George, then met Blasić when he'd positioned the van, and driven him off."

"Pity about the ambush," said Bhardwaj. "Sounded a really cool idea."

"But why kill George? Why now?" asked Moira.

"Maybe he'd uncovered something new," said Blue, "or maybe they just weren't sure what he knew, and didn't want to take any chances. Or maybe it's just to scare us, show what they can do."

"Look, Angus, I'll head over to George's. I'll take Deirdra. If necessary I can leave her to guard the crime scene. The paramedics have already called the doc, so I'll talk to her when I get there. She might be able to give us a time of death."

"How did they know George was involved?" asked Blue. "There must be someone here who's talking to them. And, given what happened in Glasgow, we should have someone at the hospital to keep an eye on Enver."

Moira turned to Sergeant Walker. "Bob, can you get back to the station now? Send Blackett, if he's there, that is, over to the hospital. Stay at the station. I'll call you there."

"What about the site here, boss?"

"I think the SOCOs should go straight to Portnahaven now. Can you call them from the station?"

"Sure, boss, no problem."

"And Bob, be careful," warned Blue. "There is a possibility that Blackett may have been got at."

"Yes, sir, I'll take care." Walker set off at a brisk march back into the town.

"We need to think carefully now," said Blue. "They could be anywhere. Could Blackett be working for them? Is he just sending them information, or more actively involved?"

"You're not suggesting Boris could have killed George?"

"I don't know. Look, I'll go and get Alison. I need to know she's safe."

"Meanwhile, we should try to contain them on the island. I'll get Bob to ask Calmac to hold the next boat until we can check the cars and passengers waiting. And the same with the airport."

"Good idea," said Blue. "I don't want to alarm you, but do you have any weapons at the station?"

"Yes, there are two pistols in the firearms safe. It needs Bob and myself to be there to unlock it. I can give you my key. Are you authorised?"

"Yes, I am. Thanks. I'll go to the station first and pick up a weapon. I'll feel happier."

"OK, Angus. Keep in touch." Moira handed over the key. Then she and Craig took the car Bhardwaj had brought in, and headed off towards Bridgend and the road to Portnahaven. Blue and Bhardwaj took the battered but still roadworthy vehicle which had hit the van, and headed for the police station. The car was fine apart from a grinding and scraping noise from somewhere underneath. But this wasn't the time to visit McCall's repair shop.

70

They arrived at the station to find Sergeant Walker unlocking the storm doors. "Curious, chief," he said to Blue, "These doors should be open. Maybe Boris got called away." He opened them, then the inner glass door. The reception desk was unmanned. There was a smell of burning.

"Something's up," said Blue. "Arvind, check downstairs. I'll do upstairs. Bob, can you man the door. Phone the ferry terminal and the airport. Tell them to hold everything till they hear from us."

He dashed up the stairs to his office. The door was ajar – not locked, as he'd left it. Inside he saw at once that someone had been searching the room. Or clearing it out. Any papers which had been lying on any surface were gone, along with all the files from the deep drawer in his desk. And his laptop was missing. The base room was the same, all the paperwork gone, even notepads and jottings on scraps of paper. And the PCs had been zapped, a taser-like device, he guessed. Moira Nicolson's room had been similarly treated. Even though she had no material on the case, they weren't taking any chances.

He almost bumped into Bhardwaj in the downstairs corridor. "Someone's been rummaging about in the work-room, chief," he gasped. "The PC's been got at. Smells like it's been burnt out."

"It's the same upstairs. They've taken the laptops too. What about the back door?"

"Back door's OK, chief. I'll check the windows."

In the foyer, Sergeant Walker reported, "That's the boat and the plane held up, sir."

In minutes Bhardwaj was back. The windows had not been forced.

"OK, so they must have simply walked in the front door," said Blue, "but where was Blackett? Did he let them in and then clear off?"

"No, I can't see that," replied Walker, "Boris is careful. He would pay close attention to anyone coming in the door. He must have known them. He may be odd, but I don't see Boris for a traitor, chief."

"Maybe they showed him some police ID," said Blue.

"You mean King?" asked Bhardwaj.

"What if it was King who killed George, a couple of hours ago?" suggested Blue. "Then he's got plenty of time to come over here. He waits, maybe in a car, till he sees Enver leaving. Then he phones Blasić and sends him after Enver in the stolen van. He waits until the rest of us have gone – he knows it won't take long for news of the attack on Enver to reach here, and it'll draw us out. Then he comes in, shows Blackett his ID, and…"

"Boris might let him in, but he would call me right away," said the sergeant.

"So where is he?" asked Blue, "Anybody got any ideas?"

"Maybe they've abducted him? You know, as a hostage," suggested Bhardwaj.

"I suppose it's possible. So let's say King ties him up. Then he collects all the stuff he thinks is relevant to the case, including the laptops, zaps the PCs, just to be on the safe side, and clears off."

"That must have been happening whilst you and Deirdra were chasing Blasić," said Bhardwaj.

"Hmm. Who's got keys for the storm door? King must have locked that when he left."

"The boss and me, that's all," said Walker. "If anyone else is to open up, they have to borrow one of ours. And sign for it."

"Who's done that recently?"

"Well, only Clara, back in July, I was on holiday, and the Inspector was going to be in late."

"Clara? Wait a minute, Bob. Could Clara, and not Blackett, be King's contact?" Blue was annoyed with himself. He had not weighed all the possibilities equally. He had assumed. "What do you think? It looks like *one* of us is working for them. Feeding them information. Poking about in my office earlier. And now letting King in. If that's how it went."

"Well, I don't know, chief?" said the sergeant thoughtfully, "As I said before, I wouldn't have put Boris down as a traitor. But Clara, I just don't know."

"How long's she been working here?"

"Let's see, must be a couple of years now. She and her husband came here when he retired. That must have been about ten years ago. He was a DI over in Edinburgh. Died three years ago. That's how she got the job, copper's widow in need of support and all that. We've never had any difficulty with her. I mean, she can be a bit abrupt, keeps things to herself, but…"

"What was her husband's name?"

"Terry, no, Jerry, that was it, Jerry Gilmour. He were even more secretive. We reckoned he'd been in Special Branch or anti-terrorist. Never gave anything away." He paused. "Oh, I see what you're getting at. He and Clara could have known DCI King."

"Perhaps she was placed here," suggested Bhardwaj, "You know, as a sleeper. To be activated when needed."

"I don't think anyone anticipated the bodies being discovered," said Blue, "So it's more likely King recruited her after it happened. Perhaps like with WPC Baines in Glasgow, he spun a yarn about national security issues, asked her to help stop the plods messing up a secret operation."

"She did have a pretty poor opinion of us, I must admit," muttered the sergeant, "My wife did hear about some of the things she'd said at the Poetry Group. Mind you, they all think they're a bit superior there. But that's just my opinion, never could get my head round poetry. I mean…"

"Let's bear in mind that Clara could be with them. Now we need to move carefully. We also need to be armed. Are the weapons still here?"

"Yes, sir, no-one's tampered with the firearms safe. No-one else ever gets the keys to that."

"Good. I'll phone Oban, let them know what's going on. Arvind, can you phone Islay hospital and check on Enver. Tell them that he's to have no visitors whatever, until we get there. That includes anyone who turns up claiming to be a doctor, an official of any sort, or a tradesman. Bob, can you check the evidence cupboards?"

Blue went back to his office, and phoned Oban. He got through to the Super right away.

"What's going on down there, Angus? Reception said an emergency."

"Yes, sir. McCader's been run down. Not dead, thankfully, but in the hospital. One of our informants murdered. And the station here broken into, case files and laptops stolen, PCs zapped."

"All right. Give me all the facts now, Angus. Five minutes, fewer if you can."

Blue rapidly outlined what had happened that day.

"Dammit!" muttered the Superintendent. "Those people have gone too far. Who the hell do they think they are?"

"People beyond the law, sir."

"We'll see about that. Nobody takes out my people and gets away with it. I'll send the armed unit over right away in the patrol boat. We'll get them. Including this Gilmour woman if she's with them. I think I met Jerry Gilmour a couple of times. Nasty piece of work, you never got a straight answer from him. Always working to a different agenda. That's the trouble with these guys who don't do proper police work. By the way, have you got any firearms there?"

"Yes, chief."

"Get them out. These people are dangerous. Don't be afraid to shoot if you have to."

As soon as Blue had rung off, his phone rang again. It was Moira. "Looks like George let someone in. Made him a cup of coffee, there are two mugs still on the table. Then at some point the visitor just shot him, straight through the head. Close range, probably a silenced pistol. No sign of ransacking of his house, searching, that sort of thing, but we'll have to wait for a proper examination. We have a witness to the killer leaving the house. A neighbour was washing her front windows and saw a man come out of the house, walk to a car at the bottom of Kirk Lane, and drive off. Medium height, hat, overcoat and scarf. Clean-shaven, wearing glasses, round lenses. Not so young, she thought."

"King! He's doing his dirty work in person now. The car?"

"Silver Mercedes. Or something like it."

Blue told her about the situation at the station.

"Looks like things are escalating," was her comment. "Deirdra and I will secure the site here, then I'll leave her to wait for the SOCOs. They're on the one o'clock boat. I'll tell her to keep the doors locked. Just in case they go back there. Sheena's going to stay here too – that's Dr. Halsetter – so at least there will be two of them. I'll get back to the station."

"What do you think about the possibility that Clara's working with them?"

"Frankly, it wouldn't surprise me. I've had to have words with her a few times about doing things without informing me, or running them past me."

"Moira, can you go to Grace Keltie's on the way and wait there for me – I'm coming out to collect Alison."

"I could bring her in myself. Though I think you may be there first. I'm not sure how long it'll take me to get away from here."

"I think we should bring Grace in too. If they know we've got something from her, she may not be safe at home. I'll see you at Grace's."

He met PC Bhardwaj in the downstairs corridor. "Enver's out of immediate danger, sir, but needs to be moved to Glasgow. Helicopter's on its way."

Sergeant Walker called them into the workroom. "Evidence cupboards stripped. Everything."

Blue sent Bhardwaj out to see if he could find anyone in the other buildings on the street who'd seen anything suspicious earlier. Then he and Sergeant Walker opened the firearms safe in the workroom, took out the two automatic pistols and boxes of ammunition, and filled out the Weapon Access Form for each gun.

"What do we do now, chief?" asked the sergeant.

"As soon as Arvind's back, keep him here till you hear from the armed unit. I'm going to the hospital, then to collect Alison, then we'll come back here."

There was a heavy thud from the foyer. Someone had slammed the storm door shut. Blue released the safety catch on his automatic and eased himself into the corridor, Sergeant Walker behind him. He tiptoed up the corridor, readied his gun and burst into the foyer. "Freeze!!"

PC Blackett was standing motionless. He was soaking wet, water running off him, forming little pools on the floor. Then Blue realised he was weeping.

"They pushed her into the harbour, right under the water, she had no chance. No chance."

"Oh God, what's happened, Boris?" said Bob Walker.

"Who's in the water?" demanded Blue "Quickly!"

"Tatiana. I got a call saying she was in trouble, and I had to go right away. And found her there."

"Who's Tatiana?" urged Blue. "We can still get there."

"It's his car, sir," said the sergeant quietly. "His yellow Lada."

"The only one," wailed Blackett.

This is crazy, thought Blue. But before he could do anything Sergeant Walker put his arm round the weeping Blackett. "Don't you worry, Boris, we'll get her out again. She'll be right as rain again, you'll see. Just as soon as we've sorted these villains out."

71

Blue took the unbattered car and drove the few hundred yards to the cottage hospital. The doors were locked, and he had to ring, and then be scrutinised by a nurse through the glass pane in the door. McCader was lying strapped onto a trolley, blocks of polystyrene on either side of his head. He was well-bandaged, especially around the chest and shoulders, and one arm was in plaster. He was conscious, but heavily sedated. He managed to raise his good arm from the elbow. "Sorry, chief, wasn't looking."

Blue squeezed his hand. "Glad you're alive, Enver. Stay that way." He asked the duty sister how he was.

"We've done as much as we can here. We had to truss him up like this, in case his neck or spine are fractured. We've X-rayed them and can't see anything, but he'll need a scan, in Glasgow. Dr Halsetter is over at Portnahaven right now, but Dr Gibson's on call in case he's needed. No-one's tried to get in to visit him. The helicopter should be here any minute."

That reminded Blue of something. He called Glasgow and spoke to Inspector Taylor, who readily agreed to place McCader in the secure ward at the Southern General. "And this time it will be secure, you have my word on that, Angus."

Two minutes later he heard the heavy drone of the engines as the helicopter landed behind the hospital. Soon afterwards a couple of paramedics arrived. Blue scrutinised their IDs before allowing them to go in. Once the men had wheeled the sergeant out towards the helicopter, and the noise of its ascent filled the air, Blue felt more relaxed. He set off for Kilchoman. It was still sunny, though not warm. Autumnal.

Twenty minutes later, having turned off the main road onto a single track road, and finally onto a passable track between hedged fields, he pulled up outside a small cottage on a hillside. The track went on up to a substantial farm complex. The door was opened by Grace Keltie, a small and lively-looking woman in her early eighties, slightly bent by age, and with her grey hair in tight curls. "Come in, come in, Mr Blue, you're just in time for some tea." She led Blue into her living-room-cum-kitchen, where Alison was sitting in an armchair by an electric heater, holding a cup of tea. A small table contained a plate of pancakes with butter and dark jam.

Blue explained to Grace that she would have to come to the police station, as she might be in danger.

"I wouldn't want to put you to any bother," she said. "I'll just stay here, if you don't mind."

"We don't want to lose you," said Alison. "They've already killed George Outhwaite. Anyone we've talked to could be in danger."

"Do they want to shut me up? Is that it? Just like all those years ago. All right, I'll come along. I don't want to see them win again."

"Did they win last time?" asked Blue.

"Yes. They took away poor Murdo, and we never saw him again. Never knew what happened to him. When he didn't come back we suspected they'd done away with him. But what could we do? Just asking questions was enough to put you behind bars then."

"Grace has a very interesting story to tell," said Alison. "Actually, I think her whole life is an interesting story. You should write your autobiography, Grace!"

"Hah! If I did that, they'd be suing me till the day I die."

"But Grace, when you die, all your stories die with you."

"Well, we'll see. I have an awful lot to do. The geese will be coming soon, and I keep a watch on them. They need the numbers, you see, to work out the compensation for the farmers. Won't you have some tea, Mr Blue. I've made pancakes too. And…"

"No thanks, Grace, we really should go, soon as Inspector Nicolson gets here."

Alison interrupted. "Angus, you've got to hear Grace's story first."

"Did you record it? We could play it at the station…"

"No! I mean, yes, I did record it. But you should hear it now."

The old lady settled herself in her armchair and began. "Though I come from Islay, my family were living in Greenock when the war started. My father was a radio engineer, putting new systems into warships. After the attack on Clydebank – that was in March 1941 – my parents thought Greenock might be next, so I was sent to stay with an aunt of my father, Isa Shaw – Isa's short for Isabel – who lived in Port Ellen, in one of the houses on the front. I was only six then. My brothers went to another relative, on Lismore.

"The house was wee, there was just the one bedroom up the stairs, but that was kept for visitors. Great-aunt Isa – I just called her Aunt Isa then – slept in the bed recess in the kitchen, and I had the recess in the living room. So I suppose we had a spare room. The next thing is that she was told – this was maybe in 1942 or maybe 1943 – that she'd have to have someone billeted on her, a Flight-Lieutenant Murdo McLeod. You'll know that Murdo McLeod is a name like John Smith in the Western Isles. He was from Lewis, and he and Aunt Isa could talk to each other in Gaelic. That was a great comfort to her, it made her feel he wasn't so much of a stranger. I'd learnt a bit of the Gaelic too, from my parents, and that helped me fit in. In those days there were plenty of Ileachs who spoke it.

"Murdo was very nice, polite and always helpful, if there was coal to bring in or peats to cut, and he was able to get us little extras, like one day he brought us a tin of strawberry jam. Well, Aunt Isa had never seen jam in a tin – she always made her own – and she didn't have a tin-opener, she had to borrow one from one of the neighbours. He was married too, not long before he came to us. His wife was called Rowena Sinclair – he showed us a picture – a lovely-looking girl. They'd got engaged before the war, planned to wait till it was over, but when it began to look as if might be a while, they decided to get married sooner. So, if anything happened to Murdo, they'd have been husband and wife, even for a little while."

"So when did Murdo disappear?" Alison prompted.

"Oh, now that would have been in late November I think. 1944. It wasn't long after my tenth birthday, and that was on the first of November. We had a lovely celebration." Grace stopped and sniffed. Even good memories can bring sadness. "I'm sorry. Oh dear, talking like this brings those times back so vividly. The smell of the peats in the kitchen range, and the taste of the cake that Aunt Isa baked for me, with a little bit of icing on it, and strawberry jam between the layers. I even had a candle – one little bit cut from a bigger one. We needed the candles then, there was no electricity in the house. Yes, it was two or three weeks after that.

"We were sat round the kitchen table one evening, playing cards. We usually played whist, although Aunt Isa was trying to teach me canasta, but she said we needed four people to play it best. It was quite late, past my usual bedtime, and Aunt Isa and Murdo had a cup of tea on the table too. It was cold and dark outside, but nice and warm in the kitchen – that was the only room in the house that was warm, from the range, so we stayed in there as much as possible. And took hot water bottles to bed.

"All at once there was this loud banging on the door. That wasn't unusual – they were very strict about the blackout, with the base, you know, there were patrols every night. So Aunt Isa assumed that's what it was, and went to the door. As soon as she opened it, these two men just marched into the room. I didn't like the look of them. One had gingery hair and a little moustache, a bit like Hitler's, looked like a wide boy from the markets. The other was bigger, more like a bouncer. The first one called him Les. I've no idea what the ginger one was called, but he seemed to be in charge.

"He said, 'Flight Lieutenant McLodd' – that's how he pronounced it. Murdo says, 'Yes, that's me' and the ginger man saluted him in a careless sort of way, 'special order from Colonel Dawkins, sir, you're to come with us.' Murdo said, 'I'm in the Air Force. I don't know any Colonel Dawkins. What would it be about?' The ginger man gave him a piece of paper. 'Not for me to say, sir. Maybe a special operation.' Murdo looked at the paper. 'I'm still not sure what it's about, but I better go,' he said. 'You'll need to bring your things,' said the ginger man. 'Might not be back for a while. We'll give you five minutes.'

"So Murdo went upstairs. 'We'll just take a look around,' this was the ginger man. 'Les, you check the other room.' The bigger man went out and into the living room – it was at the other side of the little hallway. We could hear him opening and shutting the cupboards. The ginger man did the same in the kitchen, just snooping into everything. Aunt Isa asked him what they were doing. 'Just normal security precautions,' he said. The other man came back with a tin of corned beef, that was in the sideboard in the living room, and asked Aunt Isa where she got it. 'At the shop. In Bowmore. We're saving it for Christmas,' she said. 'We'll have to take this,' said the ginger man. 'Suspicion of black market trading. You could go to prison for that, Grandma.' I didn't like the way he grinned at her. Well, I thought that was very unfair, and said so to Isa, in Gaelic of course. She told me to stay completely quiet, say nothing at all.

"Then Murdo came down, with his kitbag. 'I'm ready,' he said to them. 'I'll just say goodbye to my aunt, and my niece.' I thought that was odd, as we weren't related to him at all. He came over and gave Aunt Isa a big hug. He gave me a hug too, lifted me right up into the air, and whilst he was doing that he whispered in my ear, in Gaelic. He said, 'Tell Isa to hide my book. It's under the bedroom floor.' That was all. 'Hey!' shouted the ginger man, 'None of that Irish stuff. Bloody Irish is jerry-lovers, all of 'em.' Murdo ignored him, and said to Isa, in English this time, 'Write to Rowena, that I've gone, in case I don't get a chance for a while.' And he went away with them."

"I'm pretty sure that makes our last man Murdo McLeod," said Alison quietly.

"And that would be Tony and Les in action," said Blue.

"There's a little bit more," said Alison. "Grace, did you see Murdo again?"

"No, he never came back. But those two men came back the next night, about the same time. Barged in again, said they had to search the house. 'For evidence of black market dealings,' they said. They went up to the bedroom first, where Murdo had slept, and spent quite a while there. We could hear them clomping about, and even shifting the bed and lifting the loose floorboards, of which there were one or two. Then they came down and rummaged through the rest of the house. They made such a mess. This time they took some leeks one of the farmers had given Isa, and a pair of silver cuff-links that had belonged to her husband, as 'evidence'. Then the ginger man questioned Aunt Isa. He wanted to know if our guest kept a diary. She said she didn't know about any diary.

"Then he turned to me. But Isa had told me while they were upstairs, 'You only speak the Gaelic, remember that.' I took the hint right away. So when the man asked me, 'Did the man upstairs keep a little book somewhere?' I just looked at him and said, *'Chan'eil fhios agam.'* That means 'I don't know'. And Aunt Isa said, 'She only speaks the Gaelic. She's not had a chance to start at the English school yet. The war.' 'Bloody gibberish,' said the ginger man, 'soon as this war's over and we can knock that nonsense out of the kids here, the better. It's like being in a foreign place, ain't it, Les?' The other just grunted. Then they went."

"And was there a diary?" asked Alison.

"Oh yes. It was under a loose floorboard in the bedroom, just as Murdo had said. As soon as we'd heard them drive away with Murdo the previous night – they'd come in a noisy Jeep – Isa led me up to the bedroom and we looked for it. And found it soon enough. Isa hid it again, wrapped in a piece of oilcloth, in the roof of the outside toilet. So it was gone by the time the men looked under the floorboards the next day. Nobody came back after that, so one day – it would be February or March of 1945 – Aunt Isa got it down again and we had a look at it. But it wasn't very detailed, just jottings here and there. 'Got married…mother's birthday…Sent to Islay.' That sort of thing, in Gaelic, of course. We didn't look beyond the first few pages."

"What did Isa do with the diary?" asked Blue.

"After the war ended, she posted it to Rowena in Lewis. But a fortnight later it came back with 'Addressee unknown' on the envelope.

Later the same year, she got a postcard from Rowena, saying she'd been told Murdo had been killed on a secret mission behind enemy lines. He'd even been awarded a posthumous DFC. She thanked Isa for the hospitality she'd shown him. There was no address, the postmark was Inverness. But it was a lie, wasn't it? He never went on a mission at all, did he? I know what you're investigating, those bodies found in the peat. Murdo's one of them, isn't he?"

"That could be the case," said Blue.

"They just took him away and killed him, didn't they? And then lied to his wife. Gave her a medal to cover up what they'd done. It makes you sick, doesn't it?"

"What happened to the diary, Grace?" asked Alison.

"Och, I'll still have it somewhere. I got most of Isa's things when she died. Probably up in the loft. I've been meaning for the last twenty years to read through it."

"Could we take a look at it?" asked Blue. "Just in case there's something in it that might help us."

"If you don't mind clambering up there. There's a folding ladder that comes down. I think it'll probably be in a brown suitcase by the cold water tank."

Ten minutes and a few sneezes later the suitcase was recovered. In amongst the old newspapers, postcards and knitting patterns was the brown envelope with 'Returned Post. Addressee unknown' stamped in red on the front. Blue put it in his pocket.

72

He must have dozed for an hour or two. He woke again when the door was flung open. "Right oh, matey, get your clothes off and these ones on. Any tricks, Mr Batty's back." He'd got very stiff, and it was hard to get out of his clothes and into the fresh ones. Then he limped into the dim light in the corridor and as he emerged, the man hit him again with the bat, a vicious blow right on the elbow which sent daggers of pain down to his hand and up to his shoulder. He turned to face the gaoler and got another blow on the side of the head that left him dazed, but still on his feet. He fought to clear his head, and felt his arms being grabbed and roped behind him by the bigger man, the one called Les. "Don't give us any trouble, mate," the man said. "It just annoys Tony and he'll hit you again with that bat. I'm going to gag you now, so's you don't try to call out." The man used a strip of coarse cloth to gag him.

It was only now he saw the others. One by one, they were dragged out of their cells, bound and gagged. He recognised them all: Dafydd and his friends Peter and Terry, and his fellow pilot Arthur Walforth. Now he knew why they were here, why they would never be released. He guessed they were now going to be taken to some place far from Islay, where they could be safely forgotten, left to rot until no-one knew or cared about the events of the previous day. The mysterious visitors whose plane he and Arthur had rendezvoused with over Tain, on the North East coast beyond Inverness, and escorted on a carefully planned course to Islay which avoided any town or city, flying through a corridor of darkness right across the country.

Then he saw the Russian, standing just inside the door to the building, behind the guard's chair, his back against the wall, his pale skin, sandy hair and long overcoat almost blending into it. Now he knew their fate was not to be forgotten, but to be extinguished. He knew the man, had heard him talking in the officers' mess.

"I admire the German soldier," he had said, to disapproving frowns. "He is brave and loyal. Even in a bad spot, he fights on; though he knows he is doomed, he fights on. Our Russian soldiers, bah, they are just peasants, they think only of their cow and their fat wife back home. If we're winning, they're good. They can kill and rape, torture and burn, create terror among the civilian population, so that the morale of their menfolk at the front is undermined. But if the army is losing, they are no use, they simply throw down their weapons and run away, back to the cow and the wife. Then they hide in the barn or in the forest until we stop looking for them. But an army that retreats must fight too, must not simply collapse. This is where my unit comes in, the Loyalty Detachment we call it. We *are behind the rear of our army, and our job is to kill any man who tries to run away. We have snipers, machine guns, flame-throwers. Sometimes we must eliminate entire units. Our peasants know for certain that if they run, they die. Their officers know too that if they allow their men to turn around, they too will die, as will their wives, their parents, their children. Their families will be utterly extinguished. To win a war it's often necessary to kill some of your own men, to ensure that the others will obey their orders. War has no time for humanity."*

73

Blue went over to the sink to wash his hands. Looking out the window as he did so, he could see the track and beyond the hedge a brown field, where stubble had been ploughed in. A couple of crows were wandering about near the centre, prodding the earth at random spots.

Something caught his eye. A brief reflection, less than a second. Behind the hedge further down the track. There was a vague shape. Nothing clear, but he knew it was Blasić. He didn't see King as the type to creep along behind hedges – he would knock on the door, have a cup of coffee, and then shoot you. Was Blasić just watching, or preparing to be more proactive?

He heard, then saw another car coming along the minor road, a police car. Moira Nicolson! If it were Blasić there, he could pick her off easily once she came up the track. She needed to be warned. Would she pick up her mobile if it rang – probably not, if she were driving. He grabbed a dishtowel from the kitchen, tied it round a long wooden spoon, and went to the front door. He opened it a little, then dashed out, ducking behind the police car parked in front of the door, and waved the makeshift flag furiously. He kept well down. Suddenly, with a crunching percussion, the car window over his head shattered outwards, showering him with glass fragments.

He remembered the gun he was carrying, and extracted it with some difficulty from the shoulder holster. There was not much to shoot at, but he was still not clear if Moira had got the message. So he crawled to the end of the car and fired a couple of shots at the spot where he had seen the reflection earlier. In response, another shot hit the car, near the headlight, the bullet disappearing into the bonnet. The next shot smashed through the kitchen window. Blue hoped that Alison had persuaded Grace to get down on the floor.

The next moment there was a scrunching of gravel and a police car swerved into sight coming off the track onto the space in front of the house and skidded to a halt, crunching its front bumper into Blue's rear bumper. Blue crawled across till he was level with the front passenger door of the other car and, still on all fours, flung it open. Moira Nicolson was lying on the seat, blood pooling on the seat from a head wound. The driver's window was shattered. "Hi, Angus," she gasped. "Ouch, that hurt!" Then she passed out. Blue grabbed her and pulled her out across the seats and onto the ground.

Where was Blasić? Blue scanned the hedge but could see nothing.

Suddenly the cottage door opened and a figure appeared in a coat and hat. Three shots rang out immediately in rapid succession. The head exploded and the hat flew off. But Blue had seen where the shots came from. He stood up and fired a volley of shots at the shadow he could see through the hedge almost across the road. He thought he could hear a brief cry, but he was not so rash as to run out on the attack, only to find Blasić was still active. He ducked down again and waited. No further shots came.

Now he dragged Moira towards the front door, staying as low as possible. Alison crawled out and helped drag her into the cottage. Grace was waiting inside. "You're both OK?" he gasped.

"Of course we are," answered Grace. "But that turnip stuck on my broom handle took a couple of direct hits, and my old hat is now, well, I would say, old hat. Let's have a look at her. Come on, I was a nurse for over forty years. Mr Blue, off you go, you can stay on guard. We'll get her nearer the back in case there's more trouble." Grace and Alison dragged Moira over to the other end of the room, leaving a trail of fresh blood on the carpet, and Grace bent over her.

Blue was back at the broken front window, peering out across the farm track to the hedge opposite. There was nothing moving. But any moment he expected Blasić to burst in the front door. Or the back. "The back door!" he shouted.

"It's fine," answered Alison, "Solid, and well bolted. He won't get in there."

Back at the window, Blue noticed a movement further up the track, and a flash of yellow. A digger was driving slowly down the farm track. Two men could be seen inside, one driving, the other crouching behind him, with a weapon. This was about to get nastier. "Look out, more of them coming, keep your heads down," he shouted in the direction of the other end of the room.

Grace came over, bent low, and peered out beside him, presenting, he thought, a perfect target. "Och, no need to worry," she said. "That's Tommy Darnwell and his son. The cavalry's coming!"

The digger turned into towards the parked police cars and shuddered to a halt. The toughened glass doors opened and two men got down, both carrying shotguns. The older knocked on the cottage door and then let himself in whilst the younger man scrutinised the hedge opposite, sweeping his gun slowly along it.

"Hi, Tommy, how are you doing?" called Grace.

"Better than you folks," came the reply. "We heard some shots, saw you were having a spot of trouble. Anything we can do to help?"

"I think there's only one of them. But he's dangerous. Armed with at least a pistol," said Blue.

"He may have run for it. The hedge looked clear."

At that moment there was a loud bang from beyond the front door. Tommy threw open the door and dashed out, Blue right behind him.

"What's doing, Jamie?" said Tommy.

Jamie Darnwell nodded to Blue. "Saw him go across the field. He was limping, but making a good pace. Reckon I may have nipped him with a few pellets, but it'll keep him moving." He pointed over the field. "Must have made the gate by now."

"Come on, then," said Blue, "we need to catch him. Get in the car."

He got into the driver's seat of the car which he had come in, and Tommy and Jamie jumped into the back. He reversed slowly, shunting Inspector Nicolson's car back until it hit a clothes pole, then manoeuvred past the digger and raced off down the track. At the bottom, he turned left onto the single track road towards the corner of the field where he guessed the gate was. Sure enough, they could see Blasić desperately running along the road, hampered by a limp. He heard them coming up and turned, training an automatic on the car.

Blue put his foot down. "Get your heads down," he shouted to the others, and ducked down himself. Two shots crashed through the windscreen, then there was a thump, and he slammed the brakes on as the car slewed to the right, then skidded for a few moments before the front driver's side wheel dropped off the road into a ditch and the vehicle ground to a halt.

They all clambered out, the Darnwells brandishing their shotguns. Blasić lay on his back motionless in the left hand ditch. Blue checked his pulse. He was alive, but it wasn't obvious how much damage he'd sustained. What he could see, was a gunshot wound just above the belt of his trousers, on the left side. He didn't want to move him in case there was spinal damage. He took out his phone. No signal! "Have either of you a mobile?" he asked, and two phones immediately appeared, both of the latest, smartest type. "Can you call the police station and let them know what's happened? Tell them there are two injured people, one here and one at the cottage."

"Some driving, Mr Blue," said Tommy. "I'll do the phoning. Jamie, you nip back and bring the digger, and we'll get this car out of the ditch."

Two minutes later Alison arrived from the cottage in the other police car. She saw Blasić's inert form. "Is he dead?" she asked.

"No," replied Blue. "How's Moira?"

"Oh, not so bad. According to Grace, the bullet glanced off her skull, so there's a lot of blood but hopefully no real damage. She's bandaged her up and called an ambulance, and the police."

"Good. Though I don't know if we've got any police to spare at the moment."

"How are you, Angus?"

"Fine. Just a little glass in my hair." Blue ran his hand through his hair and brought it back bloodied. "Oops! I think I'm bleeding somewhere." He pulled out a handkerchief and dabbed it vaguely on his head.

"Give it me, and bend your head over," said Alison gently, and took the handkerchief. She dabbed it herself where she could clearly see the bleeding. "You'll need that cleaned at the hospital. We were watching from the cottage. That was very dramatic."

"Yes, had to be done," said Blue, trying to stay in charge of the situation. "Anyway, can you get back to the cottage, wait there for the ambulance for Moira, then take Grace in the car to her niece? I'll go with Blasić and Moira to the hospital. I'll see you later. Take care."

74

The ambulance collected Blasić, then picked up Moira at the cottage. She was conscious again, but still groggy. She recognised Blue from her stretcher, and gave him a smile. At the hospital, and whilst the other two were wheeled to the ward, Blue's head was treated. The wounds were washed and dabbed with iodine, which caused him more pain than anything else. "Come on, you wee softie," said the nurse. "Stop wincing. You're like a bad actor."

Alison was waiting for him, drinking coffee from the machine. She had dropped Grace already at her niece's, and offered to drive him to the police station.

"Thanks, Alison, that would be great, if you don't mind waiting a bit. I need to see how Blasić is and get somebody round from the station to keep an eye on him."

"No problem. Can I get you some coffee? My treat!" She smiled.

The sister soon appeared. "Ah yes, Mr Blaasitch. He's not going to die just yet, but he's sustained a lot of injuries. Gunshot wound in the lower abdomen, broken shoulder and collarbone, collapsed lung, bruising to skull and ribs, several shotgun pellets in the back. Enough to be going on with, I'd say. He'll have to go to Glasgow when the helicopter arrives. Second time today. And Moira, she's not doing so badly. Bullet just grazed her skull, nothing fractured by the look of it. But we'll have to keep her under observation for a while. Maybe she'll get a brain scan in Glasgow, just to be on the safe side. She's a tough lady. And I hope you don't mind, Mr. Blue, but I called Alasdair to let him know she's here and OK."

Blue thanked her and went back to where Alison was sitting in the foyer. "I'll wait here until Blasić is picked up. I daren't risk someone turning up to silence him. Then we can go to the station."

Half an hour later Blasić was on his way to the Southern General, where Taylor's people would escort him to the secure ward. Blue and Alison were back at the station. Soon PC Craig arrived, having got a lift back with Dr Halsetter. By now it was after five. Sandwiches had been got and Blue called a meeting of Islay's surviving police force: Sergeant Walker, and PCs Craig and Bhardwaj, along with Alison. Blackett was there too, but too distraught to take part in the meeting. He'd also taken a heavy dose of whisky to calm down.

Blue reviewed events. It seemed King had either gone to ground or was already off the island.

"Could he have gone to Clara's house?" asked Alison.

"Anyone know where she lives?" said Blue.

"Yes," said Sergeant Walker. "Out beyond Port Ellen, just past Lagavulin. Big house, there's just her in it now."

"So it's near the coast?"

"Yes, that's right, chief. You go past the distillery about 200 yards, there's a gap in the wall on the right and there's a track runs down to the house. It was built for the distillery manager about a hundred years ago. It's on a sort of bluff, opposite Dunyvaig Castle."

"Could a boat get in there?"

"I would think so, if they knew the waters, that is. Could King be there?"

"It's possible," concluded Blue. "He won't have heard from Blasić, and may conclude that he's either dead or wounded, or we've got him. Either way, he's no more use to King. He may have other people, but we've not seen any sign of them."

"Could he call in more of them?" asked Alison.

"It's possible, but he'll realise we'd have sent for reinforcements as soon as McCader was attacked. His window of opportunity has passed. Now he may just lie low till he can get away."

"His best chance is to wait somewhere near the coast," suggested Bhardwaj, "then get picked up by a small boat after dark."

"Clara's place would be just right for that," said Sergeant Walker. "Out of the way."

"Couldn't they send a helicopter for him?" asked Craig.

"Too visible during the day, too noisy at night," put in Blue. "And he'd have to get to a suitable spot to meet it. If he'd done that this afternoon, he'd have got clean away, we were so overstretched. But I guess then he still thought they could do us a lot of damage. Now he's lost Blasić, things are not so good. Bob, any word on when the extra men'll get here?" He glanced at his watch. Ten past five.

"Should be at the pier here around half past, chief."

"Good. Then we can move on King. If we can get to Clara's and if he is holed up there…"

"What'll happen if he does get away?" asked Alison.

"We've got both Blasić and Vrasko, with a bit of luck at least one of them will talk. Hopefully incriminate King. If we can put him on trial, justice will be done, and seen to be done. On the other hand, if he can get out this evening, we've lost him for good. He'll be hidden somewhere 'for security reasons' and we'd never get him. His bosses will manufacture an alibi proving he wasn't even here, and any evidence we have would be challenged by the best lawyers and 'experts' our taxes can buy. By the way Arvind, did we get any witnesses to the break-in here?"

"Yes, chief." Bhardwaj consulted his notebook. "Two figures seen fiddling with the front door and then going in. A number of flashes were noticed."

"That must have been after Boris was enticed away with the call about Tatiana," observed Walker, "go on Arvind."

"About twenty minutes later, the two figures came out and went down the lane alongside the station, presumably to a car. One witness gave a positive identification of Clara Gilmour. The other was muffled, wearing an overcoat, scarf around the face, and flat cap pulled low over the eyes. But it does sound like King."

"Good work," said Blue. "By the way, I think we've got our final name. But the secret that King and his creatures are trying to protect is still eluding us. Once we've dealt with the present threat we'll get back to that. Don't forget, it's that secret that's driving all this."

75

The tension was palpable, as the dusk settled like fog round the building. But they felt things were moving their way. Blackett began to pull himself together and accepted a cup of coffee, laced with more whisky. The others watched the clock, and when the phone rang they all jumped. Bhardwaj sprang up to answer it. "They're at the pier, chief. Want us to meet them with transport."

There were two battered police cars at the station, so Blue and Bhardwaj drove them down to the pier. They could see in the gloom a police launch tied up at the quay, black shapes climbing out onto the pier. Blue went down to greet them. A tall figure came forward. "Ah, Blue, good to see you. Sounds like you're having a hard time of it."

"Yes, sir, glad you're here. I didn't think you'd come in person."

"Don't worry, Angus, this is your case," said Superintendent Campbell. "I'm only here to observe and assist. Good work on catching Blasić. Is King still around?"

"I think so. He may be holed up at Clara Gilmour's house. By Lagavulin Bay. He could have arranged for a boat to pick him up there. Or he might be anywhere else."

"If there's a lead, follow it!" said Campbell, "If they've a boat, we'll send ours round too."

"How many men have you got?" asked Blue.

"Eight, plus me. All armed. Have you got transport?"

"It'll be a squeeze."

"I'll take a couple of them in the boat," said Campbell. He signalled to two of the men, and they headed back to the boat. "See you at Lagavulin," shouted Campbell as he also made for the boat.

As he got to the car, Blue could hear the boat's engines revving up. The rest of the men, plus Blue, and Bhardwaj, were crushed tightly into the two cars. Blue insisted that the guns be put in the boot. He didn't want one going off by accident.

He had a hard job keeping up with Bhardwaj as he raced along the straight towards Port Ellen. They found the gap in the wall after Lagavulin village, and drove down the rough track. There was still a glow of red in the west and they could see the dark bulk of the house on the bluff ahead of them. There was a gravel parking area by the wall round the garden, and the silver Mercedes was parked there. A gate in the wall led to a door at the side of the house. A light was on in a downstairs room. Further to the right, the ruinous hump of Dunyvaig Castle stood on an isolated rock, across a low grassy area which ran down to the shore of Lagavulin Bay. The long, low white rectangular facade of the distillery glowed dully across the base of the bay, the huge black letters still just visible.

Radios were checked, and Blue discussed the situation with the armed squad commander, a sergeant. The commander nodded, and his men, clad in black, with black helmets and bulletproof vests, crept through the gate and gathered on either side of the house door. The squad commander rapped on the door, and called out, "Police, open up!"

No response. The commander looked at Blue, standing further back, who nodded. Two men ran forward wielding a steel battering ram and smashed at the door, which shuddered and creaked but refused to open. The men swung back the ram, and then brought it swinging forward again, aimed directly at the handle. This time, with a splintering crash, the door burst open, and the other men rushed into the house, one of them shouting, "Armed police. Surrender at once!"

After a few minutes the commander reappeared at the door, flicking on his radio. "Body of middle-aged female in downstairs room. Shot in the head. Otherwise the place is empty." As the men filed out of the building, Blue considered their next move. The parked car suggested King was not far off. He could still be hiding in the house or have fled into the surrounding darkness. "OK," he radioed back. "Send half the team in again to search the house thoroughly." The commander gave rapid instructions and three of the men went back into the house.

There was a low moon now, and in its ghostly light Blue scanned the area below him, from the distillery to the castle, and then up to the house. The castle marked the start of a series of rocky outcrops fringing the coast as jagged skerries. The only safe passage he could see was beyond it, where a boat could come into the bay quite easily. There was a silver sheen on the dark water, in which dark holes seemed to open and close as the deep water moved and rippled. He half expected something large and glistening dark to emerge from the water. Something primeval.

Bhardwaj materialised at his side. "Where do you think he is, chief?"

"Could he have got further round the bay? What about the distillery pier? They could pick him up there."

"Unlikely. He could certainly have picked his way round on the shore. But that would be too easy to spot, and a police car would just need to drive round to the distillery to pick him up."

"Anything further round the bay?"

Bhardwaj thought for a moment. "There's a small jetty right across the bay. I suppose he could also make his way round there on the rocks. But that would take a while, and again, one of our cars could get there in no time. If he wants to lie low till his boat appears, a good pickup spot would be the shore this side of the castle. He could hide in the ruins till he sees the boat, then get down to the shore as fast as he can, and hope we don't spot him."

"Thanks, Arvind. OK, we'll go with that."

He called over the squad commander. He didn't want to panic King by having a troop of armed men march towards him. If King was well positioned in the castle, the thing could end in a bloodbath. So his plan was hatched. The men at the house would make plenty of noise, hopefully enough to make King think they were all there, taking the place to pieces. Then three of them, plus Blue, who was now struggling into his Kevlar breastplate, would move as stealthily as possible towards the castle, hoping that in the darkness their approach would not be spotted.

Unfortunately the moon was not their friend on this occasion, and neither were the policemen trained to move unseen like commandos. After all, their main function was just the opposite, to be highly visible. Soon a shot rang out from the castle, and one of the men screamed, hit in the arm by a bullet which had glanced off his breastplate. Now at least they knew for sure where King was. Time for another plan.

This time Blue asked the armed squad to keep up a sporadic fire on the castle, to keep King pinned down. Then he and Bhardwaj would creep by a roundabout route to the shingle beach where Bhardwaj reckoned the boat would come in. The shooting began, and they set off. Blue noticed soon that King was not replying to the shots fired at the castle. Where was he?

He and Bhardwaj worked their way across the boggy land towards the shore, giving the castle a wide berth. At the shore they found a mixture of rock and mud, with the occasional tussock, and various bits of seaborne debris. A small wellington boot and a rubber glove, caught up in the ruins of a pallet. An empty whisky bottle. A black woollen hat. A dead seagull. From here at the edge, the water looked oily and viscous, merging into the mud, moving sometimes among the rocks like a dark living tongue. He was assaulted by an inexplicable sense of unnamed things moving about in the darkness. What was that film where the dead sailors came back, bowed by the weight of water that had held them for so long. Concentrate!

They made their way along the shore towards the castle. The sporadic shooting continued, but now Blue could hear another noise, the whine of the engine powering a fast inflatable boat. They were coming in to collect King. He must have signalled from the other side of the castle, unobserved by the police, and the boat was coming at speed, to snatch him quickly from the shingle beach.

As they came to the shelter of a ruined wall, beyond which was the shingle, Blue caught sight of King. He was making his way carefully down from the upper part of the castle, and would soon be on the beach.

Bhardwaj nudged him. "The Bad Step," he whispered.

"What do you mean?"

"It's what the locals call it, sir. To get out of the castle, you have to step across a gap that's right above the beach. It's the only way down. It's easy to get up because the step is angled to the left, towards a safe footfall. But the other way, it needs an awkward step round a boulder over empty space, and the footfall isn't easily visible. He may not know it."

Which is quite possible, thought Blue. Nevertheless, even if he knew it, it would not be easy.

They could see King hesitate now, and feel his way round the boulder, using both hands to try to get some grip on the smooth surface. Then he swung himself out and round, and slipped. He crashed down onto the shingle. He groaned and tried to get up, but one of his legs would not respond. Blue could see from the weird angle that it was broken.

"Now's our chance to take him," he whispered to Bhardwaj.

Bhardwaj grabbed his arm, and pointed to the water. The inflatable was now clearly visible, heading for the beach, the steersman a black shape in the centre, flanked by two other men, whom Blue assumed were armed. They would need to act quickly.

King was dragging himself down the shingle towards the water's edge. Blue stepped out from behind the wall, his pistol extended: "Stop right there! Armed police. Hands up!"

King turned painfully and peered at him. "You're causing a lot of trouble, Mr Blue, a great deal of trouble," he said quietly, and winced as he tried to pull himself forward.

"Was it the meeting you were trying to cover up? Back in 1944?" asked Blue.

King frowned. He didn't know how much Blue knew. Or how little. "You little people are always trying to disrupt the flow of history. You don't realise, Blue, it's the job of rulers to make history. And to shape the way people see it. So they can play their part."

"Dying in the trenches, fighting illegal wars, toiling for absentee landowners, working for a pittance in factories whilst employers enjoy the high life and avoid paying taxes. Is that their part?"

"That kind of history has no value. It doesn't inspire people. It's not history, it's just invective."

"It's what makes us what we are. It gives meaning to words like right and wrong, good and evil, justice and injustice."

"Quite the philosopher, eh? Well, time for me to go now. You see, Blue, History is what *we* make it. Us, not you."

Blue felt himself grabbed by the arm and wrenched backwards down behind the wall, just as a volley of shots rang out and bullets ricocheted off its upper stones.

"You forgot about the boat, chief," whispered Bhardwaj. They could see the vessel easily now; its engine had powered down and it was moving into the shore slowly. King had dragged himself into the shallow water towards it, a trail of blood on the shingle.

"Don't move, we are armed!" shouted Blue, but this only drew another volley of shots in his direction, making him duck down again,

"We can't let them get away so easily," whispered Bhardwaj. He had a large rock in one hand, and with a practised swing flung it straight at the dark shape of the steersman. There was a crack and a loud cry, then a clatter as the man fell into the bottom of the boat. Another volley of shots followed, but Bhardwaj was behind the wall again.

Then they could hear another noise, the deep pulsating drone of the police launch's twin diesel engines. Now the beam of a powerful searchlight panned into the bay from beyond. The inflatable had come to a halt, as another of the men took the helm, then began to turn it away.

"I'm just here," shouted King. "Come closer. Your orders are to get me out!" As the boat continued its swing away from the shore two shots rang out in quick succession. King's body shuddered convulsively, and the back of his head seemed to bulge out before he slumped backwards with a splash into the shallow water.

Blue leapt from behind the wall and emptied his pistol at the two shapes on the boat now speeding towards the distillery. He thought he heard a cry from the boat, which was lit up briefly as it raced across the searchlight beam and disappeared into the gloom. "Where are they going?" he thought aloud.

"Round the edge of the bay to avoid the launch and get out the other side," Bhardwaj answered. "It's going to be close."

As their eyes adjusted to the weak moonlight again, they watched the boat as it sped past the distillery pier and then the jetty at the other side of the bay, gaining speed all the time. Now they could see the launch too, moving slowly across the mouth of the bay to cut the smaller boat off.

"I think they're going to make it," gasped Blue.

"I don't think so," said Bhardwaj. "The skerries."

At that moment there was a loud bang, and the speeding inflatable seemed to spring upwards into the air, and then turn over several elegant cartwheels on the surface of the water before falling away out of sight.

"He wouldn't have made it, even if he'd got to the boat," commented Bhardwaj.

"No," said Blue.

He realised there were other figures on the beach now. The armed officers, unfamiliar with the lie of the land, had arrived only in time to see the very last act of the drama. His radio crackled. It was Campbell: "Coming in to the distillery pier. Meet you there, Blue. Out."

Blue turned to see that Bhardwaj was no longer by his side. A flash alerted him to that fact that he was using his mobile to photograph King's body. He went over. King stared up at him from the water, a red stain spreading around his head. The shot had smashed the left-hand glass of his spectacles, and gone into his eye, then exited from the rear of his skull. There was another shot in his chest. Efficient work.

"Taking some shots of its original position. Tide's coming in, so we'll have to move it. Is that OK, chief?"

"Yes, yes, good thinking, Arvind."

Blue alerted the commander of the armed team to what had happened, asking for the body to be moved and the house search completed. Then he began to pick his way round the shore towards the distillery pier.

76

The launch was tied up by the time Blue got there, and Campbell was waiting on the pier. "Angus, well done, successful operation, minimum loss of life."

"Thank you, sir. But we didn't get King alive. We could have got a lot out of him."

"Believe me, Angus, we wouldn't have. These people are well trained, they know what to do. Short of pulling his fingernails out, which I believe is illegal, we'd get nothing from him. Even if he did talk, it would likely be misinformation. And, sooner or later they'd either manage to get him out, or eliminate him. Now King is dead, and we can prove it. We've still got the Croats, and we'll get something out of them. And once you can tell us what they were trying to cover up, we've got a fair outcome. Better than we could have hoped for, knowing King's connections."

"Which we can't prove."

"Of course not. We won't find a top civil servant's phone number at the back of his diary. In fact, no link will lead us back to the person who gave him his orders. His line manager, AC Adam Farborough, will simply say that King had gone rogue. As usual, they'll remain invulnerable. Someone may get a black mark in the ministry, and fewer dinner party invitations from the boss, but we won't know that. It's a different country, Angus, a network that's alien to us, that closes round its own, and is protected by its members in the highest offices."

"It still leaves a bad taste."

"Well now, I've a cure for that. I'm going back to that distillery tomorrow to get a couple more bottles of that Madeira Cask Special, and you can try it yourself."

"Er, that reminds me…"

"I know, Angus, I haven't paid you for the last lot yet. Have no fear, I'll give you a cheque this evening at the hotel. Or first thing tomorrow morning. Anyway, we better sort this lot out now. What do you suggest?"

"The SOCOs are at George Outhwaite's now, so I'd like to get over there and have a look. Maybe we'll get enough forensic to tie it to King. Could you handle things here, chief? I'll send the SOCOs and the ambulance over as soon as they're done at George's, then come back myself."

"Leave it to me, Angus, happy to help. Good to get away from the desk for a while. No need for you to come back. I'll take a look for their boat with the launch – they've a pretty good searchlight – then get over to the house and see what they've found. I'll report to you in the morning."

As Blue made his way back round the shore, he could hear Campbell giving orders and the launch's engines revved up again, before it backed away from the pier.

He caught up with Bhardwaj at the house. "Come on, Arvind, let's go over to George's now. Superintendent Campbell will be in charge here. Have they found anything so far?"

"Yes, sir. It seems that Clara wasn't as security-conscious as she might have been. She printed out some de-crypted emails from King which do point to criminal activities, and in particular, identify targets for 'treatment.' We've also found King's travel case, which I've sealed till we get it back to the station. And most of the stuff taken from the station seems to be there too. Including the laptops."

"That's a relief. Let's go. Do you mind driving? Which of these cars looks the most likely to get us there?"

Scene-of-crime were finished by the time Blue and Bhardwaj got to George's house. They had prints of two fingers and a thumb from one of the two mugs on the table, and more from the back of a wooden chair, which Blue presumed King had moved back to sit down at. The ambulance men were waiting to remove the body, as soon as Blue had had a look. George had a surprised expression on his face, and had been shot cleanly in the centre of the forehead. Blue okayed the removal of the body and the house was sealed. The SOC team went on to Lagavulin.

There was a text from Alison: 'At hosp x' Did she always put an x, he wondered, or was it for him.

Then a call from the Super. "Everything under control here. Spotted the wreck of their boat, thrown up on the rocks, and some other bits and pieces, but we can't do anything more till the morning. Still working on the house, SOCOs here too. Now get some rest. You sound exhausted."

"Next stop the hospital," Blue said wearily to Bhardwaj. "We'll see how Moira's doing."

Blue and Bhardwaj were shown into the room where Moira lay, apparently asleep. Alison and Alasdair were at her bedside. Alasdair got up and shook Blue's hand. "Thank you, Angus."

"How is she?"

"Dozing. Sore head. Morphine. Apart from that, *gle mhath*."

Moira began to stir, and opened her eyes.

"How are you feeling, love?" asked Alasdair.

"Everything is beautiful."

Alison drove Blue back to his hotel. As he was about to get out of the car, she put her hand on his arm. "Thanks for coming to get me at Grace's, Angus."

"Er, yes, no problem."

"And I heard you did very well down at Dunyvaig." She kissed him on the cheek. "Now, get off and get some sleep. You're knackered."

Blue was too tired to eat. But in his room he did open one of the miniatures he'd been given at Kilbrocheann Distillery. As the heavy sweetness of the liquor relaxed him, he let the events of the day replay themselves through his consciousness, more than once. So much. And King's last words still echoed, as the cartwheeling boat disappeared into the darkness.

Day 10. Saturday

77

Even before he was out of bed, Blue's phone pinged. John Striven. Coming over on the morning plane.

Blue met Campbell at breakfast. "Successful conclusion last night, sir?"

"Yes. Got the bodies off and the house sealed. Shame about Mrs Gilmour. I doubt we'll ever know exactly why she got involved. I'm sure if we'd got her alive she'd have told us plenty. No doubt King knew that too. We'll have another look this morning for their boat. You don't mind if I handle that end of it?"

"Not at all. It's good to have someone really experienced here."

"How close are we on the Peat Dead case, Angus?"

"We've got all the names now. And maybe a reason." He explained.

Campbell listened carefully. "Hmm," he concluded, "the motive for the killings does seem clearer now. But there's still something we don't know. About this meeting. Something that makes the reaction today more understandable. We won't get it from the Croats. Maybe one of your dead people can tell us more."

"I'll see what I can do. What about the press? We can't keep yesterday quiet."

"Hmm. Sooner we let this out the better, or someone will try to cover it up. We won't get people flocking out here for a press conference, so that'll have to be in Oban. Maybe tomorrow morning."

"As it happens, John Striven from the *Nation* is on his way to the island now. What about if we give him an interview today? Give him the scoop. They'll make a big splash."

Campbell looked suspicious. "How come he's over here right now?"

"He was following the murders in Glasgow. Deduced that they were linked to this case."

"Most journalists these days are simply working to an agenda. Will this one give us a fair report?"

"Yes. I know him from university days. He still believes that journalism is about searching for truth. He's not afraid to reveal what others want hidden."

"Sounds just the man for us. Let's meet him this afternoon. That gives us time to get things sorted out a bit more. If we see him at say three, that still gives him time to file his copy for tomorrow. Can you let him know?"

"Yes, will do."

"Oh, and Angus, one other thing." Campbell slipped a folded cheque across the table to Blue. "Many thanks, and sorry to keep you waiting. Hope it didn't break the bank, eh?"

"Thanks, chief. Glad to help. By the way, do you want a lift into Bowmore?"

"Thanks, but no need. Launch is picking me up at Port Ellen pier at 8.30, then we'll get back to Dunyvaig and tidy things up there, hopefully find some wreckage and bodies. If they've not been swept out to sea, that is. I'll report back once we're done."

"Thanks, that's very helpful."

"Remember, Angus, the sooner we get the old case sorted out, the better. The Justice Ministry need to have that definitive account."

Blue was at the police station by 8.30 and called a meeting for nine. He invited Elspeth too. The museum people had been with them from the start, it was only fair they should be there at the end. Then he texted John Striven suggesting a meeting at the police station at three.

The gathering comprised Blue himself, Elspeth, Alison, Sergeant Walker, and PCs Bhardwaj and Craig. Blackett had phoned in sick. Blue reviewed the previous day's events. He reported on the injured: Blasić still in intensive care, now stable. McCader no longer serious, thankfully no fractures to his back or neck. And Moira Nicolson seemed fine, although she was being flown to Glasgow that morning for a precautionary brain scan. Until she recovered, Sergeant Walker would stand in as officer commanding Islay police. He also reported that the case against Blasić, Vrasko, King and Clara Gilmour was being transferred *in toto* for Glasgow to deal with. Inspector Taylor was placed in charge. Although King was dead, his role in the business had to be clarified and made public.

There was a general sense of relief that the Now case seemed to have been tied up. However, Blue repeated Campbell's point that in order to explain the current events, the nature of what was being covered up needed to be fully disclosed. They still had a job to do, and his priority was therefore to tie up that case.

"Deirdra, where are we on the identifications?"

"Aye, chief, we have three names confirmed by DNA comparison with family members: Dafydd Thomas is body number 4, Peter Bishop is body number 5, and Terence Darwin is body number 2, and we're still waitin for results concerning Arthur Walforth as body number 3. But I think it'll come positive. And it seems clear that Murdo McLeod is number 1. That's all five."

"Thanks, good work, Deirdra. Well done. Though I'd still like your check on the marriage registers for Murdo McLeod. I think, given Tony's reference in his book, and Grace's evidence, we don't need the DNA to confirm, though it wouldn't do any harm as a double-check. So, we've got the victims, the killer, that's Burovkin, and his accomplices, Greeley and Rogers. That just leaves the motive."

"Murdo's diary?" said Alison, "Might be worth looking in there. Someone knew he kept a diary. Otherwise why would Tony and Les be so keen to get it?"

The envelope containing the diary was in the file he had in front of him. He took from it a dark green exercise book with hard covers. He flicked through it. It was all in Gaelic, as Grace had said. "Elspeth, can you help us? This is in Gaelic and I don't think mine's up to it." He leafed through to 15th November 1944, and pointed to the entry. "Can you read this bit, it's not very long."

Elspeth took the book, and peered at the page. "OK, let's have a shot. '15th November. Me and Arthur bring in a German plane, right across the country. Siebel Fh 104. Very nice plane. Can't believe who got out – Himmler himself! And Churchill in the big house waiting for him, so Arthur says. What's going on? Are the Germans going to surrender? Let's hope so.' That's it. Er, is this real?"

"Himmler meeting Churchill. Holy shit!" said Bhardwaj.

"Thank you Elspeth," said Blue, "That's joined a lot of the dots together."

"Why Himmler and Churchill?," asked Alison, "What was going on?"

"Towards the end of the war Himmler, through various interme-diaries, indicated to the Allies that he wanted to do some sort of deal, and join them in a grand alliance against Soviet Russia. It's long been known there were contacts between the British and Germans, using diplomatic channels. But no-one imagined a direct meeting between Churchill and Himmler. And on British soil."

"Ch and Hm," said Alison, "in Group Captain Stamford's wine diary. He was telling us too."

"Wow!" said Bhardwaj. "Awesome!"

"So those five poor men were killed simply because they caught sight of Himmler, and recognised him?" said Alison.

"That's what it looks like," said Blue. "Remember that Churchill was obsessive about secrecy. He may have ordered these men's deaths himself. If word ever got out Himmler and Churchill had met, it would have damaged Churchill's reputation, especially with the Russians, whom he wanted to keep on board as allies for as long as possible."

"This is a gift for historians," said Elspeth, "and I can imagine it won't do Churchill's reputation any good. But it hardly seems enough to justify all this killing today. I mean, they could just say it was a clever ploy on Churchill's part to find out what the top Nazis were thinking."

"It does seem an over-reaction," said Blue, "though maybe they're paranoid enough. Looks like the alien-hunters got the story right, after all. Their third theory was correct. Seeing two men, who should not be seen together, was enough for five others to be killed."

"Just one wee thing," put in PC Craig, "yon man Stamford told George he knew lots of secret stuff, but it wasn't any more than what Murdo knew. Wasn't he supposed to be high up?"

"Maybe there was something in the rest of the wine diary," said Bhardwaj.

"Dammit!" said Blue. "No, no, it was a decoy! It's just dawned on me."

"What was?" asked Alison

"The diary. And his whole approach to George. He could easily have gone to George much more discreetly. But he did it when he knew his watcher was there. He wanted her to see them. And to get the diary – that's why he stuck a few real clues in it, to make her think it was his revelation. He relied on the fact that George would talk to people about it."

"You mean, he wanted people to think he had more secrets than he had?"

"No. I'm sure he did have more secrets. Look at it this way. Both he and Murdo know that Churchill met Himmler. But only Murdo gets executed. What does that say?"

"Stamford was on the inside," said Bhardwaj. "Maybe he co-ordinated the meeting. And ordered the killings. He'd know all about it then."

"But he must have known that talking to George could get him killed," said Alison.

"Yes, maybe he knew he was close to death anyway. Found out he was terminally ill. Something like that. Didn't want the secrets to die with him."

"So what happened to them?"

"He must have got them out some other way. That he thought would be more secure. Any ideas?"

There was silence for a few moments, then Elspeth cleared her throat. "Ah. I think perhaps I can help. When I moved here, that was a couple of years after Mr Stamford had died, I offered to catalogue the library at the museum. They had lots of books, but they were just piled in heaps, mostly still in the boxes they'd come in from donors. Among them was a box from Group Captain Stamford. I asked Ina about it, and she said there had been loads of books at his house, and papers, too, but Amanda Tomkins had taken them all away. Ina didn't know when the box had been sent to us."

"So he sent it himself, before he died, without Amanda knowing?" asked Blue.

"Looks like it."

"Where are those books now? Catalogued and shelved, I suppose. Did you look at them closely?"

"Yes, I catalogued them. And no, I didn't look closely at them, just got the details off them and stuck them back in the box. There were loads of books altogether, and his weren't very relevant to Islay history, so they didn't go on the shelves, and I just put the box in store."

"What were they about?"

"Aeroplanes. History of flight, types of plane, planes of all countries. Nothing very rare."

"Can we see them?"

"You think something might be hidden in them?" asked Alison.

"It's worth checking," said Blue. "Elspeth, can we send a car over for it?"

"Yes, of course. I can go in my own if you like."

"No, that's not necessary. Arvind, can you drive Elspeth over and fetch the box?"

"No problemo, chief!"

"Everyone else, coffee break!"

78

They did not have to lie in the darkness in the back of the van for long. He heard a sentry's call, and guessed they were leaving the base itself. Soon afterwards he could feel it was climbing, then bumping onto rough ground, where it stopped. The doors were swung open, and they were dragged out by the legs, and dumped on the wet ground. There was a little light, it would be dawn soon. Enough light for their killers to see what they were doing, not enough for anyone out and about at that time to see what was going on. If there were, they'd hear the shots of course. But there was a war on, and a military base there, people knew not to ask questions, not to challenge anything that looked suspicious, not to do anything that might get you noticed too much.

"Get up, you bastards," shouted the man with the bat, while the other one tried to help them to their feet. The Russian stood a little off, just a dark shape in the pre-dawn gloom. They were manhandled over to the edge of a pit dug into the peat. It seemed to him they were on the muir just behind the base. He looked beyond the base towards the sea, thought he could detect a glimmer, but he could hear it clearly enough, and smell the salt on the air. He remembered a time, in a previous life, the two of them, alone on the beach at Mangersta, back in Lewis. The broad beach bookended by the rocky headlands shining wet under the cascading water, the Atlantic rollers taking their time to flop themselves onto the white sand, to rest after the endless advance across the ocean. The white sand, that squeaked as they walked on it. You could make it sing if you walked a certain way, so they said.

"If only time could stop for a while," she said, "and make this moment last."

"We won't forget it," he replied. "We'll keep it always, and we'll know we have it. A memory to unite us in a time of trouble."

Dafydd was the first. He could hear him whimpering behind the gag. The Russian seemed to materialise from nowhere behind him and there was a shot, Dafydd made no sound, pitched forward into the blackness of the pit. Then Terry, and Peter. Arthur still seemed dazed, Les had to hold him steady, keep him pointed forward, until the shot.

So he was to be last. Reverse order of rank, perhaps, or just the way they happened to line up. As he felt the Russian come up behind him, he turned round, and looked into his face. There was no expression, he wasn't in a hurry, his face showing palely in the gloom. His eyes were pools of blackness, and staring into them was like peering into an abyss. An infinity of emptiness. He could not speak under the gag but as he looked into the dead eyes of the Russian he knew the man had sensed that he, Murdo McLeod, possessed something the other did not.

He turned back round, and stared into the distance and listened to the sea. Then he was falling, holding her close as they swooped down into the light.

79

Back in his office, Blue called the Super, asked how things were going.

"Made progress this morning. Fished three bodies out of the bay. Got most of the bits of the boat. Can't trace ownership, which is a pity. We're finished at the house, too, so I'll head back in a short while. Tremendous thrill, being back at the coalface again. I'm most grateful to you, Angus."

"Don't mention it, chief. See you soon."

Next Blue phoned Taylor in Glasgow.

"Morning Angus. Things are moving here. We're getting more out of Vrasko now. She's angry Blasić was almost killed – there's clearly something between them. She blames King for that, and is telling us what she knows. Once Blasić can talk, he won't be able to plead ignorance. We've certainly got enough to put King at the heart of this. McDonough's giving a press conference at six this evening."

"That sounds good. Thanks for your help, Donald."

"Not at all. It's good to have a case that we've tidied up completely. And thanks for your assistance too, Angus. Any time you need more help from the real policemen, just let me know."

He sipped his coffee and looked out the window. The red Range Rover was parked opposite. The man with the white stick got out, and started tapping his way towards the whisky shop. But this time Sergeant Walker marched across the street to intercept him. Blue couldn't hear what was being said, but eventually the man flung the stick down on the pavement, took his dark glasses off and thrust them into his pocket, straightened up, and marched into the shop. The sergeant picked up the stick and came back across the road.

There was a knock at the door and Alison came in. "I just wanted to say thank you for letting me work on this. You could easily have sent me back after the dig at the peat cutting site. I've really enjoyed it."

"Makes you want to be a policeman?"

"No, not quite. I do like my own job better. But sometimes a bit of excitement wakes you up again. By the way, you've got two very good people there. I mean Arvind and Deirdra."

"Thanks again. Sadly, they're not mine. I'll probably have to hand them back to Sergeant Walker by the end of today. Back to dealing with blind drivers, dogshit and loud parties on the beach."

"You will give them some encouragement to go further?"

"Of course I will. You can be sure of it. By the way, Alison, I've enjoyed working with you too." Alison coloured, then smiled and left the room.

Blue checked the news on the internet. There was an interesting new item. The Metropolitan Police had issued a statement describing Chief Inspector Gregory King as a good officer who had 'gone rogue' because of his (unspecified) 'particular political views' coupled with a 'personal psychological episode', again of an unspecified nature. So, the process of distancing had begun. Before long, nobody would admit to ever having heard of Gregory King.

Twenty minutes later, with Elspeth back, they reconvened. A large cardboard box sat on the table.

"Here goes," said Blue, "I'll give everybody two or three books. Just go through them, page by page please, in case anything's been written or stuck in." He handed the books out. They weren't particularly old, mostly hardbacks from the 1970s and 1980s, still in the dust jackets. Nevertheless a musty smell emanated from them. They began the task of working through them.

It was Sergeant Walker who found it. "Sir, I've got something here. In *The Encyclopaedia of Aircraft of World War Two*. Curiously, it's at the page for the Siebel Fh 104. The one Murdo McLeod mentioned."

"What sort of plane is that?" asked Alison.

Walker peered at the book. "Small, twin-engined plane used for transport and communications. First flew 1937, advanced aerodynamic design, all-metal construction. Noted for reliability in flying long distances. Often used to transport top Nazi generals and officials. Hmm, interesting. Hadn't come across that one."

"Bob, can we see what you've found?" asked Blue.

"Oh, sorry, sir. Yes, there's an envelope here, taped to the page, the one with the photo on it. I don't want to just rip it off, might damage the picture." After what seemed an age of careful peeling, he passed the envelope over to Blue.

A light blue Basildon Bond envelope, sealed. Blue opened it along the top with a pair of scissors, and extracted three sheets of paper, folded together. Thin, almost transparent paper, with blue typed text on it. A carbon copy, each character fuzzy but readable. "Minutes of a meeting," he read out, "15th November 1944. Present: W. Churchill, H. Himmler, four other names I don't recognise, one of them German, perhaps they were civil servants. Oh and one other, Squadron Leader Stamford, secretary." As he read through the text, he was reminded of another meeting. At a villa by the Wannsee, on the edge of Berlin. Politicians and civil servants discussing in businesslike terms how to exterminate a whole people. He remembered the chill he'd felt as he read those minutes at university. Focus. "They're discussing a treaty between Britain and Germany. Main points are, let's see, one, Germans to arrest and try Hitler for war crimes, two, Germans to withdraw from occupied areas of western Europe. Three, a conference to reorganise eastern Europe. Four, Britain to declare immediate war on the Soviet Union. USA to be invited to join Britain and Germany to form a North Atlantic Alliance. And five…bloody hell!"

"What?" said Alison.

"Sorry. Five, immediate sharing of British nuclear explosive work and German rocket developments, to prepare a new weapon to be deployed against the Soviets."

"Churchill was going to give the atom bomb to the Nazis?" gasped Bhardwaj.

"To start a nuclear war!" added Craig.

"That's what it looks like."

There was a moment's silence, as they all took it in.

"That would certainly have changed history!" said Alison.

"But why kill people today? What does it matter if the story gets out? It's history." asked Bhardwaj.

"The cult of Churchill is still very important to British governments," said Elspeth. "He's at the centre of the British identity campaign. The epitome of Britishness. The brave Brit who stands strong against the shifty foreigners."

"A True King Arthur," quoted Blue.

"Quite. Churchill meeting Himmler could be presented as a clever trick. But not this. Not offering the Nazis the atom bomb. His iconic status would be demolished. The British Studies module will look a bit hypocritical."

"Think of all those banknotes they'd have to reprint," added Alison.

"And they knew it all along," said Blue. "The top copy of this will have been in London since 1944. It's been kept secret ever since. They couldn't have it coming out right now. They didn't know what we'd find when we started poking around. Couldn't take the chance we'd find it."

"So who gave King his orders?" asked Craig.

"Farborough, I presume. But who whispered to him, that we'll never know. It'll all be covered up. And there will be nothing on record."

"So they win," said Craig.

"No. The story is out, or it soon will be. They won't be able to suppress it any more."

"What they may try," added Elspeth, "is to declare that it's a forgery. It looks genuine to me. But I know someone at Falkirk Uni who's an expert in documents from this period. I'm sure he'll be on the first plane over as soon as I phone him, and if he says it's genuine, it'll be lot harder for them to rubbish it. And once this is public, historians will start looking closer at that period, and who knows what else they'll find."

"One other thing," put in Bhardwaj. "Why would Churchill come up with this? Weren't the Allies winning the war by then?"

"Yes, quite so. But by this stage of the war Britain had become very much the junior partner. It was the Americans and the Russians who had the resources and the manpower to beat the Germans. Churchill didn't like that. He already suspected he was being left out of the loop. He was still under the illusion that the British Empire was a world power. I suspect he was looking for a way in which Britain could secure a historic coup that would show he was still top dog. As an aristocrat and an imperialist, he was by nature rabidly anti-communist. He must have thought this would be a clever move which would kill two birds – Hitler and Stalin – at one stroke. And put Britain, and especially himself – he was very self-centred – at the centre of history."

"So why wasn't the treaty put into effect? We know it didn't happen."

"My suspicion would be that the Americans vetoed it. After all, it was mostly their work Churchill was planning to hand over. And a third world war straight after the second wasn't how they saw the future. The truth is that whatever Churchill signed, he wasn't in a position to deliver. He was often going off on his own with things, so it may even be that as soon as his colleagues in the War Cabinet saw it, it was dead. Once the historians get onto it, I'm sure we'll know more."

80

Half an hour later, Superintendent Campbell arrived at the station, looking years younger than when he had arrived on the island. He listened to a brief review of the morning's revelations from Blue. "Well, well, who'd have thought it. What a stupid waste of life. What planet do these people live on? Sooner we get this stuff out into the light of day, the better."

"Don't you need to check with somebody higher up?" asked Blue.

"Give me five minutes and a quiet room."

Ten minutes later Campbell was back. "I've spoken to the Minister. She wants it all in the public domain, nothing covered up. And she needs a full report as soon as possible. When's this journalist coming? Sooner we see him the better."

"Three."

"It's 12.15 now. Can we get him in sooner?"

Blue called Striven's mobile. "John, Angus here. Can you come for the interview a bit earlier?"

"Five minutes?"

"Where are you?"

"In a cafe just around the corner."

The interview with Blue and Campbell lasted an hour and a half, and gave Striven an account of the whole case, then and now. Plus a digital copy of the minutes from the 1944 meeting, which Craig had scanned. Elspeth had emailed them to several historians she knew, one of whom had already put it up on *Wikipedia*. The text had gone viral almost immediately.

"Fantastic," Striven concluded. "This is huge. The very least it will do is pull the rug from under the British Studies module. And maybe make people think twice about where this xenophobia's taking us. They're already holding the front page for me."

Campbell excused himself after the meeting. "Congratulate your people for me, Angus. I have to go now – the boat will be waiting for me at the pier. They're taking me to Kilbrocheann Distillery before we go back to Oban – to get more of that Madeira Cask Special. Once you're back in the office, I'll give you a dram to taste. Oh, and don't forget that report."

Blue led Alison, Bhardwaj, Craig, and Sergeant Walker to the Italian restaurant for lunch. Constable Blackett even managed to raise himself from his sick-bed to join them, looking somewhat hung-over.

"Thanks for coming," Blue announced, as they waited for the food to be prepared, "Islay can do without its police force for a couple of hours. My treat. You can even have wine, as long as no-one's driving!" During the meal, he complimented each one of them individually for the part they had played. "We couldn't have got to this point without every single one of you. And Inspector Nicolson and Sergeant McCader too. We've made a good team. Deirdra and Arvind, I'm commending you both to Superintendent Campbell. You've both got a great future ahead. Bob, you've held the fort with exemplary calm. Alison, you've been an inspiration. Boris, you've played your part too, and I'm sure Tatiana will be herself again. Now let's drink a toast to the memory of the Peat Dead. Human beings are never expendable."

Later, as he and Alison waited at the airport for the plane to Oban, his phone rang. It was McCader.

"Enver, good to hear from you. How are you?"

"Not doing badly at all, chief. Hear you tied everything up neatly. Got a little information for you myself, which I managed to get off one of my contacts. I was heading out to somewhere private to phone him when that van hit me. Anyway, I reached him from the hospital and persuaded him to open a file. You were looking for a Russian, Burovkin?"

"Yes, that's right, Burovkin."

"Fyodor Burovkin, that would be. He was settled after the war in Portsmouth, under the name Frederick Burke. Ran a taxi company there. Made quite a bit. Some suggestions of connection with organised crime. Died in 1975. An odd accident. Walking down a street at night when a load of bricks fell off some scaffolding, right onto him. Killed instantly."

"Ah! Maybe he was writing his memoirs too."

As Blue sat in the plane, next to Alison, he watched Islay disappear beneath them as the plane rose into the low cloud that was now covering the west coast. He felt the touch of her hand.

"We should do this again sometime," he said.

"Yes," she said. "That would be good."

The End

Note on Islay Places

Ileachs and visitors to Islay will notice a few small tweaks to Islay's infrastructure, for artistic purposes only! I've added a cafe to the excellent Museum of Islay Life, so please don't be annoyed if you go there and you can't get Jessie's carrot cake. The Islay police station I've upgraded from a modest bungalow to an Edwardian villa. No more than they deserve! The remains of the wartime airbase are still be seen around the airport.

Kilbrocheann Distillery is fictitious, so don't look for it. However, you'll have to visit all Islay's distilleries to work out which one it's based on. The descriptions of the whiskies tasted by Angus Blue are all his own, based on actual tasting, and not copied out of a book. This was difficult and time-consuming research, undertaken for the greater good of the artistic enterprise.

Otherwise Islay is as described. Visit if you can.

Note on Historical Plausibility

There is no evidence that the meeting described in this book actually happened. However, it is entirely plausible. In the months after Britain abandoned Belgium and France, there was a real possibility that a peace would have to be negotiated with the victorious Germans. Churchill was let off the hook by the German invasion of Russia in 1941, as that campaign occupied most of Germany's fighting force, and the invasion of Britain was postponed and then dropped. In fact, it was the Russians, and then the Americans, who bore the brunt of fighting against Germany and secured the eventual victory. By 1944 Churchill was bitterly aware of this, and on the lookout for any opportunity which enable him to steal a march on his allies. A surprise deal with Germany which could be presented as Churchill personally bringing the war to a triumphant close would have seemed to him a brilliant move.

In the years since the war, partly through Churchill's own selective writing of history, and partly through his being mythologised as a British hero, accounts of him have often been somewhat one-sided. For a more balanced view, see Clive Ponting's magisterial Churchill (Sinclair-Stevenson, 1994). For Churchill's activities during the war, see also Nigel Knight's Churchill. The Greatest Briton Unmasked (David & Charles, 2008).

About the Author

Allan Martin

Allan Martin worked as a teacher, teacher-trainer and university lecturer, and only turned to writing fiction after taking early retirement.

He lives in Glasgow and with his wife regularly visits the Hebrides and Estonia.

He has had several short stories published, notably in *iScot magazine* and *404Ink* magazine.

He has also translated from Estonian a 'closed-room' mystery, *The Oracle*, originally published in 1937.

Also from ThunderPoint

In The Shadow Of The Hill
Helen Forbes
ISBN: 978-0-9929768-1-1 (eBook)
ISBN: 978-0-9929768-0-4 (Paperback)

An elderly woman is found battered to death in the common stairwell of an Inverness block of flats.

Detective Sergeant Joe Galbraith starts what seems like one more depressing investigation of the untimely death of a poor unfortunate who was in the wrong place, at the wrong time.

As the investigation spreads across Scotland it reaches into a past that Joe has tried to forget, and takes him back to the Hebridean island of Harris, where he spent his childhood.

Among the mountains and the stunning landscape of religiously conservative Harris, in the shadow of Ceapabhal, long buried events and a tragic story are slowly uncovered, and the investigation takes on an altogether more sinister aspect.

In The Shadow Of The Hill skilfully captures the intricacies and malevolence of the underbelly of Highland and Island life, bringing tragedy and vengeance to the magical beauty of the Outer Hebrides.

'...our first real home-grown sample of modern Highland noir' – Roger Hutchinson; West Highland Free Press

Madness Lies
Helen Forbes
ISBN: 9781910946312 (Kindle)
ISBN: 9781910946305 (Paperback)

When an Inverness Councillor is murdered in broad daylight in the middle of town, Detective Sergeant Joe Galbraith sees a familiar figure running from the scene.

According to everyone who knows him, the Councillor had no enemies, but someone clearly wanted him dead.

The victim's high profile means the police want a quick resolution to the case, but no one seems to know anything. Or if they do, they're not prepared to say.

This second novel of Highland Noir from Helen Forbes continues the series with a crime thriller that moves between Inverness, North Uist and London, reaching a terrifying denouement at the notorious Black Rock Gorge.

"You would expect Helen Forbes to write well of an exile's experience of Sollas, Vallay and west side of North Uist, and she does. She evokes the machair, the changing sky and sea, the flowers, birds and waving grass, the dunes, the people and above all the peace." – Roger Hutchinson, West Highland Free Press

Toxic
Jackie MacLean
Shortlisted for the Yeovil Book Prize 2011
ISBN: 978-0-9575689-8-3 (eBook)
ISBN: 978-0-9575689-9-0 (Paperback)

The recklessly brilliant DI Donna Davenport, struggling to hide a secret from police colleagues and get over the break-up with her partner, has been suspended from duty for a fiery and inappropriate outburst to the press.

DI Evanton, an old-fashioned, hard-living misogynistic copper has been newly demoted for thumping a suspect, and transferred to Dundee with a final warning ringing in his ears and a reputation that precedes him.

And in the peaceful, rolling Tayside farmland a deadly store of MIC, the toxin that devastated Bhopal, is being illegally stored by a criminal gang smuggling the valuable substance necessary for making cheap pesticides.

An anonymous tip-off starts a desperate search for the MIC that is complicated by the uneasy partnership between Davenport and Evanton and their growing mistrust of each others actions.

Compelling and authentic, Toxic is a tense and fast paced crime thriller.

'...a humdinger of a plot that is as realistic as it is frightening' – crimefictionlover.com

The Deaths on the Black Rock
BRM Stewart
ISBN: 978-1-910946-47-3 (Kindle)
ISBN: 978-1-910946-46-6 (Paperback)

It's been a year since Rima Khalaf died in a fall from the Black Rock, deemed to be a tragic accident by the police.

But her grieving parents are dissatisfied with the police in-vestigation, so DS Amanda Pitt is sent north from Glasgow to the small town of Clachdubh to re-examine the case.

Despite the suspicions of the distraught parents, all the cir-cumstances seem to confirm Rima's death was indeed a tragic accident, until another woman is also found dead in the town.

Frustrated by the lack of any real evidence, DS Pitt pushes the limits of legality in her quest for the truth.

Stewart writes with a gritty intensity that places the reader in intimate contact with the darker side of society, in a way that forces you to empathise with the uncomfortable idea that sometimes the end justifies the means for those who are supposed to uphold the law.

The Oystercatcher Girl
Gabrielle Barnby
ISBN: 978-1-910946-17-6 (eBook)
ISBN: 978-1-910946-15-2 (Paperback)

In the medieval splendour of St Magnus Cathedral, three women gather to mourn the untimely passing of Robbie: Robbie's widow, Tessa; Tessa's old childhood friend, Christine, and Christine's unstable and unreliable sister, Lindsay.

But all is not as it seems: what is the relationship between the three women, and Robbie? What secrets do they hide? And who has really betrayed who?

Set amidst the spectacular scenery of the Orkney Islands, Gabrielle Barnby's skilfully plotted first novel is a beautifully understated story of deception and forgiveness, love and redemption.

With poetic and precise language Barnby draws you in to the lives, loves and losses of the characters till you feel a part of the story.

'The Oystercatcher Girl is a wonderfully evocative and deftly woven story' – Sara Bailey

Changed Times
Ethyl Smith
ISBN: 978-1-910946-09-1 (eBook)
ISBN: 978-1-910946-08-4 (Paperback)

1679 – The Killing Times: Charles II is on the throne, the Episcopacy has been restored, and southern Scotland is in ferment.

The King is demanding superiority over all things spiritual and temporal and rebellious Ministers are being ousted from their parishes for refusing to bend the knee.

When John Steel steps in to help one such Minister in his home village of Lesmahagow he finds himself caught up in events that reverberate not just through the parish, but throughout the whole of southern Scotland.

From the Battle of Drumclog to the Battle of Bothwell Bridge, John's platoon of farmers and villagers find themselves in the heart of the action over that fateful summer where the people fight the King for their religion, their freedom, and their lives.

Set amid the tumult and intrigue of Scotland's Killing Times, John Steele's story powerfully reflects the changes that took place across 17th century Scotland, and stunningly brings this period of history to life.

'Smith writes with a fine ear for Scots speech, and with a sensitive awareness to the different ways in which history intrudes upon the lives of men and women, soldiers and civilians, adults and children'
– James Robertson

The False Men
Mhairead MacLeod
ISBN: 978-1-910946-27-5 (eBook)
ISBN: 978-1-910946-25-1 (Paperback)

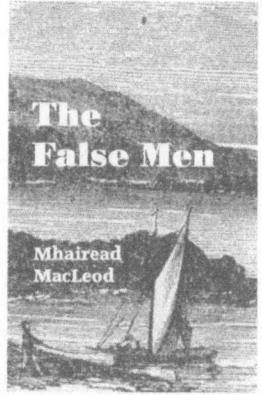

North Uist, Outer Hebrides, 1848.

Jess MacKay has led a privileged life as the daughter of a local landowner, sheltered from the harsher aspects of life. Courted by the eligible Patrick Cooper, the Laird's new commissioner, Jess's future is mapped out, until Lachlan Macdonald arrives on North Uist, amid rumours of forced evictions on islands just to the south.

As the uncompromising brutality of the Clearances reaches the islands, and Jess sees her friends ripped from their homes, she must decide where her heart, and her loyalties, truly lie.

Set against the evocative backdrop of the Hebrides and inspired by a true story, *The False Men* is a compelling tale of love in a turbulent past that resonates with the upheavals of the modern world.

'...an engaging tale of powerlessness, love and disillusionment in the context of the type of injustice that, sadly, continues to this day' – Anne Goodwin

Dead Cat Bounce
Kevin Scott
ISBN: 978-1-910946-17-6 (eBook)
ISBN: 978-1-910946-15-2 (Paperback)

"Well, either way, you'll have to speak to your brother today because...unless I get my money by tomorrow morning there's not going to be a funeral."

When your 11 year old brother has been tragically killed in a car accident, you might think that organising his funeral would take priority. But when Nicky's coffin, complete with Nicky's body, goes missing, deadbeat loser Matt has only 26 hours in which to find the £20,000 he owes a Glasgow gangster or explain to his grieving mother why there's not going to be a funeral.

Enter middle brother, Pete, successful City trader with an expensive wife, expensive children, and an expensive villa in Tuscany. Pete's watches cost £20,000, but he has his own problems, and Matt doesn't want his help anyway.

Seething with old resentments, the betrayals of the past and the double-dealings of the present, the two brothers must find a way to work together to retrieve Nicky's body, discovering along the way that they are not so different after all.

'Underplaying the comic potential to highlight the troubled relationship between the equally flawed brothers. It's one of those books that keep the reader hooked right to the end' – The Herald

The Wrong Box
Andrew C Ferguson
ISBN: 978-1-910946-14-5 (Paperback)
ISBN: 978-1-910946-16-9 (eBook)

All I know is, I'm in exile in Scotland, and there's a dead Scouser businessman in my bath. With his toe up the tap.

Meet Simon English, corporate lawyer, heavy drinker and Scotophobe, banished from London after being caught misbehaving with one of the young associates on the corporate desk. As if that wasn't bad enough, English finds himself acting for a spiralling money laundering racket that could put not just his career, but his life, on the line.

Enter Karen Clamp, an 18 stone, well-read wann be couturier from the Auchendrossan sink estate, with an encyclopedic knowledge of Council misdeeds and 19th century Scottish fiction. With no one to trust but each other, this mismatched pair must work together to investigate a series of apparently unrelated frauds and discover how everything connects to the mysterious Wrong Box.

Manically funny, *The Wrong Box* is a chaotic story of lust, money, power and greed, and the importance of being able to sew a really good hem.

'...the makings of a new Caledonian Comic Noir genre: Rebus with jokes, Val McDiarmid with buddha belly laughs, or Trainspotting for the professional classes'

The Bogeyman Chronicles
Craig Watson
ISBN: 978-1-910946-11-4 (eBook)
ISBN: 978-1-910946-10-7 (Paperback)

In 14th Century Scotland, amidst the wars of independence, hatred, murder and betrayal are commonplace. People are driven to extraordinary lengths to survive, whilst those with power exercise it with cruel pleasure.

Royal Prince Alexander Stewart, son of King Robert II and plagued by rumours of his illegitimacy, becomes infamous as the Wolf of Badenoch, while young Andrew Christie commits an unforgivable sin and lay Brother Brodie Affleck in the Restenneth Priory pieces together the mystery that links them all together.

From the horror of the times and the changing fortunes of the characters, the legend of the Bogeyman is born and Craig Watson cleverly weaves together the disparate lives of the characters into a compelling historical mystery that will keep you gripped throughout.

Over 80 years the lives of three men are inextricably entwined, and through their hatreds, murders and betrayals the legend of Christie Cleek, the bogeyman, is born.

'The Bogeyman Chronicles haunted our imagination long after we finished it' – iScot Magazine

The Birds That Never Flew
Margot McCuaig
Shortlisted for the Dundee International Book Prize 2012
Longlisted for the Polari First Book Prize 2014
ISBN: 978-0-9929768-5-9 (eBook)
ISBN: 978-0-9929768-4-2 (Paperback)

'Have you got a light hen? I'm totally gaspin.'

Battered and bruised, Elizabeth has taken her daughter and left her abusive husband Patrick. Again. In the bleak and impersonal Glasgow housing office Elizabeth meets the provocatively intriguing drug addict Sadie, who is desperate to get her own life back on track.

The two women forge a fierce and interdependent relationship as they try to rebuild their shattered lives, but despite their bold, and sometimes illegal attempts it seems impossible to escape from the abuse they have always known, and tragedy strikes.

More than a decade later Elizabeth has started to implement her perfect revenge – until a surreal Glaswegian Virgin Mary steps in with imperfect timing and a less than divine attitude to stick a spoke in the wheel of retribution.

Tragic, darkly funny and irreverent, *The Birds That Never Flew* ushers in a new and vibrant voice in Scottish literature.

'...dark, beautiful and moving, I wholeheartedly recommend' scanoir.co.uk